Former copywrit
financial security
notion of embarki
become a crime fi
wordsmithery was
for All and its seque

Steven is thirty-six years old and lives in Norwich with his wife, editor-in-chief and harshest critic Lisa, and his chocolate Labrador, Murphy. He is a sucker for all things Americana, and he's currently working hard on his next novel.

Find out more about Steven at www.mirabooks. co.uk/stevenhague

Also available by **Steven Hague**

JUSTICE FOR ALL

BLOOD LAW

STEVEN
HAGUE

MIRA

All the characters in this book have no existence outside the imagination
of the author, and have no relation whatsoever to anyone bearing the
same name or names. They are not even distantly inspired by any
individual known or unknown to the author, and all the incidents are
pure invention.

Published in Great Britain 2009.
MIRA Books, Eton House, 18-24 Paradise Road,
Richmond, Surrey, TW9 1SR

ISBN 978 0 7783 0305 3

59-0809

MIRA's policy is to use papers that are natural, renewable and
recyclable products and made from wood grown in sustainable forests.
The logging and manufacturing processes conform to the legal
environmental regulations of the country of origin.

Printed and bound in Spain
by Litografia Rosés S.A., Barcelona

Acknowledgements

Thanks to my agent, Broo Doherty, and my editor, Catherine Burke, for believing in me, and for their continued hard work on my behalf.

The following books and websites were useful sources of information for *Blood Law*:

Do or Die by Leon Bing
My Bloody Life by Reymundo Sanchez
Illegal Drugs by Paul M. Gahlinger, M.D., Ph.D.
Dead or Alive by Geoff Thompson
Native American Religions by Arlene Hirschfelder & Paulette Molin
www.streetgangs.com

To my family and friends for all their love and support. Writing may be a solitary business, but you can't be a writer on your own.

"In wise hands, poison is medicine.
In foolish hands, medicine is poison."
Giacomo Casanova

PROLOGUE

Three Months Earlier

DREADNOUGHT had just three days left to serve on his latest sentence, but he was about to put his release date in jeopardy. He'd been banged up on an assault beef, and the six months that the judge had handed down had passed relatively uneventfully up until now. During his time in Pelican Bay, three inmates had ended up in the hospital wing and two had been laid out on a slab in the morgue, and none of them could be traced back to him. Like he said—the stretch had been a quiet one.

He was standing on the first-floor gantry, looking down at the bulls and the inmates below, watching for anything out of the ordinary. All aspects of the human condition were on display, well, all *negative* aspects, anyhow. Envy, greed, cruelty, fear, hatred—you name it, it was there, many times over, coursing through the blackest of hearts, and by black, he didn't mean negro, because Dread was a man of colour himself, and the one thing he'd learnt in his thirty-odd years on the planet was that all muthafuckas had the capacity for evil, no matter their race, colour or creed.

He flexed his considerable biceps then ran his hand down the prison ink he'd had inscribed on his left arm. The sleeves of his blue penitentiary shirt had been torn off to make sure everyone got the message. The words, rendered carefully in Gothic script, read, 'Only God Can Judge Me.' He wasn't a religious man, but he'd seen the phrase spraypainted on a wall somewhere and had liked it immediately. It made him stand out from the crowd. The cops, the courts, the whole damn legal system could do what the hell they liked, but it didn't mean shit to him. No one but *God* could judge him. All the rest could go hang.

'You ready?' he asked, turning to the brute alongside him.

All he got in response was a grunt. Cyclops. When that cat was in the zone he was all the way gone. Cyclops was Dread's number one go-to guy when it came to busting heads. He'd been a violent son of a bitch since kindergarten, and he'd been known by many different names over the years, his most recent coming after a prison fight in which a member of the Aryan brotherhood had gouged out his left eye. Cyclops may have lost fifty per cent of his vision, but the white supremacist prick had come off far worse—he'd lost all motor function from the neck downwards.

Dreadnought strode along the walkway until he'd made it as far as the shower block. He exchanged a quick nod with the brother standing guard by the door, waited for him to turn up his boombox to a near deafening level, then stepped inside. The sinks were laid out in a row to his left, while the communal shower area was off to his right, kept separate by a dividing wall that had gaps for ingress or egress at either end. There were three people using the facilities—a geriatric career crim washing up at one of the sinks, and a pair of Latino faggots soaping up in the showers. When Cyclops gave the old guy at the sink one of his looks, he quickly realised that personal hygiene was off the agenda and slunk out the door in a hurry.

'Well, ain't this nice and cosy…' said Dreadnought, as he walked into the shower area with shiv in hand—a shard of glass with a length of bed sheet wrapped around one end to form a makeshift handle.

The two Latinos turned as one, both of them sporting impressive erections, their members standing proud like twin flagpoles yet to receive their standards.

'You don't wanna start no shit, Dread…' said the taller of the two. 'You'd have to be loco to mess with da Mex Mafia.'

'Yeah, well, my pops always said I was a crazy son of a bitch.'

The Latino took a half-step forward with fists raised while his companion wilted into the background.

'You wanna dance with me, Rodriguez?' asked Dreadnought, keeping his back to the wall and forcing his target to circle around and face him.

'Rodriguez! Look out!' shrieked the other Latino, his voice high-pitched and feminine.

Rodriguez started to turn but it was too late. Cyclops, who had entered the shower area from the far end, came up fast to deliver a piledriver of a punch to the naked man's kidneys. Rodriguez slumped onto the wet tiles, mewling like a kitten as he curled into a ball.

'Now you're gonna tell me all you know,' said Dreadnought. 'Or you're gonna find yourself in a world of pain.'

CHAPTER ONE

ZAC HUNTER took another pull on his ice-cold Asahi as he walked to the edge of his deck and leant on the balustrade. He was a big man, around six feet tall, with a powerful, athletic physique, and the length of pine creaked slightly to acknowledge his presence. The view that confronted him was spectacular: a 150-foot sheer drop down his own private cliff face, then the land evened out and ran gently away to the valley that stretched out below. Rocky foreground, followed by thick clumps of sagebrush and chaparral, followed by civilisation—the sprawling megalopolis of Los Angeles.

Hunter lived up high in the hills that ringed the north side of the city, in a one-storey adobe house that was just off Mulholland. Prime real estate. The house had been left to him by his mom, who'd succumbed to cancer when he was just sixteen. Thanks to her prudence and foresight, he now owned it outright, although that didn't stop the other bills from rolling in. He finished his beer and went back inside, where Rage Against the Machine's 'Battle of Los Angeles' snarled out of the micro hi-fi unit in the far corner. These days, mid-afternoon meant beer, rock music, relaxation— just one of the many perks of being self-employed.

Once he'd retrieved another bottle from the fridge, he turned on the TV, muted the sound, and settled back into his sofa to scan the banner headlines that scrolled across the bottom of the screen. The TV was tuned to the news on a local Fox affiliate, and the reports were full of anger, violence and despair. Gang activity was on the rise, turf wars were getting ever more vicious, and the body count was headed for the stratosphere. Hunter watched on as a talking head brought the latest update from East LA, her perfect make-up and expensive coiffure distinctly at odds with the blood-splattered wall that loomed large behind her. Two more African Americans wiped out in a drive-by, plus an eight-year-old facing life as a paraplegic after she'd caught a stray bullet in her lower spine. And it wouldn't end there. One violent act would demand another, retribution would be the order of the day, and the cycle of violence would continue. Random death was a way of life in the poor parts of town, but something sure had riled the protagonists into a frenzy this summer. East LA was an increasingly Hispanic enclave, and it looked like any black family left in the region was now being driven out. In days gone by, it would have been Hunter's job to do something about it, but now that he was no longer with the LAPD it was someone else's problem.

His departure from the department had been acrimonious. After sixteen years of dedicated service, an internal affairs review board had stripped him of his badge and shown him the door. It had all boiled down to a difference of opinion. The board believed that police officers should respect a suspect's rights at all times, whereas Hunter didn't—not when you were dealing with the dregs of society and innocent lives were on the line. But what was he going to do now? He couldn't live off his savings forever, and being a cop was the only job he'd ever wanted, ever since his mother had sat him down as a six-year-old and gently explained why he'd never met his father. Two stick-up kids, a local diner, his father the bystander gunned down in cold blood. Just another act of random violence in the City of Angels. The senseless killing had shaped Hunter's life from that point on, prompting him to join the cops. He'd wanted to clean up the city's mean streets, but now that he was no longer on the payroll, he didn't see why his mission had to change. Maybe he'd be more effective than before, now that there were no rules or regulations to get in his way.

His plan was to become a PI, but not the kind of licensed PI that spent most of his time working divorce cases, no, he'd set his sights a little higher than that. What he wanted to do, what he needed to do, was to make a difference. To fight crime, to take down the bad guys, to save lives—but first he had to find himself a client.

The telephone buzzed to life as he took another slug from his beer. He reached for the handset and answered it on the third ring.

'Yep?'

'Hunter? Is that you?'

The voice was low, sensual, and on edge—to the

trained ear the mixture of desperation and fear bubbling just under the surface stood out like a screech owl in a choir. The voice was also familiar. He scanned through his memory banks trying to match it to a face.

'Who wants to know?'

'Hunter? It's Angel…'

And in a flash, there she was in his mind's eye. Angelica Cortez—Angel to her friends—a Latino gangbanger who ran with the Santa Ana Ghosts. Long brown hair, free flowing and wild. Big doe eyes that sparkled with passion. A curvaceous figure that turned heads wherever and whenever.

'Angel,' he began. 'It's good to hear from you.'

'Hunter, you gotta help me, I'm in a lotta trouble…'

'What's wrong?' he asked. This wasn't the Angel he knew. She was tough. She had no choice. When you grew up in the gangs any sign of fear was a sign of weakness, and weakness meant you'd be culled from the herd.

'I don't know where else to go, Hunter, you're my only hope,' she sobbed. 'They're gonna kill her, I know they are…'

'Kill who?'

Hunter flinched as a sharp slap reverberated down the phone line.

'No! *Hijo de puta!* Leave me alone!' shouted Angel.

'Angel! What's going on? Where are you?' he yelled, but all he got in reply was the sound of a brief struggle before the connection was cut.

CHAPTER TWO

HUNTER climbed into his black Plymouth Barracuda and fired the engine. He wasn't sure where he was headed, but he knew that he had to head somewhere. He'd tried to reverse-trace Angel's call, but the number had been blocked. He'd also called in a few favours and tried to track her via the usual methods—social security, credit card, utility bills—but everything had come back blank. To all intents and purposes, Angel didn't officially exist, which wasn't all that uncommon for an illegal immigrant. Fake IDs were a whole lot easier to get than a green card. But although he had no idea where she lived, he couldn't just sit on his hands. He decided to head for East LA. That's where she'd grown up, and that's where her gang, the Santa Ana Ghosts, had their base of operations, so it seemed like the best place to start. It didn't do much to narrow the search, though—East LA wasn't exactly a dot on the map.

He backed the 'Cuda out of his driveway onto a small slip road, then nursed the car through a series of switchbacks until he was motoring along Mulholland.

As he made his way east, he thought back to their first meeting. Dispatch had sent him to a homicide scene just off Mariachi Plaza, where a Hispanic male had been gutted with a butcher's knife. A crowd of spectators had formed, and Angel had been amongst them. When he'd asked for witnesses, she'd given him the same empty expression as everyone else, but a few days later she'd tracked him down via the switchboard at Parker Centre to request a meet at a downtown bar.

She'd told him that she could ID the killer, but if he wanted a name she was going to need a little financial incentive, so he'd put her on his list of paid informants and stumped up some cash. Her info had been golden. The killer had been a member of the Latino Locos, one of the most dangerous gangs in town, and the fool still had the murder weapon in his possession, thereby buying himself some hard time at Pelican Bay. From that point onwards, Angel had passed on intel every once in a while. As he'd gotten to know her better, his feelings for her had started to grow—not in a romantic way, but more like that of an older brother. He'd wanted to protect her, get her out of the life, because running with a gang rarely had a happy ending, and he couldn't bear the thought of her going the same way as so many faceless others.

When she'd told him she was pregnant, he'd decided to act. The father was another member of the Ghosts, a guy called Lunatic, who'd been as laid back as his moniker suggested. Hunter had done everything in his power to help Angel get out of the life, providing some stake money, setting her up with family services, but at the very last moment she'd changed her mind and gone back to banging, and to this day, he didn't know why. Angel was the one who'd gotten away. The young woman who'd stood at a fork in the road, bright future off to the left, inner-city hellhole to the right, and she'd made the wrong choice. They'd crossed paths a few more times over the years, whenever an investigation had taken him to the Ghost's East LA enclave, and their relationship had remained cordial, despite her chosen profession. Against all odds, she was still with Lunatic, which pretty much qualified them for relationship of the decade in gang terms, and her child was now a beatific six-year-old called Graciela.

He shook his head and forced himself to concentrate as he raced the 'Cuda along the Hollywood Freeway towards downtown LA. By the time he'd worked his way through the traffic and rolled past Union Station, he knew where he was headed. The Gutter—a small bar on the south-western outskirts of EastLos. Back in the day, it had been one of the favoured hangouts of the Ghosts, maybe even their base of operations, and one thing that all gangs did well was adhere to tradition.

As he pulled up by the bar his nerves started to jangle. When he'd been a cop, entering a gang stronghold in broad daylight wouldn't have held too many fears, as any banger with an IQ over fifty was ultra-wary when it came to dealing with five-oh. One of the street dealers had explained it to him. He'd said that it wasn't the prospect of incarceration that they were afraid of, but the police department itself. The police were the most organised and most powerful gang in the city, and that made them a force to be reckoned with. Now that Hunter was just a private citizen, he was vulnerable the moment he stepped inside the bar, but if he wanted to find Angel, he didn't have much choice. He climbed out of his car and loosed his Beretta in its shoulder holster as a police chopper buzzed overhead. Although he'd decided to take a softly-softly approach, the gun might come in handy if things turned to shit. Someone had wedged open the bar's front door with a trashcan. He shifted his head from side to side, popping the muscles in his neck, then stepped over the threshold.

The inside was gloomy, save for a narrow strip of sunlight that backlit him from behind, and the temperature was near stifling. An old wooden counter was on the right, and the elderly barman behind it was working his way through a generous measure of Scotch. The counter ran for three yards or so before giving way to doors marked 'Playaz' and 'Hoes'. A pool table stood in the middle of the room, its faded blue baize marked with myriad cigarette burns, while to the left was a motley collection of chairs and tables that looked like they'd been picked up during a scavenger hunt at a junkyard. Hunter took it all in at a glance, then focused his attention on the group of Latino youths that were kicking back in the far corner by a fire door. There were six of them slumped around a table full of empty bottles, and they were dressed all in black, apart from the white fist logo on their bandanas. The logo signified their allegiance to the Ghosts, and the eldest of them didn't look to be much more than sixteen years old. Hunter walked over to the bar.

'Two pitchers of Bud.'

'*Sí,*' muttered the barman, showing no great enthusiasm for the task.

When the pitchers were ready, Hunter picked them up and walked slowly to the back of the room. By the time he'd covered half the distance, six sets of eyes glared at him from the shadows.

'Peace offering,' he said, depositing the beer on the table. No one moved.

'What you want?' asked the biggest of the kids, working hard to put an aggressive edge on his voice.

'No drama, I'm just looking for some info,' Hunter responded, his palms held aloft in a submissive gesture.

'Don't know nuttin'.'

'What's your name?'

'My crew call me Capone.'

'Well, how about you take your hand out from under the table, Capone, so we can have a civilised conversation. Like I said, I'm not here to cause trouble.'

The banger's hand stayed right where it was.

'Jeez, you guys are jumpy,' muttered Hunter, coolness personified.

'Streets are mad dangerous. Gotta do or die.'

'That's got nothing to do with me. When it comes to turf wars, you can call me Switzerland.'

'Huh?'

'I'm strictly neutral. Hey! Take it easy!' warned Hunter, as one of the others rose from his chair and headed for the fire door.

'Gotta take me a leak,' squeaked the kid.

'Something wrong with the rest rooms?'

'They fucked up.'

'This is a business meeting. Cross your legs till we're done.'

The kid looked at Capone, who nodded for him to sit back down.

'You heard of Angel Cortez?' asked Hunter.

Capone's eyes drifted up and to the right as he answered, 'Ain't no angels in this hood. Just skanky-ass hoes.'

'What about Larry Lloyd? Better known as Lunatic?'

Capone shrugged.

'C'mon, you must have heard of them—you're wearing Ghost colours and they're way up in your gang.'

'You a knowledgeable muthafucka, huh? What you want?'

Hunter started to relax as Capone brought his hand out from under the table to reach for his beer. Big mistake. A moment later the sound of a shell being jacked into the chamber of a shotgun rang out behind him.

'Who sent you, son?' asked the old barkeep.

'You're pretty light on your feet, pops,' acknowledged Hunter, keeping dead still. 'No one sent me—I just need to find Angel, and I need to find her fast.'

He ran through his options. The barkeep had the drop on him, but his reactions were probably shot—a stiff Scotch on a hot afternoon tended to have that effect on the elderly. But while it might not be too difficult to deal with the threat from behind, the group of surly young men sitting in front of him could prove more problematic. He elected to let things play out for a while.

'What business you got with Lunatic and Angel?' asked Capone. 'They not just high up in the gang, they top dogs.'

'I just need to find her. She's an old friend of mine. Give me an address, I'll be on my way. And I'll pay for the info. How does a hundred bucks sound?'

'Show it!'

'Sure, as soon as the old timer points his gun elsewhere.'

Capone gave the barkeep a nod. Hunter withdrew a wad of bills from his pocket, peeled off five twenties, and laid them on the table.

'That's a lot of green you're holding,' said Capone with greedy eyes. 'You go all in, I'll give you an address.'

Hunter laid down the rest of the cash without argument and stared expectantly at his young adversary.

'They on Eagle—right by the cemetery. Gotta stack of old tyres in the front yard.'

'You sure?' asked Hunter.

'Sure I'm sure,' replied Capone, pocketing the cash, 'Now get gone.'

Hunter backed out of the bar with his hands in clear view, maintaining eye contact with Capone all the way to the exit. Once he was back on the street he climbed into his car, gunned the engine, and drove off, but as soon as he'd taken the next bend, he pulled up and doubled back on foot. Having settled behind a dumpster in the side alley, he waited for the fire door to swing open. After ten minutes or so his patience was rewarded when Capone emerged blinking into the sunlight. Hunter didn't make his move until the young man had unzipped his fly and started to urinate against the wall.

'Careful son, you'll splash your sneakers,' he whispered, pushing the barrel of his Beretta under Capone's ear. 'Keep real quiet. It'd be a shame to spoil this tender moment by inviting someone else along. Besides, you probably wouldn't want your crew to know that you're packing a Derringer downstairs, huh?'

'Fuck you!' choked Capone, as he stuffed his shrivelled manhood back in his pants.

'Not with that. Now, about that address you gave me. Who lives on Eagle with all those tyres?'

'Crazy Joe. He a sherm head. Does nuttin' but PCP all day long.'

'Nice. I think I'll pass on a visit to Crazy Joe's. How about you cough up Angel's real address? And make sure you get it right this time, my patience has its limits.'

'She on Verona—'bout midway down near South Ferris. Lunatic's ride'll be out front—got himself a pimped-out Caddie.'

'And when did you last see either of them?'

'Dunno—maybe last week.'

'And they were okay?'

Capone shrugged. 'Yeah, they cool.'

Hunter's brow wrinkled. What the hell had happened in the last few days to prompt Angel's cry for help?

'Been nice talking to you, son. Sleep tight.'

With that he holstered his Beretta and snaked his arm around Capone's neck, clasped his right hand with his left, then dug the bony part of his wrist into the banger's windpipe. Capone struggled for a few seconds then his body went limp as lack of oxygen to the brain had an effect. Hunter lowered him to the ground, rolled him on to his side, then checked that his airway was unobstructed.

'And you won't be needing this any more,' he said, as he reached into the banger's pocket to retrieve his roll of cash, before heading back to his car.

CHAPTER THREE

FROM the outside, Angel's house looked peaceful enough. It was a two-storey affair, constructed from stucco, brick, and timber, and separated from the street by a small patch of yellowing lawn and a white picket fence. Just as Capone had predicted, a '78 Cadillac Eldorado was parked in the drive, pimped out to include headlight covers, grille caps, lake pipes, and a thick-padded vinyl top that mirrored the vibrant crimson of the bodywork. Apart from a couple of over-sized crows perched on the house's side gable, there were no other signs of life.

So how best to advance? Given that he might be facing a hostage situation, a cheery knock on the front door seemed out. Rear entrance it was, then. Hunter ducked into the neighbour's yard and worked his way to the rear of the property. A six-foot brick wall marked the boundary line. He hauled himself up, then dropped down on the far side to take shelter behind a large bay laurel. If anything, the back of Angel's house was even quieter than the front. Two picture windows were positioned within a few feet of each other, closely followed by a wire mesh screen door, then a pair of sliding glass doors that opened onto a stone-slab patio.

Hunter kept vigil for a few minutes from the relative safety of the laurel, waiting for movement from inside the house, but none was forthcoming. He freed his gun from its holster, released the safety, then broke cover and ran forwards in a half-crouch. Having reached the edge of the building, he edged up to the first of the windows and risked a peek inside. Dining room. All clear. He stared at his reflection for a moment, noting that his eyes now sparkled with the buzz of adrenalin, then he moved on to window number two. Kitchen. Another empty room. The screen door beckoned. He covered the distance, gave the handle a twist, then eased the door open. Nothing happened. No screams of fear, no yells of rage, and, best of all, no gunshots. He stepped inside and crept down the hallway, thankful for the thick carpet that helped mask his advance. When he reached the first of the interior doors, he took a deep breath and pushed it open, his Beretta swinging round in search of a threat.

Angel was slumped in an easy chair at the far end of the room, her eyes shut, her pallor sickly. She wore a sleeveless white shirt that was knotted just below her breasts, while her jeans looked like they'd been spray-painted on. She'd added some blonde highlights to her hair to complement its natural chestnut colour, and her face, although just as beautiful as he remembered, was clouded with a look of despair.

'Just leave me alone,' she said, drawing her knees up beneath her.

'Angel? It's me, Hunter,' he said, returning his Beretta to its holster.

Her eyes snapped open and widened in surprise, then she rose to her feet and stood before him.

'Hunter? What are you doing here? You've gotta leave…'

'But I thought you needed me? I thought you were in trouble?'

'I am,' she said, as fresh tears started to well in her eyes, 'I'm in so much trouble I don't know what to do. But we can't talk now.'

'What's wrong, Angel? Whatever it is, I can help.'

'Hunter, listen to me—you've got to go.'

'Muthafucka ain't going nowhere!' commanded a deep voice from the hallway.

Hunter raised his hands slowly above his head, then turned around to find that a large Latino male filled the doorframe. The newcomer was tall and muscular with the look of an athlete, a look that was reinforced by his choice of clothes—white Converse All-Star tennis shoes, black sweatpants and a white Nike sweatshirt. His hair was cropped short, and his handsome features were distorted into a mask of rage.

'Lunatic,' said Hunter, 'Long time no see.'

'What the fuck is he doin' here? I said no cops,' Lunatic spat in Angel's direction.

'We need help, Larry,' said Angel, putting herself between the two men.

'We don't need no help, 'specially not from him. You just made things worse. What the fuck you told him?'

'Not a thing,' interjected Hunter, electing to keep the

fact that he was no longer with the LAPD quiet for now. 'Except that she's scared and in trouble.'

'Shit! They find out about this, she's as good as dead.'

'Let him help, baby, please,' begged Angel, resting a hand on her partner's muscular forearm. 'We can't do this alone.'

'We *gotta* do this alone. Ain't no other way. Bringin' him here is the worst thing you coulda done.'

Hunter watched the big man closely. A vein jumped in his forehead, his eyes were red-rimmed and bloodshot, and his hands kept clenching and unclenching. Lunatic was a street veteran, the boss of an inner-city gang who'd lived through numerous episodes of extreme violence, and yet he was scared stiff. What the hell was going on?

'For crissakes, Lunatic, listen to her. Whatever you're into, you're in way too deep—that's plain to see. I haven't seen you this nervous since you went one on one with Cedric Walters. Let me help.'

'Who the fuck's Cedric Walters? An why the fuck you wanna help me? You ain't blood an' you never will be.'

'I'm not here for you, I'm here for Angel,' said Hunter. 'Why she's stuck with you this long is a mystery, but I don't hold that against her—everyone's allowed one mistake.'

'Larry—no!' cried Angel, as her boyfriend raised his fists.

'Stay the fuck outta my business, and get the fuck outta my house! I ain't gonna tell you twice.'

'My pleasure,' said Hunter, making for the door.

CHAPTER FOUR

NOT many people dared enter the park once the sun had gone down, but the path that twisted through the gnarled trees and overgrown shrubs held little fear for Gopher. Sure, some of the addicts that lived deep among the darkened recesses were dangerous, but to them, Gopher was a hero. The park was home ground, part of his territory, and that made him feel safe—no, better than safe, more like a god. He'd just turned sixteen, his cash flow was right and his game was tight, and whenever he needed his axle greased, any one of a dozen young hoes were happy to get buck wild between the sheets. In short, Gopher's life was sweet.

So when he first thought he was being followed, he didn't panic. Instead, he stopped, turned around, and called out in a clear, confident voice, 'Ain't got no yayo, cuz, gonna have to wait till sun-up.'

He waited a moment, heard nothing but the distant rumble of the diesel big-rigs on the 105, then shrugged his shoulders and continued onwards. His crib was on the far side of the park, and the cut-through shaved fifteen minutes off his journey. His mom would be watching some Cosby reruns on the TV while working her way through a bottle of liquor. He didn't know what sort of liquor, as her daily selection was governed by whatever happened to be on special at the market. When it came to getting loaded, Moms wasn't choosy.

He swaggered onwards, his shoulders back and his chest pushed out, working on his strut, then he heard it again. Another noise, only this time not from the rear but from the side. He stopped and stared at the thick wall of greenery that bordered the path, his anger on the rise.

'I'm telling you, cuz, I'm all out. Come find me in the a.m. an' I'll hook you up fo' sure, but right now you gotta leave a niggah be.'

The bushes stared back at him silently. He waited for a few seconds then moved on, but when he rounded the next bend he found himself face to face with two sets of gleaming eyes.

'Fuck!' he exclaimed.

The two large dogs ignored his outburst and continued to stare at him like he was dinner. When one of them began to emit a low growl, Gopher took a half-step backwards.

'Get the fuck outta the way, this niggah be strapped!' he yelled.

'Is that so?' asked a voice softly over his shoulder.

Gopher reached for the .38 he kept stashed down the back of his pants but the gun was already gone. He turned around to find six-foot-three's worth of muscle blocking his path. The newcomer had long dark hair that had been pulled back in a ponytail and eyes that

shone black in the moonlight. When he'd finished un-
loading the .38, he threw the shells in one direction and
the gun in another, then folded his arms and waited.

'Fuckin' red man!' cussed Gopher. 'You a long way
from the reservation.' As he finished the sentence he
stepped forward and threw a wild right towards his adversary's jaw. The Indian swayed inside it, caught
Gopher's arm in a vice-like grip, then twisted it up
behind his back until his fingers were touching his
scapula. For the first time that night, Gopher felt afraid.

'Where's Dreadnought?' asked the Indian in a dull
monotone.

Gopher kicked back with his right heel but connected with nothing but thin air. The Indian responded
by pushing his hand higher. The pain was excruciating.

'Where's Dreadnought?'

'Ain't never heard of no—'

Gopher felt another surge of white heat explode
through his shoulder as his rhomboid muscles were
stretched close to breaking point. When something
popped in the joint, he cried out in agony.

'Where is he?'

'Dunno,' he gasped.

'Not good enough.'

More pressure on his shoulder, more pain. The
Indian maintained the hold for what felt like a lifetime
then, just as Gopher's bladder gave way, the pressure
eased off.

'Dreadnought be on the down low,' he choked out,
'Ain't nobody seen him in a while.'

The Indian considered this for a few seconds, then

released the hold and gave Gopher a sharp kick in the butt that sent him sprawling to the ground.

'You're lucky—I believe you. But consider this your first and final warning—you'll have more than a dislocated shoulder to nurse if you don't change your ways. Clean up your act. I'll be watching.'

From his foetal position in the dirt, Gopher blinked through the tears and watched the Indian stride off into the darkness, the two dogs trotting obediently in his wake.

Stone walked quickly away from the whimpering kid he'd left lying on the ground. He took no enjoyment from inflicting pain upon so weak an opponent, but blood law governed his actions now. This was the sixth member of the gang that he'd questioned, and more violence would doubtless be necessary if he was to find the elusive Dreadnought, but the prospect didn't trouble him at all. A long journey consisted of many footsteps.

He exited the park with his two dogs in tow and headed over to his Triumph Rocket III. The behemoth of a motorcycle sat under a streetlamp like a lion under the savannah moon. Stone straddled the beast, fired the engine, and felt the vibrations course through his body. He engaged first gear, let in the clutch, and twisted the throttle, easing the bike along the ribbon of tarmac, his dogs keeping pace on the sidewalk. Another night, another dead end, but Dreadnought was out there somewhere, and finding him was just a matter of time.

CHAPTER FIVE

HUNTER pulled his leather jacket tighter around his broad shoulders and checked his watch. He'd been waiting for the best part of three hours now, and he didn't plan on staying out all night—Calvary Cemetery wasn't the most hospitable of places to wile away the time.

He leant against the tree trunk and let his eyes dance over the nearby headstones. LA's past was buried here, the plots harbouring both famous and infamous remains—where else could the likes of comedian Lou Costello rub decomposing shoulders with Jack Dragna, the most successful but least known of the old LA mob bosses? On the way in, he'd walked past Jose Diaz's plot, the guy whose body had been found over in Sleepy Lagoon back in 1942, prompting a near race war. Six hundred Latino youths had been arrested in connection with the crime, twenty-two of them charged, and seventeen convicted. As anger and mistrust had flared among the communities, the Zoot Suit Riots had exploded, and the melting pot of LA had threatened to boil over. Race against race in the City of Angels—sixty years later, not much had changed.

But the headstone that interested Hunter that night marked the final resting place of a certain Cedric R. Walters. Cedric had been born on 6 September 1885, he'd lived without fanfare for sixty-five years, then he'd died on 21 October 1950. Other than that, Hunter didn't know the first thing about him, but he'd made a point of dropping Cedric's name into his heated conversation with Lunatic, and he was hoping that Angel had picked up on the reference.

Back when Hunter had been a cop and Angel had fed him snippets of info on gang activity, Cedric's grave had been one of their meeting places. With Angel now desperate for his help, and Lunatic equally as desperate to keep him at arm's length, the only way Hunter was going to learn anything was to get Angel out from under the clutches of her bad-tempered boyfriend. Only problem was, he had no idea if she'd understood his clue. Just as he decided to give her another half-hour, a cab rolled slowly down the private road that dissected the cemetery, its headlights cutting a swathe through the gloom. The door popped open and Angel climbed out, wearing the same tight jeans that she'd had on earlier, along with an oversized plaid workshirt that gave her a tomboyish quality. Hunter watched as she had a brief conversation with the cab driver before hurrying across the grass to their old meeting place. Once he was certain she hadn't been followed he slipped out from behind the tree and walked over to her.

'Hey,' he said. 'You remembered old Cedric, then?'

'Sure did,' she said, with a half-smile that failed to hide the worry in her eyes. She turned around and waved the cabby off. 'We gotta be quick, I'm not sure how long I've got. Larry stormed out of the house after you left, he could come back any time.'

'So why don't you tell me what's happening?'

'It's Gracie—she's gone missing.' Her shoulders sagged as she slumped towards Hunter. 'I don't know what to do.'

He only just caught her as she started to weep. Gracie was her daughter, her only child, and she hadn't been present at the house. It had been late summer the last time he'd seen the kid, playing with her dolls in Bristow Park while he'd caught up with Angel. Before he'd left, he'd bought Gracie an ice cream and had got a huge smile in reward, then it had been back to the day job, chasing down a lead on a serial rapist who'd been terrorising the surrounding area.

Once Angel's tears had subsided he asked his next question.

'How long has she been gone?'

'Since around four o'clock, yesterday afternoon. She was at the playground, but she never came home…'

'And you're sure she's not just run off with a friend—maybe gone on a sleepover, something like that?'

'No way. She always lets me know where she is. My Gracie's a good little girl.'

'Have you notified the police?'

'Larry told me not to. He said I mustn't tell anyone—not even the Ghosts.'

'Why?'

Angel slipped out of Hunter's embrace, blotted her eyes, then reached into her shirt pocket to withdraw a matchbook and a cigarette, which she proceed to light with shaking hands.

'I don't know. He won't talk to me. He won't talk to anyone.'

'Do you think he's involved?'

'No way! He loves his little girl.'

'No, not like that, I meant could he have done something to have put Gracie in jeopardy? Somehow made himself a target?'

Angel shrugged in response.

'So why'd you call me?' asked Hunter.

'I had to call someone. You're a cop—I thought you'd know what to do. I thought you'd be able to look for her on the quiet? Without Larry or anyone else, knowing? Use your contacts, stuff like that?'

'I'm not with the department any more, Angel, I quit last year. Well, I didn't exactly quit, they threw me out for hospitalising a…suspect,' said Hunter, deciding not to reveal that the suspect in question was a paedophile who'd been responsible for the brutal deaths of seven children.

'You're not a cop any more? Then what the hell am I gonna do? I got nowhere else to turn, Hunter, you gotta help me, you just gotta,' she said, stubbing out her cigarette, her lower lip trembling. 'She's my daughter, she's all I've got.'

He thought it through for a split second. A missing child needed rescuing. A six-year-old. An innocent. He pictured the look on Gracie's face when he'd given her the ice cream, and came to a decision.

'Of course I'll help. Don't worry, Angel—I'll find her. Everything will be fine.'

She threw her arms around him and hugged him fiercely. When he inhaled, the delicate scent of apple blossom rose from her hair.

'Thank you, Hunter, thank you so much.'

She held on for five seconds that seemed a whole lot longer, then broke away and delved once more into her pocket.

'Here, I've got a photo. It's pretty recent—just a few weeks old.'

He took the photo and stared at it, and Gracie stared back at him. Her short brown hair was cut in a bob, she had a cute smile on her face, and a mischievous glint in her eyes.

'Where's the playground she was last seen at?'

'On Verona—a couple of blocks east of my place, no more than five minutes away. I don't usually let her go there on her own, but she'd been bugging me all afternoon, so I said she could go on ahead, then the phone rang, and I got held up…'

'Can you remember what she was wearing?'

'A baby blue skirt and a pink T-shirt with some flowers on the front.'

'And one more thing—have you any idea where Lunatic went after he stormed out of the house tonight?'

'No. But you gotta leave him alone. You saw how he was.'

'I'll leave him for now, but I'm gonna have to talk to him at some point. You need a ride?'

She nodded and followed him out of the cemetery, the two of them walking in silence along the lamplit path that cut through the neat rows of headstones. A missing child, plus a father who was running scared. What was it Lunatic had said earlier? 'If they find out about this, she's as good as dead.' Who were 'they'? And how was Lunatic involved?

CHAPTER SIX

CASSIUS elbowed his way past the junkie in the doorway and stumbled into the room. The only light came courtesy of a streetlamp outside the boarded-up window, but he could still make out the bodies that were strewn all around him—near zombies propped against the side walls or curled up and shaking on the bare wooden floor. The smell of rancid sweat that rose from them was enough to make a grown man gag, but Cassius wasn't fussed, as at that moment all he wanted was to get his load on.

He kicked one of his companions in the ribs and made himself a spot by the wall, then set about preparing his fix. Having placed a couple of small lumps of yellowish rock into the bowl of his crack pipe, he sparked a lighter and began to gently ease the flame around the underside of the glass, prompting the rock to start popping as it heated up. Once the crystallised chunk had melted, he took his first hit off the rising fumes, then began to shake with anticipation.

The vaporised molecules of cocaine hydrochloride flowed into his lungs where they were absorbed into his bloodstream via the tiny vessels lining the air sacs. From there, the molecules journeyed swiftly northwards to diffuse from his blood into the fluid that bathed the nerve cells in his brain, where they immediately began to stimulate the dopamine receptor in the mesolimbic sector, while simultaneously blocking the re-uptake of a number of other neurotransmitters that also played an important role in the stimulant-reward cycle. The whole process took around ten seconds to achieve, and the result was a mind-numbing rush of intense pleasure.

Cassius lowered his crack pipe to the floor and stretched out his legs, his anxieties draining away as a feeling of immense wellbeing washed over him. His whole body felt like it was going into orgasm. His senses were heightened to a razor-sharp level, while energy coursed through every fibre of his being. But ten minutes later, he started to crash, and while he was slipping into the first stages of withdrawal, things took a further turn for the worse.

'I found him, Diaz, get your ass in here!' yelled a figure in the doorway.

The familiar voice hit Cassius like a slap in the face. The guy in the doorway was Mason, and he'd been blackmailing Cassius for what seemed like forever. As his demands had become increasingly outrageous, Cassius had taken to hiding out in crack dens, but now that he'd been found, he was pretty certain that Mason and his muscle-bound partner Diaz wouldn't take kindly to being stiffed. They had him in a tight spot. He couldn't earn cash fast enough to keep them at bay, but if he didn't pay his dues he'd wind up being public enemy number one.

Everything had first turned to shit when they'd shown up at his pad a few months back.

'Let's do this smooth and fast. Get in and out before anyone realises we were here,' muttered Mason, as he eased his aging Oldsmobile Cutlass to the kerb and loosed his gun. He looked at his companion for confirmation and was rewarded with a monosyllabic grunt.

Mason climbed out of the Olds and sighed as the heat pummelled him like a cruiserweight on steroids. It was another hot day in the City of Angels and the sun was fast approaching its midday zenith, but at least he was suitably dressed—an electric blue Hawaiian shirt dotted with large red hibiscus over a pair of tattered blue jeans that had more holes than denim. He threw a furtive glance up and down the street to make sure that the locals were keeping their distance. Although he'd visited the Imperial Courts Housing Project on numerous occasions, he knew better than to start feeling at home there. The residents didn't view outsiders with distrust, they viewed them with outright hostility. They had to. They lived slap bang in the middle of a war zone.

He hurried around the hood of his car and waited as his companion stretched out his impressive six-foot-five frame before smoothing the creases from his slacks.

'C'mon, hurry it up, will ya? You can worry about looking pretty later.'

Diaz cocked one eyebrow above the rim of his mirrored Ray-Bans then gestured for Mason to lead on.

'You remember where we're headed, right? Li'l Cass's crib is on the second floor, right down the end. Chances are, we're ahead of the game, so our visit should come as a complete surprise,' Mason motor-mouthed as he hurried across the sidewalk to the apartment block known as the Pill Head.

The two men bounded up the steps three at a time, ignoring the indecipherable graffiti that covered the stairwell walls. When they arrived at the second floor, they drew their guns in unison and strode out onto the balcony that ran the length of the building. Loud rap music pumped from the far end of the block, where a frail figure sat slumped in a lawn chair directly outside their target's front door. Diaz levelled his Desert Eagle.

'Don't sweat it—it's just his mom,' said Mason, pushing the huge barrel down. 'She won't give us no trouble.'

As they neared the old woman her physical state became apparent—eyes rolled back in her head, drool running from her mouth, open sores and pus-filled abscesses marking every visible part of her body.

'Some sentry, huh?' whispered Mason with a smirk. 'Jeez—he's even tied her up,' he said, as he eased up the cuff of the old woman's house dress with the barrel of his Sig Sauer Pro to reveal that her wrists had been lashed to the arms of the chair. 'And what about that smell?' he continued, wrinkling his nose in distaste. 'No wonder she's out on the balcony.'

The apartment's front door stood wide open and a heavy bass line rumbled out of the opening like a charging rhino. Mason had no idea who the artist was— all rap music sounded the same to him. He stepped past the unconscious woman and raised his Sig. A hallway stretched out ahead of him, two doors to the left, two to the right, all of them closed. He checked his memory. The kitchen was behind the first door on the right, the living area behind the second. He motioned Diaz down the hall, then eased open the door to the kitchen. A tirade of expletives greeted him, as the rap music flooded into the room via the archway that led to the living area.

A mountain of dirty crockery was stacked high in the sink, and a half-eaten pizza sat on the small Formica table. He crept forward, noting that a fresh steel bolt had been sunk into the floor, and reached for a slice. Once he was alongside the archway, he scarfed down a couple of bites. Pepperoni and meatballs. Outstanding. He threw the pizza to the floor, took a couple of deep breaths, then stepped into the living area with gun held high, Diaz crashing through the far door a split second later.

Cassius was laid back on the sofa, his eyes shut tight, a thin smile on his face. His blue penitentiary shirt was open to the waist to reveal his skinny torso, while his black Levis were bagged up around his ankles. A young black girl with straggly hair extensions was kneeling in front of him, her head bobbing up and down vigorously to the booming music, her spine standing proud on her naked back.

'Love's young dream,' muttered Mason, as Diaz yanked the stereo's plug from its socket, killing the music stone dead. Cassius opened his eyes to blink rapidly against the daylight while the girl continued to chow down.

'How y'all doing?' he slurred.

'You're slipping, Cass, letting us walk straight in here unmolested. This ain't no time to be partying, you're in deep shit,' replied Mason, eyeing the crack pipe that lay on the sofa. 'Shit—I thought all you playas watched *Scarface?* Don't get high on your own supply, that's a sucker's game. Now lose the whore—we've got business.'

'Got-to-get-gone, bitch,' said Cassius, running the words together as he pushed the girl's head away from his crotch and yanked up his jeans. She rose unsteadily to her feet then turned around, her expression barely changing when she saw that there were two more men in the room. As she tottered towards the doorway to the hall, her small breasts jiggled against her scrawny frame. Diaz sent her on her way with a playful slap to the rump, the barest hint of a smile tugging at the corner of his mouth.

'You fucked up good and proper this time, Cass,' began Mason. 'Should have stuck to the projects, where another dead body don't matter.'

'What the fuck you talkin' about? Li'l Cass don't ever be fuckin' up.'

Diaz stepped forward and hit the young man in the face.

'You've been selling outside your remit,' continued Mason, as if nothing had happened. 'You know the

rules. Now you gotta pay the price for breaking 'em.
Where's your stash?'

'Huh?'

Mason sighed in disappointment then offered a nod
to his partner. Diaz grabbed Cassius by the ears and proceeded to lift him to his feet. The smaller man's legs
flailed in mid-air as he let out an anguished scream.

'Enough,' muttered Mason, prompting Diaz to throw
Cassius back down on the sofa. 'The stash?'

'Look, Mason, I been meaning to talk to you… I'm
all out… I need to re-up…'

'You're lying, Cass. We gave you a fresh batch just
a couple of days ago. You made a sale, then you came
back here to get your dick vacuumed. You keep on
lying, there's only gonna be one result.'

This time, Diaz didn't need any encouragement. He
threw a short, sharp right into the bridge of Cassius's
nose, prompting blood to burst forth from his nostrils.
Mason stepped forward and pushed the barrel of his gun
against the winded man's temple.

'We ain't got time for this shit, so here's how it's
gonna play out. Diaz is gonna break your fingers one by
one, and when he's done with the fingers, he's gonna start
on your toes, and if you haven't spilled your guts by
then, well, you don't wanna know what he's gonna break
after that. Diaz—why don't you start with a pinky?'

Diaz grabbed Cass's left hand and bent back the
little finger until there was an audible crack. When
Cassius had finished screaming Mason leant in close.

'The stash?'

'It ain't here, Mason. I swear.'

'Bullshit. You're too paranoid to hide it anywhere but right under your nose. Diaz?'

The next digit went the same way as the first. Cassius tried his best to turn a shade of white.

'Eight to go, Cass, and bear in mind that you're not gonna be of much use to me with two busted hands.'

'H-hold up, hold up,' stammered Cassius. 'I remember…'

'Now, that's more like it. Where?'

'Loose floorboard, under my bed…'

Mason nodded to Diaz, who left the room in a hurry. When he came back a minute or so later he was carrying a beat-up backpack. Inside the backpack was a bunch of plastic baggies, and inside each of the baggies were hundreds of small vials.

'There—see how simple that was? But you ain't on easy street just yet,' Mason said, as the beginnings of a plan started to coalesce in his mind. 'What we got here is a bad batch. Supplier cut it with rat poison to maximise his profits, only he went and fucked up the mix. People are dead, and I'll bet your prints are all over those baggies.'

'So what? Shit looks like all the other rock out in the hood. How's five-oh gonna prove I sold it?'

'Chemical composition tests, you dumb fuck. If this gets into the wrong hands, your ass is gonna get nailed to the wall. But don't you worry—me and Diaz will keep it safe for you. Course, we're gonna have to charge for the service.'

'Y'all sell me bad shit, then you wanna charge me for taking it back? That ain't right.'

'It ain't about right, Cass, it's about might, and right now we're the ones with the power. Let's say ten Gs, shall we? Plus we're gonna have to renegotiate all future deals.'

'Fuck dat!' shouted Cass, trying to rise to his feet, but Diaz pushed him back down.

'You ain't got much choice, son, you either play ball, or you end up turning sissy in Lompoc. You got one week to come up with your first down payment. I suggest you get busy.'

With that, Mason exited the room with Diaz following suit. Once they were clear of the apartment they strolled along the balcony and made their way back down the stairs. The Cutlass started with a splutter, then Mason floored the gas and headed out of Imperial Courts.

'Sweet,' he said, breaking into a grin. 'We've turned a potential disaster into a money-maker. Looks like we might get out from under sooner than we thought.'

Diaz hefted the backpack with a raised eyebrow.

'LA River,' muttered Mason. 'The sooner that shit's gone, the better I'm gonna feel.'

'Fuckin-A,' said Diaz, nodding in agreement.

Cassius began to panic as Mason strode past the zombie-like junkies, planted a boot on his wrist to stop him reaching for his gat, then gave him a long hard stare.

'So this is where you've been hiding, Cass? Well, I gotta tell ya, I don't think much of your new room-mates, but fair's fair, you do fit right in.'

Cassius tried to focus, but it wasn't easy—all he

could think about was scoring another fix. Christ, how he needed one. He was so damn tired, plus the worries about paying off Mason seemed to have amplified now that his nemesis had materialised in front of him.

'We've spent the last few days trying to find your skinny ass. Checked out all the downmarket hangouts that a lowlife such as yourself might frequent. All the juke joints, fleapits and titty-bars we could think of. I shoulda known you'd turn up in a crack house. What did I tell you about smoking your own product? It's liable to mess with your head, Cass. Make you do something against your better judgement. Like trying to skip out on a payment, huh? You're in hock, boy, and you gotta pay your dues. Maybe you need a little reminder of what happens to guys that try to cross the Mason-Diaz line. Diaz—teach him a lesson.'

Diaz loomed large over Mason's left shoulder, blocking out what was left of the light. The Puerto Rican pulled on a pair of latex gloves, bent his considerable frame to the floor, relieved Cassius of the Micro Uzi that he had wedged down his pants, then stood back up and cracked his knuckles.

'No, Mason, you got it all wrong. I was just comin' to find you,' spluttered Cassius. 'I been havin' a little cash flow problem is all…'

The first kick from Diaz landed deep in his gut, driving the air out of his lungs. He slumped to the floor and rolled up into a ball, his arms instinctively going to his head.

'I don't wanna hear it, Cass,' Mason shrugged.

A few of the junkies slipped out of the room, but

most of them stayed right where they were, either too high or too scared to make a move. Diaz let fly again, and this time the point of his boot connected with Cassius's lower ribs with a loud crack. Pain exploded through his chest like a forest fire as tears began to leak from his eyes.

'See, Cass, you gotta man-up and pay your debts, it's as simple as that,' continued Mason. 'And this is the last time I'm gonna cut you a break. So listen up.'

Cassius rolled onto his back and drew in a series of deep, gasping breaths, wincing at the onset of each inhalation.

'You've got two more days to find the cash, otherwise that package I'm holding for you is gonna end up in the wrong hands. And no more hiding out in crack dens—I'm through playing. Diaz—why don't you show him just how serious I am?'

Cassius looked up as Diaz pointed the Micro Uzi straight at him. His whole body started to shake as he stared at the barrel, then it went rigid as Diaz's latex-clad finger eased down on the trigger. At the very last moment, Diaz swung the gun to the left and loosed off a burst at a nearby addict. In the enclosed space, the sound of automatic gunfire was deafening. The bullets made chopped liver of the junkie's face, sending arcs of blood splattering over Cassius.

'Now look what you've gone and done,' said Mason. 'Killed an innocent man and left your prints all over the murder weapon. Trouble just seems to follow you around. You've got two days. Consider this a final warning.'

Cassius felt his heart sink as he watched the two men

leave. He hauled himself into a kneeling position and crawled for the exit. How the hell was he gonna come up with Mason's cash in just two days?

CHAPTER SEVEN

STONE walked out of the Seven-Eleven with a camera case hung off one shoulder and a brown paper bag in one hand. He glanced upwards to establish the sun's position in the sky and estimated the time to be a little after nine a.m. The day was fixing to be a hot one. His long hair was pulled back in a ponytail, a soft sheen of sweat glistened on his forehead, and the sleeves of his checked shirt were rolled up to display a pair of powerful arms.

He took a couple of steps forward until he was at the kerb, then reached inside the bag to retrieve a bottle of Jack Daniel's. Two passing businessmen threw him a pair of condescending looks, but he paid them no mind. He held the bottle up to the light and stared into its amber depths for a moment, then he broke the seal and unscrewed the cap. He raised it to his face and inhaled deeply, allowing the scent of the liquid to explode inside his nostrils, then he lowered the bottle once again. Having passed the test, he sank to his haunches and proceeded to pour the entire contents of the bottle into the gutter. The river of whiskey bubbled and sloshed its way down the street until it disappeared into a nearby drain, forever removed from temptation.

'Caleb! Joshua!'

At the sound of his voice, two large dogs rose from their prone positions on the sidewalk and fell into place alongside him. They were male Akitas, one a pinto, the other pure white, powerful animals whose long snouts and pointed ears gave them a passing resemblance to huskies. He'd owned them since they were pups, having rescued them from one of LA's many animal shelters, and for now they were all the family he had. As he strode down the street, the dogs kept pace with him on either flank, their noses twitching.

Fifteen minutes later he'd reached his destination. He was in a rundown alley, standing next to a large dumpster that was overflowing with trash. A chain-link fence stood in front of him, and behind that fence was a dirty asphalt playground that led up to a three-storey building with a domed structure butted onto its right flank. Acorn Elementary School where according to their motto, they were busy 'Nurturing The Seeds Of All Our Futures'. The school was situated at an intersection, and Stone could look right across the playground to observe the passing traffic on Willowbrook Avenue.

'Caleb, Joshua—down.'

The two dogs prostrated themselves at his feet. He sat between them, the dumpster providing cover from the street, then he freed his Canon camera from its case and settled into a comfortable position. The playground was empty, save for a small group of boys that leant against the fence on the far side, for whom lessons were presumably optional. Once he'd attached a powerful zoom lens to the camera, he turned it on, aimed it at the boys, then made some adjustments until the image came into sharp focus. There were five of them in total, four black, one white, and they all looked world-weary despite their tender years. They wore baggy jeans, oversized T-shirts, and lots of cheap gold, but this wasn't what captured Stone's attention. Instead, it was the single word rendered in gothic script that was tattooed on the back of their necks—'Knights'. A conflicting mixture of anger and sorrow began to build inside him, and the scene through the viewfinder began to shake. Caleb let loose a soft whine and Joshua edged closer, the two dogs seemingly aware of their master's inner turmoil. Stone took a deep breath, set his jaw, and got himself under control, then he began to take a few pictures of each of the kids.

When he'd finished, he lowered the camera and petted his dogs, his eyes flicking back and forth along Willowbrook Avenue. Twenty minutes passed in this manner, until the sound of an approaching engine combined with a heavy base beat prompted Stone to tense up. A Ford Maverick 4x4 rolled slowly into view before coming to a gentle stop alongside the kids in the schoolyard. He raised the camera to his eye and targeted the new arrival. The door of the Maverick swung open and a small black man with an impressive Afro climbed out of the vehicle, his bushy black hair encircling his head like a giant halo. Stone grimaced. This guy was no angel. His hands tightened on the camera as he began to take picture after picture. Snap—the man rounding the hood of his Maverick. Snap—the vehicle's licence plate. Snap—the man's face in close-up.

The Canon's shutter kept whirring as the man walked up to the fence to converse with the five loitering kids. Stone was beyond anger now—a feeling of pure rage blasted from his every pore. As he watched on, the conversation continued for a couple more minutes then exchanges were made through the bars. The kids turned as one and walked back inside the main school building, while the guy with the Afro returned to his Maverick. Stone didn't lower his camera until the vehicle had pulled away. He'd taken over fifty photos in a three-minute period. He unscrewed the zoom lens, packed the camera away, then rose to his feet.

'Caleb, Joshua—come.'

The two dogs leapt up to assume their flanking positions, then the three of them walked off down the street.

CHAPTER EIGHT

HUNTER eased down on the Barracuda's brakes and brought the car to a gentle halt. He'd been up early that morning, eager to start looking for Angel's daughter, but he'd had to kill a little time before setting out for his destination, as he knew that it was likely to be deserted until the neighbourhood moms had completed their school run. He checked his watch—it had just got nine-thirty—perfect timing.

The playground from which Gracie had disappeared was just a few blocks from Angel's home on Verona. It was a relatively small affair, wedged in between the surrounding houses and contained on all sides by a steel mesh fence. The space was sectioned in two: on the left, a sandy area stocked with a collection of swings and slides for the kids; and on the right, an expanse of concrete that was home to a few wooden picnic benches and not much else. Hunter noticed that the benches had been bolted to the concrete. Everything was fair game in some neighbourhoods.

A couple of large, home-made placards had been attached to the fence bordering the kids' area. The writing was in stark black letters and it proclaimed that this was a drug-free zone. A couple of Latino pre-schoolers were taking turns on the slide, their mothers watching on as they drank take-out coffee at one of the picnic benches, while an emaciated black woman lay draped over the bench furthest from the street. The two mothers seemed to be doing their best to ignore her, although neither could resist throwing an occasional disapproving look. Hunter walked towards them, their conversation becoming clearer as he closed the distance.

'...I still think that Miguel is cheating on her. And have you seen the way he looks at me? Like I'm a piece of prime rib just waiting to be devoured.'

'Morning, ladies,' he said. 'Sorry to cut in. I need a little help.'

'I'll bet you do, honey,' said the woman nearest him, her eyes roving the length of his body. 'Ain't you a fine-looking specimen. I'm Carla.'

As she spoke, she ran a hand through her hair and fluttered her lashes provocatively. She was quite the looker—her bright crimson halter top accentuated her bust, while her cut-off jeans left little to the imagination.

'And I'm Luisa,' said the other woman quietly, seemingly embarrassed by her friend's behaviour. Luisa was dressed much more conservatively in a floaty knee-length skirt and plain white blouse. Her expression was guarded and she seemed upset by the interruption.

'Well, it's nice to make both your acquaintances.' Hunter smiled. 'You come down here most days?'

'Pretty much,' said Luisa. 'Our kids love to play on the slides.'

'We only come in daylight, though,' muttered Carla, as she tapped loose a cigarette from the pack that lay on the table in front of her and proceeded to light it. 'It ain't safe after dark. The junkies take over.'

'They leave their filth everywhere,' continued Luisa, gesturing angrily towards the black woman in the corner. 'First thing I do every morning is clean up as best I can. I can't sit by and leave needles laying around so close to where our kids play.'

'How about the Wednesday just gone? Were you here in the afternoon?'

'Why'd you ask?' said Luisa, her mouth tightening.

'A little girl went missing. Here—I've got a photo…'

Hunter slid Gracie's picture across the table towards the two women. Carla gave it a lingering look but Luisa's eyes skipped straight over its surface to look off into the distance.

'You recognise her at all?'

'I think I seen her before, but not on Wednesday afternoon—I was getting a manicure at the salon,' said Carla, holding out her nails for inspection.

'How about you, Luisa?'

'No, I never seen her,' she said refusing to meet Hunter's gaze.

'Yeah, yeah, you have,' pressed Carla. 'Her mom thinks she's all that, remember? Weren't you down here on Wednesday?'

'No. No, I wasn't. And her mom's tied up with the gangs. It's time I was going.'

'Hey—wait a minute,' said Hunter. 'What did you see?'

'I didn't see anything. And even if I had, I make it my policy to keep out of gang business.'

'But a little girl's life is at stake.'

'I'm sorry, I can't help you. I got a kid of my own.' She shook off his hand, rose to her feet, and dragged her friend away. Hunter watched on as the two women held a hushed conversation en route to their respective children. When it came to finding Gracie, Carla was a dead end, but Luisa was holding something back. He took a step forward before a frail voice stopped him cold.

'I be Elsa… I be here on Wednesday…'

He looked around to find that the emaciated woman by the fence was beckoning him over.

'You see this girl?' he asked, walking over and showing her the photo.

'Uh-huh.'

'So what happened?'

'Gonna cost you.' Elsa coughed, rubbing a hand across her dirt-streaked face. She looked like she was all-star when it came to drug use—a lost soul that would ingest anything she could lay her hands on. A fetid stench of stale sweat enveloped her, torn rags hung loosely off her bony shoulders, and deep scratch marks ran up both her arms. Hunter had seen marks like that before. They were caused by a mental illness known as formication—a hallucination suffered by some coke-heads that convinced them that bugs were crawling under their skin.

'How much?' he asked.

'Forty?'

'Twenty.'

'I be needing forty.'

'The offer's twenty—take it or leave it.'

She nodded glumly, so Hunter pulled a couple of ten-dollar bills out of his pocket and slid one of them towards her.

'Tell me what you know, and if it's any good I'll give you the rest.'

Elsa grabbed at the cash and began to talk.

'I see that girl here on Wednesday, but not for long. She come down on her own, play for a li'l while. Then a black van pull up and two guys jump out.'

'What make was the van?'

'Dunno…'

'Did it have any distinguishing marks? Maybe a defect in the paintwork or a dent in the fender?

'Dunno…'

'What did the men look like?'

'Jus' guys, you know? They was all in black, wearin' hoods—one of 'em had marks on his arm.'

'Tattoos?'

'Yeah.'

'What sort of tattoos?'

'Can't recall,' she muttered, snot dribbling from her left nostril.

'So two guys jumped out of a van—what happened next?'

'They grabbed the li'l girl.'

'Was she on her own? Or were there other kids present?'

'Other kids…maybe three or four.'

'But they went straight for this one?' he asked, holding up the photo.

'No doubt…she was right at the back. They walked past the rest like they wasn't even there.'

'And nobody tried to stop them?'

'They big and they fast. They grabbed her, then stuffed her in the van and took off.'

'You get the licence?'

Elsa shook her head and muttered 'Goddamn bugs!' before starting to rake her fingernails over the scars on her forearm until she drew blood.

'What about that woman over there?' asked Hunter, gesturing to where Luisa played with her child. 'Was she here too?'

'Maybe…but she ain't gonna talk to you…she scared…' Elsa said dismissively.

'She'll talk,' said Hunter, turning to leave.

'Hey—what about the rest of my money?'

'I figure ten bucks is all you were good for.'

'But I ain't finished—I gots more…'

'Make it quick.'

'There were some cars too…'

'So?'

'When the van pulled off, the cars left straight after…maybe they was followin', you know?'

'Or maybe they weren't. Describe them.'

'Blue Dodge sedan—dirty-looking ride with two brothers up front. I remember coz they music was so loud…'

'Anything else?'

'Yeah…red Chevy…two-seater with a cargo bay in back. My pop used to run one back in the day…'

'A two-seater with a cargo bay? Like a pick-up truck?'

'Yeah. Like my pops used to have.'

'Get the licence on either of them?'

'Nah. But the Chevy was all pretty on the side. Like it was burning up, you know?'

'You mean flames? From a paint job?'

'Uh-huh.'

'And what about the two brothers in the Dodge? They look like bangers to you?'

'Honey, everyone in the life around here. It's all we got.'

'And that's all you remember?'

'Yep.'

As Hunter slid her the rest of the cash she made a grab for his arm.

''Less there's anything else I can do for you? I'll suck your cock for another twenty?'

He shook off her hand and walked away.

'Come on, mister, I got a kid to feed,' she called after him. 'He a bit slow—I gotta help him…'

A bit slow? No wonder, when he had a drug addict for a mother. But at least Zac now knew that Gracie had been abducted, and experience told him that meant one of two things—either a kidnap demand would follow, or she'd been taken by sex freaks. His blood ran cold at the thought of the latter. He hurried towards the Latino mothers and their kids in the play area. Carla offered a half-smile as she saw him approaching, but Luisa didn't look overly pleased.

'I've done talking to you. Why don't you just leave us alone?' she said coldly.

'Just one more question, and this time you don't even need to answer. Just keep quiet if what I say is true. Black van, two hooded men, one abducted child.'

Luisa looked scared but she kept quiet.

'Thanks. And do me a favour? Bring her some food next time you're here?' he asked, handing over a few dollar bills as he gestured to the crack addict Elsa. He walked back to his Barracuda, his frustration on the rise. He'd learnt a little, but it was nowhere near enough.

CHAPTER NINE

STONE was up high, four storeys above the ground on the roof of an empty department store, legal commerce having long since departed the locale. He'd grabbed a spot by the side wall between two air-conditioning vents, while the stairwell that led to the store's interior was thirty yards to his left. The midday sun beat down on him remorselessly, and every minute or so a bead of sweat would trickle down his forehead to sting his eyes. As the temperature ticked another degree higher, he unbuttoned his shirt and drained the last of his bottled water.

He'd been up there for over two hours, near motionless for most of that time as he studied his prey. The waiting didn't bother him. In years gone by, his ancestors would have sat countless times as he did now, virtually invisible until the moment to strike was at hand, at which point they'd have burst from their cover and attacked—their target either the mighty buffalo for sustenance or their human foes for vengeance. His parents were Plains Apaches, thus hunting and warfare ran deep in his blood. He'd turned his back on this rich heritage for a while, distracted by the dark temptations of the modern world, and although that sorry period was now behind him, he still had a lot to make up for.

He placed the empty water bottle by his feet and returned to the task at hand. His perch on the roof allowed him to look down on a large open square situated on the far side of the street. An aging apartment building provided the backdrop, while the buildings that had once been on either side of the square had both been demolished, leaving piles of rubble in their wake. A couple of lawn chairs sat in the middle of the space, and on those chairs sat two black youths in relative comfort, leaving their four less fortunate companions to stretch out on the surrounding concrete. Four gleaming mountain bikes lay nearby and lunch had just been served courtesy of McDonald's.

Stone focused the zoom lens of his camera on the small group and snapped off a few more pictures as they devoured their burgers. The two on the chairs appeared to be in their early twenties, and each wore pristine Timberland boots, dark blue jeans that hung low to expose their boxer shorts, and plain white Ts. Their actions thus far marked them out as the senior members of the crew, and they were there to make sure that the wheels of inner-city commerce turned smoothly. The four guys lounging around on the concrete were all younger, ranging in age from around ten to eighteen, their clothes less stylish, their demeanours less confident. Every once in a while one of them would be dispatched to carry out some menial task—the last had been to fetch the burgers—at which point they'd jump to their feet, grab their bikes, and ride off quickly. These four were the runners, there to provide their betters with whatever they demanded.

As Stone zoomed out to get a wider view of proceedings, a man wearing ripped slacks, a dirty raincoat and little else stumbled into the frame. His rolling gait was akin to that of an old timer, but on closer inspection he looked to be somewhere in his mid-forties. As he approached the group of youths, one of the runners walked out to meet him. The man fumbled inside his raincoat then handed something over. The runner nodded towards the apartment block at the back of the square, then turned to go back to his homies. The man set out once again, his stride now slightly more purposeful. Stone angled his camera at the apartment block where the walls were daubed with a mixture of obscene graffiti and monochrome gang signs, focusing the viewfinder on the far entrance on the left, which was the only one that still had a door in its frame. When the man arrived, he knocked once, then shuffled from side to side. The door snapped open and a hand snaked out to drop something into his palm. No sooner had this occurred than the man was off once again, making his way around the side of the building in search of chemical stimulation.

Stone swung his camera back to the gang of youths who were busy counting greenbacks after their latest deal. Their accrued total must have reached some pre-agreed level, as two of the runners began stashing wads of dollar bills down the fronts of their pants before grabbing their mountain bikes to set off for some unknown destination. Stone sighed. It had been this way all day. Every few minutes some half-alive junkie would stumble towards the cashiers in the middle of the square, hand over the remains of his welfare check, then head off to the apartment block to pick up his order. Of course, it wasn't just men who were out here buying an escape from reality—in the last two hours Stone had seen just as many women make the same sorry purchase.

For the guys riding point on the chairs, it was a pretty neat system. If any passing member of LA's finest was to roust them, all they were holding was cash, and even then never enough of it to arouse suspicion and fall foul of the law. As a result, they were fairly safe from any random police incursions, although their actions wouldn't hold up to the scrutiny of a surveillance programme like the one Stone was running now. As he watched on, something sparked the four remaining gangbangers into action. They leapt to their feet, formed a half-assed line, and folded their right arms across their chests, fists clenched with little fingers extended. Stone had seen this before. Their gang sign—thrown to either warn off rivals or welcome fellow brethren. He searched the area for the sign's intended recipient. A red El Camino was parked at the front of the square. The door swung open and a small man climbed out. He was wearing a pair of baggy jeans along with a blue penitentiary shirt that billowed around his frame like an oversized kaftan. When he saw the four youths throwing their salutes he stopped dead in his tracks.

CHAPTER TEN

HUNTER marched straight up to Angel's house and rapped on the front door. On the face of it, he was calling in to update her on the search for her daughter, but he also had a secondary motive: to confront Lunatic. From what he'd learnt at the playground it sounded like Gracie's kidnapping might have been gang related, and if it was gang related, then Lunatic might know something about it. Maybe he'd run foul of a supplier. Maybe a turf war had gotten out of hand. Maybe he'd already received a ransom demand and kept it quiet. Hunter rapped hard on the door once again. It was time the gang leader started talking.

The door swung open and Angel appeared in the frame wearing a mauve towelling robe, her face care-worn and make-up free. When she saw who'd come calling, her expression flickered with hope, and Hunter felt guilty that he hadn't come armed with better news.

'Have you found her?'

'Not yet. But I've made some progress. Is Lunatic home?'

Her eyes clouded over as she shook her head.

'You'd better come in.'

She led the way through her home with heavy steps. When they arrived at the kitchen, she gestured for him to take a seat at the small wooden table in the centre of the room.

'Coffee?' she asked, reaching for the pot by the sink.

'Please.'

'How'd you take it?'

'Black, two sugars.'

She poured him a cup, refilled her own, then sat down opposite him, her robe falling open to reveal some cleavage. He looked away quickly, feeling embarrassed, but she didn't seem to have noticed.

'So what have you found out?'

He ran through the conversation he'd had with the drug addict at the playground, detailing how Gracie had been snatched by two hooded men and bundled into a black cargo van. As he told the story, tears began to leak from her eyes.

'The good news is, it looks like she was targeted,' he said softly.

'Targeted? How in the hell is that good news?'

'The kidnappers walked straight past three or four other kids to get to Gracie. Why? If the abduction wasn't random then they must need her for something. And if they need her, it stands to reason they'll keep her alive.'

'But why would they need her? She's just a kid.'

'A kid with important parents. Both you and Lunatic are well known around these parts. The two of you head up a gang, and that makes you a big deal, and a big target. The most common motive for abduction is profit. Have you had a ransom demand?'

'No.'

'What about Lunatic?' he asked. 'Maybe he's heard something?'

'I don't think so—he's not saying much. All he's told me is that he'll sort everything out. He says no one else can help. Says if they try, then Gracie's gonna wind up dead.'

'But you called me?'

'I was desperate. But he was real mad when he found out. I never seen him so angry. Said it'd be my fault if Gracie died…'

'None of this is your fault. You did the right thing in calling me.'

'Did I? Gracie's still missing and now Larry's gone too.'

'Gone? What's happened?'

'He never came home last night. I'm all alone,' she said, strands of brown hair falling over her eyes as she lowered her head.

'You're not alone, Angel,' he said, as he gently raised her head until she looked straight into his eyes. 'I'm here for you. And we're going to find Gracie. But I still think you should contact the police.'

'No! I can't. The one thing Larry was clear about was that we couldn't involve the cops. The only reason I called you was because I knew you'd help. And anyhow, what are the cops going to do for us? We've been running with the Ghosts all our lives—police ain't got no love for gangbangers.'

'But they've got the manpower, the resources—they know what they're doing when it comes to missing persons. You've got to trust them.'

'Trust them? You've gotta be joking. I can't get them involved. I can't take any more risks. It's up to you, Hunter. You gotta help me. You promised.'

He decided to leave it for now. What with her partner having just pulled a disappearing act, she was even more emotionally fragile than before, and the prospect of calling in the cops seemed set to push her over the edge. Lunatic's absence was a major problem. Hunter had a hunch that he was the key to everything that was happening, and without him, making progress was going to be tough.

'So Lunatic never came home last night. Have you tried calling him?'

'I tried his cell and his beeper but there's no response.'

'Any idea where he might have gone?'

'Nope.'

'What's he been doing since Gracie went missing?'

'Not much. Just hanging out in the 'hood.'

'Like he's been waiting for something to happen?'

'I guess.'

'Get some clothes on. We need to find him.'

Angel rose to her feet, tightened her robe, and headed out of the kitchen. Hunter drained his coffee and watched as she walked away. With no other obvious leads to chase down in the hunt for Gracie, questioning Lunatic had become top priority.

CHAPTER ELEVEN

CASSIUS slammed the door of his Camino, straightened his frame to its full five feet eight inches, then froze as a burst of pain shot through his cracked rib. He looked out across the square to find that his bomb squad were standing in a line up ahead, throwing out the hand signal that claimed their set. He responded in kind, feeling a burst of pride about the family ties he'd forged with these men and others like them. The elder two he'd known for years, the youngsters only weeks, but as fellow members of the Imperial Knights he viewed them all as brothers. The Knights meant everything to him. Each and every one of them had his back, just like he had theirs. There wasn't one member of the gang that was blood to him, but they all might as well have been. One thing was for sure—they were a whole lot more reliable than his actual family.

From what he could remember of his childhood, it had been one shitty year after another. His father, Luther, had been a feeble excuse for a parent who had been absent for the most part—and those had been the good times. Luther had been a drunk who'd never held down a full-time job, unless you counted petty robbery as a profession, and to make matters worse, he'd been a terrible burglar, probably on account of the fact that he'd always been half-loaded when he'd set out in search of easy money. In the end, his visits to the state pen had become so regular he'd practically had his own cell there. Cassius had spent his childhood either smothering a grin as he'd waved his father off on another short-time stretch, or hiding his fear as he'd welcomed the son of a bitch back home.

And it was the home times that were the worst. Luther took his belt to him at the slightest provocation, regularly thrashing him until the skin on his back was red raw. Forgot to put the trash out? Time for a beating. Finished the last of the Cheerios? Time for a beating. Looked at him funny? You get the picture. Cassius was forced to sleep on his stomach, or else the wounds on his back would stick to the bed sheets. And where was his mom while all this was happening? Where had she been when he'd needed a champion? She'd been nowhere, as she'd had problems of her own, problems that continued to haunt her every waking moment to this day.

In the end, his father's seemingly endless ability to fuck up had brought Cassius some respite. Luther, naturally right handed, had tried to hold up the local five and dime store while holding a bottle of rotgut whisky in one hand and a Colt revolver in the other. As he'd placed more importance on the booze than on the robbery, he'd had the bottle in his right hand and the gun in his left. When the clerk had gone for the sawn-off shotgun that he'd kept hidden below the counter, Luther had missed high with his first shot and he'd never got off a second. At such close range, the clerk's double-ought buckshot had demolished Luther's chest, and he'd bled out long before the ambulance had arrived. On hearing the news, Cassius had felt nothing but sweet relief.

So family ties had never meant all that much to him in his formative years, at least not until he'd been jumped into the Knights, where he'd discovered family of a whole different kind. It had been the Knights that had given him a sense of belonging. The Knights that had shown him respect. The Knights that had shown him love. To be a pure-blood Knight you had to hail from the Imperial Courts Housing Project and, once sworn in, you had to be ready to die for your turf. Cassius had signed up at the age of nine, eager to be a part of something, whatever the cost, and for the next fifteen years he'd never looked back.

He'd passed every test with flying colours, standing firm with his brothers on the streets and keeping his game tight when he found himself locked down—first in juvie, then youth authority, then prison, with each successive bout of incarceration bringing longer and harder time, but to his credit he'd never dishonoured his crew. Being locked up had never worried him. It was an inevitable consequence of banging—part of the job description—and thanks to his father's exploits it had played a large role in his childhood anyhow.

Over in the middle of the square, the four members of his crew lowered their arms and ceased their urban salutes. The pride he felt was suddenly tempered with another emotion—pity—because the day was about to head south for one of them. It was a shame, but he had no choice. Mason and Diaz had backed him into a corner. They wanted their money, and they wanted it fast. If he failed to pay up, the whole city was going to hear of his sins, including his boss. A shudder ran through his skinny frame at the thought of that. Dreadnought would tear him limb from limb. No matter that they'd been close friends for over a decade, Cassius knew that his actions of late would demand the ultimate censure.

He pushed back his shoulders and began to pimp strut across the square, just fast enough to look purposeful but not so fast he looked in a hurry. Every ten yards or so he'd cast an eye at the passing addicts to ensure they maintained a respectful distance. Some of them were real sick, and he had no intention of contracting a disease during his brief visit to the shop floor. As he neared the centre of the space, the crowd thinned out.

'Wassup, Cass?' asked Zombie, the senior of the four, so named as his love of the weed often left him near senseless. The other man, Slowpoke, nodded a lazy hello, while the two boys shuffled around and looked nervous.

''S all good,' said Cassius, throwing his skinny arms around Zombie's shoulders in a brief embrace. 'You?'

'Same ole, same ole. Hangin', bangin' and slangin'…'

'How's bidness?'

'Decent. Been a steady flow of cluckheads down here jonesing all day, mostly desperate for nickel bags, though we sold a few dimes too. Had a couple of college boys show up in the a.m.—whiteys that be well heeled—say they comin' back to re-up if the shit's good.'

'They be back—everyone know our shit's the best in the west.'

'True, dat.'

'That's righteous, Zombie, but you gotta push the product harder. We gotta make more sales, bring in new custom. How these shorties pannin' out? They down?'

'Yeah, they down. They ready to die for the 'hood.'

The two boys visibly swelled on the spot.

'So send 'em out to the crack dens,' continued Cassius. 'Have 'em roust anyone that ain't lit up, remind 'em there's good times to be had down here for only five bucks a pop.'

'What's the hurry, Cass? Addicts know where we be—they come down sooner or later.'

'Let's make it sooner,' said Cassius, lowering his tone as he led Zombie away from the group. 'We been losin' some of our premium dealers lately, and profits are slidin'—Dread ain't gonna be happy if the weekly numbers be down again.'

'We lost more dealers?'

'Yup. Some muthafucka put Cockroach in the hospital with a busted collar bone, plus Gopher pulled a disappearing act.'

'Cockroach grab a look at who done for him?'

'Nope. One second he be walking along all fine and dandy, next he be lying on the ground, all fucked up.'

'Ain't gonna be easy uppin' profits overnight, Cass, we got a lotta new guys learnin' the ropes.'

'Just get it done, any which way. Get the product flyin' off the shelf, and if those white boys come back, give 'em a deal on a bulk buy.'

'And what we gonna do with the cash? If shorties be out rousting crackheads there be no one to handle the money run.'

'Don't sweat it. Sit on the green till late in the day, then get Slowpoke to take care of delivery.'

'Slowpoke? With a heavy load? You sure?'

'Sure I'm sure. Slowpoke be fine. And I want you to keep representin' right through the night. From now on, we runnin' at full capacity for twenty-four hours a day, seven days a week. We gotta keep our game tight, Zombie, what with all the turf wars going on, we can't afford to be showin' no weakness. Now get to it. I got other bidness to attend to.'

Cassius clapped Zombie on the shoulder then spun on his heel and hurried back to his El Camino. He'd been out in the open way too long—what with Mason and Diaz on the lookout for him, he'd been trying to keep a low profile. Coming to the square had been a high-risk strategy as it was one of the Knights best-known dope spots, but as he'd wanted to raise some quick revenue, he'd had little choice. Now he had to hope that the move would pay off.

CHAPTER TWELVE

HUNTER coaxed his Barracuda along South Arizona Avenue at a snail's pace, his eyes constantly roving the sidewalk.

'See anything?' he asked Angel, who sat alongside him in the passenger seat.

'Nope.'

It was mid-afternoon and the two of them had been criss-crossing the neighbourhood for the past hour or so on the lookout for Lunatic. Prior to that they'd checked out all his usual hangouts—bars, diners, and the like—where a few other Ghosts had been present, although none of them had seen their glorious leader.

'You hungry? How about we pull over and grab some lunch?' he asked, his stomach rumbling at the sight of an approaching taco stand.

'Wait a minute! Back up!'

Hunter hit the brakes and shifted the car into reverse.

'Over there,' said Angel, pointing down a side alley. The alley was stationed between a derelict plot of land and a neighbourhood bar, and it was bordered by ramshackle wooden fencing. 'Those guys are Ghosts.'

He followed her gesture to observe three men stepping through a hole in the fence. Once they'd disappeared from view, he turned back to Angel.

'Should we check it out?'

'If it's Ghost business, Larry might be around. Not much goes down without his say-so.'

'So what are we waiting for?'

When Hunter cracked open the door, Angel laid a restraining hand on his arm. He turned and looked at her, noting the spark of concern in her eyes.

'You gotta keep a low profile—they don't like outsiders. Plus if Larry's there, he mustn't see us together—he'd go ballistic.'

'Got it.' He nodded, before leading the way to the mouth of the alley. A stack of empty beer crates and an overflowing trashcan were positioned halfway down on the left-hand side, while a piss-stained mattress sat a few yards further ahead. He edged around the mattress, and crept forward, straining his ears for signs of life, but all he heard was the sound of Angel following stealthily in his wake. As the two of them neared the gap in the fence, shouts of encouragement suddenly broke the silence, the voices a mixture of baritone and soprano. A fresh fear entered his mind. What if the bangers' actions demanded that he intercede? He'd find it pretty hard to stand by and do nothing if they were brutalising a citizen, regardless of his pledge to Angel. He drew his gun then craned his neck until he could see through the hole.

The bar's rear parking lot was on the other side of the fence. Nine men and four youths were arranged in a loose semi circle by the side of a beat-up white truck. Lunatic was in the middle of the group. A skinny boy, who wasn't much more than ten years of age, stood in front of him, shifting from one foot to the other. Angel squeezed in close to get a better view of proceedings, curling her right arm around his waist for balance. He felt her body stiffen when she recognised her partner, but she made no move to go to him. The sweet scent of her perfume began to dance over his nostrils. He forced himself to concentrate on the action that was about to unfold.

The shouts of the group rose in volume. They seemed to be yelling encouragement to the lone boy. And then they suddenly stopped. One of the men checked his watch and said *'Uno minuto'* in a sombre tone. At that, Lunatic burst into action.

His first punch was delivered straight to the boy's gut, doubling him up in an instant. Hunter took a half-step forward, but Angel stopped him cold.

'It's an initiation,' she whispered. 'Leave it be.'

A gang initiation. He'd heard about them, but he'd never actually witnessed one. He forced himself to watch as Lunatic threw another punch, this one thudding into the boy's lower ribcage, then another, a right hook to the kidneys. Tears ran freely down the boy's cheeks, but as the gang boss doled out the punishment, his face remained impassive.

'Treinta sobras!' shouted the man with the watch.

Two more blows, one to the gut, another to the heart, and the boy was beginning to sag, prompting two of the onlookers to step forward and haul him up by the arms. Lunatic now changed tack as he crashed the instep of his foot against the fleshy part of the boy's calf before drawing back his boot to lash out again at the side of his victim's right knee. The lot was silent now, save for the sound of the boy's whimpers escaping through a set of firmly clenched teeth. Hunter's heart went out to him. It wasn't easy watching a kid get taken apart like this, but what could he do about it? No one would thank him for interfering, least of all the human punchbag. The kid had volunteered for this beating in order to become a proud member of the Santa Anna Ghosts. When the gangs were your best option in life, something was seriously wrong.

'Diez sobras!' yelled the man with the watch, as Lunatic went back to his fists. His next blow was a vicious uppercut that connected with the point of the boy's chin, snapping his head backwards. A couple of the onlookers gasped in shock, signifying that some line had just been crossed.

'Time's up!' came the shout, but Lunatic went on as if nothing had changed, sending a powerful left straight into the bridge of the boy's nose. A few of the gang members looked at each other uncomfortably, but no one made any effort to stop the violence. The boy had just enough time to register a look of abject fear before another punch exploded into his face. Lunatic wore a mask of fury while his fists glistened with the blood of his latest recruit.

'Stay here,' whispered Angel, and then she was gone, stepping though the gap in the fence to run over to her fellow gang members.

'Larry! That's enough!' she yelled. 'I said that's enough!'

Lunatic pulled his punch at the sound of her voice and turned as if waking from a dream, while in sharp contrast the boy was allowed to slip to the ground, where he lay twitching in the throes of a terrible nightmare.

'What the hell do you think you're all doing?' shouted Angel, rounding on the rest of the group. 'Letting him take the kid apart like that? We need new blood to stay strong—a few more seconds and he'd have been no use to no one.'

'Sorry, Angel,' muttered one of the men.

'Enrique—take him back to your pad and get him patched up.'

A stocky Latino stepped forward and helped the kid to his feet, then began to lead him towards the alley.

'Sweet Jesus! Not on foot!' said Angel. 'You might run into a black and white! Manuel—drive them.'

A second man broke off and helped get the kid into a nearby Impala. The engine spluttered to life, then the wheels spun on the gravel as it pulled out of the lot.

'Now the rest of you—get gone. All that commotion will have drawn some attention.'

Angel then wrapped her arm around Lunatic and led him towards the bar's rear entrance. As he moved forward, his footfalls were ponderous, like he was wading through deep mud. Once the two of them had disappeared inside, Hunter slipped quietly away, and by the time he was back in his Barracuda, he'd had a chance to consider all that he'd seen.

Angel had been impressive. She'd marched head-long into a group of dangerous men high on testosterone and read them the riot act, taking charge of the situation in an instant, and not one of them had thought twice about arguing with her—she'd had their total respect, and when it came to the streets, respect always had to be earned. Even Lunatic himself had kept quiet while she'd handed out her orders, at a time when his famous temper had just got the better of him. Lunatic might have been the boss of the Ghosts, but it was clear that Angel was pretty high up the food chain as well. Hunter set his jaw as he had a sobering thought. With Gracie still missing, Lunatic was on the edge of a precipice, and that made him more dangerous than ever.

Hunter yawned and cracked his knuckles. Angel and Lunatic had been inside the bar for the best part of an hour and he was starting to get impatient. The rest of the gang had dispersed shortly after the initiation, and Hunter had ducked down low in the Barracuda's front seat as they'd drifted away. As he'd sat there, he'd found himself replaying the initiation in his head. It had been a chilling spectacle. To think that someone volunteered for such punishment was scarcely believable, yet he'd seen it happen with his own eyes. Most of these kids had nothing—they were the lost generation. They'd become disconnected from their families either by crime, poverty or drugs, and they were in search of something, anything, that would give their lives meaning, and that was where the gangs came in. It was the lethal lack of hope that caused the gangs to flourish—they provided a sense of belonging, and sometimes it was better to belong to something bad than to nothing at all.

He looked up as the front door of the bar swung open. Angel paused in the frame for a second, then walked over to him. Her hips rolled gently as she approached, while her chestnut brown hair bounced on her shoulders.

'He's not talking,' she said, as she leant against the side of the car.

'Not a word? Not even to say where he was last night?'

'Nope. Though I'd guess he spent most of it in a bar.'

'And he didn't say a thing about Gracie?'

'Only that I should leave everything to him, and that it'd all be over soon.'

Hunter climbed out of the car and dug a twenty out of his pocket.

'Get yourself a cab home. There's a phone box on the corner.'

'What are you gonna do?'

'Talk to him.'

'But he'll go loco if he finds out you're still involved! You saw how he was out there, he would have beat that kid to death if I hadn't stepped in.'

'I'm no kid, and I've got to talk to him. He knows something about Gracie's abduction—maybe I can convince him to open up.'

'How?'

'I have my ways.'

She considered his meaning for a moment before continuing. 'If you're going in, I'd better come too.'

'No—it's better I do this alone. It'll focus his anger on me, not you, plus if things turn physical, I'd rather you weren't around. Here, take the money,' he said, pushing the twenty into her hands, 'And get a cab. I'll call you later.'

'Okay,' she said, although he could see she wasn't convinced. 'But be careful.'

As she walked off down the street, he locked the 'Cuda, then strode over to the bar. He paused outside for a moment, as the reality of the situation hit him. He was about to question a Latino gang boss about the whereabouts of his own missing daughter, and he was being paid to do so by the gang boss's better half. Talk about surreal. When he leant on the door, it yielded with a groan. His gaze flicked quickly around the interior to take in the layout. The room was small and the blinds were drawn. Tables and chairs were dotted about the wooden floor in no discernible pattern, while the counter was straight ahead, nestling against the rear wall. Framed posters of the Lakers' 1988 World Championship squad hung all around, with the twin legends Kareem Abdul-Jabbar and Magic Johnson taking pride of place on either side of the counter, where a youthful barman was busy wiping down glasses. Lunatic was the only patron, his fellow gang members having realised he wasn't in the mood for company. He sat at a table on the left-hand side, his back to Hunter, his attention focused on something in his hands.

Hunter approached the table on the balls of his feet, but he needn't have bothered as the gang boss's concentration was so intense that a herd of charging elephants would have failed to rouse him. When Hunter was a few yards shy of his target, he discovered that Lunatic was staring at a photo.

'Who's that?' Hunter asked, bringing the gang boss back to the here and now with a start. Lunatic hurriedly stashed the snapshot in the pocket of his sweatpants, but not before Hunter had managed to grab a peak at its subject. The photo was of a tough-looking Hispanic man, and it looked like it had been taken with a zoom lens, as the man seemed oblivious to the fact that he was being captured on film. His head was shaven, his face made to look angular by a sharply pointed beard, while his arms were festooned with tattoos.

'No one,' Lunatic snarled, his eyes burning with hostility. 'What the fuck you want?'

'I've come to cut through the bullshit,' said Hunter, pulling up a seat. 'I'm here to help.'

'Like I said before, I don't need your help. You're just gonna fuck things up.'

'From where I'm sitting, things are fucked up already. Gracie's gone, Angel's at her wits' end, and you're running around with a hair-trigger temper. Why don't you just admit it? Your little girl's missing, and it's all your fault.'

'What the fuck you talkin' 'bout? I don't know jack.'

'Yeah, right. You won't talk to Angel, but you promise her that everything's gonna turn out fine. That's not the sort of promise you'd make if you were still groping around in the dark. The kidnappers must have been in touch with you.'

'So what if they have? I'll say it again, just so we clear—this ain't none of your business. Who the hell made you our protector? You're sticking your nose in where it ain't wanted, just like you did all those years ago, when you tried to take Angel away from me.'

'I tried to get her out of the gangs—you think that's a good environment for a mother to bring up her firstborn?'

'It's the only environment we got. I didn't pick the Ghosts, the Ghosts picked me. I got jumped in when I was eight years old—three kids kicked the shit outta me on my way home from football practice and said that from then on I had to protect my block, no matter what. They said they'd kill me if I wasn't down for La Raza, and that ain't the kind of invitation you can decline. And once you in, you in—there ain't no going back.'

A little bit of the fire went from Lunatic's voice as he reminisced. Hunter decided to take on a more conciliatory tone in the hope that it would get the gang boss to open up.

'Football, huh?'

'Damn straight. Middle linebacker. Best in the district. Coach said I was headed for a college scholarship till I ruptured the tendons in my left knee. Never the same after that. Lost my speed. Lost my one shot at making something of myself. Lost my dream. Ghosts was all I had left.'

'Apart from Angel?'

'Yeah. She gave me back some ambition. Put some fire in my belly. Then you tried to take her away.'

'Like I said, I had her best interests at heart.'

'You ain't got the first idea what that girl's best interests be.'

Hunter's hands tightened beneath the table. 'Angel just wants her daughter back. She thought I could help.'

'You can't. There's nothing anyone can do. It's all on me.'

Lunatic closed his eyes, lowered his head, and laced

his fingers around the back of his neck, leaving Hunter to experience a new sensation—he felt sorry for the gang boss. Now that his bravado had faded, Lunatic seemed full of despair, like he was waist deep in shit that he couldn't wade out of.

'Gracie's my little girl. Chances are, I ain't never gonna see her again. You know how that feels?'

'No,' said Hunter quietly, 'but if you level with me maybe I can help you out of this mess. The kidnappers have been in touch, haven't they?'

No answer. Hunter tried again.

'C'mon—how much did they ask for?'

'How much?' Lunatic said bitterly. 'All I got an' all I'm ever gonna have.'

'What's that mean?'

'Figure it out.'

'Listen—back when I carried a badge, I saw plenty of people in your position, and they all learned one thing the hard way.'

'What?'

'You can't trust a kidnapper. I know what you're thinking—right now, paying the ransom seems like the best thing to do, but, trust me, it's not. Even if you stump up the cash, they're only gonna want more. And what about proof of life? Have you had that yet? Your best bet is to get the authorities involved. They handle this stuff all the time. They know all the angles.'

'Fuck that. I'd be giving my daughter a death warrant. I'm being a goddamn fool just talkin' to you. Money ain't a problem. I know what's gotta be done. And I got no choice but to do it.'

Lunatic's cellphone started to ring before Hunter could respond.

'Speak,' said the gang boss, the phone pressed hard to his ear. After a few seconds the knuckles on his hand stood proud while a tremor ran the length of his arm. He acknowledged the message with a grunt, cut the call, then rose to his feet.

'I gotta get gone. From now on, me and Angel are dead to you. Leave us the hell alone.'

Lunatic stormed out of the bar, his athletic stride eating up the distance to the exit. The call had clearly rattled him. But who the hell had made it?

CHAPTER THIRTEEN

HUNTER watched Lunatic stake out the restaurant. He'd tailed him from the bar, maintaining at least three cars' distance between them at all times, and he was pretty confident that he hadn't been seen. At first he'd been worried that the gang boss might have checked for activity in his rear view, but his concerns soon faded once he realised that Lunatic had slipped into a fugue-like state of introspection.

The joint was a Tex-Mex establishment, with the emphasis firmly on the Mex. It was set back from the road with a gravel forecourt out front, and judging by the number of vehicles that were parked there, business was good. Lunatic had stationed his crimson Cadillac Eldorado directly opposite the joint on the other side of the street, and Hunter was about forty yards further back, the Foo Fighters' latest album playing softly on his car stereo. According to the hand-painted wooden sign that hung on the wall, the restaurant went by the name of Desperados. The Mexican flag flew proudly from a makeshift flagpole that had been crudely attached to the eaves of the roof, and the red-brick façade was decorated with paintings of saguaro cacti and guitar strumming Mariachis. A double glass door on the left of the building served as an entrance, while two picture windows allowed a further glimpse of the interior, although the view was somewhat obscured by the chilli garlands and piñata donkeys that hung in each frame.

Since his arrival almost an hour previous, Lunatic had remained inside his Caddie and had made no move to leave it. As Hunter resigned himself to a lengthy stakeout, his thoughts turned back to Angel. With her daughter missing, she had to be going through hell. If she'd quit the gangs when he'd given her the chance, then none of this would be happening. The day she'd turned him down had been a black one for all concerned.

'Coffee?' asked Hunter, as he offered the take-out cup to Angel, who accepted with a smile. The two of them were in Calvary Cemetery, walking among the grave markers, safe from the prying eyes of the 'hood. It was a cool mid-January morning, and Angel was wearing a pair of tight-fitting jeans and a denim jacket, beneath which the first signs of her pregnancy were starting to show. She'd made contact with Hunter at the crack of dawn, and demanded that he meet with her as soon as possible, although she'd refused to reveal why.

'So what have you got for me?' he asked, taking a seat on one of the remembrance benches that lined the cemetery's walkways.

'It's big,' she began, nestling up alongside him. 'Real big. If I give you this, you gotta guarantee that you'll keep my name out of it.'

'Don't I always?'

Angel had been a confidential informant for a while now, feeding him nuggets of information on gang activity in her neighbourhood, always on her rivals, but never on the Santa Anna Ghosts, the gang that she counted as her *familia*. Her real parents, Ernesto and Inez, had disowned her, partly because of her decision to run with the gangs, and partly because they objected to her boyfriend.

'This one's real dangerous and I gotta be extra-careful now that I got two people to think about,' she said, gently rubbing her belly. 'If it's a girl, I'm gonna call her Graciela.'

'That's a cute name. And you've got your priorities right. When it comes to you and your child, there's no need to worry—I've got everything set up with Social Services. You want out of the gangs, just say the word.'

She went quiet for a moment, as if realising that what she was about to do would change her life forever, then she nodded once and began to talk.

'I've got King Chino. I can give him to you on a plate.'

Holy shit! King Chino! The leader of the Santa Anna Ghosts and one of the most wanted men in all of East LA. Hunter had laid off the Ghosts in recent times, not as a result of any conscious decision to do so but because Angel was giving him such good intel on the other street gangs he had his hands full busting the Ghost's rivals. In recent weeks, the word was out that Chino had brokered a deal with a new supplier to shift more Mexican Tar into EastLos, the cheap brown heroin that proved especially popular with the financially challenged. Hunter had known that he was going to have to do something about it, so Angel's decision to inform on her own boss couldn't have come at a better time.

'King Chino? You've never informed on one of your own before. Why start now? And why start at the top?'

'Because he's lost his mind. You hear about the body found in Crenshaw late last night?'

'In Gilliam Park?'

Who hadn't heard about it? An as yet unidentified Hispanic male had been slashed multiple times before being propped up and left on a park bench. Only thing was, he'd been left there without his head. It had been manna from heaven for the news media. In a city plagued by violent death, run-of-the-mill homicides didn't cut it any more. To make it on to heavy rotation, a death had to be gruesome, and the more gruesome, the better.

'Yeah, that's the one. That body belonged to Gunsmoke, current boss of the 6th Street Crew. He's been in charge while his brother, Bullseye, was banged up on a two-year stretch for burglary. By taking out Gunsmoke, the King's gone and started a full-on gang war. He's put all the Ghosts in danger.'

'How d'you know all this?'

'I got my sources. People talk in the barrio. King Chino was bragging about what he was gonna do before he set out to do it.'

'Hearsay isn't gonna cut it as evidence. Anything else you can give me?'

'How about Gunsmoke's missing head?'

Hunter's eyes widened. 'Where is it?'

'The King's got it stashed in his garage like some kind of trophy. Bullseye gets out of Lompoc today. Word is, the King's planning on hand-delivering the head to show him who's boss.'

'That's great work, Angel. I'll get straight on it,' he said, pulling an envelope from his pocket and offering it to her.

'Keep your money, this one's on me,' she replied. 'Call it community service.'

'Okay. Have you come to a decision about my offer?'

'Once you've taken down Chino, we'll talk some more. But I do know this much. My neighbourhood's no place to bring up a child. I can't be a mother and a banger. Little Gracie ain't gonna grow up an orphan.'

Hunter nodded in agreement, pleased that she'd accepted the reality of her situation, then strode quickly out of the cemetery with thoughts of a major gangland arrest on his mind.

'Okay—everyone ready? We go on my mark,' Hunter said softly into his radio. He was sitting in the back of an unmarked white truck a block north of King Chino's residence in Boyle Heights. Space was at a premium as four heavily armed SWAT guys in full body armour were also present, one of them hefting a battering ram. Another van with a similar payload was stationed a block south of the target. When Hunter gave the command to go, both vehicles burst into life, engines roaring as they accelerated towards each other, brakes squealing as they came to a halt outside the King's house.

'Go! Go! Go!' Hunter yelled as the vans' rear doors burst open and men spilled out. He raced up the drive and took a position by the main entrance. The rest of his team fanned out alongside him, while the secondary unit headed for the cinderblock garage to the left of the property. Once everyone was ready he gave the signal for a full breach. The battering ram made light work of the door, sending it flying inwards on shattered hinges, prompting yells of fear from inside.

'Police!' Hunter shouted as he stepped through the opening and headed down the hall, his eyes flicking around in search of a threat, his gun arm following suit.

Three doors awaited him, one on either side, staggered about six feet apart, with the other at the end of the hallway. He motioned that he'd take the one on the left with support from the man at his heels, while the rest of his team should take the one on the right. He crouched down, then swung around into the opening, his field of fire being the right-hand side of the room, just as his colleague went through the same motion above him, his field of fire being the left.

'Clear!' he yelled, prompting the rest of his team to scurry past and repeat the process at the second door. When the first of them stepped into the frame, a shotgun roared out. The blast caught the officer full in the chest, lifting him off his feet and propelling him backwards into the far wall. The other team members responded instantly, their guns barking loudly as they poured lead through the opening. The assault continued for a full five seconds until Hunter called a halt and stepped forward to check out the carnage. A youth lay slumped on the kitchen floor, the shotgun having fallen from his grasp, his body pockmarked with bullet holes. Blood was splattered across the cabinets behind him to mark his passing with a crimson salute. Why had the kid come out firing? If he'd surrendered peacefully, he'd still have been drawing breath. Back in the hallway, the officer that had taken the shotgun blast was rising to his feet and dusting himself off, his Kevlar body armour having served him well. When the door towards the rear of the property swung open, the team turned as one with fingers tightening on triggers.

'Don't shoot! Don't shoot!' yelled an obese Hispanic man as he emerged from the bathroom, hoisting a pair of sweatpants over some dark blue jockeys. 'Can't a guy take a dump in peace no more?'

'Raise your hands, Chino! Raise them now!' yelled Hunter.

'What the fuck you gringos be shootin' up my place for? I ain't got no beef with five-oh,' said the King, his hands held high overhead.

'Secure that son of a bitch,' commanded Hunter.

Two men raced over and cuffed the King, then took up positions on either side of him, interlocking their arms around the gang boss's massive triceps.

'What the fuck you been shootin' at? Where's my li'l vato, Wallace?'

'Your li'l vato just opened fire on a uniformed officer and paid the price,' responded Hunter.

The King let loose a howl of rage and threw himself forward, dragging the two SWAT guys along for the ride. Hunter set his feet in a forty-five-degree stance and launched a murderous right cross, simultaneously thrusting with his right hip to throw his body weight into the punch. His fist connected with the point of the King's chin with a loud crack, rocking him just enough for his escorts to grab the initiative and wrestle him to the floor.

'I'll say one thing for you, you can take a punch,' said Hunter, nursing his knuckles. A normal man would have been out cold, but the King was still bellowing loudly as he tried to break free of his captors. During the course of his thrashing, his head twisted around to the left to give him an unencumbered view of the kitchen, at which point his struggles came to a halt.

'Wallace,' he mouthed, as he looked at his brother's corpse. 'Wallace—what they done to you?'

'Don't go blaming us,' said Hunter. 'You brought this on yourself. Live by the gangs, die by the gangs. It's little wonder the kid came out firing when you're all he's got as a role model. But at least you'll be off the streets from now on—you've fucked up one time too many.'

'What the hell you talking about?'

Before Hunter could answer, the lead member of the secondary SWAT unit, a swarthy guy who went by the name of Bishop, appeared at the entrance with a grocery bag in his hands.

'We checked the garage and found this in the freezer,' he said, reaching inside the plastic bag with a gloved hand.

When Bishop's hand emerged it held a severed head. The jagged edges of skin that hung around the neckline suggested that the decapitation had been brutal, while the face was a mass of inch-deep scars, droplets of ice clinging to the frozen blood. The head looked like something from a sub-zero horror flick.

'If that's what you keep in the deep freeze, then count me out for dinner,' said Hunter.

'That's Gunsmoke!' exclaimed the King. 'What the fuck's he doin' in my icebox?'

'Like you don't know, you sick fuck,' said Bishop.

'Last time I saw that pug ugly face it was attached to a body. Dead cholo got nothin' to do with me.'

'Bullshit! We've got you this time,' said Hunter. 'Gunsmoke's decapitation made the front page, and all that publicity has got the DA's office excited. There's nothing they like more than a big win in the press. They're gonna go all out to burn you, and I'm gonna grab a front row seat to watch you go down.'

'It was there—just like you said it would be. Had the damn thing hidden inside his deep freeze like it was some kind of popsicle,' said Hunter, as he offered Angel some gum. She accepted with a smile and popped the stick in her mouth. The two of them were back in Calvary Cemetery on their usual bench, and the shadows thrown by the nearby headstones were getting longer as the sun disappeared over the western horizon in a blur of ochre.

'Hey—like I keep telling you, my info is golden. And you've got a watertight case, right? King Chino's gonna get sent down for a long time?'

'Count on it,' responded Hunter with a grim smile.

'He's trying to plead his innocence, but having Gunsmoke's head stashed in his ice-box is kinda undermining his case. Our crime-scene technicians didn't get any prints off the head itself, but they took a few partials off the grocery bag, plus the King's status as a known gang leader is gonna count against him big time.'

'That's great. I took one hell of a risk giving him up, but now he's out of the picture, at least we've got a chance to make peace with 6th Street.'

'We? You're still thinking like you're a Ghost. That's a habit you'll have to break once you're out.'

'Yeah, about that,' Angel said softly. 'I kinda changed my mind.'

'You've what?' Hunter was stunned into silence for a moment. He stared at Angel, but she refused to meet his gaze. 'But I thought it was all agreed? You hand-deliver the King, I arrest him, then you and your first-born get out of the life?'

'That's just it—it's about my baby. I had my scan this morning—it's a girl. She's Larry's kid too—I can't just take her away from him.'

'You're kidding me? You want to raise a child with a man whose nickname is Lunatic? You know how he earned that street name? By beating a man to death with an iron pipe after an argument over a ten-buck poker game. The only reason he's still on the street is because no one would come forward and ID him as the killer.'

'I know he's got a temper, but he's working on it. He's different now. He loves me.'

'But, Angel, you won't be safe. You said it yourself,

the gangs are no place to bring up a child. You've gotta get out and start afresh while you still got the chance.'

'I can't. The Ghosts are all I know. And Larry says we're gonna be a family—I gotta give him a chance. Family's important—a girl needs her father.'

'But, Angel…' Hunter was lost for words. He'd come here tonight thinking that he was going to give her a leg up in life, to rescue her from her the violence of her surroundings, only to find that she'd decided to turn her back on him at the death.

'It's best this way,' she said, rising to her feet. 'I'm going to make a go of it with Larry for Graciela's sake. Thanks for everything—I'll see you around.'

She turned and walked away without a backward glance. Hunter watched her leave with a sour feeling deep in the pit of his stomach.

Hunter's fists were clenched so tight his nails were digging into his palms. Not many events from the past still hit him hard, but Angel's eleventh-hour change of mind continued to hurt. He'd thought he was doing the right thing in offering her a way out of the gangs, had thought that she'd jump at the chance of a better life for her and her child, yet when push had come to shove she'd turned him down. At the time, he'd felt cheated, not so much by Angel, more by the gangland environment that had gotten its hooks into her and refused to let go. But opting to stay with Lunatic to raise her daughter had taken guts, and the fact that the two of them were still together now said something about the strength of their relationship. Broken homes were the norm in gang circles, with the men often changing their female companions on a whim, so Lunatic deserved some credit for sticking around.

Hunter stared at the Eldorado parked further down the street, where the gang boss continued his vigil of Desperados. Why did it hold such fascination for him? Did he think that Gracie was being held there? And if he did, why wasn't he doing something about it? As Hunter watched on, the gang boss broke his paralysis and began to beat furiously on the steering-wheel with his ham-like fists. Once the ferocity of the blows had dissipated, his shoulders began to rise and fall in great heaves. Lunatic, a gang war veteran, was crying, and the restaurant seemed to be linked to his emotional outburst. Hunter looked back at the brightly coloured building, with all it's cacti, mariachi and piñata decorations, his mind made up. He had to find out what was going on in there. It was time to book a table for one.

CHAPTER FOURTEEN

CASSIUS checked his watch as the sun crept lower in the sky, the dull orange orb edging towards the distant horizon like a dying ember. He rubbed a little powdered cocaine along the length of his gums and worked his tongue hungrily against the roof of his mouth as the initial buzz coursed through his brain. A low moan of pleasure burst from his lips as the drug took the edge off his nerves. He was sitting on an old hunk of cinderblock, and directly in front of him was an expanse of pockmarked wasteland, and on the far side of that wasteland was the square where Zombie and his juvenile crew had been turning a tidy profit selling crack to the disenfranchised all afternoon. Cassius had ordered that Slowpoke handle the money run that night, and Slowpoke made a habit of walking straight across the wasteland en route to the drop-off. When the dim-witted drug dealer finally appeared, his shambling gait was instantly recognisable through the gloom. Cassius rose from the cinderblock and walked towards him.

'Yo, 'Poke—wassup, cuz?'

Slowpoke's hand went instantly to the rear of his

jeans where he kept his Ruger Redhawk, then he relaxed when he saw who'd hailed him.

'It's all good, Cass. Whatcha doin' out here?'

'Need to borrow one of Zombie's shorties for a while, but seein's you're here, you can do me a solid.'

'I's on the money run, Cass,' said Slowpoke, looking a little bemused. 'Zombie said I had to get back asap.'

'No drama, I just be needin' you for a few minutes, then you can fade.'

'Okay. Where we headed?'

'I got a business meeting. Just need you to stand guard, make sure we ain't disturbed. C'mon—it's on your way.'

Cassius set off at pace across the wasteland, prompting Slowpoke to fall in behind him.

'How were sales in the p.m.?' he asked. 'Those white boys come back?'

'Yeah—they said somethin' about a frat party then ordered a heavy load.'

'Outstanding. And how'd the roust of the crack dens go?'

Slowpoke shrugged. 'Half the cluckheads were too chalked up to move, while most of the rest were broke, but a few come down to the square to make a purchase.'

'Shit,' cursed Cassius, as he stepped over a broken bicycle. That wasn't good news. Still, what with the frat-party score, plus the usual street traffic, takings ought to be halfway decent. He put all thoughts of the finances from his head and turned to look at the man alongside him. 'How long I known you, 'Poke?'

The question seemed to take his companion by surprise.

'Dunno. Maybe five years?'

'Yeah, that sounds about right. Remember your first day in Imperial Courts?'

'No doubt—I joined the Knights on that same damn day.'

'And you was a natural. Took to it like you'd been bangin' all your life. C'mon, it's this way,' said Cassius, heading towards a back alley. 'Remember your initiation?'

'Yeah. We burglarised that Korean bodega over in Watts, then busted a cap in the owner. I woulda got plugged too if you hadn't seen his son come out of the storeroom strapped with a gat. Remember how we celebrated after? Got ourselves a couple of forties then went at it with the Williams twins in they parents' bedroom. Man, what a day. Those girls knew how to fuck. Whatever happened to them?'

'One got the virus off a needle, the other's on ice in Valley State, three-year stretch for assault. Still, you right, though, those girls sure knew how to fuck.'

The two men headed deeper into the alley, their feet crunching on glass as they walked under a busted lamp that Cassius had seen to earlier.

'We had some good times, huh?' he continued.

'Yeah, we did.'

'And I always had your back, ever since that day in the bodega?'

'Yeah, cuz, you cool.'

'That's why I'm so damn sorry 'bout this.'

His hand whipped out from under his penitentiary shirt holding a Micro Uzi. Slowpoke's eyes widened in surprise. Cassius let off a short burst, raking the barrel across his friend's torso. The sound of the gunfire bounced off the alley walls, amplified in the enclosed environment. Four bullets punctured Slowpoke's chest, one of them burrowing straight through his heart. He was dead before he even hit the ground. Cassius knelt by his side and watched the blood bubble out of the holes.

'Sorry, cuz, but needs must, you know?' he said gently. He looked into Slowpoke's face for the last time, which he'd purposely left untouched in order to give his family the dignity of an open-casket funeral, and wished him a speedy ascent to the afterlife, then he stuck his right hand down the front of the dead man's pants and rummaged around. Dreadnought, their boss, had passed the rule two months previous. When making a money run, all cash was to be stored alongside the ball sack, as a man would protect his nuts above all else. A look of distaste crossed Cassius's face as he pushed aside Slowpoke's member, and that look turned to outright disgust when he felt the sweaty heat of the dead man's testicles, but then he broke into a grin. When his hand emerged it was grasping a thick wad of bills. He rose to his feet and totted them up. The day's takings totalled a shade under six grand, and what with the money he'd already put aside, he now had enough to pay off Mason and Diaz. A sense of relief washed over him as he headed out of the alley.

CHAPTER FIFTEEN

HUNTER felt his adrenalin kick in as he approached the entrance to the Mexican restaurant. When Lunatic had driven off into the night just moments earlier, he'd decided to let him go, as his gut had told him that he needed to stay at Desperados. The place was somehow related to Gracie's abduction, and the fastest way to find out how was to march straight into the lion's den and ask.

He wedged his Beretta down the back of his pants, took a deep breath, and reached for the door handle. When he opened it, a loud burst of 'La Cucaracha' blared out from a speaker wired to the entrance at ear-shredding volume, prompting everyone inside to give him the once-over. Mercifully, the tune cut off after a few seconds and the patrons went back to their food, leaving Hunter to pull the door shut and claim a table of his own. He opted for one in the corner of the room, as it provided a view of both the entrance and the rest of the diners. Some saloon-style doors were stationed halfway along the wall to his left, while the bar was situated at the far end of the room, where the short wooden counter was staffed by a pretty serving girl dressed as a *vaquero*—leather chaps over faded blue jeans, a checked shirt knotted above her midriff, and a wide-brimmed cowboy hat perched at a jaunty angle on her head. A greasy-haired waiter came banging through the swing doors carrying a tray laden with sizzling fajitas and burritos, also wearing the attire of a Mexican cowboy. It looked like Desperados took its status as a theme restaurant pretty seriously.

Hunter switched his attention to the paying customers. Everyone in the place was Hispanic. Of the fifteen wooden tables dotted around the tiled floor, only three were busy, discounting his own. The closest of them was home to a teenage couple, and it was to them that the greasy-haired waiter was headed. The other two occupied tables were next to the bar, and each of them was home to a group of laughing youths who were eschewing sustenance in order to concentrate on their margarita intake.

Four boys and four girls made up the party, and most of them were smoking joints. Hunter's nose wrinkled as the smell of industrial-strength skunk reached his nostrils, then his eyes flicked over each of their faces, taking them in at a glance. None of them looked to be out of their teens but, despite their youthful demeanours and relaxed attitudes, they still gave off an aura of menace. Short-sleeved white shirts and long khaki shorts were the order of the day for the boys, while the girls seemed intent on showing as much bare flesh as possible. A blue item of clothing, usually a bandana knotted around the forearm, featured in every ensemble, expensive gold chains hung around most of the necks, and tattoos fashioned from thick black ink abounded on uncovered forearms. Low-level gangbangers on a drunken night out. Most of them would be packing, which made them a threat no matter how old they were. Hunter knew from experience that there were enough baby-faced assassins in LA to put a dent in your life expectancy if you weren't on your guard.

As he watched on, the loudest male in the party started to rag on one of the others, criticising him for running up in some syphilitic girl called Maria. The rest of the crew burst out laughing and joined in with the seemingly good-natured ribbing, but the guy who was the butt of the jokes clenched his hand into a fist. Hunter made a mental note to keep an eye on developments, then waved over the waiter.

'*Señor?*' The metal tag pinned to his chest said his name was Pancho. Hunter raised an eyebrow.

'That really your name?'

'If the boss says I'm Pancho, that's good enough for me. You want a menu?'

'Who runs this place?'

'The boss is out back. What's the problem?'

'I'm not talking about the guy who gets to order a fresh lorryload of tortillas on a Monday morning. Who's really in charge?'

The waiter gave a slight pause before answering, which was enough to confirm Hunter's suspicions. Desperados wasn't the family-run joint it appeared to be. The restaurant was owned by a gang or, at the very least, it was paying protection money to someone with sharp claws.

'Dunno what you're talking about,' spluttered the waiter, turning to leave. Hunter grabbed him by the arm and rolled up his shirtsleeve to reveal a series of black tattoos that looked almost identical to those sported by the kids over by the bar.

'Really?' asked Hunter.

'Wait here,' muttered a resigned Pancho, 'I'll be back in a minute.'

Hunter drummed his fingers on the wooden table as he killed time, keeping one eye on the gangbangers to ensure he'd be ready for any drama. By asking the waiter about the restaurant's true ownership, he'd taken a calculated risk. Gangs didn't take kindly to outside attention, but he needed to do something to set wheels in motion. When Pancho returned he looked jumpy.

'Come with me,' he muttered, throwing a nervous glance towards the counter.

Hunter followed him through the swing doors and into a dimly lit corridor that smelled faintly of refried beans.

'Where are we going?'

'Boss wants to talk to you.'

They walked in silence till they came to another pair of swing doors. Hunter battened down his sense of growing trepidation. Pancho gestured that he should go ahead, so he barrelled through the doors like a gunfighter entering a saloon, to find himself in the world's least hygienic kitchen. The sink in the corner was full to the brim with dirty crockery, patches of mould blossomed across the ceiling, the faded wallpaper was peeling away in large strips, and enough rat traps were dotted around the floor to suggest that a major infestation was under way. A wizened old guy stood straight ahead, chewing on a toothpick, his meagre hair greased back over a shiny bald pate, while a large pan of chilli bubbled gently on a nearby hot plate.

Hunter had just enough time to take all this in before a pair of giant arms encircled him from behind to crush him in a vice-like grip. The arms were as thick as tree trunks and packed with sinew and muscle. He winced as the pressure on his thoracic cavity intensified, forcing the air from his lungs. Every breath burned the back of his throat, and as his gasps became ever more ragged, black spots began to dance in front of his eyes. As his head began to droop, the old guy watched on impassively, working the toothpick around the side of his mouth.

CHAPTER SIXTEEN

STONE pushed open the door and stepped through the opening to be greeted with some over-enthusiastic moans of sexual ecstasy. A flight of stairs descended in front of him while rows of plastic-covered seats were laid out to his left. He stood in near darkness, which suited his purposes for the time being, although soon he'd have to venture towards the front half of the auditorium, which was bathed in the sickly glow of wan light that emanated from the big screen. The fleapit cinema was on the outskirts of Hollywood, and tonight's double feature consisted of two low budget pornos, imaginatively titled *Rimmerama 3: Fire in the Hole* and *Topless Brain Surgeons.* His eyes flicked to the screen where a man the size of a small house was currently engaged in a frenzied bout of cunnilingus with a pneumatically breasted blonde who bucked and writhed like she was sitting on an electric sander. The scene had all the eroticism of a French kiss from your buck-toothed grandma. Stone looked away quickly away and began to scan the rest of the room for signs of life.

Four other people were present, and although the

subdued lighting meant he couldn't be sure that they were all men, it seemed like a pretty reasonable bet. The closest of the cineastes was four rows in front of him, slumped down low in a central seat, loud snores emanating from his person. Stone worked his way steadily along the preceding row, pulling up short and retracing his steps once he realised that it wasn't the man he was looking for. The next guy was six rows further forward and closer to the aisle, while the remaining two were stationed front and centre, their poor eyesight suggesting that they came here a little too often.

Stone started to descend the flight of stairs, his muscles tensing when he recognised the nearest of the three remaining men—a small, shifty-looking guy with a big Afro—the same guy who'd shown up at Acorn Elementary School to rap with the delinquent kids. His street name was Rocket. Stone stilled his breathing and gently withdrew a hunting knife from the leather sheath cinched to his thigh. The silver blade glinted dangerously in the half-light. He'd been going easy on his enemies thus far, but the time had come to send out a clear message—non-compliance with his demands would no longer be tolerated.

He worked his way down the row and sat directly behind Rocket, whose eyes remained focused on the screen, although he obviously wasn't worried about following the film's serpentine plot, as he was plugged into his iPod. The gangbanger's right hand was jerking frantically away in his pants, while his left was grasping an extra-large Coke. Stone leant forward and grabbed Rocket's forehead from behind, pulled backwards to expose a scrawny neck, then jammed the blade of his hunting knife against the banger's throat. Rocket went rigid with fear, all thoughts of impending orgasm banished from his mind. Stone yanked the headphones from his ears and leant in close.

'What the f-fuck you want?' stammered Rocket.

'Keep your voice down, hold onto your drink, and keep your other hand in your pants,' commanded Stone.

'You some kind of fag? Wanna watch me get off?'

'No. All I want is Dreadnought.'

'Ain't never heard of no Dreadnought.'

'Don't lie to me,' rasped Stone, digging the knife deeper, prompting a trickle of blood to sully the blade.

'Fuck! It's you, ain't it? The crazy muthafucka that's been hittin' on our gang. We all been lookin' for you. You're gonna get got. No doubt.'

'You're in no position to be making threats. Dreadnought. Where is he?'

'I dunno where he's at…no one does…'

'Take a wild guess,' offered Stone, sawing the blade gently back and forth. The gangbanger squealed in response, the sound drowned out by the grunts and groans emanating from the big screen.

'I tole you—I don't know. He bin laying low since he come outta the pen.'

Stone's mouth hardened. Rocket had the same story as all the others. It was exactly as he'd expected. But this time he was going to make sure that his warning had some effect.

'You were outside Acorn Elementary yesterday.'

'So what? Just trying to get me an education.'

'If I ever see you there again, you're a dead man. On your feet.'

The two men rose as one, Stone holding the knife to Rocket's jugular, the banger holding on to his Coke and his dick. They worked their way out to the aisle, then Stone transferred the blade to the middle of Rocket's back.

'Keep still,' he commanded, glancing around. The patron at the rear of the cinema was still slumped forward in his seat, while the two on the front row had yet to notice the drama unfolding behind them. In one fluid motion Stone crouched down and slashed the knife across the back of the gangbanger's heels, slicing straight through both of his Achilles' tendons. Rocket went down face first into one of the lower steps like a fighter on the take, blood exploding from his mouth as he bit through his tongue, his subsequent screams of agony cutting through the porno soundtrack. Stone grabbed a chunk of the banger's Afro and raised his head from the steps, before pushing the point of his knife into the soft skin just under his left eye.

'Stay away from the school. Leave the kids alone. And make sure that the rest of your crew gets the message.'

With that, he released Rocket's hair to let his head slam down once again, then hurried out of the cinema, leaving three astonished pornography lovers and one screaming gangbanger in his wake.

CHAPTER SEVENTEEN

'GO EASY, you fool!' croaked the old man in a thick Mexican accent from the rear of the kitchen. 'How'm I gonna talk to him if he's unconscious?'

The pressure on Hunter's chest lifted enough for him to suck down a little oxygen, then he raised his head to look his interrogator in the eye.

'Why you here, *hombre?* What's with all the questions out front?'

'Guess I'm just interested in the restaurant trade,' wheezed Hunter, earning another flex of the giant's arms against his chest.

'Comedian, huh? Well, that ain't gonna get you far. Let's try again. You wanna know who owns this place? The Emerald Vipers. And now you've gone and poked their nest with a stick. Why the hell you so interested? You some kind of cop?'

Not any more, thought Hunter, although the protection offered by an LAPD badge would have come in handy right about now. But at least he'd got a name for the gang that used Desperados as a base, and it was a name he was already familiar with. The Emerald Vipers were a mid-sized organisation with a reputation for being one of the major drug suppliers in East Los Angeles, and they were known to have strong ties to a few of the other Latino outfits. Were they now in the process of mounting a major offensive against Lunatic and the Ghosts? Had they nabbed Gracie as some sort of pre-emptive strike? Hunter drew some more air into his lungs as he considered how he was going to get answers to these questions. As things stood, the old guy in front of him had the upper hand, and as long as that continued he wasn't likely to prove amenable to partaking in a quick Q and A. Somehow, Hunter needed to flip the situation on its head.

'The Vipers? They sound like a friendly bunch. How about I talk directly to them, instead of their hired lackeys?'

'Cracking wise, huh? Well, if that's the way you want it,' said the old man with a shrug. 'I tried to cut you a break by bringin' you back here—if I'd left you to the kids out front you'd be full of holes by now and I'd be stuck slap bang in the middle of another crime scene. But if you're in a hurry to die, then so be it. Jose—turn out this guy's lights.'

On hearing this, the giant known as Jose began to squeeze down hard on Hunter's ribs. After putting up a brief struggle, he allowed his head to sag forward and his whole body to go limp. The pressure on his chest started to recede as his assailant assumed that the fight was almost over. Big mistake. Hunter drew his knees to his chest then pistoned his legs backwards to send his heels crashing into a pair of unprotected patellas, while simultaneously throwing a reverse head butt that landed on the bridge of Jose's nose with a satisfying crunch. The giant let out a bellow of pain and released Hunter from his grasp, allowing him to suck down a huge gulp of air before launching his next attack—an elbow deep into Jose's solar plexus that gave him some breathing difficulties of his own.

Hunter backed away towards the nearby stove, using his peripheral vision to check on the other men present. The old guy had yet to move a muscle, while Pancho, the greasy-haired waiter, was frozen in place by the swing doors. Hunter refocused his attention on Jose, whose shabby cook's apron now counted human blood amongst the myriad stains down its front. His nose kinked sharply to the left and blood ran from each nostril in a glutinous torrent, while the blows to his kneecaps seemed to have left him unsteady on his feet. Hunter tensed as the cook came at him with a clubbing right hook aimed straight for his heart. He twisted out of the way at the last moment, grabbed Jose's huge arm, and used the larger man's momentum to drive his hand into the pot of chilli that was bubbling on the stove.

Hunter wasn't sure what was worse. The sound that the giant made as the skin bubbled off his hand or the smell of charred flesh that choked the air when he withdrew his hand from the pot. He shoved Jose backwards to put some distance between them, then used the break in hostilities to reach down the back of his pants for his Beretta.

'Enough!' he commanded, levelling the gun, although Jose showed few signs of wanting to continue the fight. 'And where the hell do you think you're going, Pancho?'

The waiter stopped trying to slip out through the swing doors and raised his hands.

'Okay, let's have all of you sitting on the floor against the rear wall.' Hunter reached for a washcloth, ran it under some cold water, and tossed it to the cook. 'Wrap that around your hand.'

Once the three men were in position, Hunter started with the questions, concentrating on the old man.

'What's the deal here? You run the joint and the Vipers skim off the profits?'

'*Sí*—something like that. The business has been in my *familia* for three generations, but when the Vipers came calling, I didn't have much choice but to hand it over.'

'My heart bleeds. Why did I get such a warm welcome after asking a couple of simple questions out front?'

'I got my instructions…if anyone shows any interest in the Vipers I'm to find out why, then call the boss.'

'Since when?'

'The order came down a couple of days ago.'

Alarm bells went off in Hunter's head. That was right about the time that Gracie had been snatched.

'And why have the Vipers got you running interference?'

'Ask him,' said the old man, nodding at the waiter. 'He's in the gang. It's the only reason he's got a job.'

'How about it, Pancho? Wanna tell me why the

Vipers are so jumpy?' asked Hunter, gesturing with the Beretta for the waiter to take up the tale.

'We're just lookin' out for our own is all. There's been a lotta trouble recently, and the boss wants us to be ready—get our retaliation in before we get hit.'

'And that's it? You're just keeping your defences tight? You had any trouble with the Santa Anna Ghosts lately? Or their leader, Lunatic?'

'The Ghosts? Nah, man, they cool. Ain't never had a beef with them.'

'How about a little girl called Gracie? Heard anything about her?'

Hunter watched all three of them for the slightest spark of recognition but none was forthcoming.

'Little girl, huh? That what this is about? Someone sticking it to your underage bitch?'

'You watch your mouth,' barked Hunter. As far as he could tell, the waiter was telling the truth, but that didn't really mean all that much. Pancho was a bottom feeder, and the chance of him being privy to any important information on Viper tactics and strategies was pretty remote.

'This place got a rear exit?' asked Hunter, prompting a nod from the old man.

'Over there—through the storeroom.'

Hunter backed over and checked it out. Inside the storeroom there were two rows of shelves stacked with a mixture of Mexican foodstuffs, plus a heavy external fire door that had been wedged open with a sack of rice.

'You! *El Gigante!* On your feet,' commanded Hunter.

Jose stood up, his right hand still swathed in the wash-cloth, the blood from his nose congealing on his face.

'See that chiller over there? Shift it in front of the swing doors.'

The giant placed his huge hands against the side of the chiller and began to heave. The muscles in his arms stood proud like iron bars laced through concrete, while sweat ran down his forehead in thick rivulets. After a few minutes of intense exertion he'd managed to shift the chiller across the front of the doors, effectively blocking the way to the dining area.

'Now sit back down with your buddies,' said Hunter. 'It's time I said my goodbyes, and unless you've got a taste for hot lead, don't try to follow.'

With that, he ducked into the storeroom and strode towards the exit, pausing only to shift the sack of rice so that the door swung shut behind him. He emerged into the gloom to find himself in a side alley. The alley was fenced in on three sides, and it was home to an old black dumpster and a stack of beer crates. He pushed the dumpster in front of the fire door, sealing the three men inside, then skirted along the side of the building to find himself back in the front lot. A quick glance through the restaurant's picture windows confirmed that the juvenile gangbangers were still busy with their margaritas, oblivious to what had just gone down.

He slipped quickly away and hurried down the street to his waiting Barracuda. His decision to take the direct approach had been worthwhile. He'd confirmed that the restaurant was effectively gang owned and, more im-portantly, he'd put a name to that gang. But if he wanted to find out what tied Lunatic to the Vipers, and what implications those ties had for Angel and Gracie, he was going to have to discuss it with someone higher up the Viper chain of command.

CHAPTER EIGHTEEN

STONE stood by the window and watched as the sun emerged on the eastern horizon. Dawn was his favourite part of the day. It signified a new awakening. A rebirth. A second chance. And right now that was all he wanted from life.

Below him, the warehouses and factories that dominated the surrounding area were bathed in a golden glow, the metal roofs of the food-processing plants glistening in the morning light. This was Vernon, the economic powerhouse just to the south of downtown LA, home to industries as diverse as steel and agriculture, apparel and cold storage, plastics and recycling, and also home to Stone, at least for the time being.

His window on the world was six storeys up, on the top floor of a building that was owned by a garment manufacturing company that specialised in producing exotic clothing for the film industry. For exotic, read fetish; for film, read porn. When the company's owner, a flame-haired Amazonian who went by the name of Peaches, had taken him on a tour of the lower floors, he'd seen row upon row of Asian immigrants furiously beavering away at sewing machines, their apparent goal in life to attach chains and studs to strips of leather. Peaches, a former porn starlet herself, had told him that the business was all about product placement. If her outfits featured in a successful adult flick, their sales would quadruple overnight. When she'd offered him a place on the payroll, he'd accepted on the spot.

His position was that of night watchman for Fetishwear Inc. This exalted position came with a modest salary and one major perk—he got to live rent-free on the top floor of the building. Even his dogs, Caleb and Joshua, were welcome, as Peaches realised that the presence of two well-trained Akitas could only enhance security. It was the first job Stone had been able to pick up in a while, ever since he'd assaulted his last boss and left him in County USC Medical Centre. As references went, giving your former employer a fractured cheekbone wasn't much of a selling point.

He'd been working as a bouncer at a low-rent night-club when it had happened. His asshole of a boss had made one racist remark too many, something to do with savages and their squaws, the sort of rubbish that usually sailed right over his head, but on this occasion something had snapped inside him, because on this occasion Stone had been drunk. Now, being drunk hadn't been out of the ordinary for him back then, indeed, it had been his usual physical state, but on this particular night he'd yet to vent his frustrations on any of the nightclub's more violent patrons, so he'd been a powder keg waiting to blow. When his boss had mouthed off, he'd lit a fuse. Stone had swung his right

fist like a hammer and laid the guy out on the edge of
the dance floor, and it had taken three of his co-
bouncers to drag him off. No squealing sirens and arrest
for assault had followed, though—the nightclub had
been one of those places that preferred to keep police
involvement to a minimum. Instead, the boss had
ordered the other bouncers to take Stone out back and
administer a good kicking. By the time they'd accom-
plished the first part of their task they'd all sported
fresh cuts and bruises, so they'd wisely elected to pass
on the second part and let him stumble off into the
darkness unmolested.

He turned away from the window and let loose a
loud yawn. He'd been up all night—first at the porno
cinema, where he'd left a hobbled gangbanger in his
wake, then back at Fetishwear Inc., where he'd completed the second half of his duties as night watchman,
having left Caleb and Joshua in charge for the first few
hours. When he was otherwise engaged, he gave them
the run of the building by wedging all the stairwell
doors open with trashcans, confident that the pair of
them could handle any intruders should the need arise.
He knelt down to where the two dogs were stretched
out on the floor and petted the tops of their heads. Once
they were satisfied that neither food nor exercise were
on the immediate agenda, their eyes rolled shut and they
went back to sleep.

Stone rose to his feet and surveyed his domain. For
a bolthole, it wasn't half-bad. The space was large,
maybe a hundred feet long by forty feet wide, with
bare brick walls, exposed wooden rafters and a cold

concrete floor. Windows were spaced every ten feet or so on both the north and south faces to provide plenty of natural light during the day and a wonderful view of the celestial constellations during the night. Access was via the stairwell positioned in the far left corner of the room or the service elevator positioned in the far right. The elevator, with its large cargo bay and wide doors, was particularly useful, as it allowed him to bring his Triumph Rocket all the way up to the top floor, where he could ensure that the motorbike would be safe.

When it came to mod cons, the room had relatively few. Just a single cot bed by the west wall and a series of recently acquired possessions lined up along the east: an old refrigerator that hummed softly to itself, a Weber barbecue plus a large bag of charcoal, and a stainless-steel kettle. What few clothes he owned were draped across a length of rope he'd secured between two of the rafters, while his collection of razor-sharp knives was stashed safely under his bed. Other than that, the space was largely bare, except for the swathes of paper that dominated most of the walls.

Everywhere he looked he saw the fruits of his labour. A large map of East Los Angeles with key areas of interest highlighted in red. Diagrams of drug and cash movements between dope spots and safe houses. Lists of manpower in each locale and timings of shift changes. The routes that the LAPD prowl cars took around the neighbourhood when they were on sweeps. A series of location photos of crack houses, rundown apartment buildings, inner-city schools, bars, nightclubs, restaurants and private residences. Surveillance snaps of twenty-one men, arranged in a pyramid fashion with a big empty space at the top. Fourteen of the photos had street names listed underneath, along with additional notes concerning their known associates and suspected roles in the gang, be it spotters, runners, soldiers or dealers. The pyramid was arranged in terms of seniority, with the more numerous, and more youthful, spotters and runners listed along the base, while the veteran lieutenants were positioned closer to the summit. Survival was everything in the gang world—when you first joined you were cannon fodder, but if you could somehow stay alive long enough you earned the right to prosper, at least for a while.

There were seven faces that had yet to be identified and, more importantly, one identity that had yet to be apportioned a face. Dreadnought. The gang boss. The space for his photo was at the very apex of the pyramid, but despite Stone's best efforts he was no closer to tracking him down. He stared at the name on the wall for a moment, then dragged his eyes down until they were focused on the photo of Rocket, the banger he'd accosted at the cinema. Rocket was a mid-level street dealer, and by temporarily crippling him Stone had hoped to send a strong message to Dreadnought and the rest of the gang. With any luck, his attack would work on two levels—first, the simple act of removing a dealer would hit the gang's ability to function, and second, the manner of that removal should sow a little consternation among the ranks as to the kind of threat they were now up against. Stone was just one man while the gang were many, and when facing a foe with superior numbers, guerrilla warfare was the order of the day. You had to emerge when least expected, strike hard and fast, then vanish back into the shadows. Raise doubt and fear in your enemy's heart until his fighting spirit was weakened, then annihilate him. That was the Apache way.

Stone retrieved a marker pen from the floor and drew a thick red cross through Rocket's photo. With his ability to walk now severely hampered by the fact that both his Achilles tendons had been detached, this was one drug dealer who could consider himself removed from the conflict. Five other photos, each featuring another surly-looking dealer, all sported similar red crosses. Stone had been busy. But there was a lot more work to be done.

CHAPTER NINETEEN

CASSIUS eyed the payphone with trepidation. It was stationed just outside his apartment block in Imperial Courts, a graffiti-covered metallic eyesore that somehow remained in working order despite being located in one of the most rundown parts of the city, and although the phone wasn't all that scary in itself, the call that Cassius was about to receive filled him with fear.

It hadn't always been this way. Conversations with the boss had once been a thing to look forward to. A daily occurrence that boosted his ego and filled him with joy, or at least something that felt like joy, his life thus far not having given him the emotional frame of reference to be sure of how joy actually felt. Pain, envy, anger, fear—he considered himself expert in these dark emotions—but throughout his twenty-four years on the planet, joy was something that had always remained just out of reach.

But if he'd had to pinpoint a time in his life when he'd been at his happiest, it would have been back when he'd first joined the Imperial Knights and hooked up with Dreadnought. Dreadnought had been a few years older than him, but a whole lot stronger, and a whole lot more respected, and he'd taken Cassius under his wing and had let it be known that the new kid wasn't to be touched. He'd taught him the way of the streets, such vital skills as how to defend your block to the death, how civilians were your meal ticket, how to hide your fear, how to throw fear into your enemy, and how to show deference to the police without losing face, and Cassius had taken it all in as best he could. As Dreadnought's ever more violent actions had ensured that he'd risen fast through the ranks, Cassius had been at his side to bask in the reflected glory. Even then, he'd had no delusions about his place in the scheme of things, but he'd figured that it was better to ride to the top on the back of someone else's coattails than to stay at the bottom on your own.

He withdrew a small baggie of dull white powder from his pocket, then proceeded to rub some of the cocaine along his gums. Just a little something to help him focus. To make sure he was on top of his game. He'd phoned the bakery ten minutes ago. It acted as a relay station, taking calls from Cassius before passing them on to Dreadnought, who in turn would call back from some secret location. Security was ultra-tight at present, and Cassius was no longer in the inner circle, his privileges having been revoked ever since Dread had returned from a stay at the big house a couple of months back. Dread had heard rumours that Cassius was on the pipe, and despite his assurances to the contrary, Cassius had found himself out in the cold. He had no idea where his best friend was now holed up, and the fact that he was no longer trusted with such information was a bitter pill to swallow. He harboured dreams of proving himself worthy once again and reclaiming a seat at the top table, but dreams were all they were for now, as he could see no way out of the self-created shit-storm he was blundering around in. When the phone rang, he reached out with a shaking hand to place the receiver to his ear.

'What up, cuz?' he asked.

'I've told you before, lay off of the gang speak.' The deep voice rumbled down the phone line like an armoured division on manoeuvres. 'You talk like a savage, then that's all you'll ever be.'

'Sorry, boss,' muttered Cassius. Dreadnought had used his prison time to educate himself, and Cassius was still struggling to come to terms with his new and improved vocabulary.

'What payphone you at?'

'One outside a McDonald's, over by the freeway,' Cassius lied. He'd been warned not to use the payphones that were close to home, as it increased the risk of them being wire-tapped, but just lately he'd struggled to find the enthusiasm for travel.

'You sure?'

''Course I'm sure, Dread, I ain't slippin'. I be doin' just what you tole me.'

'So what have you got for me?'

Cassius took a deep breath and decided to bite the bullet. If he could barrel through the bad news in a hurry, maybe he'd make it to the good stuff before Dread got too upset.

'We down a couple more men, cuz.'

'Who?'

'Slowpoke 'n' Rocket.'

'They dead?'

'Rocket be in the hospital after getting his ankles all cut up and shit.'

'How bad?'

'Went into surgery in the a.m. Doc reckons he'll be on his ass for a while. Gonna need a wheely-chair, Ironside-type shit.'

'He get a look at his attacker?'

'Nope. It was real dark and the muthafucka came at him from behind.'

'So they're making their move...' Dreadnought said softly.

Cassius kept quiet. The boss's low tones were a cause for concern. The angrier Dreadnought got, the quieter he became. After a five-second pause, a half-whispered enquiry came down the phone line.

'You got any further in tracking this guy down?'

'Nah, cuz, he like some kinda ghost. I axed everyone on the street, but no one's talking. Don't worry, boss, I'll find him.'

'You'd better. At this rate we aren't going to have much of a crew left. How many does that make now? Seven men he's taken out of the game? Eight? This is coming at a real bad time, and if it carries on much longer it's going to throw a serious wrench in my plans. Find him. Find him fast.'

'You got it.'

'What about Slowpoke? What happened to him?'

'Got caught in a sneak attack. Poke was handlin' the

money run from the apartments late last night when someone sent him to his maker.' Cassius swallowed hard as he tried to hide the tremor in his voice. 'They left him perforated then ran off with the cash.'

'Goddamn it! What the hell's going on? I left you in charge of the day-to-day, but if you're not up to it, just say the word.'

'It's all good, cuz—I can turn this around. Just some minor problems is all.'

'Your loyalty got you this gig, but loyalty only gets you so far. You've been slipping. You've lost your edge. Are you using again?'

'Using? No way, boss. I cut out that shit long ago and I ain't never goin' back.'

'You'd better not. Addiction is another form of en-slavement. Drugs are for victims, and I don't employ victims in positions of power. You got any good news for me? How are we set for today?'

'Everything's sewn up tight, just like you wanted. It'll go down at noon, so there'll be plenty of bangers on hand to put the word out once it's done.'

'Excellent. But make sure it gets done right. I want you to handle this personally. Start repaying my faith.'

'You got it, boss. Leave it to me.' Cassius replaced the phone in its cradle and ran through the plan one last time. Everything was in place—he was sure of it. If it all went down exactly as Dread had ordered, he'd win back some respect. And once that was done, he could hook up with Mason and Diaz to pay off his debts. Then he'd be back on his way to the top.

CHAPTER TWENTY

WHEN Angel answered her front door, her red-rimmed eyes told Hunter that she'd been crying. She stood barefoot before him on the carpet, wearing a baggy blue T-shirt and a pair of cut-off jeans, her hair pulled back in a ponytail, her face devoid of make-up, and she looked stunning. When she stepped back to let him enter, her arm brushed against his, and he felt the breath catch in his throat.

She'd called him a half hour earlier and asked him to come over. When she'd asked about Gracie the hope in her voice had tugged at his heartstrings, and he wished that he could have told her that her daughter was as good as found, but thus far his progress had been slow. After leaving Desperados late last night he'd tried to track down someone senior within the Vipers to brace them about their involvement in events, but gang bosses were an elusive breed at the best of times, and now that the streets were on red alert, finding the head of the snake had proved nigh on impossible.

Angel gestured for him to head towards the living area, and when he settled into the large sofa that faced the window, she sat down next to him. A photo album lay open alongside her, its pages covered with pictures of Gracie, her smiling face staring outwards.

'Larry didn't come home again last night,' she said quietly.

'Well, I know where he was for a while. I tailed him to a Tex-Mex restaurant called Desperados. Have you heard of it?'

'Desperados? That's a Viper hangout. What was he doing there?'

'Not much. Just sat outside in his Caddie like he was casing the joint, then drove off into the night.'

'Where'd he go?'

'I don't know. From the way he was looking at the restaurant, I figured it had to be important, so I went inside and dug around a little.'

'What did you find?'

'That the place was Viper owned and everyone inside was jumpy. Very jumpy,' he muttered, remembering how he'd had to fight his way out. 'Have you had any problems with the Vipers lately?'

'No—just the opposite. We've got a loose alliance with them. We back each other up on the streets every now and again. I know a few of their chicas from back in the day.'

Hunter's brow furrowed. Pretty much the last thing he'd expected to discover was that the Ghosts were best buddies with the Vipers. That certainly hadn't been the impression he'd got while Lunatic had been casing the restaurant last night. Maybe there'd been some kind of fall-out between the two gangs that Angel was unaware of? With her daughter missing, it would be understandable if a recent change in allegiances had passed her by. In the gang world, friends became enemies overnight, usually for one of two reasons. Number one—a violent episode led to bad blood, and when this occurred, it was usually very public, very noisy, and very messy, so the likelihood of no word of such an event having reached Angel's ears was not that high. So that left reason number two—a breakdown in a business relationship, and the business that all gangs were involved in to at least some extent was that of drugs.

He rubbed at the light stubble on his chin as he considered the possibilities. Maybe some drug deal between the Ghosts and the Vipers had turned sour. Maybe the Vipers had grabbed Gracie as collateral to force Lunatic's hand. That would go some way to explain why he was so adamant that the police should not be involved in the search for his daughter. He'd always said that only he could guarantee Gracie's safe return, almost as if he knew exactly what had to be done, but for some unknown reason had yet to get around to doing it. Everything led back to Lunatic and the fact that he knew more than he was willing to share. For Gracie's sake, Lunatic had to talk. But the gang boss had gone missing again.

'We've got to find Lunatic,' Hunter said softly. 'He's involved in all this, I'm just not sure how. I've got to talk to him again, and this time…I've got to take the gloves off.'

Hunter watched Angel closely for a reaction, but

none was forthcoming. She seemed almost dead to the world, her fears for her missing daughter leaving her an emotionally spent force. She reached out for the photo album that sat on the sofa, and began to stroke one of the larger photos of Gracie with the tips of her fingers.

'Whatever it takes,' she said. 'Just do whatever it takes. I've got to get her back, Hunter. She's the only good thing in my life. I can't go on without her.'

'I might have to hurt him.'

She turned from the photo album to look up at him from close range, a small spark of fire shimmering deep in her eyes. 'If Larry knows anything about what's happened to Gracie…anything at all…then he'll deserve every damn thing he gets.'

Her eyes dropped once more and she nestled in close to him. He wrapped his arm around her as he considered her emotional turmoil. Her daughter was missing and her long-term partner was somehow implicated. It was a wonder she was keeping it together at all. The two of them remained that way for a while, until the phone by the sofa broke the silence. Angel withdrew from his embrace and stretched out full length to reach for it.

'*Ola?*' she said into the handset, then she swung her legs around to sit upright, her body crackling with electricity. 'Larry? Is that you?'

'Put him on speaker,' mouthed Hunter. Angel quickly obliged, and a series of deep, gasping sobs filled the room. Something was wrong. Something was very wrong.

'Larry? Is that you?' Angel asked again.

'Yeah…it's me, baby,' he said, his voice choked

thick with emotion. 'I just called to let you know that everything's gonna be fine. I'm gonna take care of business in a little while, then Gracie'll be back with you.'

'What are you talking about? What are you going to do?'

'It don't matter. Only thing that does is little Gracie. I'd do anything for her—you know that, don't you?'

''Course I do, baby. Where are you?'

'You and Gracie were the best things that ever happened to me…I love you guys more than life itself. Everything I ever done, I done for you two.'

Before Angel could reply, Hunter's face lit up as he heard a familiar sound in the background.

'Keep him talking—you've gotta keep him talking,' he whispered in her ear, and then he was running for the door, down the hallway, and out onto the street, where his super-fast Barracuda awaited.

Hunter spun the steering-wheel through his hands and launched his car round the next bend, then punched the gas as he came out the far side. The seat belt tightened across his sternum as a burst of gravitational force pushed him back into his seat. The power under the 'Cuda's hood was so immense that its high-performance suspension sometimes struggled to keep the vehicle on the road, and Hunter was going to need every last ounce of that power if he was going to make it to his destination in time.

The streets flashed by in a blur on either side, the midday sun glinting off the hoods of the cars that lined the sidewalks, the heads of startled pedestrians turning to watch him as he raced by. His only hope of getting to Lunatic in time was if Angel managed to keep her partner talking on the phone, and something told him that wouldn't prove easy. Lunatic had sounded like a man who'd come to a decision. Like someone who was about to set out on a path from which there could be no turning back. What the hell was the gang boss going to do?

He rolled the 'Cuda around the final bend to find that Lunatic's Caddie was parked just up ahead, right outside the entrance to Desperados. The drive from Angel's house to the restaurant should have taken him twenty minutes but he'd covered the distance in ten, hurtling down the East LA back streets to avoid the midday traffic that clogged the freeways. The Caddie appeared to be empty. He eased off the gas and coasted forward. As he neared the Caddie's rear bumper, the front lot of the restaurant came into view. The sight that confronted him was alarming.

Lunatic stood outside the main entrance in full gang attire, wearing a baggy white T-shirt, knee-length shorts and a black bandana that featured a clenched white fist logo. There was no phone pressed to his ear, signalling that his call to Angel had been terminated. Instead, a can of spray paint hung loosely in his right hand, and he'd just completed redecorating Desperado's front door with a hastily drawn Ghost logo. Hunter watched on as Lunatic pulled a TEC-9 from his shorts. When the gang boss opened the door, the familiar chimes of 'La Cucaracha' rang out at public-nuisance volume, the same tune that Hunter had heard in the background while listening in on Lunatic's last call to Angel. Before the chimes had finished, a less melodic sound burst from the restaurant to assault his eardrums. The sound of automatic gunfire.

Hunter drew his Berretta and clicked off the safety. As he climbed out of his car, the sound of Lunatic's TEC-9 spitting out bullets at a rapid rate chilled his blood, while intermittent lower-pitched booms signalled that the Vipers were returning fire. If Gracie was somehow caught up in the middle of this, she wouldn't stand a chance. Was the gang boss on some death-or-glory mission, putting his only child's life at risk in the process? Hunter pictured the heartbreak on Angel's face as he told her that her daughter was dead. No—that wasn't going to happen.

He set out for the restaurant at a sprint, but he'd barely got halfway across the street before Lunatic staggered back outside, his gun hanging limp by his side, blood pumping from a wound in his stomach. Hunter came to a stop as the gang boss fell to his knees, his TEC-9 clattering away into the dirt, and then things got really interesting. A skinny black guy appeared by the side of the building, emerging from the very same alley that Hunter had used as an escape route just one night previous. He was wearing a pair of stiff black jeans and a blue shirt that was three sizes too big, while the white hockey mask that obscured his face left him looking like he'd just stepped out of a Halloween movie. Lunatic was oblivious to the newcomer's presence as he was busy trying to keep his guts in his torso. The guy in the mask took three steps forward, his hand swinging out from behind his back to reveal that he was holding a snub-nosed revolver, then he placed the gun against the back of the gang boss's head and pulled the trigger.

The bullet burrowed through Lunatic's cranium and exploded out of his forehead, sending a shower of blood, brain and bone onto the dirt. The gang boss tottered for a moment then slumped face first into his own mess, his life force forever extinguished. Hunter broke his paralysis and raised his Beretta, but before he could shoot, his eyes registered a flicker of movement from inside the restaurant, then his instincts took over and he was diving headlong to his left, just as a picture window shattered to signal that one of the Vipers had joined the fray with gun blazing. As Hunter rolled to a stop and drew a bead on this new threat, Lunatic's assassin made a break for the alley. The Viper that stood swaying in the window was blood drenched and near death, the broken shards of glass that framed him somehow adding to the sense of macabre. Before he could fire again, the barrel of Hunter's Beretta came to rest on his chest, the gun coughed once, then the Viper tumbled out of view. Hunter jumped to his feet and ran forward, his eyes flicking between the restaurant and the alley, wary of further attack.

When he reached the front of the building he risked a peek inside. A scene from the depths of hell awaited him. Bodies were strewn everywhere, some slumped over tables, others lying twisted in unnatural positions on the tiled floor, all of them drenched in blood. Most of the victims seemed to be gangbangers, although the girl who served at the bar was also among the fallen, her once pretty face now destroyed by a 9-mm Parabellum cartridge. With the field of fire confined to such a small space, the blast from Lunatic's TEC-9 had been murderous in the extreme. With mounting dread, Hunter ran inside and picked his way through the carnage.

The first body he stepped over was strangely familiar. He paused for a second to take in the man's features—shaven head, angular face, small pointed beard—and then it came back to him. It was the guy from the photo that Lunatic had been studying the day before, and he was bleeding profusely from two matching wounds to his torso. Hunter pushed on, his gaze dancing over the corpses as he searched for the body of a small child. Once he was satisfied that Gracie wasn't present, a great sense of relief washed over him.

He rushed back outside and hurried to the far end of the building. The side alley looked empty, so he advanced with his Beretta aimed at the one piece of meaningful cover—the dumpster that sat by the boundary fence. When the far end of the trash receptacle came into view, all he found was the corpse of a dead rat. The fire door that led to the kitchens was secured from the inside, which left Lunatic's killer with just one other means of escape.

He climbed onto the dumpster to be rewarded with a clear view of the neighbouring side street. The stretch of potholed asphalt was lined with liquor marts, cut-rate clothing stores and bargain eateries, and it was largely deserted, the familiar sound of gunfire having convinced most of the locals to run for cover. He looked both ways to find that there were two cars on the block—a beat-up white station wagon heading south and a red El Camino heading north. When the Camino made a turn at the end of the street, the far side of the vehicle flashed into view to reveal an electric yellow flame decal over the rear wheel rim. The face of a broken-down drug addict appeared in Hunter's mind's eye. The addict he'd spoken to at the kids' playground where Angel's daughter had last been seen alive. The addict who'd said that an El Camino with a flame decal had been present when Gracie had been bundled into a black cargo van. He watched as the car with the matching description disappeared from view. It had to be one and the same.

Hunter raced back out front to where his Barracuda sat waiting, his nerve ends sparking with excitement. This was the first major break in the case—the guy that had just killed Lunatic was somehow involved in Gracie's abduction. He couldn't let him get away. A pair of sirens began to wail in the distance, prompting him to jam his keys in the ignition and fire the car to life. He had no desire to meet up with his former comrades and explain his presence at a gangland shootout, plus Angel had made it clear that she remained petrified of police involvement, although maybe that would change now that Lunatic was out of the picture. The 'Cuda's tyres spun as he roared away from the kerb, then he swung the car around the corner and stamped on the gas, his pursuit of the flame-licked Chevy now firmly under way.

* * *

Hunter was hemmed in on all sides, stuck in traffic on the Seven-Ten. Five cars forward and two lanes over, the El Camino with the flame decal sat idling. The early afternoon gridlock was giving him time to consider the events he'd just witnessed. The first conclusion he'd drawn was that Lunatic's actions made no sense. If the Emerald Vipers had swiped his kid, then what good was embarking on a suicide mission? Had the gang boss expected to find Gracie somewhere in the restaurant? Or had the frustration of losing her got too much for him? A chilling thought crossed Hunter's mind. What if Lunatic knew that she was already dead? What if the shootout had been all about revenge? But that didn't tie in with what he'd said in his last phone conversation with Angel, when he'd promised that Gracie would soon be back in her arms.

A break in the traffic opened up in the lane to his right, so he swung his Barracuda over to gain another car length on his target. He pictured the tag that Lunatic had spraypainted on the door to Desperados prior to the massacre. By leaving the Ghost's logo there for all to see, Lunatic had thrown down a challenge that the Vipers would be forced to respond to. The one thing you could be sure of in gangland was that any violent act would be answered with a swift and even bloodier reprisal. An eye for an eye didn't exist any more— these days it was all about escalation. But how on earth was starting a gang war with the Vipers going to help?

And who was the skinny black guy in the El Camino? Was he some stray guard who'd slacked off to take a piss by the dumpster? Had it been sheer good luck that he'd emerged from the alley at just the right time to punch

Lunatic's ticket? It sure hadn't looked that way. When he'd come around the corner there had been no sense of surprise in his actions—his gun had been cocked, locked and ready to rock. It was almost as if he'd known what was going to happen—as if he'd expected Lunatic to be standing right there. Was the guy even a Viper? The fact that he was black would suggest otherwise. And how did he fit into the big picture? The one thing Hunter was sure of was that he needed more information. His only link to Gracie was up ahead, and he couldn't let him get away.

As he mused over these thoughts, the El Camino took the off-ramp at exit 12B to head towards Wright Road. Taking advantage of a minuscule gap in the traffic, Hunter pulled in front of a diesel bigrig and accelerated down the ramp, just in time to see the Camino turn west onto Imperial Freeway. Lunatic's killer was headed straight into the heart of Watts, and Hunter was right on his tail.

CHAPTER TWENTY-ONE

CASSIUS swung his El Camino into the Imperial Courts Housing Project, his face sporting a wide grin, his brain enjoying a dual buzz, one chemically induced, the other natural. The chemical buzz came courtesy of his second vial of crack cocaine of the day. He'd taken the first before stepping out of Desperado's side alley to steady his nerves ahead of the big event, then he'd lit up another to celebrate while he was stuck in traffic on the way home. The drug was now melding perfectly with his natural high, which had come courtesy of the fact that he'd successfully offed Lunatic, boom, one shot to the cranium, a death that had left him a little more confident when it came to his future prospects.

Not much in his life had gone to plan lately, hell, not much in his life had ever gone to plan, but this time things had turned out okay, and for that he was grateful. Later this afternoon, he'd get in touch with the boss. In stark contrast to yesterday, it was a phone call that he now looked forward to. Dreadnought was going to be pleased. Lunatic's very public demise had gone as planned, so Cassius's stock would be back on the rise, but before he could get his props, he had one more pressing matter to attend to. The grin fell from his face as he saw what awaited him up ahead. An Oldsmobile Cutlass streaked with a lifetime's worth of grime sat directly outside his apartment block, with one man propped casually against the front fender and another loitering nearby. Mason and Diaz had come to collect. He'd contacted them earlier that day to tell them he'd raised their cash, and despite his best efforts to convince them otherwise, they'd insisted on showing up at Imperial Courts for the pay-off. If he was seen with them it would be bad for his rep. Very bad. But for now they were in charge, and he had little choice but to go along with whatever they wanted. He hoped that they hadn't been waiting long. Mason was an impatient son of a bitch at the best of times.

Cassius brought his El Camino to a stop just behind the Cutlass and climbed out. His blackmailers watched as he approached, their faces sporting matching expressions of thinly veiled disgust, like he was something they'd just stepped in. Mason, who leant against the hood of the Olds, was his usual slovenly self, his faded jeans full of holes and his surfer shirt a garish collection of mismatched colours, while Diaz, who stood nearby on the sidewalk, was resplendent in a light tan suit and lilac shirt, his eyes hidden behind a pair of black Ray-Bans. As Cassius stopped a yard shy of them, the effects of his last crack hit began to wear off. His hands started to shake as the confidence drained from his body, leaving only a cold hunger for more chemical stimulation in its place.

'G-guys…whassup?' he stuttered, folding his arms across his chest.

'You're late,' said Mason coldly.

'But I'm here now, so it's all good, right?'

'You think me and Diaz like to be kept waiting by the likes of you, then you're sadly fucking mistaken. Where's our money?'

'Chill…it's in my crib…'

'So what the fuck are you doing down here?'

As Cassius turned to go, he received a firm kick in the ass that sent him tumbling forward, his outstretched arms only just managing to stop his face from making hard contact with sidewalk. The two men laughed as he scrambled to his feet.

'Take care, now, you'd better not drop our cash on the return leg,' Mason called out as Cassius broke for the stairwell that led up to his second-floor apartment.

Fucking wiseass, Cassius fumed silently. One day, Mason and Diaz were gonna get what was coming to them. He took the stairs two steps at a time, then stumbled along the balcony as he fumbled his key out of his pocket.

'It's just me, Moms,' he shouted as he entered the apartment, headed down the hall, then ducked his head into the kitchen to make sure she was okay. The old girl was right where he'd left her—sat in a chair, slumped over the Formica table. A manacle was attached to her bony right ankle, and from that manacle ran a length of welded steel chain that was secured to a steel D-ring set in the floor.

He'd been doing this for a while—confining her to

the apartment for her own safety. Her addiction was now so bad she could barely function. If she was left to wander the streets on her own, God knows what she'd get up to. The last time she'd slipped away she'd been missing for over two days. When he'd finally found her, she'd been stretched out on the back seat of a burned-out car in a vacant lot, passed out in a dried pool of blood and vomit. The inside of her right arm had sported a series of fresh tracks, and her ratty old housedress had been covered with jizz stains. How the hell someone had got off over a scraggy-assed heroin addict who was well into her sixties beat Cassius, but he knew damn well that the streets were packed with sexual predators, and to make a list of all their perversities would take more time than he had to spare.

Since that day, he'd added the manacle, chain and D-ring to his armoury in the fight to keep Moms inside. 'Course, it was also important for his own street rep that she didn't get out and embarrass him. You tended to lose face when your mom was around the way, offering toothless blowjobs in return for a nickel baggie. But his decision to keep her confined meant that he had to care for her—feed her on those rare occasions that she'd take food, wash her emaciated body down every once in a while, even score a regular supply of drugs and cook up her fix. Helping his mom to get high was nothing new to him—he'd been doing it on and off since he was eleven years old. He could still remember the day she'd talked him through the process step by step, her hands shaking too much to do it herself. Cook the heroin on a soupspoon, then filter the liquid through a small piece of cotton into a syringe. Insert the needle into a vein between the toes and draw blood. Let the blood and heroin mix together, then depress the plunger. Even at the age of eleven, Cassius had been pretty sure that this wasn't the sort of education that the white kids got in the suburbs.

His mom had been fighting a losing battle against the drug ever since. Every once in a while she'd try to clean up her act, but it had never taken her long to succumb to the awful urges of withdrawal. So the only thing left for him to do was to help her see out her remaining days in relative safety, and that's where the manacle came in. The funny thing was, she didn't even seem to mind being confined to quarters, just as long as she got a fix before he went out, then another on his return, she was as happy as…well…as a heroin addict on heroin. And he was lucky that her drug of choice was Mexican tar, as its depressant properties made it easier to keep her under control. All in all, things could have been worse.

'I'll sort out your fix in a few, okay?' he said, as she raised her head a half-inch and gave him a pleading stare.

'Need it now,' she mumbled, her voice cracking. 'Hurts so much…'

'You gotta wait, I be busy.'

'Cocksucker—I'm gonna kill you!' she rasped, before abruptly changing tack. 'Want some pussy? I give you some pussy, boy, you fetch my stash? Momma make you feel real good…'

'Just sit fuckin' tight,' he commanded, ducking back out into the hall, a plaintive wail following him out of the door. He shrugged it off and made for the bathroom at the rear of the property. Her emotional blackmail hadn't had much effect on him in a long while. She could beg, cuss and make as many sexual offers as she wanted but, as far as Cassius was concerned, she may as well have been speaking Chinese. He'd long since accepted the fact that she was an addict, and that, like any other addict, she'd say and do anything in order to secure her next fix.

He entered the bathroom and walked over to the window, then wrapped both his hands around the latch and tugged upwards. Shit. The damn thing was stuck fast again. Whenever the temperature nudged above eighty the old wooden frame swelled up and the window refused to budge. He clenched his meagre muscles and redoubled his efforts, letting loose a cry of relief when the glass moved upwards with a jerk. When he ducked his head through the opening he was rewarded with a hot blast from the rear of the air-con unit that serviced the apartment next door. His eyes darted around to make sure no one was watching, then he reached over to the unit, pried up the back of its casing, and snaked his hand inside. A few seconds later his hand emerged grasping a ziplock baggie stuffed with dirty dollar bills. The score he'd nabbed from Slowpoke's last money run, along with all the cash he could lay his hands on. He pushed the casing back in place, ducked back into his apartment, and hurried down the hall. As he passed the kitchen his mom let fly with another string of profanities, and then he was running along the balcony, his eyes flicking over the balustrade to where Mason and Diaz waited below. By the time he was standing in front of them, he was struggling to catch his breath.

'Looks like your hustler lifestyle ain't all that conducive to good health,' cracked Mason with a sneer. 'I believe that belongs to me?'

Cassius handed over the baggie with a heavy heart and watched as Mason started to count. Coughing up his hard earned dough was a real pisser, but he didn't have much choice.

'Fucking drug money—it's always so goddamned filthy,' Mason moaned as he leafed through the crinkled bills. 'But I guess it all gets spent the same. Hey? What the fuck's this, Cass? You're five thousand bucks short. Where the fuck's the rest?'

Diaz cracked his knuckles and moved forward a step, throwing a shadow over Cassius as he squirmed on the sidewalk.

'But, Mason, that's what you asked for, so that's what I got…'

Diaz drew back his right arm and gave him an open-handed slap across the side of his head that almost knocked him off his feet.

'That's your fucking problem, Cass,' sighed Mason. 'You just don't listen. Now, there's enough cash here to cover your original debt, but what about the vig? That's an extra five g's. You're gonna have to make good on that too.'

The stinging pain in his right ear was nothing compared to the twisting sensation that rose in his gut, like someone was tightening a set of steel bands to choke up his insides. The truth finally dawned on him. Mason was never gonna let him off the hook. One demand for a payoff would follow another, as sure as lights out followed head count in the pen. From here on in he was Mason's bitch, and there wasn't a damn thing he could do about it.

'But, Mason…you gotta be reasonable…'

Diaz grabbed him by the scruff of the neck, lifted him off his feet, and slammed him over the hood of the Oldsmobile.

'You trying to ass-fuck me, son? Do me out of what's rightfully mine? We had a deal, and you ain't gonna back out now. You gotta man up and do the right thing. Otherwise the whole world's gonna hear about what you done.'

'Okay, okay, but you gotta give me more time,' said Cassius, squirming as the heat from the Olds's sun-soaked bodywork burned the side of his face. 'It ain't easy comin' up with that sort of dough in a hurry…'

'Like hell! You're in a cash-rich business, Cass. You got a steady stream of dead presidents passing through your hands each and every day. All you gotta do is divert a few of 'em in my direction. Is that too much to fucking ask?'

With that, Cassius was plucked from the hood of the car and sent sailing through the air to land in a bedraggled heap on the sidewalk. When he caught his breath and looked up, Diaz was wiping down his hands with a Kleenex, as if physical contact with the gangbanger had somehow sullied his being.

'Get busy, Cass, we'll be back real soon,' promised Mason, 'You can count on it.'

Cassius blinked back a tear as he watched the two men climb inside their vehicle and drive off. Why was life so goddamned unfair?

Hunter slid lower in the front seat of his Barracuda as the two men in the Oldsmobile flashed by. He considered following them, but opted to stay where he was—however interesting those guys were, he couldn't link them directly to Gracie, so he'd have to put them on the back burner for now. Instead, he settled for taking a note of their licence tag. He was sitting at the head of one of the side streets that criss-crossed Imperial Courts, an old housing project that had been built back in the early 1940s to provide homes for workers in the war industry. He'd positioned his car in such a fashion that he could keep an eye on his target while also minimising his chances of detection, but as things had turned out, he needn't have bothered, as Lunatic's killer had had more than enough to keep him occupied.

But who were the two guys that had just driven off? And how did they fit into the mix? The deeper he got into the case, the more unanswered questions it threw up. A scruffy-looking white guy and an impeccably turned-out Latino, and neither of them looked much like gangbangers. So what were they doing consorting with one? Were they mid-level drug dealers? Guys that acted as a link between the gangs and the out-of-state suppliers? Or were they somehow linked to Gracie's disappearance? Slave traders? Pimps? Organ harvesters? Anything was possible in the City of Angels.

Whoever they were, one thing was for sure—they were higher in the food chain than Lunatic's killer. He watched as the skinny black guy picked himself up from the sidewalk and dusted himself down. The interplay between the three of them had made it pretty clear as to who was in control, who was the muscle, and who occupied the least coveted role of bottom feeder. The good news was that when the black guy had entered one of the second-floor apartments he'd let himself in with a key, suggesting that he lived there. So Hunter had a choice. He could either march over and demand information regarding Gracie's whereabouts, or he could take a more circumspect approach. His brow furrowed as he thought things through. Although time was of the essence, coming up empty would leave him back at square one, so the first option was just too risky. He had to play it cool. Come up with a plan that would get him close enough to the black guy to find out what he knew, and find out quickly. Only problem was, now that the gangs were on a war footing that was easier said than done.

CHAPTER TWENTY-TWO

THE pale moon climbed higher overhead as Stone hefted his rucksack and made ready to depart. His two dogs, Caleb and Joshua, were watching him expectantly, their ears pricked and their tails beating softly on the concrete floor, as they'd known that something was amiss ever since their usual dining time of around seven p.m. had come and gone without so much as a sniff of food. He'd decided to take them with him that night, so their stomachs needed to be empty to ensure they were at their sharpest. This also meant that he'd be leaving the premises of Fetishwear Inc. totally unguarded, but he wasn't going to lose much sleep over that.

He lifted his motorbike off its stand and wheeled it into the service elevator, then called the dogs to heel, prompting them to bound over and take up flanking positions on either side of him. The cart set off with a slight bump, then groaned and clanked its way down six storeys before coming to a halt. He stepped out onto a raised walkway and headed for the metal roll-up door that was set in the wall in front of him. To the left of the door were two large buttons—one red, one blue. When he pushed the red one, the door rolled upwards to reward him with a view of the rear lot, which was bordered by an eight-foot wall topped with razor wire. He turned and went back to the elevator, where his motorbike and dogs waited patiently.

'Caleb, Joshua—go!' he commanded, to send the dogs sprinting for the exterior. He climbed on his bike, fired the engine, and followed in their wake. Once outside, he punched the 'close' button on an aging keypad, prompting the door to roll shut again. By now, the dogs were whining excitedly as they paced the lot. The Akitas had a strong pack instinct, and there was nothing they craved more than the chance to join their master on a late-night excursion.

Stone pointed his Triumph north and set off at a genteel pace, Caleb and Joshua following gamely on the sidewalk. The streets were near deserted, the traffic having faded away like an ebbing tide, and his target was just under three miles away. By the time he'd arrived, the Akitas were panting steadily with their tongues lolling from the corners of their mouths, although the sharp glint in their eyes suggested they were a long way from spent. He pulled up alongside a street sign, then secured the Triumph's front wheel with a padlock and chain. Having slipped off his rucksack, he dug out a large metal bowl and a bottle of water. Once the dogs had taken their fill, the three of them set off towards the one business that was still open—a café called The Grease Pit. Once they were thirty yards from their target, Stone called a halt by a battered Ford Taurus.

'Caleb, Joshua—down,' he commanded. The two dogs fell obediently to the ground, leaving the car between them and the café. He hunkered down next to them and stared over the hood of the vehicle. The café's front window was full of neon signs advertising burgers, pizzas and kebabs. Inside, a handful of insomniacs were sitting at the tables, all of them eating alone. Stone glanced at the moon and estimated the time to be around one a.m. Not long now.

He'd come here in search of a member of the Imperial Knights who went by the street name of Ziggy, a Rasta-loving drug dealer who wore his hair in a cascade of thick dreadlocks that reached halfway down his back. Ziggy was one of the most successful dealers in the southwest quadrant of the Knight's territory, largely because of his dedication. Every day, he'd be up at the crack of dawn to make regular sweeps of the dope spots under his control, haranguing his underlings to push the product ever harder to ensure he maximised his profits from human misery. And at the end of each day, his routine was always the same: after leaving a rundown courtyard in Watts where the bulk of his business went down, he'd stop off at The Grease Pit for some late-night refreshment.

After fifteen minutes or so, Ziggy emerged from the café, pulling a large white bubble jacket over a striped T-shirt. He paused for a moment to plug in some headphones, then set off down the street in a loose-limbed swagger. Stone rose to his feet and tapped his hand twice against his thigh, prompting Caleb and Joshua to fall into place alongside him.

'Target,' he whispered, pointing at the gangbanger. The dogs went straight into alert mode, ears pricked and hackles rising, eyes focused on the man that was walking away. Once Stone was satisfied with their state of readiness, he led them off in a controlled pursuit, the three of them flitting from shadow to shadow like vengeful wraiths. Two blocks later, his stomach tightened as the time for action approached. He quickened his pace, closing the distance between them until the gangbanger suddenly ducked out of view down a side alley. This was the moment that Stone had been waiting for. He jogged to the head of the alley and looked around the corner. Ziggy was now just thirty yards ahead, his head bobbing to the music as he picked his way through the trash, his white bubble coat acting as a homing beacon in the gloom.

'Hunt!' said Stone, and no sooner had the word left his mouth than Caleb and Joshua were streaking away from him to vault over upturned supermarket carts and abandoned lawn chairs, their long strides eating up the distance to their target in a hurry. They covered the last few yards in two matching bounds, then bunched the muscles in their hind legs to spring forward as one, their lithe bodies arcing through the air like guided missiles. Ziggy never knew what hit him. The dogs crashed into him from behind, driving him face first into the dirt, where they proceeded to clamp a set of powerful jaws around each of his arms and shake him into submission. Stone unfolded a hunting knife with a drop-point blade as he made his way down the alley.

'Hold,' he called to the dogs, who immediately stopped shaking their prey, although their jaws remained clamped to Ziggy's bloodied forearms. Stone crouched down behind the gangbanger and spun the knife in front of his eyes, the steel glinting dangerously in the moonlight. Once he had the Ziggy's undivided attention, he jerked the knife backwards, detouring at the last moment to pull the headphones out of his ears.

'I dunno where he is man, I got no idea,' Ziggy spluttered.

'Did I ask you a question?' said Stone. He was through talking to these guys. None of them seemed to know where Dreadnought was hiding, or at least none of them would admit to it if they did, so it was time to up the ante once again.

'What the fuck you want?'

'Shut up and keep still, otherwise I'll let my dogs tear your jugular from your throat.'

That wasn't strictly true, as the dogs were a long way from being trained killers, but the prostrate Ziggy wasn't to know that, and he started to tremble with fear. Stone gathered his dreadlocks in a bunch, then yanked them back to raise the gangbanger's face out of the dirt.

'Nah, man, keep those wolves off me—you gotta find some bakery, that's all I know.'

'A bakery? Where?'

'I got no clue.'

'Last chance.'

'I swear that's it—I got nothing else.'

'Then you're of no use to me.'

Ziggy yelled in pain as Stone began to hack through his hair with the hunting knife, severing the first of the matted ropes from his head.

'I said *quiet,*' he muttered, punctuating the last word by bringing the haft of the knife down on the back of Ziggy's head to knock him unconscious. A bakery. That would narrow the field a little. But in all his hours of surveillance he'd never seen any of the gang at a bakery. A few minutes later, he stood up and surveyed his work. The gangbanger's appearance had changed dramatically. With no mass of dreadlocks tumbling down his back, Ziggy looked more like a boy than a man.

'Release,' he said to the dogs, then he rolled the gangbanger onto his back, stared at the contours of his face for a moment, and went to work. Having placed the tip of his knife on Ziggy's forehead, he broke through the skin, prompting a small dot of blood to well from the wound. When he dragged the knife downwards, the skin tore open and the drop of blood turned into a thin river. After a number of further strokes, the thin river had been become a crimson delta, and four letters had been carved into the gangbanger's dome to brand him for all to see.

Stone tucked the knife back in his pocket, then picked up Ziggy and hoisted him over his shoulders. With his dogs in tow, he set off at pace, as if he was carrying nothing more cumbersome than a sack of grain. When he reached the mouth of the alley, he checked that the street was clear, then headed towards a yellow cab. The cab wasn't going anywhere—its tyres were long gone, having been replaced by four stacks of bricks, while its interior had been burnt out.

'Stay,' he muttered to the Akitas, before striding across the sidewalk to dump the gangbanger on the vehicle's hood. Having retrieved a set of plastic restraints from his rucksack, he placed Ziggy's right hand through one of the loops, slipped the other over the off-side wing mirror, then tightened the restraint until it cut into the skin. Once he'd repeated the process on the other hand, he went to work on Ziggy's ten outstretched fingers, bending each one of them back until all ten metacarpals had snapped with a resounding pop.

His work done, he headed off down the alley with his two dogs following faithfully behind, leaving the gangbanger stretched out in a crucifixion pose on the hood of the cab, with a single word cut into his forehead.

N-A-R-C.

Maybe that would throw a crimp in his sales patter.

CHAPTER TWENTY-THREE

HUNTER awoke on Angel's sofa with a crick in his neck and a throat that felt like someone had been working on it with a sheet of industrial-grade sandpaper. His body ached with a lethargy he hadn't felt in some months, and his eyes were near blinded by the early morning sunlight that streamed in through the glass doors stationed opposite. He was still wearing the same clothes he'd had on the day before—a pair of faded blue jeans and a black denim shirt—and he suspected that he was in dire need of a shower. He hauled himself to his feet, stretched his arms overhead, and let loose a long yawn, before pulling on his desert boots and heading for the kitchen.

He'd returned to Angel's yesterday afternoon to find her place empty, the cops having already collected her to make a statement regarding her boyfriend's bloody demise. No matter that Lunatic's body was still warm on the slab—there'd been five other gang-related murders in East Los Angeles that day and the local homicide detectives were stretched thin, so they'd been keen to get Lunatic's death out of the way in order to move on to the next one. When it came to the demise of a gangsta, official sympathy was in short supply.

Hunter had found all this out from one of the neighbours, an elderly woman who'd taken great delight in detailing Angel's cries of anguish as she'd been bundled into the back of a black and white. By the time he'd tracked her down at the local precinct, Angel had been so distraught that the desk sergeant had thought it best if she was transferred to the nearest hospital for observation, but as soon as she was outside the station, she'd insisted that they return home. Once back at her crib she'd dry-swallowed some tranquillisers and retired to her room, only breaking her silence once to ask Hunter to stay close at hand. Finding himself with time to kill, he'd grabbed a spot on the sofa and planned his next move. Getting close to the skinny black guy that had killed Lunatic looked like a tall order, but after a while he'd come up with something that might just work, and after that his thoughts had turned back to Angel.

One of the first things he'd been told when he'd been learning the ropes as a young detective was to not get emotionally involved with someone linked to the investigation. The training officer had said that emotion clouded the issue—that it dulled your senses and messed with your instincts—but Hunter didn't agree. He'd found that he only brought his A-game when he really cared about the outcome—when his need to help someone left him ready to walk through walls to get the job done. As far as he was concerned, emotional investment wasn't a mistake, it was essential. After all, wasn't it the very presence of emotion that separated man from beast?

And he certainly felt something for Angel. Spending time with her had awoken feelings within him that he'd never even known he had. She was a strong, resourceful woman who'd not just survived in a savage urban environment, she'd flourished. She'd earned the respect of her testosterone-fuelled companions, and she was street smart and tough. But she was also tender. She'd held her family together, and her love for her daughter was plain to see.

As he entered the kitchen and set about fixing himself some coffee, he revisited the doubts that had kept him awake long into the night. Getting involved with her was not a smart move. No matter how attractive she was, her lifestyle remained ugly. She ran with a street gang, which meant she was at least indirectly involved with all the drug dealing and casual violence that membership entailed, and right now her head was a mess. Her daughter was missing and her partner had just been gunned down in cold blood. So the right thing to do would be to back off. To be there as a friend, but to make sure he didn't cross the line. Trouble was, he wasn't sure he could do the right thing.

He poured the steaming black liquid into a mug, then heard movement behind him as he reached for the sugar. When he turned around, Angel was standing in the doorframe wearing a knee-length pink silk robe. Her hair was pulled back in a loose ponytail, although one strand had escaped to hang over the left side of her face.

'Hey,' she said, as she pulled up a seat at the breakfast bar.

'Morning. I was fixing a coffee—can I get you one?'

'Sure.'

'How are you feeling?'

'Like some vampire's spent the night clamped to my neck, sucking all the life out of me. I'm not sure how much more of this I can take.'

'Cream or sugar?'

'Straight up's fine.'

'I'm sorry about Lunatic,' he said, resting the mug in front of her.

'You were there when it happened?'

'Yes.'

'Was it…quick?'

'It couldn't have been any quicker. He didn't feel a thing.'

'I can't even think about that now. Not while Gracie's still missing.'

'I understand. But I do have a few questions, if you can face them?'

'Go ahead.'

'The other day, you said that the Ghosts and the Vipers had some kind of truce in place?'

'Yeah. It's been holding for a while now. They stick to their patch, we stick to ours. No drive-bys, no retaliations. It's all about the business. As long as we keep a lid on the violence, the cops pretty much leave us in peace.'

'And there's no way the truce has failed?'

'Not as far as I know.'

'So when Lunatic went inside that restaurant with all guns blazing, having painted your gang sign on the wall out front, he was working his own agenda?'

'I guess so. I've no idea what he was up to. The last thing he said was that Gracie was coming home. So where is she? Where's my daughter? What's he gone and done?'

'I don't know. Maybe he thought Gracie was being held inside the restaurant.'

'But I just can't believe that the Vipers are involved. And even if Larry thought they were, why did he go to Desperados alone? Why didn't he take some of our soldiers? None of this makes any sense. All I want is my little girl back.'

'Yeah, about that—I've got a lead,' he said. What with all the madness of yesterday afternoon, he hadn't had a chance to update her on his movements following Lunatic's death.

'What kind of lead?'

'I followed the man that killed Lunatic. He's a skinny black guy with a shaved dome, and he lives in Imperial Courts.'

Angel went quiet for a while as she thought things through. When she finally spoke, she lowered her gaze and stared at the table.

'If he's from the Courts then he's probably a Knight. They run half of Watts.'

'But what was he doing in East Los Angeles? And why did he kill Lunatic? My best guess is that he's a freelance hitter, shipped in by one of your rivals,' Hunter said, remembering the two men that had dished out some punishment to Lunatic's killer at Imperial Courts. Had they been brokers for the hit? He put that aside for future consideration and continued to theorise.

'Or maybe Lunatic made some deal with him that turned sour. I'm not sure. But his link to Gracie is a strong one. His car was seen hanging around the playground from which she was abducted.'

'So what are we doing here? Why aren't we beating Gracie's whereabouts out of him right now?'

'What if he doesn't know where she is? What if his involvement started and finished with the abduction, and now he's out of the loop? Trust me, from what I've seen, this guy is no leader.'

'But he's gotta know something—we've gotta talk to him,' she said, rising to her feet.

'Wait—I agree with you. This guy definitely knows something, but we're gonna have to be smart if we want to find out what it is. The best way to do that is for me to get close to him and gain his confidence, then if he turns out to be a link in the chain, I can work my way up to the next level. And you're going to have to stay out of sight.'

'Why?'

'Because Gracie was selected from among a bunch of other kids at that playground. I think she's being used as leverage. It's got something to do with the gangs. Before he died, Lunatic was adamant that she was still alive, and the only way he could have known that for sure was if the kidnappers had been in touch with him. So if the kidnappers took Gracie to get to Lunatic, then they know all about him, and chances are they know all about you. If they think you're getting too close, they'll just up sticks and disappear back under whatever rock they crawled out from under. We can't take that risk.'

'But I can't just sit here and do nothing.'

'It's for the best, at least for now. There's something big going on here—this isn't just some kidnapping racket. Gracie was taken for a reason, and until we know what that reason is, we're blundering around in the dark.'

'But how are you going to get close to the Knights? You can't just walk in and sign up. You're going to need one hell of a suntan to even get a foot in the door.'

'I've got a plan.'

'Wanna share?'

'No—the less you know about it the better. You've gotta trust me, Angel. I promised I'd get Gracie back, and that's just what I'm going to do.'

'Okay,' she said, as she sat back down. 'But whatever you're gonna do, do it quick, because every second my little girl's away from me is another one she's in danger.'

'I know,' he replied. 'But, remember, they took her for a reason, and until we know what that reason is she's likely to be okay.' When she reached out to hold his forearm, a burst of electricity leapt from her fingers and snaked its way to his core.

'I can't thank you enough for this. God knows how I'd be coping without you. I've got to go down to the morgue this afternoon to identify Larry's body. So long as it doesn't interfere with finding Gracie, can you come with me?'

'I'll do my best. I'm gonna head out soon to set some wheels in motion, and if I've got time, I'll swing by and pick you up later. But before all that, I could really use a shower.'

'No problem. It's up the stairs, last door on the right.'

'Thanks,' he said, rising to his feet. 'I'll be back in ten.'

He headed out of the kitchen and took the stairs two at a time, noting the framed pictures of Gracie that hung on the wall. One particularly arresting photo caused him to stop for a moment. It had been taken at the Santa Monica pier just in front of the Ferris wheel. Gracie was wearing a blue summer dress and holding some pink cotton candy, and a dazzling smile shone out from her angelic features. Hunter drank in the photo until it was imprinted on his memory. This was what was at stake. The life of a little girl. She'd been missing for four days now. She had to be petrified. He swore to himself there and then that he was going to find her, and find her soon. He was going to take Gracie back to the pier with Angel and see that smile for himself. He swallowed his doubts and resumed the climb.

Once he was in the bathroom, he pushed the door shut, stripped off his clothes and manoeuvred his six-foot frame into the shower. He set the dial to its strongest setting, then turned it on and stepped under the water, allowing the jets to pummel his aching shoulders and unlock the tension he'd been carrying around for the past few days. It felt good as the clouds of steam billowed around him. He nudged the temperature gauge higher, closed his eyes, and ducked his head under the spray. After a minute or so, he had the feeling he was being watched. He opened his eyes to find Angel standing on the other side of the glass, still wearing her pink silk robe.

'I brought you some fresh towels,' she said softly, gesturing to the pile that lay at her feet. He didn't say a word. When she opened the door, he stood motionless before her, his heart pumping against his ribcage like a jackhammer. She put one foot inside and then stopped, as if faced with a decision.

'Angel...' he began, planning to say that this shouldn't happen, that she'd been through too much in the last few days, that this just wasn't right, but no words came out. When she put her other foot inside and pulled the door shut, the time for talking was gone.

She placed the palm of her hand against his chest and pushed him gently backwards until the hot water burst over his shoulder and splattered against the front of her robe. Within seconds, the silk was soaked and clinging to her breasts, and Hunter felt himself begin to stiffen. He ran his hands through the back of her hair and eased her body towards his. As their lips met for the first time, the kiss was soft, almost chaste, and then her tongue was darting around the inside of his mouth like quicksilver.

She reached for his shoulders, then vaulted up to wrap her thighs around his waist, his hands instinctively sliding under the base of her robe to support her ass. For a split second she looked deep into his eyes, her mouth hanging slightly open, her tongue working the edge of her bottom lip, then she drew her body higher and lowered herself onto him. She worked herself feverishly while the steam rose around them, then she let loose a stilted cry as her body was racked with a series of convulsions. He let himself go and exploded inside her, his breath coming out in ragged gasps, his mind in turmoil.

'Angel,' he said, as they began to untwine themselves, 'I don't know if—'

'Don't say a word,' she interrupted. 'Not now.'

She stepped out of the shower, grabbed one of the white towels off the floor, and walked out of the bathroom, leaving Hunter confused and alone.

CHAPTER TWENTY-FOUR

THE Latino kid on the East LA street corner looked to be somewhere in his late teens. His slicked-back hair glistened with a thick sheen of oil, his feet shuffled on the sidewalk, his eyes jumped around, constantly on the lookout for his next customer. It was approaching midday, and Hunter had been watching him for over an hour from a nearby liquor store. He'd slipped the store's Korean owner a few bucks to put up with his presence, but as soon as the old man had realised he was staking out the neighbourhood drug dealer, he'd returned the cash with a handshake and a smile.

During that time, a succession of people had approached the Latino to make their morning purchases. Their ages had ranged from pre-schoolers to octogenarians and they'd come from all walks of life. From the white soccer mom in her SUV to the gang of Hispanic kids who should have been hitting the books in the nearby junior high. From the aging Oriental lady who'd shuffled up on her walker to the hollow-eyed down-and-out with no job to go to. But despite their differences, they all had one thing in common—they were drawn there by the small chunks of whitish rock that promised them temporary release from whatever insurmountable problems they thought they were facing. When it came to fucking up your life, crack cocaine was an equal opportunity drug.

The deals went down the same every time. The buyer would approach the kid on the corner and hand over a few rumpled notes. The kid would glance around to make sure there were no cops in the vicinity, then he'd shake his client's hand, palming the goods to them in the process. Once the client had moved on, the dealer would disappear behind a nearby dumpster to replenish his supply.

Street dealers never kept much product on their persons, as they needed to maintain deniability about the nature of their business when they were rousted by the cops. Getting caught in possession of just five grams of crack could result in a mandatory minimum sentence of five years' jail time, and this sentence could not be suspended, and neither could the convict be paroled or placed on probation. Why five grams? Because it was a common unit of sale on the street. Of course, if you were caught with powder cocaine, you could get away with possessing anything up to five *hundred* grams before mandatory minimum sentencing kicked in. The system punished the low-level street dealers while cutting the wholesalers a break. But at least it was consistent with the rest of the US Federal drug policy—that didn't make much sense either.

So for now the morning was a lesson in patience. At some point the dealer's stash would run dry and he'd have to re-up, but until that moment arrived, Hunter had a whole lot of thinking time on his hands, and thus far he'd spent most of it thinking about Angel. What had happened between them kept flashing through his mind. He could still smell her hair. He could still feel her fingernails digging into his shoulders. Their relationship had changed, but was it for the better or for the worse?

Angel hadn't been keen to discuss it, shutting herself in her bedroom straight after the event, so he'd taken the hint and made himself scarce, her feelings towards him still a mystery. Maybe he was making too much of it. She was going through a lot, what with the abduction of her daughter and the death of her husband, so maybe she'd needed to feel physically close to someone to blot out the pain. It was accepted psychiatric dogma that sex and death were closely related. An undertaker had once told him that he got numerous carnal offers from women who'd been recently widowed. He'd theorised that their desire to engage in the act of procreation was in direct response to losing a loved one, or, to put it in his own words, 'to give death the finger by fucking the first man available'. Maybe that's all Hunter had been to Angel—a defiant shake of the fist at death. Maybe she'd needed something and she'd taken it, and if that were the case, he had to accept it. His feelings didn't matter, not while her daughter was missing. Whatever happened from here on in, little Gracie remained top priority. Everything else would have to wait.

'He pretty busy, huh?' asked the Korean from behind

the counter. 'Same every day, stand on corner from morning to night, selling junk to kids, turning neighbourhood into war zone. Wasn't always that way, you know? Used to be okay, but now I keep shotgun under counter.'

'With no demand, he'd be outta business,' muttered Hunter, as a car full of frat boys pulled away, having secured their weekend entertainment. Although drugs were more visible in the poor parts of town, usage was just as prevalent in the wealthier enclaves, if not more so. Despite the media's attempts to suggest otherwise, there were more addicts amongst middle- and upper-class whites than any other segment of the population, and far more occasional users. Back when he'd been with the Department, it had been a standing joke that some parts of Beverly Hills were so awash with powder you needed a set of snowshoes to wade through them.

Having successfully concluded another deal, the Latino headed towards his dumpster, but instead of stopping there like he'd done on every previous occasion, he kept on walking down the street.

'Take care, old man,' said Hunter as he made for the exit. He followed on foot, about fifty yards back, on the opposite side of the street. The kid's stash had to be close by—with no visible means of transport it wouldn't make commercial sense for him to have to walk miles every time he had to re-up. Every minute he spent on the hoof was a minute wasted and, given that his superiors were likely to give him more than just a slap on the wrist if sales were down, his time was a precious commodity.

Tailing him was a piece of cake. He strutted along up ahead, never once turning to check his six, eager to make it back to his open-air drug emporium before his next client showed up. The street itself was lined with single-storey brick abodes that had low-income housing stamped all over them. The paintwork was faded and cracked, roof tiles were missing, and front yards were little more than sandy patches of dirt. And that was just the habitable ones. Other homes had been abandoned, their windows boarded up, their exterior walls streaked with soot, while a few were missing altogether, the vacant lots now home to an assortment of trash that included items as diverse as full-length sofas, double refrigerators and burnt-out autos among the countless bags of rotting refuse.

After walking for a block and a half through this urban wasteland, the dealer arrived at his destination— a crumbling eyesore that was separated from the street by a chain-link fence. A plastic lawn chair and empty flowerpot sat on the rickety front porch, along with a rusty barbecue. When the dealer let himself in, Hunter's suspicions were confirmed. He waited for thirty seconds or so, then climbed onto the porch to find that some of the floorboards were missing. Mounds of empty beer cans stared up at him through the yawning gaps in the woodwork. He drew his Beretta, slipped off the safety, and opened the door. Clanking sounds rang out from down the hall, and a fetid aroma of skunk and fried food hung heavy in the air. He headed towards the source of the noise and stepped into the room with gun levelled.

A wooden table stood in the centre of the space with an Adidas backpack on top of it. The dealer was on his knees with his head lodged inside a kitchen cabinet, while a growing pile of pots and pans was stacked nearby on the dirty linoleum. Hunter crept over and grabbed the kid by the arms, then jerked him upwards to slam his head against the interior of the cabinet, eliciting a yell of pain. When he slammed him upwards again, no more yells were forthcoming and the body went limp in his hands. He lowered the dealer to the floor and checked him out. The skin on the back of his head was unbroken, and his breathing was fine, if a little shallow. Hunter figured he'd be unconscious for a few minutes, which would give him plenty of time to get what he'd come for.

There were two large stewing pots left in the back of the cabinet. He pulled them out to find that one was empty while the other was home to a baggie full of red vials plus a large brown envelope. Inside the envelope was a little over twelve hundred dollars. He stuffed the cash and the baggie inside the backpack. There was no such thing as dirty money. There were dirty ways to make money, and dirty ways to spend it, but the money itself was blameless, and he was confident that he'd put it to more productive use than some small-time drug dealer.

The first part of his plan had gone off without a hitch. But the next part was likely to prove a whole lot harder.

CHAPTER TWENTY-FIVE

'So HOW did it go?' boomed Dreadnought's baritone down the line.

'Smooth, real smooth,' said Cassius, shifting from one foot to the other, wishing that he'd had a hit before making the call. He was standing in a Denny's parking lot on Wilmington, a block or so south of the 105, and his nerves were jangling like crazy. When a family of four spilled out of a nearby Chevy, he looked nervously over his shoulder, but they paid him no mind, heading instead for the gourmet fare on offer inside the restaurant's four walls.

'How about you talk me through it?'

'Sure thing,' Cassius began. 'Went just like you planned. Lunatic busted into the Viper nest with his Uzi set to full spray, offed Venom, then came back out and I capped him.'

'And that's what happened?'

'Word.'

'You sure?'

'I'm bein' straight with ya, cuz…'

'Like hell you are. The only thing I can't figure out

is if you're lying or just plain incompetent. Lunatic fucked up. He killed everyone inside that restaurant except for the one guy he was meant to: Venom—the boss of the Vipers.'

'Nah, that ain't right. I looked myself, there was blood all over and shit, ain't no way no muthafucka could survive it,' spluttered Cassius.

'Don't test me, son. If I say he survived, you can take it to the bank. I caught a report on the late-night news. Venom took two shots to the torso, both of which missed his vital organs, and he ended up stable in an East Los Angeles Emergency Room. This throws a real wrench into my plans, Cass. You've let me down again.'

'Shit, boss, I'm sorry, but that Viper is one lucky spic.'

'You know what this means? You went and killed Lunatic before he could finish the job.'

'But it don't matter, right? Coz things'll work out like you wanted anyhow?'

'Maybe, but I can't afford to take the chance. The Ghosts are weaker now that Lunatic's gone, but the Vipers are still a threat. We've got to cut the head off the snake, and for that we're going to need another assassin. Lucky for you I've got someone in mind.'

'But why the fuck we goin' after these spics anyhow?'

'We got no choice. We're doing something big here, Cass, it's all about protecting the 'hood. When I was on lockdown I had nothing but time on my hands, time to think, time to strategise. I know where things are headed, and if we don't act soon, our time will be up.'

'What you talking 'bout, Dread? You a high roller, makin' crazy money, ain't nuttin' gonna happen to you.'

'Just think about it, Cass. Think about when we were on our way up. Where's Dixie these days?'

'You know where Dixie at. He dead. Beat down with a baseball bat.'

'And how about Tin Man?'

'Tin Man dead too. Got shanked back in juvie.'

'And how about Gremlin? Or Porno? Or all the others? You want me to go on?'

'Nah, man, I get the picture. Lot of homies done checked out on us. But that's always been the way.'

'And it always will be, but things are about to get a whole lot worse. The whole future of the Knights is at stake. You still love the Knights, Cass?'

'Hell, yeah!'

'And you still love the 'hood?'

'Course, Dread, it's in my blood.'

'Then you've got to trust me, and you've got to make sure everything runs smooth from now on. We can't afford any more slip-ups. Anyway—back to the hit. At least tell me you got away clean?'

'Yeah, boss, no doubt. Ain't no one saw me kill Lunatic, I was ghost.'

'Well, that's something. Is there anything else? Have there been any more attacks on our dealers?'

'Shit,' mouthed Cassius to himself. He'd been hoping that this wouldn't come up. Especially not now, not after Dreadnought had just bawled him out for fucking up at Desperados.

'Yeah, there been one. Ziggy.'

'The reggae boy? Got himself a righteous set of dreads and an iPod full of Marley?'

'No doubt. But he don't be sportin' those dreads no more.'

'What happened?'

'Someone hacked 'em off, then strapped him to the hood of a car, fingers broke, face all cut up and shit.' His voice quivered as he delivered the news. When he'd first heard that Ziggy's dreads had been removed, the symbolism had not been lost on him. The way he saw it, Ziggy had been scalped, and the race most synonymous with scalpings were Indians. All of Cassius's recent problems could be traced back to a business meeting a few months back with a young redskin, and it looked like the shit was about to hit the fan. The recent run of violent attacks on his fellow gang members was all his fault. It was his greed that had brought this plague down on them, and his alone. If the boss ever found out that he was to blame, there would be hell to pay.

'How bad?' asked Dreadnought quietly.

'Weren't pretty. Had "NARC" cut into his forehead, so a local crew went to work on him, thinkin' he be some kind of rat—sellin' out brothers to the po-lice. By the time the cops cut him loose, he'd been busted up pretty good.'

'Did he see who attacked him?'

'Muthafucka took him down from behind. Only thing Ziggy saw was his hands…'

'Were they tanned? Like a Latino's?'

'Er…yeah…and Ziggy say the guy had a couple of wolves with him too.'

'Wolves? You're shitting me?'

'Nope. Ziggy got the bite marks to prove it.'

'How long's he going to be out of action?'

'A while—with those messed-up hands he ain't worth shit to us.'

'Goddamn it! I need my dealers out making money. Make sure the rest of them work double time to take up the slack.'

'Okay, boss, I'll pass the word. Say, it'd be good for morale if you could come down to the projects and talk to 'em yourself. We ain't seen you in the Courts since you got outta jail.'

'No can do. I've got to keep a low profile until this trouble with the Latinos blows over. If you want to improve morale, come up with a way to stop the attacks on our guys—make it your number-one priority to catch whoever's behind them.'

'Sure thing,' Cassius began, but the line was already dead. He stood there with the phone still clasped to his ear, his problems beginning to mount. Venom was still alive, Mason and Diaz wanted their cash and, worst of all, by inciting the wrath of the Indian nation, it looked like he was personally responsible for the attacks on Ziggy, Rocket and all the others. He was in way over his head and he could use some help, but right now he didn't have a friend in the world.

CHAPTER TWENTY-SIX

HUNTER watched on from the passenger seat of Lunatic's pimped-out red Caddie as the car picked up speed, heading east on Cesar E. Chavez Avenue. The road was named after the great civil rights activist who'd dedicated his life to improving the lot of America's migrant workers, and Hunter was pretty sure that if old Cesar were still alive today he'd be the first to admit that the work he'd begun way back in the middle of the last century was still a long way from finished. Angel was driving, her eyes staring straight ahead, her expression devoid of emotion. The silence hung heavy between them—she hadn't uttered a word since they'd left the LA County Coroner's department.

Having secured a primo supply of crack cocaine and a little walking-around money from the Latino drug dealer earlier that day, Hunter had made good on his promise to accompany Angel to the morgue. The coroner's office had been keen to get Lunatic tagged and shifted on down the production line as soon as possible, as space was at a premium. At the last count the morgue had over 400 unidentified cadavers on ice, most of them suspected illegal immigrants, and Hunter found himself wondering what Cesar E. Chavez would have made of that.

'Traffic's light,' he muttered, as Angel manoeuvred the car through an intersection. They were now streaking alongside Evergreen Cemetery, the city's oldest graveyard and the final resting place for over 300,000 people. Hunter felt a cold shiver pass through him. Passing by thousands of headstones on the way back from the morgue—death was all around.

When Angel ignored his throw-away remark about the traffic, he decided not to push it. Seeing your loved one stretched out on a slab was tough to take, particularly if the nature of their death was as violent as Lunatic's. As for himself, he was busy trying not to feel a little jealous over her reaction to the gang boss's passing. He glanced at her as she wrestled the stick shift up into fourth. Her side window was wound down and the wind tugged at her hair, blowing it back to reveal her face. As he drank in her features he wondered what would have happened had Angel gotten out of gang life back when he'd first given her the chance. Where would the two of them be now? Nowhere. The plain truth was that had Gracie not been kidnapped, they'd have gone on crossing paths once in a while, and their relationship would have remained purely platonic. Angel would never have invited him back into her life, and the realisation that he was glad to be sitting alongside her anyway brought a sharp pang of guilt.

'Stop staring,' she said, her eyes never deviating from the road.

'Sorry,' he muttered, just as a blue Econoline van

began to labour up alongside them. The guy in the passenger seat glared at Angel. When he raised his hand in the shape of a gun and dropped the hammer, Hunter burst into action. He snaked his left hand behind Angel's head while his right grabbed the top of the steering-wheel, just as the cargo door of the van rolled open to reveal three men levelling automatic weapons. Hunter wrenched the wheel and pulled Angel down. The roar of gunfire filled the air, and for a split second a hail of bullets exploded through the Caddie's side windows, and then they were out of the firing line and slewing into the path of the oncoming traffic. Angel screamed as she stamped on the brakes, sending the vehicle into a tailspin. The grille of a UPS van loomed large, and then Hunter was bracing himself for impact.

At the very last second the grille of the van swung away as the driver tried to avoid them. Hunter's arm tightened around Angel's shoulder as the nose of the Caddie ploughed into the side of the van. His muscles flexed as she lurched forward and his ribs burned as the seat belt dug into his sternum. The Caddie came to a stop in the middle of the road just as the Econoline van and its team of assassins screeched to a halt fifty yards up ahead.

'Angel? You okay?' he asked quickly, already working on the release catch for her seat belt.

'I think so…'

Her voice was a little groggy and her eyes were struggling to focus.

'C'mon, we gotta hurry—we're not out of the woods yet. Follow me—quick!'

He opened the door and slid out onto the tarmac, then

turned to find that her movements were sluggish, like a 45 playing at half-speed. He laced his hands under her arms and dragged her out of the car, then propped her against the side of the Caddie, leaving the vehicle positioned between them and their would-be death squad.

'Keep down,' he said, as he reached for his gun. 'This might get ugly.'

When he peeked over the hood he saw three men strutting towards him, their weapons cradled lazily in their arms, their over-confidence just asking to be punished. His first shot kicked up dust in front of the guy on the left, while his second missed the guy on the right by mere inches, ploughing instead into the fender of a Nissan Sentra that was parked by the kerb.

'Next time, I'm aiming for your heads!' he yelled, as the three men dived for cover.

He loosed off another couple of shots then ducked back down as one of them strafed the Caddie with a quick burst. Some people never learnt. He took careful aim and squeezed the trigger. The bullet drilled through the shooter's forearm to elicit a squeal of pain.

'Last chance, guys, or the gloves come off…'

'*Vato*—let's get outta here,' cried one of the gunmen. A few seconds later Hunter heard the sound of screeching tyres then he watched as the van roared past him, heading back up Cesar E. Chavez Avenue towards the heart of EastLos. He was halfway to his feet before Angel yanked him back down again.

'It's a trick!' she spluttered. 'They'll have left someone behind.'

He stretched out on the tarmac and looked around

the base of the front tyre to check for danger. At first, all was still, then a sole pair of feet emerged from behind a parked car and began to advance towards them.

'Son of a bitch,' he muttered. He worked his way back past Angel to the Caddie's rear, then swung out from behind the bumper in a half-crouch, levelled his gun, and eased down on the trigger. The first bullet took his adversary high in the shoulder, knocking him back a half step and spinning him forty five degrees to the right, while the second whistled just past the kid's right ear. At this point, the banger decided he'd had enough, and he turned tail and stumbled towards the nearest side street.

'All clear?' Angel asked.

'Thanks to you,' Hunter replied. 'How are you feeling?'

'Better—a lot better. I went kinda fuzzy there for a while…'

'That's good, because we've got to get out of here fast, unless you want to hang around and give the cops a statement?'

Angel shook her head in response.

'I thought not,' he continued. 'Let's see if the Caddie still runs. And given your wooziness, I think I'd better drive.'

He cracked open the driver side door and swept the glass from the seat, then climbed inside and tried the engine. It caught on the third attempt, coughing and spluttering to life like an old man awaking from an afternoon nap. Angel swung her ass into the passenger seat then grabbed his arm as he went to push the stick into first.

'You just saved my life,' she said, her eyes staring deep into his. 'I never even saw them coming.'

'I'm not surprised what with everything you've got on your mind. Anyhow, you returned the favour when you stopped me falling for that screeching tyre trick. Another couple of seconds and I'd have been a sitting duck. Who the hell were those guys?' he asked, although he'd already drawn his conclusions.

'Vipers—it looks like our truce is well and truly over. Thank you,' said Angel, then she leant over and kissed him gently on the mouth.

His heart began beating double time, and it was still in that state half an hour later when he pulled the Cadillac into her drive.

CHAPTER TWENTY-SEVEN

'C'MON, Mom, you gots to eat,' said Cassius, as he dug another spoonful of lukewarm soup from the bowl and raised it towards his mother's mouth. She was slumped at the kitchen table, her eyes glassy, her expression one of beatific detachment thanks to the heroin that coursed through her veins. Cassius had administered the dose five minutes earlier and since then he'd been trying to get her to accept a few mouthfuls of chicken broth. Experience had taught him that she was easiest to feed just after a fix, as the drug made her more compliant, but sometimes she slipped so far into a state of bliss that she forgot how to swallow, and today was one of those days.

Getting her to take on sustenance had been hard for a while, but just recently it had become almost impossible. Her frame was now so emaciated her skin seemed to hang off her bones, and a thin, yellow-tinged excretion oozed steadily from the open sores that were dotted along the length of her body. Cassius was no doctor, but deep down he knew that the end was in sight, and while that realisation brought him a feeling of sadness, the prospect of his mother's passing also brought him a sense of relief.

'It's your favourite, Mom, just have a little…' he coaxed, although in truth his comments were aimed more at filling the silence than eliciting any kind of response. Although he'd become immune to the tirades of abuse she spouted in the throes of her addiction, the periods of quiet brought on by the heroin were becoming increasingly unsettling. During these times his mother was little more than a corpse with a pulse, and a weak pulse at that. He eased her mouth open with his left hand and manoeuvred the soupspoon inside, then held her jaw shut and massaged her throat in an attempt to get her to swallow. When he released his hold, her jaw fell open and the majority of the soup dribbled down her chin.

'Fuck it!' he exclaimed, hurling the bowl at the far wall. Then his day took a turn for the worse.

'What's up, Cass? The old girl giving you some problems?' asked Mason from the kitchen doorway. 'Looks like feeding time at the fucking zoo in here.'

Cassius's heart sank. This was all he needed. An impromptu visit from the guys who had his nuts in a vice.

'Mason…hey…I'm workin' on getting your money, but things is tight, man, I ain't ready yet.'

'You're ready when I say you're ready,' said Mason, stepping into the room to allow Diaz to fill the doorframe behind him. 'Anyways, I got some good news for you—it's your lucky day. I've figured out a way you can make good on your debt, and it ain't gonna cost you a dime.'

'Fo' real?'

'Sure, "fo' real". All you gotta do is complete one little task for me then you're off the hook.'

'One little task?' asked Cassius, as a multitude of Class-A felonies flashed through his mind. 'I dunno man, I'm in deep enough shit already.'

'Damn straight you are, and that's why you're gonna help me out, 'less of course you want to explain how a gun covered in your fingerprints killed a junkie?'

Cassius thought back to the crack den where Diaz had taken his gat and used it to execute one of the patrons, then he shook his head slowly in defeat.

'Nah, man, I don't want that. So you're talkin' 'bout a one-time thing? Then I'm done?'

'That's right. Clear your debt, then we reinstate our old partnership—get back to making money like we used to.'

'What I gotta do?'

'See, Diaz, I told you Cass would be up for it.' Mason grinned, turning to his partner. 'You've gotta have a little more faith in our friend's entrepreneurial spirit. This kid'll do anything for a buck.'

Diaz cracked his knuckles in the doorframe, his face impassive behind a pair of designer shades.

'I'm in the market for a Winnebago,' said Mason, turning back to Cassius. 'And I want you to boost it for me.'

'That's all you need? No problem, I got car-jack crews all over the city. I can get you whatever the hell you want—year, model, colour—hell, you tell me what paper you want in the can, I'll make it happen.'

'Yeah, but here's the thing—I'm after a very specific

type of Winnebago. One that's gonna be rolling into town in a couple of nights. I give you the route, the time and the plates, then you go ahead and boost it for me. Once you got the vehicle in your possession, you take it to a prearranged location, then walk away.'

'What's so special 'bout this 'Bago?'

'None of your goddamn business. I want it, and that's all that should matter to you. But you gotta boost it clean and leave no witnesses behind, otherwise the deal's off.'

'Okay.' Cass nodded. 'Is the driver gonna be strapped? There gonna be any security?'

'That's your problem, Cass, but if I were you, I'd be ready for anything.'

'Hold up—you say you're gonna give me the 'Bago's route, yeah? So I gotta boost it in transit?'

'Damn straight. You mustn't let it reach its final destination. I'll let you know where I want you to hit it nearer the time.'

'But how the fuck am I gonna take down a moving 'Bago on my own? That's a two-man job, minimum. I'm gonna need me some help…'

'So find yourself a friend—hey, why don't you ask Moms along?' Mason grinned, pointing at the form slumped across the kitchen table. 'I'm sure she'd pitch in if you asked nice. We'll be in touch.'

Cassius watched as Mason and Diaz faded from view as quickly as they'd arrived. Once they'd gone, he pulled up a chair alongside his spaced-out mom and thought about the task he'd been set. Taking down a moving Winnebago wasn't going to be easy, and as the

'Bago in question had attracted Mason's attention, it had to be involved in some sort of illegal activity, which meant there'd be additional challenges above and beyond the primary ones of stopping, boarding and commandeering a large moving vehicle. He'd need help if he was going to pull this off, but calling on his usual crew was out of the question, as he couldn't risk word getting back to Dreadnought.

As his mom let loose a loud sigh, Cassius sank further into despair. Where in the hell was he going to find a partner at such short notice?

CHAPTER TWENTY-EIGHT

'WHERE do you keep your liquor?' asked Hunter, as
Angel collapsed into the welcoming arms of her sofa
with a sigh. They'd made the trip home without suffer-
ing any further attacks from the Vipers, although Hunter
had a feeling that the gang war was only just getting
started. Once he'd seen her safely inside, he'd stashed
Lunatic's bullet-ridden Caddie in the garage and
covered it with an old tarpaulin he'd found lying under
a workbench. The vehicle had been involved in a
gangland skirmish, and while he didn't expect the cops
to expend much energy looking for it, it didn't pay to
take chances.

'Over there…' she gestured '…in the cabinet.'

He walked over to the maple-wood cabinet in the
corner of the room, then rummaged around until he'd
found a bottle of Courvoisier. Having sloshed a generous measure of the amber liquid into a tumbler, he
walked back to Angel and offered it to her.

'Drink this,' he said, noting that her face was wan
and she'd begun to shiver despite the near tropical heat
that raged outside. Now that she was safe, the adren-

alin brought on by the gunfight would dissipate and there was a risk that she might start to suffer from post-traumatic stress. It didn't matter how many violent episodes you'd already been through—coming down from an adrenalin surge never got any easier.

'You look cold—I'll fetch you a blanket,' he said, pausing to replenish her glass. Having left her alone in the living area, he took the stairs two at a time to the upper floor, then ducked inside the first of the bedrooms where what he saw stopped him cold.

The room was a pink palace. The walls were pink, the small bed was covered in pink sheets and blankets, even the carpet was pink. Gracie's room. Large posters of Shakira and the Pussycat Dolls hung on one wall, and a collection of Bratz dolls lay on the floor by the side of the bed. The dolls had been arranged in a crescent, and Hunter could see how Gracie would have filled the space when she sat down to play. Everything in the room was evidence of a life interrupted. The small pile of clothes that lay draped over the back of a chair in the corner. The half-full glass of water on the nightstand. The magazines that lay open on the bed. Hunter drank it all in. A little girl had been plucked from the arms of her family and thrown into a nightmare that was not of her making. Right now, she had to be scared out of her wits. He turned around and eased the door shut behind him. The next room along was the master bedroom. He grabbed the large white comforter from the bed, then hurried back downstairs to the living area. Angel was right where he'd left her, and from the looks of the bottle of cognac, she'd helped herself to a couple more shots. He draped the comforter over her shoulders and pulled it tight.

'That better?' he asked.

'Sure,' she replied, although he noted that a mild tremor continued to afflict her. He grabbed another glass from the cabinet and helped himself to a drink, buying some time as he worked out how to broach the next subject.

'Lunatic's attack on Desperados seems to have stirred up a real hornet's nest...' he began, taking a seat alongside her on the sofa. 'I'm not sure you're safe here any more. Now that the Vipers are gunning for you, this place is an obvious target.'

'But I can't leave home, not now...' she said, her eyes widening in panic. 'Not while Gracie's still missing. Maybe those guys weren't Vipers? Maybe it was just a random hit? Maybe they thought I was someone else?'

'Come on, Angel, you know that's not true. They came for you one day after Lunatic staged his blood-drenched last stand at the restaurant—the two events are related.'

'I guess you're right,' she said, pulling the comforter tighter, 'but I just can't believe that on top of everything else we're now at war with the Vipers. I've known some of their crew since first grade.'

'So how about we get you somewhere safer to hole up? You're welcome to stay at my place...'

'No. I can't leave home. I've gotta be here for my daughter, I'm not gonna find her by going to ground.'

'But I can't just leave you here on your own.'

'How about you move in? Just for a while. That way I can work with you on the search for Gracie while you keep me safe. And this is Ghost territory—the Vipers aren't just gonna walk in here and get to me without a fight.'

Before Hunter could answer the telephone rang. Angel shrugged off her comforter and leant full length across him to retrieve the handset from the small table at the end of the sofa.

'*Ola?*' said Angel down the line. Within five seconds her face was masked with fury. 'Maricon! Give her back, you cocksucka!'

'Put it on speaker! Now!' commanded Hunter, his heart rate surging as he manoeuvred Angel into an upright position. This was the first direct contact from the kidnappers, or at least the first that he was aware of, and the next few minutes were going to be crucial.

'You in no position to be handing out orders, bitch,' whined a voice down the line. 'You better play nice otherwise I'll hang up on your ass.'

'Keep calm,' Hunter whispered into her ear. 'We need information, not a slanging match.'

She took a deep breath and nodded, although the fire that burned in her eyes remained undimmed.

'Don't hang up. How's my little girl? Is she okay? What have you done to her?'

'We gonna get to that in a while. But first I wanna talk about your old man. He fucked up his job, and I ain't got time for no fuck-ups. If he'd done like he was axed then you'd already have your girl back, but turns out the dumb spic couldn't shoot straight. So right now I got myself a problem. I need somethin' done and I ain't got no one to do it. That's where you come in.'

'What do you want?'

'Lunatic's job was to wipe out Venom, the boss of the Vipers. You gotta take on his responsibilities. Kill the head of the snake, things'll turn out just fine. And don't you go breathing a word of this to no one—otherwise the kid dies.'

Hunter had been right. Gracie had been targeted all along. But it wasn't about a ransom, or some drug deal gone bad—she'd been taken for her value as a bartering chip, as a way to force Lunatic into carrying out a hit on a gangland ally that would lead to a full-blown war. When the gang boss had attacked a Viper stronghold, he'd done it to save his daughter. Hunter's respect for him began to grow. Lunatic had kept everything from Angel both to comply with the kidnapper's demands and to protect her from the truth. He'd have known that attacking the Vipers was a suicide mission, so the choice he'd faced had been his life or his daughter's—a choice he hadn't wanted Angel to have to make. But who was it that wanted to stir up the criminal underbelly of East Los Angeles, and what did they have to gain? Hunter silenced Angel with a look, then leant in close until his mouth was pressed to her ear.

'Ask for proof of life,' he whispered. 'Tell him you're not going to do a goddamned thing until you're sure that Gracie's alive.'

'You gotta let me talk to my daughter,' began Angel. 'I gotta know she's okay.'

'I ain't gotta let you do shit. You forgettin' who's in charge. 'Less you carry out that hit, your kid's gonna be coming home real slow, one piece at a time. First I'm gonna cut off her toes. 'Less you wanna get them in tomorrow's mail, you better do as I say.'

Angel's mouth fell open in shock, but Hunter knew she had no choice but to tough it out. Back when he'd been a detective, the first thing you were taught in hostage negotiating 101 was to force the kidnapper to prove that their hostage was still alive. This had a dual benefit, one obvious, one not so. First, it gave you some confidence that the person you were trying to rescue was still drawing breath, and without that, all bets were off. And, second, it unbalanced the kidnapper, forcing them out of their comfort zone. As long as they remained in total control of the situation, they expected their demands to be met, which meant that they were far less amenable to any form of negotiation. As you chipped away at their control, you chipped away at their omnipotence, and the more unsettled they became the more likely they were to make a mistake.

'Be strong, Angel,' he whispered. 'Stick to your guns. Until you hear Gracie's voice, you're not going to agree to anything. You're not even going to whistle Dixie, much less kill a man.'

She took a deep breath and set her jaw before continuing.

'Touch one hair on my daughter's head and I'll kill you. Let me speak to her, now.'

'Your hearing fucked up, bitch? I say jump, you say how high…'

Hunter was starting to get worried. The kidnapper's refusal to put Gracie on the line might signal that she was already dead. They had to force the issue. He took the phone from Angel's hand and cut the call.

'What the hell are you doing?' she yelled, as she turned her fiery gaze in his direction. 'He was our only link to Gracie and you cut him off?'

'Trust me, he'll call back. He wants something. Hurting Gracie isn't part of the plan—at least, not yet. And we need to make him realise that he's entering a negotiation—he's not going to have everything his own way. From now on, it's all about give and take.'

'You better be right, Hunter, you better be god-damn right…'

The two of them sat in silence as they waited for the phone to spark back to life. Within thirty seconds it obliged, prompting Angel to gasp with relief.

'Remember, keep cool, and don't stop asking about Gracie until he agrees to let you talk to her. Be firm, but don't antagonise him, whatever he says.'

When she answered the call, the air was filled with a burst of expletives.

'You done?' she asked when the kidnapper finally paused for breath. 'It's quite simple—all you gotta do is let me speak to my daughter, then we can move on.'

'You're a fuckin' pain in the ass, lady, ya dig? All right. I'll get shorty on the line, then I'll tell you what you gotta do if you wanna see her again.'

Hunter felt a sense of hope surge through him. The kidnapper had backed down, which meant Gracie was still alive.

'Thank you,' said Angel. 'All that matters to me is my daughter. If you prove she's okay, I'll do whatever the hell you want.'

'I'll let you talk to her, but you gonna have to wait

a while, as shorty ain't here. Sit tight—you'll hear from us in the p.m.'

'I'm going nowhere,' said Angel, her shoulders sagging when the kidnapper cut the line. With shaking hands she plucked a pack of cigarettes and a matchbook from her shirt pocket and proceeded to spark up.

'You did great,' said Hunter. 'Played it perfect. Getting through the first contact is as hard as it gets. In a few hours' time you're gonna hear your daughter's voice, and then we can start working on getting her home.'

'Yeah,' replied Angel glumly. 'And all I gotta do to achieve that is to kill a gang boss who's gonna be surrounded by more security than the goddamn president.'

Hunter tried to keep his concern from showing. Angel had a point. There was a long way to go if Gracie was going to come out of this unscathed. But the good news was he had a plan.

CHAPTER TWENTY-NINE

STONE was wearing a pair of faded blue jeans and cowboy boots and he was stripped to the waist, his muscular torso glistening with a soft sheen of sweat. He looked around the top floor of the building that housed Fetishwear Inc. one last time to ensure that everything was as it should be. Caleb and Joshua were stretched out on the concrete floor over by his cot. They'd been fed and exercised a half-hour previous and they had a large bucket of water to see them through the next few hours. He'd watched on as the two animals had devoured their kibble at an alarming rate, his stomach growling softly to remind him that he hadn't eaten a thing all day.

When he opened the windows on the north and south walls he felt the cool night air brush against his chest to circulate freely around his living space. The makings of a small fire were positioned in the centre of the room, and stationed next to them was a disparate collection of items—a red plastic bucket, some sagebrush, some corn shuck, a packet of Bull Durham tobacco, plus a clear plastic bag that contained a number of small button-like objects.

It was his failure to find the one they called Dreadnought that had led him to this point. Despite his weeks of reconnaissance and intelligence gathering on the mean streets of South LA, despite the escalating cycle of violence he'd visited on the drug dealers, despite the wave of terror he'd sent surging through their ranks, the gang leader remained stubbornly out of his clutches. Stone had been forced to accept that his methods were flawed. He'd underestimated the gang's loyalty to their boss. He hadn't recognised the tribe-like nature of their extended family. Results had been disappointing and he was unsure how best to proceed. The path ahead was shrouded in mist, although the goal at its end was as clear as ever. What he needed was someone to guide him through these uncertain times. Someone to show him the way. And tonight was all about finding that guide.

He retrieved a cheap plastic lighter from his hip pocket then crossed the concrete floor and knelt down by the unlit fire. The kindling at the base caught at the first attempt and the dry branches of cedar wood were soon licked with yellow flames. Having gathered up an armful of sagebrush, he spread it out on the floor in a rough crescent shape, then retrieved the clear plastic bag that contained the button-like objects. The buttons were peyote, and they'd been sacred to his people for generations, both for religious and medicinal purposes. They were harvested from the top of a small, spineless, flowering cactus that grew wild throughout Texas and Mexico, and they contained a small amount of the natural hallucinogenic mescaline. Up until three months ago, Stone had never come into contact with the drug, but then everything had changed.

He'd been a drunk when his world had been turned upside down, and that was the first thing he'd moved to address. Alcoholism had been a curse on his people for generations, so when he'd needed to quit the habit, he'd sought advice from the local chapter of the Native American Church, knowing that they had some experience in the matter. The roadman he'd spoken to had suggested he attend a peyote ceremony, and it was here that he'd first publicly acknowledged both his failings as an Apache and his desire to change.

These ceremonies were one of the few places it was legally acceptable to partake of peyote, as they fell under the auspices of religious freedom for Native Americans. At almost all other times the drug was viewed as a Schedule I substance by the authorities, putting it on a par with heroin and cocaine, despite the fact that there was no record of illness or injury due to its use, and neither was it habit forming. Thus the law smiled on you if you were an Indian taking peyote for religious purposes, but for anyone else mere possession could result in a lengthy prison term.

Having made a sacred promise to change his ways at the ceremony, Stone had then ingested peyote every day for the next couple of months, and during that time his craving for whisky had slowly been eroded until it was little more than a nagging voice in the darkened recesses of his mind. And although men of science were unsure as to how the button of a small cactus could have such a strong effect on combating addiction, few disputed its beneficial properties.

But tonight was not about the alcoholic demons of his past, tonight was about his future. He reached inside the plastic bag and pulled out the largest of the dried buttons, which he then placed on the centre of the crescent of sagebrush. This was the father peyote. Using the corn shucks and the tobacco, he rolled himself a cigarette, then lit it from the fire. After taking four deep draughts into his lungs, he laid the butt to one side and picked up a few sprigs of sagebrush. He rubbed the leaves between his hands and along his arms, then beat them four times against his chest to purify his body. The time for enlightenment had come.

He took a handful of the hard, dried buttons from the bag, popped the first one into his mouth, and started to chew. His face wrinkled in disgust as the bitter and noxious taste exploded over his tongue, and he was racked with a bout of coughing before he was able to successfully swallow it down. The second button proved no easier to eat than the first, and this arduous process continued until he'd consumed around twenty or so of them, at which point he began to chant softly in his native Athabaskan as he turned his thoughts inward.

After an hour or so, the mescaline began to have an effect. His heart started to palpitate as fat beads of sweat popped on his brow, then a dull thudding sensation began to build in the middle of his forehead, as if a sadistic drummer was calling a tribe to war just above his eyes. When he shifted slightly on his haunches a wave of nausea rocked through him and his stomach flipped over. He made a grab for the bucket, his mouth falling open. The vomit exploded out to splatter against the sides, and although the act was far from pleasant, Stone managed a smile, as he knew that he was purging himself of his physical and psychological ills. He put the bucket down, wiped his arm across his face, then waited for it to happen all over again. This stage could last for up to three hours. It was little wonder that peyote had never become America's hallucinogen of choice.

After one hundred and fifty minutes' worth of stomach cramps, sweating, dizziness and vomiting, Stone found himself entering the second phase of his peyote-induced journey. Roiling geometric patterns began to appear in front of his eyes, honeycombs, cobwebs and spirals, the form constants that the roadman had said were indicative of a divine presence. As the kaleidoscopic display of vibrant colours danced before him, his heart and soul were lifted to the heavens, the reds, blues, greens and yellows so rich he could actually hear each of the colours sing out in joy, while at the same time the mere sound of the cedar-wood fire crackling by his feet became a visual treat for his eyes. For a split second, a sense of euphoria surged through his being, and then an inner peace fell over him as he felt himself connect with each and every part of Mother Earth. This was the true gift of peyote—the small buttons served as a divine messenger, a bridge that allowed man to converse directly with the Great Spirit, and in so doing man could touch His power and seek His counsel.

'Show me the way, oh Great Spirit,' he implored silently. 'Help me return to the one true path so that I might fulfil the sacred oath of blood law.'

He repeated this mantra countless times in his head, as he sat cross-legged by the fire with sweat running in rivulets down his bare chest. Hours passed and the geometric visions continued apace, and all the while Stone waited for his prayer to be answered. For a time there was nothing other than the joy he felt at his connection with all living things, and then a sound reached his ears, a sound that hadn't been heard on the North American continent for well over a hundred years, and he knew that he was about to witness something important. It was soft at first, like thunder heard from a great distance, and then it began to swell in volume, getting ever louder until his ears throbbed with a ceaseless pounding and fat tears of joy streamed down his face.

Just when he thought that both the noise and emotion would overwhelm him, the tip of a great herd of buffalo swept through the flames of the cedar-wood fire to envelop him on all sides. Their massive heads undulated as they charged by him, and the steam that billowed from their flared nostrils warmed his face, while the clouds of dust that were thrown up by the pounding of their hooves coated his nostrils. When he reached out to touch their flanks his hand plunged deep into their thick winter coats, and then he was suddenly rising above them, ten yards, then fifty, then a hundred, like an eagle soaring on the wing, watching in awe as the buffalo crossed the plain below. Viewed from on high, the herd was a great shadow on the land, an unstoppable force of nature that was hundreds of thousands strong, united in purpose, and Stone wept with joy once again as he felt each and every one of the buffalo's hearts beating inside his chest as if it were his own.

But as the minutes ticked by his elation turned to horror as the herd began to dwindle. Gradually the buffalo fell by the wayside, peeling away to lose their footing and disappear into oblivion, until just one of their number was left to rampage onwards alone. He was a mighty beast, seven feet tall, ten feet long, the king of the herd. On he thundered, his mighty hooves eating up the plain as he strove to overcome the loss of his brothers, but in the end even his indomitable will was found wanting, his pace slowing from charge, to walk, to stumble, until he finally pitched to one side and collapsed.

Stone swooped down from on high to come to rest beside the fallen beast. The buffalo's breathing came in ragged gasps, his mighty rib cage rising and falling ever more sporadically, each breath requiring a more momentous effort than the last. Thick plumes of steam issued from the tip of his snout, and when Stone reached out to stroke it, a great sadness welled up inside him. He lowered his head and looked deep into the buffalo's eyes, and as he did so he felt like he was looking deep into all of creation. The two of them stayed that way for a while, bound together by history and an unspoken love, then the beast gave one last mighty snort before his eyes misted over and turned dead as glass. When Stone ran his hand down the animal's flank, the carcass turned to dust, leaving him sitting cross-legged on a concrete floor in front of the dying embers of a cedar-wood fire, his task now to decipher all that he'd witnessed.

It wasn't until hours later, when the dull orange glow from outside signalled that dawn was almost upon him, that Stone finally understood the meaning of the vision. As he rose to his feet, a great wave of tiredness washed over him, but the fatigue was nothing compared to the growing elation he felt in his heart. The Great Spirit had shown him the way. When the time came to act, he'd be ready.

CHAPTER THIRTY

HUNTER pulled his Barracuda to the kerb and cut the engine. Up ahead, the El Camino with the flame decal had also come to a stop. Hunter had tailed Lunatic's killer all the way from his pad in Imperial Courts to their current location, leaving Angel at home to await the kidnapper's next phone call. With any luck, he'd make it back in time to be there when she heard her daughter's voice, but that was dependent on how things went over the next half-hour or so.

He watched as the skinny black guy climbed out of his vehicle and zigzagged through the traffic, headed for the old square on the far side of the road. A handful of winos and junkies criss-crossed the concrete expanse in gaits that ranged from shambling to near crawl, while a group of youths idled around two lawn chairs stationed in the centre, their cocky demeanours suggesting they owned this stretch of sorry real estate, which to all intents and purposes they probably did. It was to this group that Lunatic's killer made a beeline, where he was met with a series of bear hugs and high fives.

Unmoved by this public display of male bonding,

Hunter climbed out of the 'Cuda, shrugged off his shoulder holster, and removed his Beretta from its custom made pouch. He wedged the gun down the back of his jeans then crossed the street to find that the square was in a state of extreme disrepair. Half the concrete slabs were absent, leaving bare patches of sun-baked earth in their stead, while the rest were laced with myriad cracks. He set off towards the group of youths at a steady pace, his nerves on the rise with each passing step. Even if Angel managed to make like a hitman and carry out the kidnappers' demands, trusting them to subsequently release her daughter was little more than a crapshoot, and a bent crapshoot at that, which meant he needed to cosy up to the skinny black guy to find out what he knew. This might be his one shot to get close to the only person that he could directly link to Gracie's abduction. He couldn't afford to strike out now.

When he was within a hundred yards of the gang the rhythmic sound of rap music reached his ears. By the time he'd covered the remainder of the distance the thudding base line that emanated from the beatbox was so powerful he felt like his internal organs were about to explode. The gang of youths eyed him balefully and a few hands slipped out of sight in search of weapons.

'You wanna turn that down a touch?' yelled Hunter, gesticulating at the beatbox. Nobody moved. He shrugged his shoulders, raised his boot, and stomped on the offending electrical device to silence the music in a heartbeat.

'Muthaaafuckaaa!' gasped a small kid, drawing the word out so it became more of a collection of vowels than an insult. A swift nudge in the ribs from one of his older companions signalled that he should keep his thoughts to himself.

'There, that's better. Now we can talk,' continued Hunter as if nothing had happened. 'So who's in charge?'

When he was met with another set of stony glares, he decided to up the ante.

'You guys aren't big on conversation, huh? That's a shame. Conversation is the lifeblood of business. Without conversation, there's no negotiation. Here I stand with a one-time, get-rich-quick offer, but if you're not willing to discuss it, I guess I'll take my generosity elsewhere.'

Hunter let his words hang out in the ether as he eyeballed each of the group in turn, his gaze flitting over the hostile faces until they came to rest on the skinny black guy who'd shot Lunatic. A brief staring contest ensued for ten seconds or so, then the fish took the bait.

'What you be wantin' with us, officer? We ain't businessmen, we just hangin out, shootin' shit an' all,' the guy whined. Hunter felt a surge of excitement. Lunatic's killer sounded pretty goddamn similar to the kidnapper who'd rung Angel earlier.

'Officer? Guess again. You've got me mixed up with somebody else.'

'So you ain't five-oh?'

'Not unless you know any cops who can supply you with primo product at discount prices. What's your name, son?'

'Cassius.'

'As in Clay, mister, coz Cass can talk up a storm,' sparked up one of the little homies.

'Cassius, huh? Cool. Well, now that you've found your tongue, let's hope you remember how to use it.'

'So what sorta product we talking? And how you know to come to us?' asked Cassius.

'The word's out on you guys—you've got one of the tightest operations in South Central. There's only one product you retail and, as luck would have it, I've got a shipment of that self same product that I need to shift fast. Like all good salesmen, I've brought you a sample.'

Hunter reached inside his jacket and pulled out a handful of the crack vials he'd liberated from the Latino drug dealer's kitchen. Cassius took the proffered vials and began to examine the contents.

'Yo, Zombie—go fetch me a lab rat.'

Hunter watched as the young man called Zombie split off from the group and strolled over to a nearby bum that lay passed out under the midday sun, cradling an empty bottle of Thunderbird. Having hauled the bum upright, Zombie dragged him backwards across the concrete and propped him up in front of Cassius.

'Wa' gives?' spluttered the old soak as he came to, his pupils mere pinpricks of light in the centre of his eyes, his lips so black it looked like his diet consisted of nothing but charcoal.

'Smile, ole-timer, it's your lucky day,' began Cassius, as he magicked a crack pipe from somewhere about his person. 'You goin' on a trip. Hold him steady, Zee.'

Hunter's fists clenched as he watched Cassius shake two vials worth of rocks into the pipe while Zombie held the bum firmly in place. Forcing some poor old derelict to take Schedule I drugs wasn't part of his plan, but there wasn't much he could do about it. He offered up a silent prayer that the guy's heart would be up to the rush, then worked on holding his nerve.

'Sweet dreams, muthafucka,' muttered Cassius, as he sparked up a lighter and heated the crack pipe, before placing it directly under the bum's hairy nostrils. For the first few seconds the old man struggled against Zombie's grip, but as soon as the vapours hit home the fight went out of him in a hurry. A thin smile etched its way onto his features, then he slumped backwards with a happy sigh. Cassius watched on without comment for a few more seconds, then turned back to Hunter, seemingly satisfied.

'That's good shit. How much you got?'

'Enough.'

'Where's it at?'

'Stashed safe, deep in my bargain basement…'

'What you want for it?'

'You ready for this? It's a once-in-a-lifetime offer. Half the wholesale value.'

'Half of wholesale, huh? That's a sweet price. But why you be comin' round here with this deal of a lifetime?'

'Truth be told, I'm new in town. I had a buyer lined up, but he went and fell face first onto an eight-inch carving knife shortly after he was caught with his dick in the boss's wife.'

'So why ain't you dealin' with the boss direct?'

'Coz I know his wife too, if you catch my meaning.'

'You run up in the bitch as well?'

'You're a smart guy. So how about it? You ready to

sign on the dotted line?' Hunter's heart was in his mouth as he made the offer. Everything had gone well up to this point. The drugs had passed their impromptu road test with flying colours, Cassius's eyes had lit up with growing interest throughout proceedings, and his crew had chipped in with the occasional nod or grunt of approval. All that was left was for the economics of the street to exert their influence. Hunter was offering a whole load of something for practically nothing, and as long as the gangbanger's greed outweighed his reluctance to deal with a stranger, he ought to be home dry.

'Nah,' said Cassius, 'I'm gonna pass.'

Shit.

'You drive a hard bargain, son,' said Hunter with a shake of the head, as he tried to keep the disappointment off his face. 'How about I sweeten the deal? Call it a special rate for new retailers. I'll sell this first batch to you at a sixty per cent discount.'

'You could give it me free and it wouldn't make no odds. You gone and fucked up your timing. Too much shit goin' down right now, and the boss ain't gonna want nuthin' to do with some white boy supplier he don't know nuthin' about. Now get the fuck off my real estate and leave a niggah in peace.'

'There's nothing I can do to change your mind?'

'Niggah say it's time to get gone,' snarled Zombie, as the mood turned from laid-back to hostile in an instant.

Hunter raised his palms in a show of surrender and backed slowly away from the group, and with each passing step he felt himself getting that little bit further away from Angel's daughter. This had been his one chance to get close to Cassius and he'd blown it. What the hell was he going to do now?

Stone felt a surge of excitement as he watched the white man make his way across the square towards the gang-bangers. This was it. The moment he'd been waiting for. He was back on top of the roof of the abandoned department store that overlooked the square, four storeys high, carrying out some routine surveillance on the drug dealers below. Caleb and Joshua were also present, curled up in the shade offered by the entrance to the stairwell on his left, and although both animals were feigning sleep, they were ready to respond to their master's call in an instant.

Stone trained his digital camera on the white man and zoomed in. The newcomer covered the ground with long strides, not fast enough to make him look panicked, and not slow enough to make him look apprehensive. He stood out, a tall man, somewhere north of six feet, his build athletic, his shoulders broad. When he arrived at the centre of the square, Stone refocused the camera on his face, eager to soak up every little detail—light brown hair, closely cropped, a pair of neatly clipped sideburns, a granite jaw. As he began to converse with the gangbangers he straightened his frame, pushed his chest out, and used his hands to gesticulate in a firm but non-threatening way. Stone was impressed. Everything about him—his physical presence, the way he held himself, his mannerisms—suggested a man that was totally at ease with himself.

Everything was coming together. It was just as his

vision had foretold. Stone thought back to the great
herd of buffalo that had enveloped him as he'd sat by
the cedar-wood fire in the grips of the holy sacrament
peyote. He remembered how the herd had slowly
dwindled one by one until only the king of the beasts
remained, and how in the final reckoning even the great
king had died and crossed over to the spirit world. The
meaning of the vision had been clear.

In days gone by, the buffalo had roamed in mighty
numbers across the Great Plains, playing a key role in
the everyday life of the Apache. Stone's ancestors
would hunt them on foot, and once a proud beast was
felled, every part of its carcass was put to use—the
meat provided food, the hide provided clothing and
shelter, the bones were fashioned into tools, even the
dung was used for fuel. The hunters would kill only as
many buffalo as was necessary to support the tribe, and
nature was in balance, but once the white man arrived,
everything changed.

The buffalo hunters, with their long-range rifles and
US military backing, began slaughtering the animals in
sickening numbers during the second half of the nine-
teenth century, the wholesale massacre designed to
undermine the survival of the Indians. In 1800 around
sixty million buffalo roamed the continent. By 1890
there were just a few hundred animals left. The Indians
had no choice but to relocate to the reservations. Stone's
great-grandparents had suffered such a fate, and many
of his estranged family remained on reservation land in
Arizona to this day.

So the death of the buffalo was inextricably linked

to the coming of the white man. This is what his vision had shown him—that a white man would enter his life and that he would somehow be all-important in revealing the location of the gang boss, Dreadnought. Stone squinted through the camera lens as the white man in question continued his discussions with the drug dealers. There could be no doubt—it had to be him. The only other Caucasians who frequented the square were broken-down addicts desperately in search of their next fix, but this man stood proud before the gangbangers—his poise, his confidence, his familiarity with the underworld all marked him out as someone noteworthy. Someone special. But who was he?

Stone snapped off a few photos and contented himself with the thought that the newcomer's identity would soon be revealed. Now that he'd seen the man foretold in the vision, he had to move fast—grab him at the first opportunity, and ask him some questions. But what if his captive were to prove as reticent as the rest of the gangbangers when it came to providing answers? Stone clasped the scabbard that was cinched to his thigh and visualised the hunting knife it contained. This was one white man that wouldn't prove reticent for long.

As he cut a swathe back through the flotsam and jetsam of human life that inhabited the square, Hunter cursed his failure to build a relationship with Cassius. Going to him in such a direct fashion had always been a gamble as inner-city street gangs weren't exactly re-nowned for their hospitality, but the urgency of the situation had left him little choice and, besides, he'd come bearing gifts. The crack cocaine that he'd stolen from the Latino dealer should have been his ace in the hole. He'd figured that by offering to sell Cassius a shipment of drugs at a knock-down price he'd get his foot at least halfway in the door, and nine times out of ten his scheme would probably have worked, but on this occasion he'd come up short. One thing was for certain—if the likes of Cassius was turning down a licence to print money, then gang tensions had to be spiralling out of control.

Hunter climbed inside his Barracuda, fired the engine, and pulled out into traffic. Ten minutes later he pulled back to the kerb. The building alongside him had crumbling brick walls that were covered in graffiti. It had no windows except for the small pane of glass that was positioned at chest height in the door. Within that glass hung a hand-painted sign that simply read 'Open'. Other than that, there was nothing to mark out the joint as a place that served liquor to the unrefined. No drunks asleep on the sidewalk, no neon signs advertising inexpensive beer, hell, the place didn't even have a name, but to those in the know it screamed watering hole nevertheless. Hunter barrelled inside to find himself in something approaching near darkness. He waited a second to let his eyes adjust, then walked over to the bar, where a deadbeat sat staring at a dog-eared copy of *Hustler.*

'You in charge?' asked Hunter, eliciting a grunt in response. He pulled some bills from his wallet and threw them down on the counter. 'This is for the

damages. And for the next few minutes you can consider yourself hard of hearing.'

It didn't look like a request that the barman would find
hard to fulfil. His face was expressionless and his eyes
had the thousand-yard stare of a man who had spent too
much time on non-prescription medication, although
his lethargy didn't stop him from scooping up the cash.

'Where's the john?'

The barman flicked his head towards the rear corner,
prompting Hunter to head in that direction and slip inside
the rest room. It was small, windowless and tiled from
floor to ceiling in dirty white tiles that gave off an acrid
stench of ammonia. A couple of cracked urinals sat alongside the solitary stall to his left, and an old sink with a
busted faucet rounded out the fittings on the far side of
the room. Hunter took a position behind the door, where
he began to ready himself for what was to come. When
the door swung open five minutes later, he was in the zone.
He grabbed Cassius from behind and swung him towards
the urinals. The gangbanger was taken by complete
surprise, and he crashed into the tiled wall with a sickening thud. Hunter was on him in a flash, sweeping his legs
away with his right foot while driving his head downwards
till his face was pressed deep in the porcelain receptacle.

'Can I help you?' he asked, as Cassius squirmed
amongst the soggy fag ends and urinal cakes.

'What the fuck?'

'I saw you tailing me in my rear-view. You've got
three seconds to tell me what you want.'

'I just wanna discuss a little business is all,' Cassius
muttered through tightly pressed lips.

'Back at the square, you didn't want anything to do with me. What's changed?'

'Couldn't talk then—too many niggahs be listenin'…'

'So you tailed me to this fleapit joint to cut a side deal?'

'Uh-huh… Now let me the fuck up…'

Hunter paused as he considered this request. If Cassius was telling the truth, maybe they could still forge a working relationship, a relationship that might ultimately lead him to Gracie. But if Cassius was lying…

'Okay,' he began, 'but bear in mind you'll have a Beretta aimed straight at your chest when you turn round. I wouldn't want you to get all riled up about this little misunderstanding—it wouldn't be good for your health.'

Hunter backed away and drew his gun in one fluid motion. The gangbanger rose to his feet, rubbed at the back of his neck, spat a couple of shiny globules onto the floor, then turned around. His eyes were blazing with a mixture of rage and shame, but his hands remained in full view with palms facing outwards.

'Why you wanna play me like that? I just wanna make a little money.'

'Yeah, well, in my line of work, you can't be too careful. If someone starts making like my shadow, they're liable to wind up in a precarious position—face down in a urinal, for example.'

Hunter knew that there were two ways he could play the ensuing conversation. Come over all apologetic about the unhygienic facial he'd just dished out and hope to squirm his way back into the gangbanger's good books, or act as if he had no regrets. Instinctively, he knew that the latter option was the only way to go. The balance of power in their relationship had shifted. Cassius had taken a dive headfirst into a piss pot and he'd still come up talking business, plus he'd come to the bar without back-up, which told Hunter two things—first, the guy was desperate to make the deal happen and, second, he didn't want the rest of his gang to find out about it.

'Anyhow,' he continued, 'why don't we forget the past and start over? I've got some product I need to shift, and you've got an eye for a bargain. The deal's the same as before—fifty per cent discount on your usual wholesale price. How about it?'

'Thought the discount was sixty?'

'That was then and this is now. Think of me like the Dow Jones—price fluctuations happen all the time. But you're still getting one hell of a bargain—primo product for a song. It's the best damn deal you'll ever make— you've got more customers than you know what to do with and by the time you retail the shit you'll be a very wealthy man.'

'I'm in,' said Cassius, 'but I got one condition.'

'Name it.'

'First, you gotta help me boost a car.'

'You're shitting me?' replied Hunter, trying hard not to break into a grin. This was going way better than he could have hoped for—the gangbanger was asking him for help. 'What the hell do you need me for? You must have a whole team of guys ready to back you up. What about those brothers back at the square?'

'I gotta keep this on the down low. You help me out, then we'll do a little business.'

'If that's what it takes to make this happen, okay. All I want to do is shift this stuff fast then get out of town.'

'Suits me, bro,' responded Cassius, offering his hand. 'What's your name?'

Hunter grasped the proffered appendage and gave the smaller man's digits a slight squeeze to reinforce his dominance.

'Call me H. How do we stay in touch?'

'By cell—let's swap digits.'

The two men traded numbers then made for the exit.

'And just when exactly is this car heist going down?' asked Hunter.

'Tonight,' muttered Cassius, 'and it ain't exactly no car.'

CHAPTER THIRTY-ONE

HUNTER nodded his thanks as Angel handed him another Dos Equis, then drained the bottle in one long pull. After striking the deal with Cassius, he'd stopped off at a Kmart to pick up some toiletries and a change of clothes, then he'd headed straight back to Angel's pad as fast as the traffic had allowed. He was sitting on the sofa in the living room, and he'd just finished updating her on the events that had transpired back at the deadbeat bar. His reward for telling the tale was to see that her spirits had been noticeably buoyed.

'So you really think that this guy, Cassius, knows where my Gracie is?' she asked, her eyes wide with excitement.

'Maybe—he's definitely involved, so by getting close to him, I'm getting closer to Gracie. Now I just need to find out what he knows. I'm meeting up with him later tonight, I'll get to work on him then.'

'Why can't we just beat whatever he knows out of him? We've gotta get Gracie back quick, we can't afford to waste no more time.'

'I've thought about it, but it's too high risk. Like I said before, what if Cassius is just a link in the chain and he doesn't actually know where Gracie's being kept? Under that scenario, the only thing we'd accomplish by interrogating him would be to blow our cover. Our best bet is to play it cool for a little while. Just give me one more day—if I haven't learned anything by this time tomorrow, we'll tear this guy a new one.'

'If you're sure.' She nodded, although he could tell that she wasn't convinced.

'Anyhow, how about you? Any problems while I was gone?'

'Just gang stuff,' she said, looking away.

'What happened?'

'There were a couple of attacks on my crew. A young kid got beat down on his way home late last night and ended up in the ER, then three others had to dive for cover early this morning when a passing Nissan pumped lead in their direction. My lieutenants are pushing for full-scale retaliation, but I've convinced them that we need to keep a low profile, at least for now. With Larry gone, they're looking to me for leadership, but if I keep telling them to turn the other cheek, they won't be looking for long.'

'You've got to keep them on a tight leash. Tell them to hold their fire. The last thing we need right now is to get sucked into a full-on war.'

'It doesn't work that way, Hunter. Once someone comes after you, you gotta fight back, otherwise you look weak, and then you're a target for everyone.'

He tried not to let his frustration show. The machismo of street-gang politics meant that backing down from confrontation was not an option. Gangs had been killing each other over land they didn't even own for decades, and historic beefs were used as an excuse to start new ones every day. And he was troubled at the ease with which Angel had assumed the role of gang leader. The fact that a bunch of hardened bangers was ready to take orders from her showed just how intelligent, strong willed and powerful she was—all traits he found attractive in a woman. It was just a shame she couldn't put those skills to more constructive use. At that moment, the telephone rang.

'Gracie!' Angel squealed, here eyes boring into Hunter's for a second before she grabbed for receiver.

'Hello?' she asked tentatively, as she placed the call on speaker.

'I got shorty here, just like you wanted. You got thirty seconds.'

This time, the voice on the line was deeper than before, more sonorous, more commanding—Cassius wasn't working alone. Hunter felt Angel tense alongside him as she waited for the silence to be broken.

'Mommy?'

Angel's joyous reaction left Hunter in no doubt that she was talking to her daughter.

'Gracie! Gracie, it's Mommy! Are you okay?'

'Hi, Mommy, I'm okay. When are you coming to get me?'

'Soon, baby girl, soon. Mommy's gonna get there as soon as she can, but till then you gotta be strong.'

'Is Papa coming too?'

Angel's jaw fell open but no words came out, then she recovered her composure and continued.

'Of course he's coming, Gracie, he can't wait to see his little princess again.'

'I just wanna come home,' Gracie whispered.

'I know, honey, I know.' The tears ran freely down Angel's cheeks. 'You'll be home before you know it, baby girl, I promise.'

'Bye, Mommy…'

'Bye, Gracie, I love you…'

'That's it, you're done,' said the kidnapper, his guttural tones at stark odds with the little girl's voice that had gone before. 'Now that you've heard your daughter's voice, you've got to do as I say. Venom must die.'

'Whatever you want…just don't hurt my baby.'

'That's more like it. We'll call back soon with a location. Till then, you make like a midget and keep your head down.'

'Let me give you my cell, just in case I'm not here,' Angel said, reeling off the digits.

'Okay. And one last thing—don't tell anyone about this, otherwise I'll slit your daughter's throat and dump her body where it will never be found.'

'I got it,' muttered Angel, as the line went dead. Hunter gathered her in his arms and held her tight.

'She's alive…she's still alive,' she sobbed.

'It's gonna be okay,' he soothed, as her body shook softly against his.

CHAPTER THIRTY-TWO

'DO NOT worry, my dear. The worst is behind us. It will all be over soon.'

Ernesto threw a glance at his wife, Rosa, who sat alongside him in the passenger seat of the old Winnebago, her hands clasped tight in her lap. Her forehead was furrowed with deep wrinkles and she kept pursing her lips as if she wanted to say something, although she hadn't uttered a single word since they'd made it to the outskirts of Los Angeles. He knew that she'd been against his idea from the start, but in the end he'd managed to talk her round. After all, what choice did they have?

It had been almost midnight when they'd set out from their rundown home in Tijuana. After making the nerve-racking pass through customs at the US-Mexico border, the San Diego Freeway had been blessedly free of traffic. In a few hours it would be jammed bumper to bumper, but Ernesto wasn't all that concerned about the driving conditions he'd face on the return trip, as before he could even contemplate going home, he had some important business to attend to.

He took one hand off the wheel to smooth down his

greying hair, then checked his watch to find that it had just gone four a.m. In his seventy-five years on the planet he'd never come close to being involved in anything illegal, but tonight he was going to lose his cherry. In fact, he'd already lost it—first when he'd climbed into the Winnebago, then again when he'd crossed the border, so it was no use getting cold feet now. And while being branded a criminal was antithesis to all that he stood for, the thought of standing idly by and watching as his only daughter was turfed out onto the streets was far, far worse.

'How about a little air?' he asked, as he cracked open the window.

'I just want this night to end,' muttered Rosa, opening her hands to reveal the silver cross in her palms. 'Please protect us, Jesus,' she implored. 'And help us to help our poor Marisol.'

Ernesto mouthed a silent prayer to himself. He wasn't sure if the Good Lord was in the habit of helping people engaged in nefarious activities, but it couldn't hurt to ask. At least they were acting for all the right reasons. They needed the money, and they needed it fast, and when you were a dirt-poor Mexican, there was only one group of people to whom you could turn for help. The local bandidos. It had all started when that no-good rat of a husband had walked out on their only daughter, Marisol, a month ago, leaving her with three young kids, a collection of final demands from the utility companies, and the threat of imminent foreclosure on the house from the bank. Ernesto had known that if he wanted to save his daughter from a life of poverty, he had to act fast, so he'd made contact with one of the surly young men who sat around drinking beer all day outside the local bar and told him he was available for hire. Now, in some countries the employment market for unskilled seventy-five-year-olds wouldn't be all that expansive, but fortunately for Ernesto, Mexico wasn't some countries. The young man had contacted him inside the hour, saying that he had an urgent job that Ernesto was perfect for, with just one proviso—he had to bring his wife along too.

Convincing Rosa to join him on the trip hadn't been easy, but she'd finally acquiesced once she'd realised that this was the only way they were going to earn enough money to bail out their daughter. So here they were, motoring through the back streets of LA at four o'clock in the morning, getting ever closer to their destination where that all important cash payment awaited. For the last half-hour Ernesto had been picturing the dollar bills that would soon be his, picturing the rumpled tens, twenties and fifties that would land in his palm, and picturing the look on his daughter's face when he handed them over. He was still busy imagining her expression morphing from one of surprise to relief when a white van pulled out right in front of him.

'Pendejo!' he cursed, as he stamped his foot down on the brakes. 'We're the only vehicle on the road and he cuts me up?' His hand went instinctively to the horn, but one word from Rosa gave him pause.

'Wait!' she said. 'We mustn't draw attention to ourselves—not tonight.'

She was right, of course. Ernesto put both hands

back on the wheel and pulled off again, following in the wake of the van that was now rumbling on ahead of them. When the stoplights turned red at the next cross street, Ernesto brought the RV to a halt a couple of yards shy of the van's rear bumper, and constrained himself to thinking dark thoughts about the driver up front. When the stoplight turned green, the van remained stationary with its engine idling.

'What in God's name is he doing now?'

Ernesto waited a few seconds then went to shift the Winnebago into reverse, but before he could complete the manoeuvre a second van loomed large in his rear-view and slammed into him from behind, sandwiching the RV against the white van in front.

Ernesto and Rosa were thrown forward in their seats like a pair of rag dolls, the old man's head banging against the steering-wheel, his wife's silver cross flying out of her hands. When they came to rest, the two of them exchanged frightened glances as they awaited their fate, both now wishing they'd come up with some other way to raise funds for their daughter.

The old cargo van was a bit of a clunker. Cassius had 'borrowed' it from a removals firm whose back lot was not as secure as it could be. He eased off the gas, trying to juggle the twin needs of keeping enough distance between himself and the target to ensure he didn't spook them, while also staying in close enough proximity to make sure he didn't lose them. Thus far, Mason had been right on the money. The Winnebago had come off exit ramp forty-six of the San Diego Freeway in the early hours of the morning, then it had rumbled along Century for a while before turning north onto La Brea to head deep into the heart of Inglewood. Cassius had been behind it ever since it had left the 405. He hadn't even bothered to check the plates against the details Mason had provided, such was his confidence that this RV was the one he'd been waiting half the night for.

Not that the hours he'd spent sitting by the roadside had been a total bust. With time to kill and his nervous energy slipping into overdrive, he'd found the beguiling call of Lady Cocaine too hard to resist, and he'd been riding high on the crest of a drug-induced wave ever since. Now, if he could only 'jack the RV like Mason wanted, maybe he'd finally get out from under. But the old Winnebago didn't look like the sort of vehicle that would buy him his freedom, which meant only one thing—if the vehicle wasn't worth shit, its contents most definitely were. Guns, stolen goods, drugs—its cargo was definitely valuable. Ever since he'd tumbled to that conclusion, Cassius had been toying with another idea—maybe he could take a little piece for himself. Not so much that Mason would notice, but just enough to get a taste. After all, he'd earned it, hadn't he? Plus he was on a lucky streak anyhow, what with the cut-price drug deal he was about to engage in.

His thoughts turned back to the newcomer who was desperate to offload his stash. Cassius knew that bringing in an outsider was a risk, but what choice did he have? Taking down a Winnebago was a two-man job, especially if that Winnebago turned out to be full of armed men. And the fact that H *was* an outsider was one of his major selling points, as there was no way that Cassius could call on any of his own crew for help. Mason and Diaz had his balls in a vice, and his only hope of survival depended on keeping his relationship with the two of them secret from the rest of the Knights. Plus H had a number of other attractive features—he was in the life, he was unknown on the scene, and he had problems of his own, problems that meant he was ready to jump through hoops to push through a fast drug deal before skipping town. All in all, H's arrival was well timed to say the least. Cassius picked up his cell-phone and hit speed dial, then waited for the call to be answered.

'Yep,' said a terse voice.

'Hey, H, they almost there. You gonna see 'em in the next coupla minutes.'

'Okay.'

The line went dead. So much for the art of conversation. As the Winnebago rumbled onwards towards the designated kill zone, Cassius hoped his newfound partner would prove more comfortable with action than he was with words.

Hunter craned his neck forward to look out of the intersection, his nervous energy on the rise. It wasn't every day he agreed to help out on a heist, but at least he could console himself with the thought that whoever he was about to 'jack was engaged in some form of illegal activity themselves. How many people rolled into LA in an old Winnebago to make a bona fide delivery at this hour of the morning?

And who were these people exactly? He had no idea what he was up against. For all he knew the RV could be jam-packed with gangbangers toting full autos, plus there was the added complication that his partner in crime struck him as a loose cannon. What if Cassius went in all guns blazing? A firefight would draw attention, even at this ungodly hour, and it could result in loss of life. Short of getting plugged himself, the last thing Hunter needed was for Cassius to walk into a stray bullet. As things stood, he was the only firm link to Gracie, and if he ended up dead in the gutter then all Hunter's efforts would count for nothing. The element of surprise was all-important. The heist had to go down hard and fast, whoever was driving the Winnebago had to be subdued and secured in a hurry, and Cassius had to be kept out of harm's way. As to-do lists went, it wasn't the most straightforward.

The ribbon of tarmac was devoid of traffic and bathed in a series of crescent-shaped glows that arced out from the streetlamps. When a pair of headlights appeared in the distance, Hunter started the van's engine and shifted the stick into first. He waited until the RV was almost on him then he swung out of the side street right in front of it, forcing the driver to stamp on his brakes. When no loud rasps on the horn followed the manoeuvre, he wasn't sure if this was a good sign or bad. The driver was either too timid to show his anger or too disciplined. Hunter fervently hoped it wasn't the latter.

The stoplights he'd selected earlier were just up ahead. He cut his speed to a near crawl as he waited for them to turn red, then came to a halt and watched the Winnebago pull up behind him. Now it was up to Cassius to spring the trap. But where the hell was he? When a second pair of headlights appeared in the distance, he let loose a sigh of relief, but it quickly dawned on him that Cassius might have left it too late. If the gangbanger didn't move fast then the driver of the RV would simply pull around him and drive off into the night.

The stoplights turned green overhead, but he stayed right where he was, imploring his partner to put the pedal to the metal. Cassius duly obliged, but in his eagerness to make up for his late arrival he came in too fast, slamming into the rear of the Winnebago with a sickening screech of metal on metal that tore through the night sky. Hunter braced himself just before impact, and was ready for the three-vehicle pile-up when it ensued. He was jolted forward in his seat, then he was on the move, reaching for his Beretta, and headed straight for the front of the Winnebago.

When he got a look at the RV's occupants he was struck with a momentary burst of confusion. The driver was a white-haired Hispanic guy who had to be seventy if he was a day. His hands were still locked on the wheel, and a thin trickle of blood ran down his nose from a nick in the centre of his forehead. Alongside him sat an equally ancient woman whose face had more wrinkles than a dried-up prune. Both of them looked scared half to death. If this was Cassius's target, it was one hell of a strange one.

'Cut the engine and get out of the RV! Now!' commanded Hunter, eager to get things under control before his partner arrived. The two old folks clambered out slowly, their hands empty and in full view, their senses seemingly addled by the crash.

'Where are you from?'

'Tijuana, *señor*…p-please don't shoot…' stuttered the old man.

Tijuana City, down Mexico way, and that made a whole lot of sense. While they might look like an old mom and pop combo on a road trip, there was a high probability they were drug mules, hired by the cartels to ferry dope over the border to the US. For this trip alone they'd probably clear more than they'd made in their entire working lives. It was the free market economy gone wild.

'We're only trying to help our daughter, please don't hurt us…'

The old man was trembling and his wife looked like she was going into shock. Before Hunter could reply Cassius appeared on the far side of the Winnebago.

'I-am-the-goddamned man!' he motor-mouthed, stringing the words together so that they sounded like a collection of vowels with the odd consonant shoved in for good measure. 'Everything-cool-up-here? You-got-these-ole-timers-wrapped-up-tight? Let's-hurry-it-up. We-gotta-move-fast.'

Hunter took a close look at him. His eyes were darting back and forth with pupils that were wide and bloodshot, a vein throbbed in the side of his scrawny neck, and he shuffled his weight from one foot to the other as he awaited an answer. Cassius was on something, and while that made him a liability under the current circumstances, Hunter had a feeling that his partner's predilection for substance abuse might prove useful somewhere down the line.

'Everything's fine here,' he soothed. 'Why don't you back up your van so you've got space to get the RV out?'

'Sure thing, H, but first I gotta off those old folks. Can't be leavin' no witnesses behind.'

'Don't worry, I've got it,' said Hunter, levelling his Beretta. 'Go move that van—we're on the clock, re-member?'

'Righteous.' Cassius spun on his heel and hurried back the way he'd come.

'You two, down that alley—quick!' said Hunter, ges-ticulating at the Mexicans with his gun.

'*Señor*…please…we won't tell no one…I promise…'

'Hurry up!' barked Hunter.

The old man offered an arm to his wife and the two of them shuffled into the alley as directed, whimpering softly in their native tongue as the tears flowed freely down their cheeks.

Hunter waited for Cassius to finish moving the van, then he took careful aim at the shadows and loosed off two shots. The twin booms of the weapon reverberated around the street for a moment, then all was quiet once more.

'They done?' asked Cassius, when he returned.

'Yeah,' said Hunter, his jaw set firm. 'They're done. Let's roll.'

'Nah, man, you off the clock now, I don't be needin' your help no more. Here on in, it's a one-man show.'

'You sure?'

'Sure as shit,' said Cassius, with one hand on the door to the Winnebago. 'You get gone, I be in touch about our unfinished business.'

'You've got my number,' Hunter said, his mind racing. Why had Cassius hijacked the RV, and where was he about to take it?

When Ernesto found himself looking straight down the barrel of the tall Americano's gun, his bladder let go and a large stain blossomed on the front of his slacks. He gripped his wife's hand tighter and sent up a prayer asking that the Good Lord watch over his daughter and three grandchildren, then he summoned up the courage to look his executioner in the eye and waited for it all to be over.

The gun barked twice and the old couple flinched as one. Ernesto felt Rosa's body sag against his as her legs gave out, then the two of them slumped to the ground. His whole body was gripped with a sudden icy cold, and as he lay back a blinding bright light appeared before his eyes. His final thought was, So this is what death feels like…

Except it wasn't his final thought. As he lay there waiting for the eternal sleep to take him, thirty seconds passed, then a minute, then another, and he realised that he wasn't going anywhere, at least for now. He ran an exploratory hand down his torso, looking for a wound, and when none was forthcoming, he cracked open one eye. The blinding bright light that moments earlier had convinced him his time was up was shining down on him from a streetlamp overhead. He opened his other eye and sat up, then quickly looked at his wife. She lay alongside him in a twisted position, her eyes clamped shut, a peaceful expression on her face.

'Rosa?' he whispered tentatively, as he reached out to touch her. His heart soared when he felt the pulse in her neck, the steady arterial throb confirming that she too was somehow alive. He gently slapped her cheeks, then watched as her eyes creaked open.

'Where am I?' she asked weakly, but he was too overcome with relief to answer, so instead he hugged her to his chest and thanked the Lord that they were still together.

'Keep quiet, my dear,' he whispered.

'The RV...hijacked...we won't get paid... What will happen to our poor Marisol?'

'I don't know...'

Ernesto climbed to his feet and helped up his wife, but before they could complete their escape, the sound of an engine spluttering to life stopped them cold. As they watched on, the Winnebago, the very vehicle that they'd nursed all the way from a grimy back street in Tijuana to a matching one in Los Angeles, passed by the head of the alley, then just when they thought the night couldn't get any stranger, they got their first look at the rear of the RV. A man was clamped to the ladder that led to the vehicle's roof, his arms and legs locked around the steel rungs, and he was staring straight at them. With a start, Ernesto realised that it was their would-be assassin, the Americano.

'That's one hell of a way to hitch a ride,' Ernesto muttered, as Rosa crossed herself alongside him.

CHAPTER THIRTY-THREE

HUNTER clung on as the Winnebago took the bend at speed, his arms and legs wrapped tight around the steel rungs of the ladder that led to the vehicle's roof. He was confident his role in the hijacking would be enough to cement his budding relationship with Cassius, but now he was after more. When the gangbanger had come to him for help, he'd inadvertently revealed that he was operating outside the auspices of the rest of his crew, and this was a situation that Hunter could turn to his advantage. By hitching a ride on the Winnebago, he hoped to learn something he could use as leverage against Cassius further down the line, something that would help him find Gracie, but the ride was turning out to be a little more uncomfortable than expected. He'd considered following the gangbanger in one of the hijack vans, but with the roads mostly deserted, the chances of being seen were too high, so he'd left them by the roadside, keys in the ignitions, confident that they'd both be gone by sun-up.

Cassius was running late, probably as a result of his decision to pull over a mile or so back and spend ten minutes ransacking the RV. As a stream of muffled curses had rebounded around the vehicle's interior, Hunter had taken the opportunity to work some of the lactic acid out of his aching muscles, but the respite had proved short-lived, and the gangbanger was now doing his best to make up for lost time.

Hunter gritted his teeth and clung on for dear life as the Winnebago exited the corner on three wheels and accelerated down the next street. He had no idea if Cassius had found what he was looking for and right now he didn't much care. He'd lost his bearings a while back, but the buildings that flashed by him on either side were industrial rather than residential—row on row of metal sheds and auto shops that looked like they catered to the lower end of the market. Wherever they were headed had better be close, as pretty soon the sun would begin to rise and the odds of him not attracting any attention, stuck as he was like a limpet to the back of a speeding Winnebago, weren't exactly in his favour.

When Cassius finally nudged the front of the vehicle towards a battered warehouse, Hunter relinquished his grip on the ladder and slipped quietly to the ground, to duck behind a stack of old oildrums. The double doors of the warehouse slid open, bathing the forecourt in a pool of light, then the Winnebago disappeared inside. Hunter made a break for the nearest corner of the building then edged along the frontage towards the entrance. Once there, he peeked inside to find that the interior was home to row on row of large packing crates stacked to the heavens on metal towers, save for a rectangular space that extended forty yards out from the sliding doors. The RV was parked in the centre of that space, and two men stood eyeballing it from close range, their attention directed straight at the driver, both of them instantly familiar.

One was a tall, dark Latino, wearing a designer suit and mirrored shades and cradling a gleaming Desert Eagle as if it were his firstborn, while the other was a short, dishevelled guy with ferrety features, whose sartorial elegance stretched no further than a pair of tattered jeans and a loud Hawaiian shirt. A white Ziploc body bag lay at their feet. They were the same two men that Hunter had seen ragging on Cassius outside his pad in Imperial Courts. How the hell did they fit into all of this?

The door of the Winnebago opened with a dull click and Cassius stepped out, his hands held high. When all three men disappeared around the front of the vehicle, Hunter slipped inside the warehouse and ducked down the nearest row of crates. Snippets of conversation reached his ears, so he drew his Beretta, thumbed off the safety, and made his way deeper into the building, walking through the thin shafts of light that bled through the narrow gaps between each metal tower until the three men had come into view.

'I got it, Mason, just like you wanted, so now we cool, huh?' asked Cassius, his tone pleading, his eyes flitting nervously between the two men and the body bag.

'You did good, Cass, you did good,' said the guy in the Hawaiian shirt, marking himself as Mason. 'But your work ain't done yet. We gotta check out the merchandise before we can clear your debt. Diaz—how about you give the kid a little direction?'

With that, the well-dressed Latino retrieved a heavy-duty sledgehammer from the body bag then headed past Cassius towards the side of the Winnebago.

'Go on, son, you go along with Diaz—he's got a job for you.' Mason smirked.

Hunter slunk further into the shadows as the three men walked in his direction. When they were midway along the RV's length, Diaz handed the sledgehammer to Cassius, opened one of the exterior hatches that ran along the base of the vehicle, and pointed at the tank contained within.

'You want me to smash it?'

Diaz nodded then backed away until he was along-side his partner. Cassius hefted the sledgehammer, his spindly arms poking out of his oversized shirt, then he swung it at the tank. It gave a dull thud and bounced off, leaving a small dent in the surface.

'C'mon, son, put your back into it,' encouraged Mason. 'Just like your mama does when she's handing out blowjobs.'

Cassius gritted his teeth, drew back the hammer, and let fly. The dent in the tank deepened and the makings of a fair-sized crack became apparent.

'That's it, son, now give it one more—third time's the charm.'

Cassius set himself, took a deep breath, and swung the hammer once again, and this time it went clean through the side of the tank, prompting a torrent of blue-coloured liquid to gush out and soak his Reeboks.

Mason started to laugh. When the strong smell of chemicals reached Hunter's nostrils he realised that Cassius had smashed into the RV's septic tank.

'Now look what you've gone and done…you've messed up your sneakers… But don't worry, son, it's all in a good cause. Now reach on inside and see what you can find,' said Mason.

Cassius dropped the sledgehammer and went to take off his shirt, but before he'd got it unbuttoned the mocking tones of Mason cut in once again.

'Nah, son—leave the shirt on. Come to think of it, roll down the sleeves.'

Hunter watched as Cassius rolled down his sleeves and squatted in the pool of blue liquid. A look of distaste crossed the gangbanger's face, then he reached inside the tank and splashed around for a few seconds. When he withdrew his arm it was soaked to the elbow, and in his hand was a large plastic baggie containing a number of brownish-coloured bricks. A look of pure joy crossed his face, then he rose to his feet and turned around.

'Give it,' commanded Mason, holding out his hands, which were now protected by thick rubber gloves. Cassius stared at the baggie longingly for a second, then handed it over to Mason, who ripped through the plastic and reached inside.

'The mother lode!' he exclaimed, holding a brick aloft with a wide grin. 'We're gonna get rich! Yeah, Cass, even you—you're off the hook.'

'Fo' real? You ain't gonna hold the poison drugs or that dead junkie over me no more?'

'Course not—we're going back to the way things

used to be. We sell to you, you sell to the street, everyone's happy. Now get your scrawny arm back inside that tank and keep digging—if our snitch is on the money there's a whole lot more where this came from.'

By the time Cassius had finished his search, another three plastic baggies were laid out to dry on the concrete floor of the warehouse. Hunter was impressed. These guys had intercepted a serious shipment from south of the border. The street value of the drugs had to run into the tens of thousands of dollars. Where the hell were they getting their intel?

'I gotta problem, Mason,' muttered Cassius, as he stared forlornly at the drugs. 'What with all the cash I given you of late, I ain't got none left for a down payment.'

Mason stared at him for a moment then led Diaz away towards the front of the Winnebago where they proceeded to hold a brief discussion. When the two of them returned Mason was sporting a smile.

'All that unpleasantness is in the past, Cass. We're partners again—and partners look out for each other. Here's what we're gonna do—we're gonna give you a brick of heroin to get you back on your feet, you're gonna shift it a.s.a.p., then we're gonna split the proceeds seventy-thirty.'

'I'm gonna get seventy per cent?'

'Hell, no, you dumbfuck, whadya think we are? Some kind of charity? You're gonna get thirty per cent, and you can thank your lucky stars we're being so generous. You give me any more lip and I'll be putting in a call to that bakery you're so fond of.'

'Thanks, M-Mason, I appreciate it—you're being r-real good to me,' stuttered Cassius, his discomfort apparent.

'Make sure you stay away from the schools on this one—you know how that turned out last time. And don't go using your crew for distribution—you gotta keep this contained. There's a bunch of spics out there right now waiting for that Winnebago to show up, and when it doesn't, they're gonna be on the lookout for anyone with a fresh supply of Mexican tar for sale.'

'No problem. I ain't exactly flush with dealers anyhow.'

'Yeah, I heard—word on the street is that someone's been taking your crew out one by one.'

'Some Geronimo muthafucka's on the goddamn warpath. You hear anything, you let me know?'

'Ain't my problem—you're gonna have to man up and fight your own battles. Anyhow, it's time we were gone.'

'What should I do with the RV?'

'Whatever the hell you want. Here's your heroin,' said Mason, tossing him a brick. 'We'll be in touch.'

With that, Mason and Diaz headed for the darkness at the rear of the warehouse. An engine fired to life, then tyres squealed as a car pulled away. Cassius stood motionless alongside the Winnebago for a second, then he picked up the brick of heroin that Mason had tossed at his feet and shuffled out of the front entrance, leaving Hunter alone with his thoughts.

The night had been a veritable goldmine of new information. The two guys that Hunter first saw berate

Cassius outside his pad at Imperial Courts were drug suppliers, only it appeared that they were drug suppliers who didn't have a regular supply of their own, hence their need to hijack the Winnebago. They were also well informed, and up until recently they'd been blackmailing Cassius over something. But how the hell did all this fit into Gracie's abduction? Neither her name nor Angel's had come up, suggesting that Mason and Diaz weren't involved.

But there was no way Cassius had pulled off the kidnapping on his own. He was a follower, not a leader—someone else had to be pulling the strings. And what was it he'd said? That some 'Geronimo muthafucka' had been taking out members of his crew one by one. So there was someone else out there who had a beef with the Imperial Knights. Who was he, and what was his angle? Hunter retraced his steps down the alley of packing crates and headed for the exit. He had a lot of thinking to do, and not much time to do it in.

CHAPTER THIRTY-FOUR

THE sun was beginning to rise as the cab pulled up in front of Angel's home on Verona. Hunter had walked for ten minutes or so after leaving the warehouse, then he'd used his cellphone to summon a ride once he was satisfied that he was far enough away not to be linked to the site of Cassius's drug meeting with Mason and the enigmatic Diaz. As the cab came to a stop, he reached for his wallet and pulled out enough bills to cover the fare, then handed them to the Arabic driver who accepted them with a thankful nod.

'*As-Salamu Alaykum,* my brother,' the driver muttered.

'Have a good one yourself,' Hunter responded, climbing out of the vehicle. The street was deserted at this early hour, except for a ginger tomcat that was nosing around an over-sized motorbike by the kerb. He walked up the driveway to Angel's house, skirted around his Barracuda, then grabbed himself a spot on the veranda. There was no need to wake her at the crack of dawn, better to let her get some rest. Plus it would give him some time to plan—time to figure out how he was going to use all he'd just learnt to turn up the heat on Cassius, to back him into a corner where he had no choice but to spill the beans about Angel's daughter.

When he'd heard Gracie's voice down the line yesterday there'd been a subtle shift in the balance of power. Now that he knew she was still alive, he was confident she'd stay that way until Angel had completed her allotted task—that task being to take down Venom, the head of the Vipers. So if he could somehow forestall the assassination, then he'd buy more time to infiltrate Cassius's organisation and discover what was going on. His eyes felt heavy and he cracked a yawn. God, he was beat. Staying up all night wasn't as easy as it used to be. He made a pillow with his jacket and stretched out on the veranda, and within seconds he'd drifted off to sleep.

When he came to a while later, he realised that his catnap had been a mistake, as the first thing he felt was a cold steel blade pressed hard against his windpipe.

'Don't move,' commanded an unfamiliar voice, and as he'd always had a soft spot for oxygen, he decided to obey. Keeping all discernible movement to a minimum, he opened his eyes to find an angry Native American bent over him, holding a hunting knife to his throat. The first word that flashed into his head was Geronimo—Cassius had said that the Imperial Knights were under attack from some Indian, and it was too much of a coincidence for this not to be the man in question. The stranger's dark brown hair was pulled back in a ponytail, his face was as weathered as a piece of old cowhide, and his eyes bristled with an ancient intelligence.

'You are the one who will lead me to Dreadnought,' he said in a matter-of-fact tone. It was the sort of voice you couldn't help but respond to—it had a hypnotic quality to it that most people would find hard to resist, especially when aided and abetted by the threat of a severed windpipe, but fortunately for Hunter, he wasn't most people.

'I'm not leading you anywhere while I'm in this position,' he responded, flexing his thigh muscles to encourage the circulation in his legs. Making a move at this point would be suicide, but somewhere along the line his attacker would give him an opening, and that was when he had to be ready to strike.

'You find this funny? I find no humour in anything that you do. You drug dealers are all the same. You bring despair to neighbourhoods that languish in poverty. You turn friend against friend, family against family. You kill children, and you turn children into killers, then you walk away with your pockets lined. You are the white oppressor. It's the same as it ever was.'

'Drug dealer? Now, wait just a minute, buddy, I'm no drug dealer—'

'I have no time for your lies,' cut in the Indian, pushing down on the blade to elicit a trickle of blood. 'Take me to Dreadnought. Now!'

With that, he grabbed a chunk of Hunter's hair and began to haul him to his feet. The pain was excruciating. He blanked it out and looked for an opening, but the knife never left his throat.

'I'm no dealer—' he began, only to get cut off once again.

'Silence. I've seen you with the gangs. I've seen you hand over drugs. No more talking. Another word and I'll cut out your tongue. You've got one last chance to redeem yourself. Take me to Dreadnought, and I might let you live.'

And there was that name again: Dreadnought. He'd never even heard of the guy, but now didn't seem like the opportune moment for that revelation. As his captor began to back away down the drive, he had no choice but to keep pace, but he kept his attention focused on the Indian's every move, waiting for that one slight slip or stumble that would signal he'd lost his centre of balance. By the time they'd reached the street, Hunter knew that a mistake of this nature wasn't going to come—the Indian was as sure-footed as a cat. They backed up a few more yards until they were alongside the large motorbike that he'd noted when he'd got out of the cab. It was a Triumph, a real behemoth, taking up as much kerb space as the average four-door compact, the early morning sun glistening off its tail-pipes, the black fuel tank buffed to within an inch of its life.

'We're going for a ride. You drive, I'll be right behind you. First, put these in the ignition,' said the Indian, dangling a set of keys over his left shoulder.

'There's not much room on there for two—how about I follow on later?' Hunter cracked, hoping to provoke a response.

'Start the bike.'

He took the proffered set of keys and thrust them into the ignition. When he turned them clockwise, the bike came to life with a throaty roar that prompted the tomcat that had been nosing around earlier to come flying out of the bushes with a yowl. The knife moved an inch from Hunter's throat for a fraction of a second. This was his chance. He twisted his head, lunged towards the Indian's forearm, and sank his teeth deep into the flesh just above the wrist. The Indian yelled out in pain as his fingers sprang open in a reflex movement, prompting the knife to slip from his grasp and fall harmlessly to the tarmac. Hunter unlocked his jaw and threw his head backwards into the bridge of the Indian's nose to elicit another pained cry, and then he was free. He pivoted on the balls of his feet, ready for action, and he didn't have to wait long.

The Indian came in hard and fast with a swinging right that he just managed to block with his arm, and then he was counterpunching, throwing a vicious right of his own straight into his opponent's solar plexus, twisting his knuckles at the moment of impact to maximise the power of the punch. When his hand crashed into the bank of knotted muscle and sinew that was the Indian's gut, it felt like he'd hit a brick wall. Before he had time to marvel at the sharp pain that was shooting up his arm, the Indian was attacking again, firing a short left straight into the side of his chin that rattled his teeth and lifted him off his feet to send him flying through the air back towards Angel's drive.

He stayed down where he'd landed, groaning on the tarmac in the foetal position, waiting for the Indian to come in and finish him off. As soon as his opponent was in range he kicked out with both legs to land a double blow on the Indian's right calf, the movement timed perfectly to catch his foe off balance and send him crashing to the ground. Both men then rolled away from each other and leapt to their feet, their fists raised in readiness for further hostilities.

'Hunter! Get down!' yelled a female voice from over his left shoulder. He reacted instinctively, diving face first into the dirt just in time to avoid a short burst from a handgun. The lethal lead projectiles zipped through the air mere inches above him as they sped on their way to their target, but the Indian was no slouch in the reaction stakes either, diving headlong towards his motorbike to leave Hunter's Barracuda between himself and danger.

Hunter rolled onto his back and leapt to his feet as the shooter went to run past him.

'Angel! No!' he shouted, catching her in his arms and holding her back. Out on the street, the motorbike let loose a guttural roar as the Indian opened the throttle and accelerated away.

'What the hell are you doing?' Angel gasped, still fighting to get out of his grip and fire another burst at the rapidly retreating biker.

'Let him go.'

She squirmed for another few seconds then her shoulders sagged as the sound of the bike's engine faded into the distance. He unlocked his arms and stepped away from her. She was barefoot, wearing an oversized white T-shirt and holding a Baby Glock.

'But he was trying to kill you!'

'If he'd wanted me dead I'd be lying in a pool of my

own blood on your veranda right now. And if I'd wanted him dead I'd have used my gun instead of engaging in a spot of hand-to-hand combat.'

'So what the hell was he after?'

'Beats me. But there's one thing I know for sure—my enemy's enemy is always my friend.'

'C'mon,' Angel said. 'Let's get you inside. Your throat's been cut and there's blood running from your mouth.'

'The mark on my throat's just a nick, and the blood in my mouth isn't mine,' he muttered, the taste of the Indian still coppery on his tongue. 'But my jaw feels like it's been hit with a hammer. How the hell did you get out here so fast?'

'I woke up when the bike started, then looked out the window to see what was going on. Once I realised you were getting your ass kicked, I grabbed my gun and ran outside.'

'Hey! I was holding my own out there!'

'Yeah, and while you were busy holding your own that guy was taking you apart,' she said, as she led Hunter back into the house. 'Go sit on the sofa, I'll be with you in a minute.'

When she returned, she was holding an icepack, a small bowl of water and a face towel.

'Here—take this for your jaw,' she said, handing him the icepack. 'Where did that guy come from?'

'First things first, let me tell you what happened last night.'

He proceeded to give her the potted version of events, how he'd helped Cassius ambush some drug mules from Mexico and how he'd subsequently tailed the gangbanger to watch him hand over the goods to two other men. While he spoke, she cleaned out the wound on his neck, her expression remaining neutral throughout.

'So the upside is that I'm in tight with the gang-banger now. Cassius trusts me, and I can use that trust to help me find out where Gracie's been stashed.'

'And what about the Indian?'

'I don't know how he fits into things but I intend to find out. Word is, he's been attacking the Knights, taking out their dealers one by one, and that sounds like the kinda guy we could use on our team.'

'When you didn't come home I was worried.'

She stopped attending to his neck, dipped the towel in the water, then wiped the blood from his lips with quick, deft strokes. The water was warm and salty on his mouth.

'Truth is, I don't think I can get though this without you,' she said, straddling him on the sofa and taking his face in her hands. She leant in close and kissed him hard on the lips.

'Angel, where are we going with this?'

The silence hung heavy between them as he waited for her to respond. When she finally spoke, her voice was soft and fragile.

'I don't know…but right now I need you more than I've ever needed anyone before…'

And that was good enough for him.

CHAPTER THIRTY-FIVE

'WHISKY,' Cassius barked at the pock-faced kid behind the bar, struggling to make himself heard over the pounding disco beat. Even though the lighting was dialled way down low, it didn't hide the fact that the joint was a shit hole, but he hadn't gone there for the decor. Once the tumbler of fluid arrived he swivelled in his seat to take in the late morning entertainment.

A small wooden stage was situated opposite, with a raised runway that led out into the centre of the room. Three metal poles ran from floor to ceiling at equidistant points along the runway, and currently writhing around the pole nearest to the bar was a silicone-enhanced blonde with masses of hair on her head and none whatsoever on her pussy. She was pushing forty, her days of working the high-class strip joints far behind her, but she still looked good in the half-light, and she still had all the moves she needed to get male blood flowing southwards at speed.

At least for most men she did—because ever since Cassius had been hitting the coke that little bit harder, he'd been struggling to bone up. Sure, there was still life down below, but it was a flag at half-mast kind of life—the kind that took far too long to summon, and even once you had, there wasn't much you could do with it anyhow. The sensible course of action would have been to cut back on the yayo, but as that idea was a non-starter, he was just going to have to live with Mr Floppy for a little while longer. Just until he'd gotten through the tough spot he was currently in. At least Mason and Diaz were off his back. He'd sold the brick of heroin to some Ukrainian guys who worked Venice Beach, which was far enough away from his 'hood to be safe. Or was it? Maybe he should have sold it outside city limits? Gone down to San Diego, hooked up down there? No—as long as the Ukrainians stuck to the coast, he'd be fine. Course, he hadn't sold them the *whole* brick—first, he'd taken enough to keep his moms quiet for a couple more weeks. When a gift horse came calling, you didn't fuck it in the mouth.

But although one of his problems had disappeared, he still had two more to contend with. Number one— to make sure that the spic whore, Angel, took out the head of the Vipers in the very near future. Dreadnought had been at pains to stress how important this was. While Lunatic's botched assassination attempt had been enough to put the Vipers on a war footing, it would be Angel's follow-up attack that would push them into open conflict with the Ghosts. Once Angel had killed Venom, the two gangs would be at each other's throats, leaving Dreadnought a happy man. Which just left problem number two—to deliver the Indian to Dreadnought, and to deliver him in a state that would mean he kept his mouth shut, and there was only one such state that came with a one hundred per cent guarantee of silence.

He watched as the stripper wrapped her muscular legs halfway up the pole then leant backwards to hang upside down, her fake tits defying gravity like two overripe melons that had been glued to her chest, her shaved genitals staring back at him invitingly. When he stuck his hand in his hip pocket to check for signs of life, a whole load of flaccid nothingness awaited him. He downed his shot and rose from his seat, then made his way to the solitary payphone out back, stopping en route to enjoy a little chemical stimulation in the john.

As the coke coursed through his veins the old feelings of supreme confidence returned to him in a rush. The Indian wasn't going to be a problem. Angel was going to do exactly as she was told. Everything would turn out okay, and it would turn out okay coz he was the goddamn man! Nothing was beyond him. Not even an erection. If he wanted to fuck a high-class ho to celebrate later on, then that's what he'd damn well do. He picked up the handset, dropped a dime, and punched in some digits. When the kid at the bakery answered, he reeled off the number of the payphone and asked that Dreadnought call him back a.s.a.p. The phone rang in under three minutes. He snatched up the receiver and held it to his mouth.

'Dread? It's Cass.'

'I know it's you, chump, you just rang me,' boomed the stentorian voice down the line. 'You got some good news? Have there been any more attacks on our men?'

'No, boss, it's been quiet for a coupla days. But don't you be worryin' yo'self 'bout that muthafucka no more—I gotta plan to take him out.'

'Glad to hear it. And make sure you bring him in alive—I'm guessing that he's some kind of freelancer brought in to fuck us the hell up. He might know something of value.'

'Sure, Dread, you got it.'

'Good. I've got a time and place for the hit. Venom gets discharged from the USC Medical Centre at two p.m. on Thursday. I want Angel to take him out on the front steps.'

'I'll give her a heads-up.'

'Yeah, but don't tell her everything at once—give her the time but not the location—keep her on her toes. I've been thinking back to Lunatic's swansong—maybe we shouldn't have told him the location so early. Maybe he got made when he was scoping it out, and that's why he didn't get the job done.'

'Yeah, boss, maybe.'

'It's got to go right this time, Cass. When Lunatic attacked Venom, he put things in motion. If Angel can finish what Lunatic started, then both gangs will be leaderless and at war, and once that happens, our position becomes a whole lot more secure. It'll mean we survive, Cass, it'll mean the 'hood survives. You still love your 'hood?'

'Hell, yeah!'

'And you still love the Knights?'

'You know I do, Dread, I got mad love for my brothers.'

'Then make sure this all goes smooth. Everything

we're doing is for the good of our people. We go back
a long way, Cass, the two of us come up together. Back
in the day, I taught you everything I knew about being
a banger, now it's time for you to step up to the plate
and make a name for yourself. Save the gang, Cass.
Save the 'hood. It's all we got.'

'Sure thing, Dread, you can count on me.'

The phone went dead in his hand. He replaced the
receiver in the cradle and made for the exit, glowing
with pride.

CHAPTER THIRTY-SIX

'THAT was good,' said Hunter, as he gulped down his last mouthful of home-cooked tamales. He hadn't realised how hungry he was until he'd taken his first bite, then he'd set about cleaning his plate with a vengeance. In contrast, Angel's plate was still half-full, and for the last few minutes she'd been pushing her food around aimlessly as if she'd forgotten why she'd put it there in the first place. She was wearing a Lakers vest and a pair of cut-off jeans, but while the highlights in her hair glinted in the midday sun, the expression on her face was growing ever more cloudy.

'What's wrong, Angel?' he asked.

'It's Larry. I've got the viewing tomorrow, then the funeral a couple of days after that. I just don't know how I'm going to get through them on my own.'

'You don't have to. I'll be right there alongside you, that is, if you want me to.'

'That'd be great, but you can't. You've got to keep looking for Gracie.'

'Maybe we'll have found her by then.'

Angel shrugged in response, her confidence in his

abilities seemingly on the wane. Before he could say anything to reassure her, the telephone mounted on the wall burst into life. She stared at the phone with trepidation. His heart went out to her. It couldn't be easy knowing that every incoming call could hold the fate of your firstborn in the balance.

'Answer it,' Hunter said softly.

'Hello?'

The look on her face told him all he needed to know. There was no speaker on the extension, so he rose from his seat and leant in close, straining to hear the voice on the other end of the line.

'You got two days to practise your shooting, bitch. You better aim straight if you wanna see shorty again, and you better not fuck up like your old man, coz I ain't got time for no more mistakes. Venom got to get got. It's goin' down two p.m. Thursday, make sure you're ready.'

'Where?' replied Angel.

'Don't you be worryin' your pretty little head about that. I'm gonna call and tell you just ahead of time, then you gonna go and do the deed.'

'I got it. But if you've laid so much as a hand on my daughter's head I swear I'll hunt you down like a dog...'

'Woof-woof!' laughed the voice, before hanging up.

Hunter took the receiver from Angel's shaking hand and replaced it in its cradle.

'Two days...all I've got is two days,' she said, as she buried her head in her hands.

'That's good—it means Gracie's gonna be fine for another two days at least.'

'But what they want is impossible. The Vipers will be out in force—how am I going to get close enough to carry out a hit?'

'You're not.'

She looked up at him in surprise.

'First of all, it's a suicide mission—just like it was for Lunatic. Even if you did kill Venom, you'd never make it back in one piece.'

'I'd die for my daughter.'

'I'm sure you would, but it wouldn't save her. As soon as Venom's dead, they'll have no more use for either you or Gracie and they'll kill you both.'

'So what the hell am I meant to do?' she screamed, her fists clenching into tight little balls. 'Wait for you to save the day?'

'In a word—yes. I promised I'd get your daughter back, and that's one promise I intend to keep. Now that I'm tight with Cassius, it's just a matter of time until he leads me to Gracie. And, remember, we've got two whole days before they make their next move, and a lot can happen in two days.'

As he finished speaking, his cellphone started to buzz.

'Give me a second, this might be important,' he said, then he held the phone to his ear. 'Yep?'

He listened intently for a few seconds, said, 'Sure, I'll see you at three,' then cut the call.

'Who was that?' asked Angel.

'Cassius. Says he wants to see me pronto. He sounded a little desperate. This might be the break we've been waiting for. Stay here. I'll be in touch as soon as I can.'

She nodded dejectedly as he headed for the door. Now wasn't the time to tell her, but Cassius was probably calling about business. The two of them had an outstanding drug deal to conclude, and the gangbanger didn't strike him as the kind of guy that would let a free lunch go to waste. Only problem was, Hunter had no intention of selling Cassius the drugs that he'd stolen from the Latino street dealer. Using a small portion of them as bait was one thing, but handing over the whole lot so they could find their way onto some schoolyard was a different matter entirely. Maybe he could stall the gangbanger for a while, buy himself more time? After all, he only had to hold out for a couple of days, then all bets would be off.

He exited Angel's house, climbed into his Barracuda, and started the engine. When he backed out of the drive, his brow creased with deep furrows as he thought things through. Somehow, he had to make sure that this meeting with Cassius yielded results. He had to keep drugs off the agenda, and get the whereabouts of a kidnapped six-year-old on it, and that wasn't going to be easy.

Hunter pulled up at the address that Cassius had given him and cut the 'Cuda's engine. Surely this wasn't the place? He was in the heart of Watts, not far from Imperial Courts, and he was staring at a rundown bungalow that looked like it was scheduled for demolition. The front door and windows were all boarded up and there were long streaks of soot on the exterior walls, while the lot was filled with trash—couches, old TVs with smashed screens, grocery carts with no wheels—it was a fly-tipper's wet dream. A scrawny arm shot out through a gap in the boarded-up windows and waved him onwards. He climbed out of the car and approached the window with caution.

'That you, Cassius?'

'Sure is. You're gonna wanna come round back.'

Hunter worked his way around to the rear of the property to find a gaping hole where the back door should have been. Cassius was standing in the frame, his eyes darting around furiously, his fists clenching and unclenching.

'Get your ass in here quick, anyone could be watching.'

Hunter raised an eyebrow as he surveyed the empty rear lot, then strolled casually over to the house.

'Move, cuz, move!' encouraged Cassius, the relief on his face plain to see once Hunter had stepped out of the sunlight and into what had once been a kitchen.

He had half a second to note that the room had been stripped bare of all its fixtures and fittings and that the lower reaches of the walls were covered with stains, and then the smell hit him.

'What the fuck is that?' he asked, choking back a gag, but Cassius was already hurrying deeper inside.

'C'mon, c'mon, can't do business in no latrine…'

He looked back at the walls. Piss stains. Nice. The gangbanger headed into the first room on the right. Hunter followed him inside to find that it wasn't in much better condition than the kitchen, although it did have one thing going for it—it didn't reek of urine. There was a large round hole through one of the interior walls at about chest height. A series of faint snores emanated from the other side of the hole. As Cassius did his best not to bounce around the small space, Hunter walked over and looked through the hole to observe a pair of spindly legs poking out from beneath a blanket.

'Who the hell's that?'

'Him? That's just ole Tom. He a smack fiend, perma-fried, you don't have to worry none 'bout him. I let him stay here coz he used to be tight with my moms back in the day…'

'I'm sure you won't mind if I take a look? I like to know who's present when I'm doing business,' said Hunter, not waiting for a response. When he went into the next room and approached the body the stench of urine hit his nostrils once again, although this time it was inter-mingled with stale sweat. He took a tentative hold of the blanket and pulled. The man sleeping underneath was all skin and bones, his cheeks sunken, his eye sockets hollow—he could have stepped straight out of Auschwitz.

'You done?' Cassius called through the hole.

Hunter let the heroin addict be and returned to the gangbanger, trying not to think about the company he was keeping these days.

'What gives?' he asked.

'First up, props for the way you handled yo'self last night. Helped me take down that RV smooth, you done me a solid.'

'No sweat.'

'And the way you took out those old timers? Buck! Buck! Cold, man, real cold.'

Hunter gestured for Cassius to get to the point.

'Yeah, well, anyhows, I know you wanna be shifting those drugs, but I'm gonna have to adjust our arrangement a little. Renegotiate terms, ya dig?'

'Now wait just a minute, I'm already selling at a knockdown price, there's no way I'm going any lower.'

'Nah, man, it ain't like that. I'm here to tell you that I'm gonna pay a bit more than we agreed—sort of a bonus—and that it's gonna go down right here, same time tomorrow, if you'll just help me out with one more thing.'

Hunter felt relieved. Handing over hard drugs to a gangbanger wasn't going to be an issue for the time being, but what the hell did Cassius want now?

'Keep talking.'

'My crew's been facing some drama from some Geronimo muthafucka. He been takin' out homies left and right, it's getting real bad for business...'

Hunter decided to keep the fact that he'd recently come face to face with Cassius's Native American nemesis to himself for now.

'Your whole crew's running scared of some Indian?'

'We ain't scared, he's just one step ahead. Muthafucka know us better than our own peeps. Knows where we deal, where we eat, hell, he even knows where some of us go snake wrestlin' at the movies...'

'So why don't you take him out?'

'Coz he's ghost man, employin' some real stealth tactics. We got no clue as to where he's holed up. So that's why I gotta draw him out to the open.'

'How?'

'I'm shutting down my dealers from tonight, 'cept

for one location. That way, when he comes after us, we'll be ready.'

'What makes you so sure he'll come?'

'Gonna use Rocket as bait. He used to do business outside of Acorn Elementary, and Geronimo's got a real thing 'bout selling to shorties. When he first caught up with Rocket, he sliced and diced his legs and put him in a wheely-chair.'

'Say the Indian shows up. How are you going to catch him?'

'Location's where it's at. Gonna put Rocket in the middle of a courtyard that's surrounded by fucked-up apartment blocks on all sides. Only way in or out is through an itty-bitty alley that leads to the street. Soon as Geronimo goes for Rocket, we gonna shut up that entrance and capture the muthafucka.'

'And then what?'

'My boss wants to have a sit-down with Geronimo to see what he knows, but that ain't good for Cass. The Indian's got shit on me that makes me look bad. Only problem is, I can't be seen to fuck things up.'

'Is your boss gonna be there?' asked Hunter, his ears pricking up.

'Nah, ever since he's been on the outs he's been keeping a low profile.'

'On the outs?'

'Out of prison, ya dig? I ain't even seen him myself since he got back in town. Security's so tight he won't even tell me where he's holed up. Anyway, that shit don't matter. What do matter is I don't want him to have no parley with the Indian.'

Shit, thought Hunter, if the boss had a safe house, then maybe that was where Angel's daughter was being held, but if Cassius didn't know where it was, then another door that might have led to Gracie's salvation had just been slammed shut. All the time he'd spent cultivating his relationship with Cassius looked like a bust. Playing nice had led nowhere fast, so maybe it was time to go with a more direct approach? But if the gang-banger didn't know where his boss was hiding, then what good would beating him up do?

Then it hit him. Maybe the Indian was the answer. If he knew as much about the gang's habits as Cassius had intimated, then he must have been gathering intel for some time, and maybe in the course of all those hours of reconnaissance he'd seen something of value, something that might give away the boss's current location. Maybe he'd even seen Gracie.

'This is all very interesting, Cassius, but where exactly do I fit in?'

'Simple, bro. I want you there tonight, layin' low, and once I spring the trap, I want you to take down that Geronimo muthafucka in a heartbeat—just like you did those old folks. Make sure he ain't got nothing to say to no one, not ever. You gotta kill the muthafucka stone dead.'

CHAPTER THIRTY-SEVEN

THE scene that confronted Hunter was all too familiar. An arid patch of wasteland stretched out before him, leading up to a ramshackle collection of cardboard boxes that were clustered under an overpass. A few yards from this makeshift village, a handful of hobos were huddled around a rusting oildrum, eking what little warmth they could from the meagre fire. The whole scene was sickening. America was the richest nation in the world, and yet the homeless population continued to grow like a cancer.

He walked towards the hobos with a carrier bag wedged under one arm, checking his watch as the sun bled below the horizon. It was almost nine o'clock, and that gave him an hour or so before he was due to show up at the apartment block. When he'd left Cassius earlier that afternoon, he'd driven straight over to the site of the Indian trap to check it out for himself. The gangbanger had chosen well. It was a natural place for an ambush with just one obvious entrance that looked simple to secure. If the Indian showed up, he wouldn't stand a chance.

'Spare some change, son?' asked one of the hobos,

jabbing his withered hand in Hunter's general direction. His eyes peered out from under hair a mass of wild hair, while his beard was matted together with some sort of gelatinous substance. Hunter gave him a quick once-over and estimated his height at a shade under six feet. Near enough.

'I think I can do a bit better than that,' he replied, opening the carrier bag. 'How about a change of clothes and enough cash to get yourself a few square meals?'

'What are you after, son? I don't turn no tricks.'

'Don't worry, old timer, you're not my type. This is business. I give you some new clothes and a fifty-dollar bill, and all I want in return are the tired old rags that you're wearing.'

The hobo couldn't strip down fast enough. Hunter handed him a new pair of work boots, some jeans, a checked shirt and a long coat, and in return he received a mangy pair of pants that were frayed to the knee, a faded Pearl Jam T-shirt that had more holes than fabric, and a tired black hoodie that was missing both of its arms. He stashed each item into the carrier bag, trying not to breathe in the noxious fumes, then his eyes strayed over to the cardboard village by the overpass.

'Where's my fifty bucks?' asked the hobo, who looked resplendent in his new duds.

'Right here,' Hunter replied as he reached for his wallet. 'Say, you got a half-decent mattress back there?'

'What if I do?'

'You sell it to me and this fifty turns into a hundred.'

'But that mattress is all I got to sleep on. How about you make it a hundred and fifty?'

'Don't hardball me, old timer, I know damn well that you'll have no problem scrounging up another one as soon as my back's turned. One hundred bucks—take it or leave it.'

'I'll take it, son,' he said, as his withered hand jabbed out once again for the cash.

With negotiations satisfactorily concluded, Hunter made the return trip across the wasteland towards his Barracuda, a bag of hobo clothes slung over one shoulder and a heavy mattress bouncing along behind him.

Hunter was standing next to his car in a dingy Watts side street, the moon waxing high overhead. An industrial-sized dumpster squatted against the wall to his left, and that wall marked one of the four exterior boundaries of the rundown apartment complex where Cassius planned to ensnare the Indian. He pulled on his recently acquired hoodie and did his best to ignore the rancid smell of stale sweat that assaulted his nostrils. His hobo ensemble was now complete, and while he didn't think that the look would catch on any time soon, there was reason to his sartorial madness. Entering the courtyard and strolling around in his usual street clothes would have been an invitation for an ass kicking. His homeless get-up was the perfect disguise. If this place were one of Cassius's dope spots then plenty of druggies and winos would be hanging out there. The rags he'd bought from the hobo would give him an authentic look and smell that you just couldn't buy off the peg. He'd blend right in like a turd at a sewage farm.

But there were always ways to improve on perfection. He reached back inside his car, pulled out a bottle of Cisco, and started to splash the syrupy hooch all over his clothes. When that was done, he crouched down and scooped up a handful of dirt, which he proceeded to smother over his face and hands. Perfect. He opened the 'Cuda's trunk, retrieved the heavy mattress that he'd wedged inside earlier, then carefully placed the soiled bedding in its natural home—inside the industrial-sized dumpster, resting on top of a mound of old trash.

Preparations now complete, he locked his car, pulled his hood down low and headed for the alley that served as the courtyard's entrance, his gait quickly morphing from that of physical specimen to drunken bum. There weren't any guards at either end of the alley, but he had no doubt that Cassius had men stationed nearby ready to shut it off in an instant. He emerged into the courtyard to find that the surrounding apartment blocks towered high all around, giving the space an arena-like feel. The rows of broken windows that stared back at him were mostly devoid of life, although the odd flickering campfire signalled where squatters had taken up residence, but the real action was out in the centre of the square itself, where a scene from the third circle of hell awaited him.

Addicts of every type strolled like zombies across the concrete, their gluttony for their vice condemning them to a life of ceaseless torment. Their bodies were frail and broken, their complexions sallow and greasy. Most wore expressions of hunger, while a handful looked more serene, marking them out as the happy few that had just ingested their drug of choice. There were even a couple of aging hookers on patrol, their mini-skirts finishing just south of their pudenda, their halter tops cut low to expose sagging breasts, although how they expected to turn a trick amongst this client base was beyond Hunter's comprehension.

He shuffled away from the entrance and headed for a spot midway along the western wall, just to the left of a crumbling concrete stairwell. Once he'd arrived, he sank down on his haunches and lowered his head, all the while surveying the space for Cassius and his men. He spotted Rocket, the drug dealer with the damaged legs, almost immediately, sitting in a wheel-chair in the middle of the courtyard with a rag-tag line of junkies strung out in front of him. Every few seconds his Afro would jerk around as he looked over his shoulder, suggesting that the role of bait was not one he was overly comfortable with.

Within five minutes Hunter had identified another five gangbangers—three interspersed amongst the lost souls that wandered the courtyard, and two more watching from the relative comfort of the first-floor balcony. Each of them was doing their best to look like a down and out, but for the most part they were failing miserably. Their outfits were fine—it was their body language that gave them away. Too straight in the shoul-ders, too confident in the walk—in fact, they were too damn cocky in general, but then gangbangers never had been known for their humility. He did some mental arithmetic. Add in a couple more guys to man the entrance, plus Cassius himself, and that meant there had to be at least nine heavily armed Knights somewhere in the vicinity.

He spent the next two hours either watching the entrance for any sign of the Indian or casing the court-yard to keep a check on Cassius's crew. Every five minutes or so he'd surreptitiously flex each of the major muscles in his arms and legs to make sure they didn't go to sleep, and he was halfway through one of these mini-exercise routines when his patience was finally rewarded. The figure that stumbled into the courtyard dragging one foot gamely behind him looked for all the world like another addict out in search of a late-night fix, but he caught Hunter's attention straight away. His clothes were decrepit, a half-empty bottle of rotgut whisky dangled from his right hand, and his head was hidden under a wide-brimmed straw hat, but despite the effort he'd taken with his disguise, it was his body that gave him away. The Indian was just too damn big. To the discerning eye, his stooped gait couldn't quite mask the fact that he was well over six feet tall, and though his shoulders were hunched, they still looked broad and powerful beneath his hobo shirt.

This was it. He rose from his spot by the stairwell and began to stumble through the sea of bodies, his at-tention flicking from the Indian back to the entrance, aware that Cassius would spring the trap the moment that Rocket was attacked. The Indian was just ten yards shy of the drug-dealing cripple when Hunter faked a half-stumble and grabbed him by the arm.

'It's a trap, they know you're coming, you've got to get out of here,' he muttered, raising his head just high enough to reveal his face beneath the brim of the hoodie.

A fleeting expression of surprise crossed the Indian's face, then he held Hunter's gaze as he digested the warning.

'Hurry, there's not much time,' urged Hunter, glancing to his left to find that the drug dealer was now eyeing them suspiciously. 'Come on! This way!'

The Indian nodded and the two of them turned on their heels and began to stumble back towards the courtyard's only exit, but they'd barely covered ten yards before an excited shout rang out behind them.

'Cass! That's the muthafucka right there!'

Rocket had recognised the Indian—now things were going to heat up in a hurry. As soon as Hunter heard the cry, he lunged to his left, heading away from the exit and deeper into the crowd, dragging the Indian with him.

'Shut it down! Shut it down now!' yelled a thin voice through a bullhorn. Hunter glanced upwards to find that Cassius had appeared on the first-floor balcony above the exit, and right on cue four gangbangers emerged from one of the abandoned rooms below to block off the alley, each of them toting an automatic weapon.

'This way,' urged Hunter, freeing his Beretta from the confines of his hobo outfit as he headed for the nearest stairwell. A burst of gunfire exploded behind him, cutting through the murmur of meaningless conversation like a lance. A junkie's forehead exploded in a geyser of crimson and his body slumped lifelessly to the ground. The shots hadn't come from Cassius, so either one of his men had panicked and disobeyed Dreadnought's orders to take the Indian alive, or maybe those orders had changed. At the sound of the first shot, two things happened. First, those who were compos mentis enough to realise what was going on began to scream and run every which way. And, second, the rest of Cassius's crew let fly.

Bodies began to fall all around as the space was turned into a killing field. Hunter raced for the stairwell and dived inside, using the waist-high walls to put a little concrete between him and the blood-crazed triggermen. He clambered upwards as ricochets whined dangerously overhead, his heart pounding against his ribcage. When a gangbanger appeared above him at the entrance to the first floor, he squeezed the Beretta's trigger twice to send two bullets burrowing deep into the kid's cerebral cortex, then looked back to find that the Indian was hunkered down on the lower steps with a hunting knife grasped in his hand.

'Some rescue!' yelled the man under his protection. 'What now?'

'We go higher.'

Hunter scrabbled up the steps to the first-floor balcony and paused at the entrance. The banger he'd just shot lay slumped right in front of him, his Uzi still in his hands. Hunter's stomach turned. The kid was sixteen at the most. He ducked his head around the corner to find that Cassius himself was running straight towards him. For a brief moment their eyes met, then Hunter opened fire, the shots accurate enough to force the gangbanger to dive into the nearest apartment, but not so accurate that he was in any real danger.

'C'mon! Hurry!' Hunter called back to the Indian, just as the reinforcements from the courtyard arrived at the bottom of the stairwell. He swung his Beretta around in a tight arc and aimed at a spot just over the Indian's left shoulder, squeezed off a burst to drop the lead pursuer, then cried out again, 'Second floor! Now!'

He laid down some suppressing fire as the Indian raced past him, then he made his move for the second floor. As he stepped out onto the balcony and rounded the switchback in the stairwell, a pair of Uzis roared out from below, prompting chunks of brickwork to explode from a nearby wall.

'Where now?' asked the Indian.

'Fourth apartment on your left, small white cross on the door.'

The two men hurried forwards in a half-crouch as the bullets continued to fly.

'It's open,' yelled Hunter. 'Get inside.'

The Indian pushed open the door and disappeared from view. Hunter paused to fire off another burst at their pursuers, then he followed him inside. The front room was empty save for a threadbare carpet and the rotting carcass of a cat. There were two interior doors, one on the west wall and one on the south.

'It's a dead end!' yelled the Indian.

'Is it?'

Hunter pushed past him and made for the door on the south wall. He threw it open and stepped through. The wooden boards that had once been used to cover the lone window were stacked neatly in one corner. The glass in the frame was long gone. Hunter made straight for the hole and stuck his head out into the cool night air. All was as it should be.

'Hope you don't mind heights…'

He climbed up onto the frame, paused for a moment, then jumped out into nothingness. The air raced by him as he plummeted earthwards, and he had just enough time to hope that his aim was true before he landed feet first on the old hobo mattress that lay on top of the dumpster. He let his legs collapse on impact as the dumpster swallowed him up, and then he was at rest. He clambered out to find that the Indian was now standing in the window above.

'C'mon!' He gestured, as he hurried over to his car. He climbed inside and started the engine, then watched as the Indian re-enacted his daredevil leap, his extra body weight causing him to land with a bigger bang.

As the dust cleared, the Indian climbed out of the dumpster, but to Hunter's surprise he bypassed the car and sprinted deeper into the alley.

'Hey! Where the hell are you going!' he yelled at the fleeing figure, just as the first of their pursuers appeared at the second-storey window. When a gun barrel poked out of the frame he knew he'd outstayed his welcome. With a heavy heart he stamped on the gas and roared off into the night.

CHAPTER THIRTY-EIGHT

CASSIUS sat at the small kitchen table in his apartment and watched as his right arm underwent a series of spastic jerks. It had been doing that for a few hours now, pretty much whenever he got distracted, and he'd discovered that only by focusing all his powers of concentration on the misbehaving limb could he hope to control it, but this time even that wasn't working. He gripped the arm tight with his left hand and pinned it down until the twitches subsided. What the hell was happening to him?

Maybe he needed some more coke to level him out. He'd taken a hit when he'd got back from the courtyard in an attempt to quell his rising panic over the escape of the Indian, and for a while that had worked, then he'd gotten straight again and all his doubts and fears had rushed back to the surface in a hurry, so he'd taken another hit and fallen into a dreamless sleep, but when he'd woken at the crack of dawn he'd found that his problems had still been right there waiting for him. What the hell had his newfound partner, H, been playing at? It was the same old story—everyone let him down. He'd had the Indian in his grasp, all his troubles had been over, but then Geronimo had gone and escaped. How was he to know that the muthafucka had an accomplice? It wasn't his fault, but the boss wouldn't see it that way. Dread was going to be super-pissed.

He looked at his mom on the other side of the table. At least she was happy. Her head was slumped forward on her filthy housedress and a thick line of drool ran from the corner of her mouth. He'd shot her up with a generous dose of tar ten minutes earlier, first struggling to find a vein that would take the injection, then plunging the syringe into one of the feeble blue lines that pulsed gently under the skin between the toes on her left foot. The bowl of chicken soup that sat in front of her was stone cold and untouched. She'd pretty much given up on food now, so he'd pretty much given up on bothering to heat it.

So how about that crack, huh? asked a little voice in his head. How about you take a little hit, just to help you relax? Help you focus.

He pulled a baggie of small whitish rocks from his pocket and loaded up his pipe. When he held the flame of his lighter underneath it, the rocks began to pop. He took a deep inhalation of those beautiful vapours and felt himself visibly swell as the welcome feelings of confidence and power returned. The Indian's escape was just a blip. He'd get the muthafucka next time, no doubt. Dread would understand. After all, the two of them had been tight since day one. He rode the wave for a few minutes then picked up his cellphone, punched in the number of the bakery, and requested an audience with the boss. Five minutes later, his phone buzzed to life.

'Tell me you're not calling from your own goddamned cell?' boomed his master's voice.

'Course not, cuz—boosted it from some messed-up ho last night. Soon as we done talkin' it's gone.'

'I've told you before—cut out the street slang. What do you want?'

'I just checkin' in with a heads-up on the Indian that's been gunning for us…'

'Indian? You mean like some totem-pole-worshipping, tomahawk-throwing son of a bitch?'

Shit! He'd let it slip that the guy attacking their gang was Indian and not Latino as Dread had suspected. He was going to have to cover this fast.

'Hell, yeah—turned out that he was some Geronimo muthafucka. I set a trap for him last night…'

'So you've caught him?'

'Cocksucka escaped. Had himself an accomplice— some hobo dude…'

'Let me get this straight—you cornered the guy that's been taking out our dealers for the last three months, then you let him escape? And the only help he had was from some old drunk?'

'It weren't like that, Dread, this hobo had mad skills—like he was some kind of one-man killing machine…'

'Words fucking fail me.'

Cassius jitterbugged around the room as the line went quiet for a few seconds, moving this way and that, first towards his spaced-out mom who'd slumped forward onto the table, then to the sink where mould ran rife amongst the mound of dirty crockery, and then to the D-ring bolted to the floor, which he proceeded to stomp over and over with his right foot, not even stopping once Dreadnought decided to resume the conversation.

'An Indian? That just doesn't make any sense. What in the hell would the Mexican Mafia be doing subcontracting to some Indian?'

'Why you so certain that the Latinos be gunning for us, Dread?'

'I got my sources.'

'Well, maybes if you filled me in on those sources I'd have more luck catching this muthafucka. Show a brother a little trust. I've had your back since the get-go. Everything I do is for the good of the 'hood. We all in this together, G.'

'Maybe you're right. Maybe it's time I gave you some more intel. You sure as shit aren't getting things done while you're in the dark. Listen up—it all started when I was on lock down in the belly of the beast…'

'What about me, Dread? You gonna let me go back to my cell?' squeaked the naked Latino, who was still cowering against the rear wall of the communal shower block, his voice barely audible over the pumping base line that emanated from the boombox outside the main entrance.

'Fuck that, sissy, your sweet ass ain't goin' nowhere,' barked Dreadnought. 'You like getting off in the showers so much, how about you stay right there and watch us go to work on your boyfriend, and if you ain't satisfied by the time I'm finished, then I won't be either—now get stroking!'

The sissy began to half-heartedly play with his member as Dreadnought turned his attention back to his other captive. This second man was also Latino, and also naked, and he was curled up in a ball on the floor, having just received a thunderous blow to the kidneys from Dreadnought's right-hand man, Cyclops. His hands were lashed tight behind his back, and his eyes were full of hatred and fear.

'Time to start talking, Rodriguez. Word in the yard is that the Mexican Mafia have got something big planned for South Central—why don't you copy me in on the details?'

'I'm warnin' you, Dread, you better leave me be…'

'You're warning me? Cyclops, remind this fool of the predicament he's in.'

The one-eyed brute drew back his boot and slammed it into the prone man's ribcage with a sickening thud, then he reached down and dragged Rodriguez to his feet by his earlobes. Someone increased the volume on the boombox outside the entrance to drown out the screams of pain.

'Let's try that again. What have the Mexicans got planned?'

'Fuck you, nigger!'

Cyclops grabbed Rodriguez by the ball sack and squeezed. The sound that came out of his mouth resembled an old tin kettle boiling on a rusty stove, while his face turned red as corpuscles popped beneath the skin.

Over by the rear wall, the sissy began to up his stroke rate as the violence turned him on. Dreadnought reached for the showerhead and turned the heat up to maximum.

'You've got yourself a dirty mouth, Rodriguez, maybe we should wash it out.'

Cyclops led the Latino to the showerhead by his testicles then grabbed the back of his neck and plunged his face into the torrent of steaming water. More screams of pain erupted from the captive man's mouth as the skin on his face blistered and burned. The sissy beat down on himself with renewed vigour.

'Spill it, Rodriguez—you're running out of time,' said Dreadnought with a shake of the head.

'You the muthafucka that's livin' on borrowed time,' Rodriguez choked through red, raw lips. 'You and your whole damn crew 'bout to be made extinct.'

Dreadnought stepped forward and grabbed Rodriguez by the windpipe, then slammed him against the tiled wall.

'What the fuck are you talking about, spic?' he yelled, as he placed the tip of his home-made shiv against the underside of Rodriquez's right eye, prompting a trickle of blood to flow down his captive's blistered skin.

'Mex Mafia are coming for you, *pendejo*. They already runnin' all of EastLos, now they lookin' to expand into South Central. Your crew ain't got a chance. Mex Mafia run thousands deep—they got their gangs fighting as one, whereas you niggers too busy fightin' each other to see the big picture.'

'Ain't no one coming into my house 'less I ask 'em. South Central's my turf, fool,' Dreadnought spat out with all the bravado he could muster, but truth was the news had rocked him. It was common knowledge that the Mexican Mafia were supremely organised and that they pretty much had all of the Latino gangs under their control. If they were planning to roll on South Central they'd be nigh on unstoppable, and according to Rodriguez, Dreadnought and the Imperial Knights were standing right on the front line.

'You already dead, cocksucka,' Rodriguez choked out.

Dreadnought rammed the razor-sharp point of the shiv through the Latino's eye and up into his brain. Rodriguez's whole body convulsed as blood erupted out from the wound in a bright red geyser to splatter the tiled floor. Over in the corner, the sissy shrieked as a thick wad of creamy ejaculate exploded from the tip of his swollen glans.

'Who's dead now?' roared Dreadnought, twisting the shiv in deeper as the first icy tendrils of fear began to wrap themselves around his heart.

'So the Mex Mafia's planning on taking South Central, huh?' said Cassius, his mouth fast drying up as the effects of the crack cocaine wore off. 'Muthafucka's gonna get got if they roll on us.'

'I wish I shared your confidence,' replied Dreadnought, his baritone rumble somehow becoming even more sombre. 'The fact is, they're too numerous, too strong and too organised. That's why I had to get them fighting amongst themselves. But this goddamn

Indian situation has come at the exact wrong time. He's taking out our dealers just when I need them the most. They should be concentrating on shifting more product, but instead they're spending their time looking over their shoulders for the next attack.'

'But the, er…Ghosts and…um…Vipers…they at war now,' stumbled Cassius, who was finding it hard to concentrate now that the familiar craving for more chemical stimulation had returned. 'So we okay, huh?'

'Yeah, for now. But it won't be long until their bosses step in and quell the infighting, and when that happens we'll be right back in the shit. You gotta make me more money, Cass, get the streets drowning in snow—I'm gonna need a mighty big war chest if I'm gonna protect our 'hood. And for chrissakes take care of that Indian.'

'I'll get it done, Dread. I'm real close now. Geronimo ain't gonna be botherin' us much longer.'

The line went dead. Cassius dropped his cell on the table and pawed at his pounding head. Goddamn, it was getting hard to think straight. He had all this shit to attend to but all he really wanted was to light up his pipe and disappear into oblivion. Surely the Mexicans couldn't really be coming for them? The Knights were all the family he'd ever known, and he couldn't face the thought of living life out from under their protective umbrella. While he was a Knight, he was a somebody in the 'hood, he had power, money, girls and easy access to as much yayo as he wanted, but if the gang went away he'd be nothing. Just him and his mom to see out their days in some rat-infested slum. He looked across to where she was slumped forward on the table.

'What the fuck am I gonna do, Moms?' he whined, but there was no response.

He stumbled over to her and gently raised her head. It was as light as a feather and her skin was cool to the touch. The drool from the corner of her mouth had dried on her chin, and a thin trail of crusted blood emanated from each nostril. Here eyes stared out life-lessly, and there was no pulse in her neck. After a lifetime of heroin abuse, Moms had finally OD'd. His heart sank and thick tears welled in the corners of his eyes. He turned to find solace in the one true friend he had left, and when he took his first hit from the crack pipe, his troubles just faded away.

CHAPTER THIRTY-NINE

HUNTER climbed out of the Barracuda, shielded his eyes against the morning sun, and let loose a long yawn. He hadn't slept well after rescuing the Indian from the clutches of Cassius and his gang at the courtyard in Watts, and when he'd finally dozed off, his dreams had been haunted by slow-motion replays of the moment he'd been forced to gun down an underage gangbanger. Taking a kid's life was a terrible thing, but when that kid was armed with an automatic weapon and no conscience, what choice did you have?

He held open the passenger side door of his Barracuda and waited for Angel to emerge. She'd forgone her usual style of dress to opt for a more modest ensemble—plain black shoes, a long black dress and a wide-brimmed black hat that obscured the upper half of her face, but despite her somewhat austere apparel, Hunter was still captivated. The curve of her calves as they emerged from the lower reaches of the dress, the steady rise and fall of her chest beneath the black fabric, the way that she brushed at the strands of hair that fell across her face—he noticed all these things, and more, but he couldn't allow himself to be distracted. Lunatic's funeral was a high-risk event, and his role was that of bodyguard. The Vipers had already made one attempt on Angel's life with the drive-by, and the public nature of today's service would make it a tempting target. He'd tried to talk her out of coming, or at least of post-poning it until things had calmed down a little, but she'd been adamant that the service should go ahead. Lunatic deserved to be at rest, and the funeral would be her final gift to him. She'd also thought it best for Gracie if her father were buried before she returned— that way, there'd be a marker at the cemetery to help her understand that he was gone.

So Hunter had accepted defeat, checked his Beretta, and accompanied Angel to their current location. The funeral home was stationed on the corner of an inter-section one block up from the Barracuda, slap bang in the middle of an East Los Angeles residential zone. He hadn't been able to park any closer as a number of cars already lined the kerb, and the prospect of having to cover a hundred or so yards of open ground to make it to the establishment's entrance was already making him nervous. His eyes roved around as they began to walk up the street. A few Latino faces stared back at him from their front yards, their expressions suggest-ing passing interest rather than hostile intent, but Hunter gripped Angel's arm a little tighter and hurried her along all the same. When they made it as far as the funeral home without incident, he began to relax a little. The sign above the door read 'Fernwood Chapel'. It was a large white angular building that was set back from the kerb via a neatly clipped lawn. A paved walk-way dissected the grass to connect the entrance to the sidewalk, and on either side of that walkway was a three-foot-high box hedge. There was nothing particularly remarkable about the place—it looked like a hundred other funeral homes in a hundred other cities—and even its residential location didn't seem all that incongruous. When a neighbourhood had seen as much death as this one, it somehow made sense to have a human disposal service close at hand.

'Are you okay?' Hunter asked, when Angel paused at the entrance.

'As I'll ever be. Let's get this over with so we can concentrate on finding Gracie.'

Gracie. Now that the Indian was AWOL, his best hope of finding her lay once again with Cassius, but when he'd swung by the gangbanger's apartment early that morning he'd found it deserted. Had Cassius recognised him when he'd helped the Indian escape from the courtyard? Was he now holed up somewhere wondering who the cut-price drug dealer really was? Or was he still oblivious to Hunter's true identity? All would become clear at the meeting the two of them had scheduled for later that day.

Hunter stepped out of the mid-morning sun and followed Angel inside. The door opened into a short hallway that led to the reception area. The décor was muted and soothing. He stood by as Angel held a brief conversation with the home's director, a be-suited man with a fast receding hairline who in the space of just a few minutes managed to say how sorry he was for her loss not once but three times. When his preamble came to a merciful close, he led the two of them through a double door into a large rectangular-shaped room. The lighting was subdued and soft music oozed gently from a set of hidden speakers. There were eight rows of chairs set out with a central aisle running straight through the middle of them, and from the looks of things Lunatic's family were sitting to the left and his gang friends to the right. The gang section was the more sparsely populated of the two, as a number of recent Viper reprisal attacks had hit Ghost numbers. At the head of the aisle was a large wooden table with ornately carved legs, and on that table sat a stainless-steel casket. The casket lay open. Lunatic's corpse lay inside.

In direct contrast to the attire he'd had on when he'd died, Lunatic was now clothed in a smart black suit, pristine white shirt and mauve tie. Hunter found himself marvelling at the skill of the undertaker. From where he stood, he would never have believed that the gang boss had been shot through the head at close range had he not seen it happen with his own eyes. After years of being at war on the street, Lunatic finally looked at peace. Hunter offered an arm for support as Angel stifled a sob alongside him, then he led her down the aisle to claim two seats at the front of the room. Within seconds, the elderly couple he'd sat next to rose to their feet and shuffled further down the row.

'What's their problem?' he whispered to Angel.

'Larry's parents…they never accepted that their son was in a gang…figured that the best way to keep up the fantasy was to refuse to acknowledge anything that linked him to the Ghosts, including me.'

'What about Gracie?'

'They have her over to visit a couple of times a year. Larry used to take her. I don't know what's gonna happen now.'

The background music slowly faded out as the priest entered the room from a small door at the rear. He was a kindly faced man somewhere in his late sixties, with liver spots dotted on his hands and upper forehead. He was garbed in a simple black cassock that had been tied at the waist with a cincture, and he had a violet stole draped around his shoulders. When he was satisfied that he had everyone's undivided attention, he cleared his throat and began the service.

'We are gathered here today to celebrate the life of Larry Lloyd…'

Hunter tuned out as the priest droned on. Celebrating the life of a dead gangbanger wasn't really his thing. He turned his thoughts back to his upcoming meeting with Cassius while Angel sat motionless alongside him. When the first hymn was announced the whole room went quiet for a moment, then the silence was broken by the sound of a number of cars screeching to a halt out front.

Hunter was already reaching for his Beretta when the first burst of automatic gunfire exploded in the reception hall.

'Easy, boy,' Stone muttered to the canine on the other side of the six-foot fence. The Indian was in a dirt alley that ran between two single-storey houses somewhere on the southern outskirts of East Los Angeles. His motorbike was resting on its stand alongside him, a light layer of dust having settled on its bodywork. The dog had just got wise to his presence and was now in the process of welcoming him to the neighbourhood with a tirade of ferocious barks. Stone kept his voice low as he talked to the animal, the process a twofold balancing act; first he had to show that he was not afraid, and then he had to show that he was not a threat. After a few minutes of gentle persuasion the barks subsided to a series of soft whimpers.

'Good dog,' he muttered, before turning his attention back to the funeral home. Fernwood Chapel was thirty yards up from him on the other side of the street. He'd watched as the white man from his peyote vision had entered the premises about twenty minutes earlier accompanied by a pretty Latino girl. Since then he'd been waiting patiently for them to re-emerge, but when two beat-up cars came screeching to a stop outside the funeral home, he knew that the time to act had come.

Doors were flung open and a total of eight Latino men leapt out, each of them brandishing an automatic weapon. They were all dressed the same—long khaki shorts, sleeveless white shirts, blue bandanas knotted around their forearms—except for one guy who wore his bandana on his head, and it was this guy that yelled out, 'La Raza!' then stepped forward to throw open the doors of Fernwood Chapel. Within seconds the sound of automatic gunfire was ricocheting around the neighbourhood. Stone was halfway across the street by the time the last of the invaders had disappeared inside the building, and he was already formulating a plan. Going in after them was out of the question, as his hunting knife wasn't much of a match for all those guns, so he'd come up with something else.

He tore off his checked shirt, twisted it up until it was a length of solid fabric, then ran to the nearest of the beat-up cars and unscrewed the old-style gas cap. Once he'd lowered one end of the fabric inside, he yanked a cheap plastic lighter from his jeans, summoned a spark, then set the flame to the shirt's trailing end, which smouldered for a few seconds before catching fire. With his plan now in motion, he turned tail and ran for cover as his makeshift fuse began to burn down, confident that he'd soon have the invaders' undivided attention.

When the chilling sound of gunfire penetrated the room, everyone froze for a moment, everyone that is bar Hunter, who was first out of his seat with Beretta already drawn.

'This way!' he urged, as he half dragged Angel to her feet and bundled her away from the aisle towards the far end of the row. On the left-hand side of the room, where Lunatic's relatives were sitting, panic broke out as people began to scream and look for an exit, but over on the right-hand side the response was somewhat different. Nothing galvanised gangbangers quicker than the prospect of imminent attack, and each of them was in the process of reaching for a concealed weapon when the double doors leading to the reception hall were thrown wide open.

'Get down!' yelled Hunter, as he stepped in front of Angel and drove her to the floor. Four simultaneous bursts of gunfire sprang from the mouths of the Viper

Uzis that now poked through the entrance to obliterate everything in their path. The first to die were the gang-bangers on the far side of the aisle—the closest any of them got to returning fire was one forlorn pistol shot that sailed high into the ceiling overhead. The second burst ploughed right into the mass of bodies that was Lunatic's family—those relations that still had their wits about them had responded to Hunter's warning and hit the deck, leaving the rest to undertake a mass dance of death, their bodies jerking spasmodically as the bullets tugged at their flesh until they finally fell to the floor.

'Stay still,' breathed Hunter into Angel's ear, taking his weight on his elbows and shielding her from danger. He worked his right hand around until his gun was angled back along the row of seats, then waited for the attackers to make their next move.

'Go grab that dead cocksucka!' yelled a voice from the rear.

Hunter watched on as four pairs of feet sprinted down the aisle towards Lunatic's casket. As they lifted the stainless-steel box that held the gangbanger's corpse from the table, Angel bucked and squirmed beneath him, and he only just managed to clamp his left hand across her mouth in time to stifle her cry. Once the Vipers had departed with their grisly trophy, he sprang to his feet and checked out the carnage. The whole place was pockmarked with bullet holes and drenched in blood, and people lay dead or dying all around. As he stood there, Angel hurried over to where her gang associates lay on the far side of the room. She bent down and rummaged amongst the bodies for a moment, then made a break for the exit.

'Angel! No!' he yelled, setting off in pursuit. She made it as far as the funeral home's front door before he grabbed her from behind and yanked her away from the opening. 'What the hell are you doing?'

'That's my man they got out there!' she yelled, as she struggled in his arms. 'Let me go!'

Another burst of gunfire sent them both diving for cover, only to realise that the bullets weren't meant for them. With one hand firmly locked around Angel, Hunter leant forward and looked outside. The scene that greeted him was surreal. The Vipers had propped up Lunatic's casket against the hood of one of their cars and were taking it in turns to rake gunfire up and down the corpse.

'What the fuck are they doing?' he asked incredulously.

'They're killing him over again—it's a sign of disrespect to me, my man and my crew,' Angel replied, her voice cold as ice. 'They're gonna pay for this.'

She started to struggle in his arms once again, but her efforts were cut short when the car that the casket was resting against erupted in a massive fireball. Nanoseconds later, the fuel tank of an adjacent vehicle ignited and the twin explosions merged into one. The percussive blast knocked Angel and Hunter off their feet, leaving them in the perfect position to watch Lunatic's casket ascend into the stratosphere.

Hunter picked himself up, helped Angel to her feet, and dusted her off. When he asked if she was okay he received a brisk nod in response, but her eyes were wide and staring and her body shook uncontrollably. He took off his jacket and wrapped it around her.

'We've gotta get moving, the authorities will be here soon,' he said quietly, giving her a nudge. 'Try not to look.'

The two of them stumbled away from the funeral home towards the site of the blast. Onlookers were already starting to gather, drawn to the carnage like buzzards to roadkill, not that there was a whole lot left to see. The two cars were little more than flaming hulks of twisted metal, and the Vipers that had arrived in them hadn't fared much better. Those bodies that were furthest from the epicentre of the blast were still pretty much in one piece, but they were burnt beyond all recognition and a foul stench emanated from their smouldering carcases. Those closer to the explosion had been partially vaporised, leaving just random body parts for their families to bury—a forearm, a chunk of torso, a foot still encased in a sneaker.

'Larry,' choked Angel, as she saw where Lunatic's coffin had landed further down the street, exploding on impact to spread its contents all over the asphalt. As she stepped towards it, a powerful motorbike roared to life. Hunter looked left to see the bare-chested Indian emerge from an alley bestride his colossal machine.

'There's no time, Angel, we've gotta leave. Quick—this way,' he said, leading her towards the alley. Given the way the Indian had lit out after the courtyard episode, Hunter half expected him to disappear over the horizon, but this time he seemed content to sit in the saddle with engine idling.

'Isn't that the guy who attacked you?' asked a confused Angel.

'Yeah. You'd better let me do the talking. He isn't the most trusting of individuals.'

Angel nodded in response.

'I take it that was your work?' asked Hunter once he was in range, noting that the Indian's torso was a wall of solid muscle. No wonder he'd been such a handful in a fist fight.

'You're welcome. Consider my debt to you paid.'

'I'm Hunter.'

'Stone,' said the Indian.

'Why'd you run off after I'd helped you escape from the courtyard?'

'Two reasons—first, I didn't trust you and, second, I'd left my bike at the other end of the alley.'

'But you trust me now?'

'Let's just say I've had time to think things through. You saved my hide from the Knights, so you must have had a good reason.'

'Damn straight. But I don't think this is the time to go into it,' Hunter said, as the wail of sirens began to swell in the distance. 'We need a place to lie low. We can't go back to Angel's as the cops will be all over it after what just happened here, and we can't afford to waste time holed up in an interview room. We could go to mine, but that's way across town. Any ideas?'

'Follow me.'

CHAPTER FORTY

STONE bent down to pick up a large chunk of rock, before manoeuvring his bike into the freight elevator. Hunter gave him a quizzical look, gestured for Angel to follow, then squeezed in behind her. The two of them had tracked the Indian to the industrial neighbourhood of Vernon, trailing his motorbike as it weaved through the warehouses, factories and food-processing plants that dominated the area, to end up at a six-storey brick-work structure. Stone had explained that he lived on the vacant top floor, employed as a security guard for the garment-manufacturing company that was resident throughout the rest of the building, and Hunter was more than happy to use the place as a bolthole. They wouldn't be here long anyhow—with Angel due to carry out her hit on Venom tomorrow, the game clock was winding down fast.

'By the way,' muttered Stone, 'there's a couple of friends of mine waiting for us up top.'

'What?'

'Don't worry—they won't say a word to anyone,' Stone said with a half-smile as the elevator clanked to a stop. When he pulled back the door two massive dogs bounded over from the far side of the room, one pinto, the other white, their initial joy at the return of their master rapidly morphing into suspicion of the new-comers that accompanied him. Angel took a step back-wards as the hackles on their necks rose as one and their lips curled upwards in two matching snarls.

'Caleb, Joshua—at ease,' commanded Stone, as he placed the rock on the floor.

All of the aggression went out of their bodies in an instant, and Hunter offered his hand to the nearest one and allowed him to take his scent.

'Magnificent animals,' he muttered, petting the pinto's muzzle. 'Which one's which?'

'That's Caleb, the other's Joshua. Can I get anyone a drink?'

'A beer if you've got one,' said Hunter.

'I only have water,' Stone replied, as he bent down and opened the small refrigerator by the wall.

'That'll be fine.'

Hunter accepted the two bottles of Evian with a nod of thanks, his eyes straying to the far wall where a large collection of photos, notes and hand-drawn maps covered the brickwork. Stone's reconnaissance work. Impressive. He passed one of the bottles to Angel and was pleased to see that she now had some of her old spark back in her eyes.

'You don't go in much for furniture, do you?' she asked.

'I have all that I need. Please—take a seat,' he replied, gesturing to the cot by the west wall. 'To business. I owe you my thanks for interceding at the courtyard—that was some rescue. But why did you help me? I thought you were one of them.'

'Me? Involved with the gangs? No way. The Knights have kidnapped Angel's little girl, Gracie. I've infiltrated them to find out where they're holding her.'

'Infiltrated them?'

'One of their lieutenants thinks I've got drugs for sale at a knockdown price. He's cutting the rest of his crew out of the deal, and he's using me to dig himself out of some kind of hole. The last task he gave me was to kill you.'

'But you didn't.'

'No—when I heard about your attacks on the gang, I figured that you had to have carried out a whole load of reconnaissance work, so I was hoping you might have seen Gracie.'

'Why was she taken?'

'To force Angel to take out the boss of another Latino gang. I'm not sure why a black gang based in South Central is so keen to meddle in EastLos street politics, but one thing's for sure—they've stirred up a whole heap of trouble.'

'What does your daughter look like?' Stone asked, turning to Angel.

'She's six years old, real cute, with short brown hair that's cut in a bob. Here—take a look.'

Angel dug a photo out of her handbag and offered it to Stone. The anxiety on her face was plain to see as she waited for him to peruse it, and Hunter felt his own nerves begin to jangle. This might turn out to be their last chance to find Gracie. Everything could rest on whether the Indian had crossed paths with her while he'd carried out his program of systematic attacks on the gang.

'I'm sorry. I haven't seen her,' said Stone, returning the photo.

'What about any *sign* of her?' Hunter cut in. 'Anywhere that might have looked like it was being used as a safe house? Maybe the boss's pad? Most likely, he's keeping her close at hand.'

Stone balled his hands into fists before he answered.

'The boss goes by the name of Dreadnought. And, trust me, if I knew where he was I would have paid him a visit already.'

'Dreadnought, huh? It's little wonder that Cassius was so keen to keep you away from him—you look like you're ready to tear the guy limb from limb.'

'And then some. I've been hunting him for weeks but no one seems to know where he is. All I've heard is that he might be holed up at some bakery…'

Hunter's brain kicked into a higher gear. A bakery? Now, why was that causing alarm bells to go off?

'That's it!' he yelled, turning to Angel. 'After I helped Cassius steal the RV, I tailed him and watched him hand it over to two men. One of them threatened to put in a call to some bakery when Cassius pissed him off, and then the gangbanger damn near shit his pants. Stone's intel is right—Dreadnought's holed up at a bakery—so maybe Gracie's stashed there too?'

'You think?' asked Angel, her face lighting up with hope.

'It stands to reason that he'd keep her close at hand—Gracie's his ace in the hole. That weasel Cassius has known where his boss has been hiding out all along. All we've got to do is force him to tell us where it is. But there's one thing I still don't get,' said Hunter, turning to Stone. 'What's your interest in all of this? And why should we trust you?'

The Indian returned his stare for a few seconds, took a deep breath, then told his story.

'My people live on the San Carlos Reservation in Arizona, in the shadow of Mount Graham, the sacred home of the Gan, the mountain spirits that guard the Apache against sickness and danger,' Stone began in a low voice. 'It all started when my nephew came to stay with me last year. His name was Daniel, he was fourteen years old, and it was the first time he'd been off the reservation for any length of time. He'd run into some trouble at home, some of the other kids had been ragging on him pretty hard, and his parents decided he needed toughening up, so they sent him to stay with me. Back then, I had a small apartment in Watts, and I was working as a nightclub bouncer and struggling to make ends meet. Daniel's parents were aware of that, but what they didn't know was that I also had a problem with whisky. Three days after he arrived I had a run-in with the boss and lost my job, then things went from bad to worse. I should have sent Daniel home, but my pride got in the way. I'd been entrusted with helping in the boy's education, and if I'd sent him straight back my tribe would have looked upon me as a failure. So I let him stay. Then money got tighter. And I started to drink more…then one day we got into a fight…'

* * *

Stone drained the last dregs of whisky from the bottle, tossed it to one side, then broke the seal on another. He was slouched on his moth-ridden couch with a torn envelope lying on his lap, having just read the message it contained. Although the words had swum in and out of focus before his inebriated eyes, he'd still managed to get the gist. The owner of the apartment wanted him out by the weekend. He was two months behind on the rent, and that put him in breach of the lease. It never fucking rained…

He took a major league hit from the fresh bottle, gulping down the firewater until everything went soft round the edges once again, then he stared at the small TV that sat on a packing crate in the corner of the room. It was tuned to a local news channel, and his eyelids grew heavy as the pretty Asian news anchor's voice began to wash over him like a soft breeze. When his nephew, Daniel, entered the room, he awoke from his slumber just in time to feel a pleasant warm feeling spread through his crotch.

'Hey,' he slurred, his face lighting up in surprise when he realised that he still had the bottle in his grasp. He raised it to his mouth and failed to see the look of despair that crossed Daniel's face.

'Hey, yourself.'

'Where are you going?'

'Out.'

'Out where?'

'Just out.'

'I'm your guardian—answer the question,' he said turning to look at the boy. Daniel was wearing a pair of faded blue Levis and a Lost Prophets T-shirt. A small Adidas backpack dangled from his right hand.

'Some guardian—you're so drunk you can't even be bothered to get up to go the bathroom,' said the kid, gesturing at Stone's crotch with distaste.

Both the words and the look should have been a reality check for Stone, and they would have been had he been halfway sober, but in his current state all they did was rile him up some more.

'You're not going anywhere!' he yelled, rising to his feet to stagger across the room. He caught up with Daniel when he was halfway out the door and grabbed the trailing end of his backpack to stop his forward progress. The backpack fell open and a plastic baggie tumbled out to land on the threadbare carpet. The baggie was full of small vials.

'What the hell?' roared Stone, wrestling the backpack away from his nephew and looking inside. 'Drugs? You bring drugs into my house? What are you? Some kind of dealer?'

'One of us has gotta earn some money! I've seen the letters from the landlord—pretty soon we're going to be out on the street, and then I'll get sent back to the res. And what are you doing about it? Nothing! You spend all day drunk on the sofa.'

Before he could stop himself, Stone went to slap Daniel with an open hand, but he missed by some distance, overbalanced, and fell to the floor.

'It's a one-time thing,' said Daniel, his voice cracking. 'I got talking to this guy who hangs around at school, and he said if I sold some stuff I could make a quick buck. I was only trying to help…'

'Help? By dealing that junk to your friends?' slurred Stone from down on his knees.

'Friends? I haven't got any friends…not here…not anywhere…'

'There's no way in hell that you're selling this stuff.'

'But I've got to—the guy runs with the Knights. I can't just tell him I changed my mind…'

'I need a drink,' said Stone, heading back to the couch with the backpack still clasped in one hand.

As he sank into the couch and reached for his whisky, he failed to observe his nephew bend down and retrieve the baggie of vials that had fallen out when the two of them had first clashed by the doorway.

'Go hide from your problems in that bottle,' Daniel whispered as he slunk out of the apartment with tears streaming down his face. 'And maybe I'll find some way to hide from mine.'

When he was safely out of view Daniel crammed the baggie down the front of his jeans and set off for the stairwell, leaving his uncle and his alcoholic demons behind for the last time.

When Stone came to a few hours later, he found that Daniel was gone, his second bottle of whisky of the day was half-empty, and the Asian news anchor on the TV was squawking with excitement. He rubbed at his eyes and groaned as he felt a familiar headache begin to build in the centre of his forehead.

'Keep it down, woman,' he muttered, as he looked around for the remote.

'And we're now able to cut live to the source of the tragedy where our roving reporter Tom Childs can bring us up to date. Tom? Have you got any more information about the terrible events that have occurred at Acorn Elementary School today?'

The mention of Acorn Elementary scythed through Stone's alcohol-induced haze. He looked up as the station cut away from the talking head in the studio to go to a live feed. A middle-aged man with a luxuriant ginger beard stood before the camera, a microphone pressed to his lips, a downbeat look on his face.

'The police have yet to make an official statement, Suzie, but I did manage to grab a few seconds with one of the paramedics who confirmed that a total of five children have died here today and a further two are in a critical condition.' The reporter paused for a moment, allowing the camera to pan away and grab a lingering shot of a stretcher being loaded into the rear of an ambulance. 'While he was unable to provide an official cause of death, he did tell me that the two children currently fighting for their lives both share similar symptoms, namely that they're racked with violent convulsions, and they're having great difficulty breathing, symptoms that are consistent with strychnine poisoning. The question of how seven inner-city school children gained access to such a dangerous chemical as strychnine remains unanswered at this time.'

Stone felt the panic begin to build up inside him like an onrushing tsunami. When his telephone rang a moment later, he reached for it with shaking hands. The female voice on the other end of the line informed him she was with the LAPD and that she was afraid she had some terrible news. An icy numbness washed over him as he listened to a complete stranger tell him that his nephew was dead, then he raised the bottle of whisky above his head and hurled it against the far wall where it smashed into a thousand pieces.

'Jesus,' said Hunter. 'I can see why you don't keep beer in the fridge any more.'

'I've been sober ever since,' replied Stone, his gaze falling to the floor.

'That's terrible,' said Angel. 'But how do the Knights fit into your story?'

Stone stared at the floor and kept silent, showing no sign that he'd even heard Angel's question. Sensing their master's distress, Caleb and Joshua began to whine and nuzzle his arm.

'Because the dope that Stone's nephew got from the Knights was cut with strychnine,' said Hunter. 'I'm guessing he sold it to the other kids then took some himself, maybe to prove it was legit, maybe because of peer pressure…'

'Or maybe because of the fight he had with me,' rumbled Stone.

'You can't know that for sure.'

'I don't have to. It's all my fault. I was a drunk, my life was coming apart at the seams, and I wasn't there for him when he needed me. I thought I'd confiscated all the drugs, but I must have missed some—and given the state I was in, that's hardly surprising. I gave up alcohol that very day, got myself straight, reconnected with my heritage, then dedicated myself to seeking justice under blood law.'

'Blood law?' asked Angel.

'When someone has carried out a grievous offence against an Apache tribe, that tribe seeks redress through killing those that have wronged them.'

'An eye for an eye?' asked Hunter.

'Precisely. I shall never rest until the man that supplied the drugs to my nephew has been punished. This is why I seek Dreadnought. As the boss of the Knights it is he that must answer for their actions. My quest is all I have left. My tribe has disowned me. I wasn't even allowed to attend Daniel's funeral. Only by succeeding in my mission will I begin to atone for my sins, and then, and only then, might I be allowed to make a pilgrimage to his grave, where I shall ask his spirit for forgiveness.'

'What did you do with the rest of the drugs?' asked Hunter.

'I still have them—when I catch up with Dreadnought, I plan to feed them to him one by one, so that he might suffer the same fate as the one he forced on Daniel and the six other children.'

'Amen to that,' said Angel.

'So we've been on a parallel course for the last few days—you want to find Dreadnought to tear him a new one, while we want to find him as he's got Angel's daughter.'

'And the key to tracking down Dreadnought is…' began Stone.

'That fucking clown Cassius,' finished Hunter. 'He's the boss's right-hand man, and he sure as shit knows something about this bakery you mentioned.'

'So how do we find him?' asked Angel.

'Finding him isn't the issue, it's what's waiting for us when we get there that might prove more problematic.'

'Explain,' said Stone.

'I'm meeting him in about an hour's time—we set it up yesterday, it's when our drug deal's meant to go down—but I haven't heard from him since I helped you escape from the courtyard. He got a pretty good look at me while I was running up the stairwell, and even though I was wearing my best hobo duds, I'm worried he might have recognised me.'

'So the meeting this afternoon might turn out to be a trap?'

'Yeah—if he even shows. Either way he'll expect me to come alone, so if I've got you as back-up we might still have the advantage of surprise. How about it? You want to team up?'

Stone retrieved the rock he'd brought in from the back lot and placed it between himself and Hunter.

'Our treaty is made by this rock, and it shall last until the rock crumbles to dust, thus as we make our treaty, we bind each other with an oath.'

Hunter took the Indian's hand and shook it firmly.

CHAPTER FORTY-ONE

THE boarded up windows meant that natural light was at a premium inside the flophouse. Hunter squinted against the gloom and checked his watch to find that Cassius was a half hour late. He popped the muscles in his neck and glanced down at the backpack that lay by his feet. He'd been waiting there for almost two hours now, having arrived early to ensure that the gangbanger wouldn't get the drop on him. The place was just as rundown and inhospitable as he remembered, and the kitchen at the rear still stank of piss, but it wasn't the surroundings that were making him nervous, it was the growing realisation that the end game was almost at hand.

Angel was due to carry out her hit on Venom the following day. If they couldn't find Gracie before then, the consequences didn't bear thinking about, which was why it was so damn important that they crossed paths with Cassius sooner rather than later. Getting him to reveal the whereabouts of the bakery wasn't going to be easy, and while Hunter had a couple of ideas as to how he might loosen the gangbanger's tongue, one in particular relied on him having enough time to put it into practice.

When he finally heard the sound of car tyres screeching to a stop, he hurried to the front of the house and peered through a gap in the boarded-up door, to find an El Camino parked diagonally across the sidewalk. Hunter felt a burst of relief as he realised that Cassius had arrived, but this soon turned to shock when he saw who he'd brought along as back-up. He looked on incredulously for a couple more seconds then hurried back to the room in which their meeting was due to occur. Once there, he picked up the backpack and walked over to the large hole in the dividing wall that served as a hatch to the front room. He placed the backpack under the hole, threw a glance at the large pile of dirty rags that lay on the other side, then retreated to await the new arrivals.

Another five minutes passed before he finally heard Cassius come stumbling through the rear door. Hunter sat cross-legged on the floor and placed his hands in his lap. When you were playing the role of bait it helped if you looked non-threatening.

'Who's your friend?' he asked, when Cassius appeared in the doorway, dragging a withered body behind him.

'My moms,' slurred the gangbanger, as he propped her against the doorframe.

'She doesn't look so good.'

'She be fine…just be taking her afternoon nap is all…'

Fine? From the way that her head lolled at such an unnatural angle to her body, Hunter guessed this was one snooze that Cassius's mom wouldn't be waking up from any time soon. Something was wrong. The gang-banger had brought the corpse of a recently deceased relative to their meeting, and if that wasn't a sign that he was unravelling then what was?

'Moms come to see Tom one last time,' Cassius said, gesturing towards the front room. 'You remember Tom—the smackhead I let stay here rent free for ole time's sake. Him and Moms go way back…anyhow, enough of this shit-chat. Where the hell you get to last night?'

'Yeah, sorry about that,' began Hunter, relieved to find that Cassius hadn't recognised him during Stone's rescue. 'I never made it to the courtyard. Got caught up in some trouble of my own…remember that ex-boss of mine I mentioned?'

'The chump whose wife you been bangin'?'

'That's the one. He somehow tracked me to the motel I've been holed up in, so I had to go to ground for a while.'

'Typical. Just when I needs you the most you go missing—you shoulda kept your schlong in your pants.'

'Tell me about it. So what happened?'

'Geronimo went and escaped, that's what happened. Had himself some help from a hobo. I lost three of my crew—it was a goddamn shit storm.'

'Tough break, but it could have been worse—at least your boss didn't get the chance to interrogate him.'

'True enough.'

'Anyhow…to business?'

'Yeah—show me the product.'

The gangbanger was now in a state of perpetual motion, hopping from one foot to the other as he clenched and unclenched his fists and jerked his head spastically to one side. Even in the gloom of the flophouse's interior, the whites of his eyes shone out like twin high beams. Cassius was cracked out to the max.

'Over there,' replied Hunter, gesturing to where the backpack sat in front of the hole in the dividing wall.

Cassius set off at a near sprint, his face lighting up like a kid's on Christmas morn when he checked out the backpack's contents.

'Out-fucking-standing,' he muttered, rising to his feet, failing to notice that the pile of rags on the other side of the wall had started to stir. 'How much we say?'

'How much you got?'

'Don't worry, man, I got somethun for ya…I call it my little surprise…I ain't gonna pay you a muthafuckin' dime…'

The gangbanger made a grab for the back of his pants, but before he could complete the manoeuvre, two powerful hands shot through the hole in the wall to restrain him from behind, clamping his arms to his sides in a vice-like grip before lifting him off the floor and yanking him backwards until his head slammed into the wall.

'And I've got a surprise for you too,' Hunter said as he walked over to where the dazed gangbanger lay in a crumpled heap. 'And it's a real doozy. Cassius—I'd like you to meet Stone.'

With that, he plucked the Micro Uzi from the gangbanger's pants and rolled him back over so that he could look through the hole to where the Indian stood glaring back at him. Even though high and concussed, Cassius still managed to register a look of abject terror.

'Tie him to that beam over there,' said Hunter, gesturing to one of the upright metal struts that supported the roof in Stone's industrial penthouse. They'd made the journey back from Watts with the Indian riding shotgun while Cassius went steerage, locked in the trunk. En route, Hunter had pulled in at a deserted lot where he'd disposed of the drugs he'd stolen from the Latino dealer, first stamping on the backpack to grind the vials under- foot, then dumping it inside a trashcan and setting it aflame.

He watched on as Stone wrestled their gagged and bound captive out of the service elevator and dragged him across the floor. The gangbanger was coming down off his crack-induced high, and his eyes swelled like dinner plates at the sight of Angel.

'Where's my daughter, you piece of shit?' she shouted, as Stone began to lash him to the beam with a length of rope. She ran over and delivered a well- aimed knee to the gangbanger's crotch, prompting the air from his lungs to rush out through the gag in a hiss.

'Tell me, you cocksucker! Tell me right now!'

Once Angel had worked the gag loose the first words out of Cassius's mouth gave some indication of his mental state.

'What da fuck?'

The look on the gangbanger's face was priceless. To say that Cassius had been surprised when he'd found out that his new drug-dealing pal was actually working with Stone was an understatement, but that surprise had now morphed into incredulity at the sight of Angel. All his chickens had come home to roost on the same goddamn day, and it couldn't have happened to a nicer fuck-up.

'Tell me where she is!' yelled Angel, punctuating each word with a slap to the face, her blows drawing a pair of angry red blotches on Cassius's skin. 'Tell me now or you're fucking dead!'

'You ain't gonna kill me, bitch…not if you wanna see shorty again…'

She drew back her hand to deliver another strike, but Stone caught it at its apex and eased her away.

'I've got it from here,' he said softly, before turning his attention to Cassius. 'Trust me—this is going to hurt.'

The Indian stripped to the waist then flexed his muscles. His torso looked like something that had been carved from solid rock. Cassius's lip began to tremble as the macho display had its desired effect. The first blow exploded into the gangbanger's guts like a piston, closely followed by another, then another.

'You're going to tell me where Dreadnought's hiding out,' Stone said as his human punch bag wheezed for air. 'Or I'm going to drill a hole clean through you…'

Hunter stood back and watched as the Indian went to work, first with a hammer blow that connected just blow Cassius's heart, then with a left cross that snapped his head back to one side. The big guy certainly knew what he was doing—every punch was designed to inflict maximum damage while minimising the likelihood of unconsciousness—but all the same, Hunter didn't expect it to work. Gangbangers were used to physical violence, and they were fiercely loyal to their set, so if they were going to make Cassius talk they'd probably have to get more creative, although there was no harm in softening him up a bit first.

'If your boss thinks he can get away with using kids to deal poisoned drugs…' grunted Stone.

A straight right pulverised Cassius's nose to send blood spraying out across the concrete floor.

'…then he can think again…'

A vicious left hook crashed into his ribcage with the sickening crunch of bone on bone.

'Don't know nuthin 'bout no poison drugs…' gasped Cassius as the Indian took a breather. Before Stone could resume the onslaught, Hunter decided it was time to put a halt to proceedings.

'Hold up, Stone.'

'What do you mean, hold up?' shouted Angel. 'We gotta beat on this dirtbag until he tells us what's what.'

'I think I can get him to talk.'

Angel threw up her hands in frustration and grabbed a seat on Stone's cot, where she proceeded to draw the blade of one of the Indian's knives slowly up and down the cot's metal frame. Over by the beam, Stone stepped aside and allowed Hunter to get a good look at the gangbanger's bloodied face. Beads of sweat popped on Cassius's brow, and his pupils had shrunken to little more than pinpricks. The time had come.

'You're in a whole heap of trouble here, Cass,' began Hunter. 'You've got more problems than a sex addict at a monastery. Your mom's just passed away, Stone wants to tear you limb from limb, and Angel would like nothing more than to put a bullet in your head for your part in her daughter's abduction.'

Cassius stared back at him sullenly.

'Then, of course, there's Dreadnought and the rest of your gang. What do you think they'd say if they found out that you were making money on the side with a few extra drug deals? I'm guessing they wouldn't be overly pleased.'

'Fuck you.'

'But right now you don't really care about any of that, do you? All these problems pale into insignificance when compared to your most pressing concern—just where in the hell are you gonna get your next fix?' Hunter held a handful of vials right under Cassius's nose. 'That's all you've got on your mind isn't it? It's the only thing you can think about. You've got the cocaine blues, coming down off a major league binge, and, trust me, your cravings have only just started.'

By now the gangbanger was barely listening to him, as all his attention was focussed on the vials that Hunter held in the palm of his hand, his eyes staring at them hungrily as his tongue darted rapidly over his lower lip.

'It's only going to get worse, son. Pretty soon you'll be ready to chew off your own right arm for one of these vials,' said Hunter, holding one up between thumb and forefinger and moving it slowly through the air.

'Remember how this stuff makes you feel? How the rush courses through your entire body to make all the pain and doubt disappear? Remember the intense feelings of pleasure? How you feel so goddamn alive? Well, if you want to feel like that again, all you've got to do is tell me where Dreadnought's holed up. Give me that one tiny piece of information and I'll give you enough product to keep you high till halfway into next week.'

As Cassius stared at the vial, a muscle spasmed in the side of his face.

'C'mon, son, whadya say? All you've ever wanted is right here in the palm of my hand. You've just gotta reach out and take it…course, you can always try and ride out your cravings while Stone systematically takes you apart, one broken bone at a time…'

'But I don't fuckin' know where Dread's at,' Cassius whined, his voice full of desperation.

Hunter kept his smile on the inside. Cassius hadn't come back with a flat 'Go fuck yourself'. Instead, he'd engaged in conversation. As his craving for the drug was only going to get more intense, it was just a matter of time before he cracked, and the gangbanger didn't strike him as someone who was blessed with hidden reserves of willpower.

'Don't bullshit me, Cass. I know that Dreadnought's hiding out at some bakery, just give me the address and this will all be over.'

'The bakery? That's out in Carson City. I can give you the address, but he ain't there.'

'Stone,' said Hunter, as he stepped aside and gestured for the Indian to resume the beating.

'Wait!' yelled the gangbanger. 'Fuck, I can't think straight, my head feels like it's gonna explode.'

'The bakery, Cassius,' prompted Hunter.

'Yeah, the bakery. Dread ain't there. I gotta call the place, then they call him, then he call me back. Ever since he got outta lockdown Dread's been fuckin' invisible.'

'So he's using the bakery as a relay station?'

'Yeah.'

'You're lying!' screamed Angel, racing over to jab the point of Stone's knife into the soft flesh just under Cassius's right eye.

'Easy Angel,' warned Hunter, while Stone looked on impassively.

'Where's my kid? Where's Gracie?'

'She's with D-Dread…I s-swear…' stuttered Cassius, as the blood trickled down his face.

'And where the fuck is Dread? Tell me, you cock-sucka, or I'll put your eye out, I swear to God I will…'

'*I don't fucking know!*'

'Angel—leave it. I believe him,' said Hunter.

'Shit!' yelled Angel, her shoulders slumping as she dropped the knife. 'If he doesn't know where Dreadnought is then we're sunk.'

'Not quite," said Hunter, as he reached into the gang-banger's pocket and took out his cellphone. 'Because now we know how to contact him, everything's changed.'

'Hey—what about my fix?' whined Cassius.

'The deal was that you get your fix when you give me Dreadnought, and as you've only half delivered up till now, you're gonna have to wait a little bit longer.'

A stream of curses spewed forth from the captive's mouth until Stone moved the gag back into place.

'Thanks.' Hunter nodded. 'Now to business. If Dreadnought's using the bakery as a relay station, he's got to have at least one person in there that he trusts.'

'Stands to reason,' agreed Stone.

'So all we've got to do is find out who that someone is.'

'And just how are we gonna do that?' asked Angel. 'Hang around by the counter and wait until one of the staff hands out a baggie with the carrot cake?'

'Not exactly. We're going to stake out the place while our good friend Cassius makes a phone call and asks for Dreadnought, at which point someone inside the bakery will react.'

'Then we grab that someone and force Dreadnought's location out of them,' Stone said, nodding in understanding.

'Exactly.'

'But what if he's only got a number to call—how's that going to help us?' asked Angel.

'I've still got friends at the phone companies—get me a number and I can have an address for it in under five minutes.'

'Even for cellphones?'

'Sure—all cellphones send a signal out to the cell towers to help route calls, and by monitoring the strength of that signal from a number of towers it's possible to come up with a general location.'

'How general?' asked Stone.

'If Dreadnought's using a cell, we can place him to within a few blocks, and given that as of this moment he could be anywhere in the greater LA basin, that would be one hell of a breakthrough.'

'But what if something goes wrong? My Gracie could get caught in the crossfire. And even if things pan out like you say, there's still no guarantee we'll find him in time,' argued Angel. 'Dreadnought expects me to take out the head of the Vipers at two p.m. tomorrow.'

'Don't worry—I haven't forgotten,' replied Hunter, 'And that's why we're going to move on the bakery tonight. You hear that, Cassius? This is how you complete your end of the deal. Put in a call to Dreadnought and the drugs are yours.'

The gangbanger's eyes lit up as he began grunting through his gag and nodding frantically.

'I think that's a yes,' said Hunter.

'So it's almost time,' said Stone, as he closed his eyes, took a deep breath, and raised his face skywards. 'After months on his trail, I am almost there. Soon I shall face the one they call Dreadnought and make him answer for all that he has done.'

Angel's cellphone chose that moment to buzz to life. She answered it then wandered away from the two men.

'Under the ancient oath of blood law my nephew Daniel shall be avenged,' continued Stone, 'and I will have set out on the road to redemption.'

'Yeah, and I'll be happy for you,' said Hunter quietly.

'But don't forget that this isn't all about you. There's a child's life at stake here and our first priority is to make sure she comes out of this in one piece.'

'Of course.' Stone nodded.

'So how many of the gang have you taken out?'

'All of the ones with a cross through them,' Stone replied, gesturing to the photos that were stuck on the wall. Hunter walked over for a closer look.

'You've been busy,' he said, as he took in the Indian's impressive collection of reconnaissance information. 'And I'm guessing that your talks with these guys weren't exactly congenial?'

Stone shrugged his powerful shoulders in response, then glanced at Angel, who was still on her cellphone at the far end of the room.

'And not one of them gave up Dreadnought?'

'No. They all pleaded ignorance on his whereabouts.'

'Having just seen your interview technique first hand, I reckon you got the truth out of them. So why is Dreadnought keeping such a low profile? I know gang bosses are security conscious but his behaviour is verging on the paranoid. What's got him so scared? Why did he abduct Angel's daughter in order to spark a gang war amongst the Latinos?'

'And how is it linked to the bad batch of drugs that killed my nephew?'

'That's another good question. Have you got any more photos of Cassius?'

'Check the file,' said Stone, gesturing towards a manila folder by the wall.

Hunter walked over and picked it up. The contents were divided into sections on each gang member. The one on Cassius was about halfway in. He leafed through the photos until he found what he was looking for, then he drained his bottle of water.

'Can I get another?' he asked, holding the bottle aloft.

'Sure,' said Stone, heading for the fridge. As soon as the Indian's back was turned, Hunter took four photos from the file and slipped them inside his shirt.

'Thanks,' he said, when Stone lofted an Evian in his direction. Both men went quiet as they watched Angel walk back towards them, a lit cigarette in her hand. The look on her face suggested that all was not well.

'Who was on the phone?' asked Hunter, knowing the answer before she replied.

'The kidnappers,' she said quietly. Stone looked at her thoughtfully.

'You might have just spoken to Dreadnought himself,' said Hunter. 'With Cassius out of play, I can't see him trusting this to anyone else. What did he want?'

'To give me the location for the hit. I'm to take out Venom when he's released from the USC Medical Centre at two p.m. tomorrow. I've gotta blow him away on the front steps.'

'It's not going to come to that,' said Hunter, as he walked over and wrapped an arm around her shoulder. 'We're going to find Dreadnought's lair tonight, then we're going to rescue Gracie.'

'I hope you're right…'

'She's going to be fine, Angel. I promise you,' said Hunter.

'But that's one promise you might not be able to keep,' she replied morosely, as she slipped out of Hunter's embrace and walked away.

CHAPTER FORTY-TWO

'WHERE in the hell is he?' asked Angel, craning her neck to look out of the Barracuda's rear window.

'I don't know,' responded Hunter, keeping his attention firmly focused on the storefront situated across the street. The two of them were up front in the 'Cuda, staking out the bakery that acted as Dreadnought's relay station out on the northern outskirts of Carson City. A thumping sound came from the trunk, where Cassius was gagged, tied and locked safely away.

'But what could have kept him? It's been almost twenty minutes now...'

When they'd left Stone's top-floor residence in Vernon an hour previously, the Indian and his dogs had been right behind them in a flatbed truck he'd borrowed from one of his co-workers, but somewhere towards the end of the journey he'd gone missing.

'Maybe he took a wrong turn,' said Hunter, watching as someone pulled the blinds on the bakery's two picture windows. The shadows were lengthening as the sun dipped below the eastern horizon, and soon the whole of Los Angeles would be cloaked in darkness.

The store itself looked like any number of family-run businesses that used to be dotted all over the city until the hypermarkets had moved in and undercut them—simple signage out front, window displays full of freshly baked bread and pastries, a welcome sign on the door—but what it didn't advertise was the fact that it had ties to an inner-city gang boss, and maybe that was why it was still in business.

Hunter was worried about Stone's disappearing act, but he was trying not to let it show. Angel could do without the stress. She was amped enough as it was, as she knew that tonight was probably her last real chance to get her daughter back, but he wasn't sure how much longer he could keep up his air of indifference regarding the Indian's non-arrival. After all, what did they really know about this guy beyond the fact that he'd been pursuing a personal vendetta against Dreadnought and the rest of the Imperial Knights for the last few months? Stone had his own agenda and, despite his assurances to the contrary, Hunter was worried that when push came to shove the Indian would act in his best interests and not Graciela's. He decided to wait for another five minutes.

'Can't you call him and see what's keeping him?' Angel pressed, the concern in her voice evident as she drummed her fingers on the dash.

'He doesn't carry a cell—I don't think he's too keen on modern technology. You saw where he lived—no TV, no computer, no phone, hell, even the icebox looked like something out of the 1960s. If he's not here in the next five minutes, we'll make our move without him.'

'But we can't,' she implored, her eyes wide and staring. 'We're going to need all the help we can get to rescue Gracie. God knows how many men we'll be up against.'

'We're going to be outnumbered whether Stone's with us or not. Our strength lies in the element of surprise, and every minute we sit around out here increases our risk of discovery. Sure, I'd prefer it if he were here, but if he's not, we can't let that worry us. After all, we've made it this far on our own, right?'

'I guess,' she muttered.

'Plus we can't afford to wait much longer—they're getting ready to shut up shop,' he said, gesturing to the bakery. 'And while I suspect that Dreadnought's inside man will stay on the premises overnight to facilitate a twenty-four-hour link to Cassius, I might be wrong.'

He checked his watch to find that two of the five minutes had now elapsed. As he waited for the remaining three minutes to tick by, Angel fell into an uncomfortable silence alongside him, although she continued to drum her fingers on the dash.

'C'mon—it's time to go,' he said, when the deadline had passed. What the hell was Stone playing at? He put it to the back of his mind. There was no time to worry about that now—instead he had to focus on Cassius and the switchboard operator in the bakery. He exited the car and headed for the trunk. When he opened it, the gangbanger greeted him with an imploring stare. His skin was covered in a light sheen of sweat, while the muscles in his face and arms were undergoing constant spasms, and a foul stench of stale sweat wafted upwards from his body like a burgeoning mushroom cloud.

'My God! Look at the state of him,' said Angel, turning away in disgust.

'Here's how this is going to work,' said Hunter, as he untied the gag then retrieved the gangbanger's cell-phone from his hip pocket. 'I'm going to call the bakery then hand you your phone, at which point you're going to ask for Dreadnought.'

'What number shall I leave?'

'Any number you like—it's not important. If you do this, I swear you'll get your next fix, but if you do anything else, and I mean anything, then you're going to stay locked in this trunk till you're nothing but a bag of bones. Is that clear?'

Cassius nodded.

'OK.'

Hunter punched the phone number of the bakery into the keypad and waited for someone to pick up, his heart rate accelerating. This was it. The final link in the chain. The last chance to find Gracie.

Hunter stared at the gangbanger as he waited for the call to be answered. Cassius had to be pretty uncomfortable, with his hands and feet lashed together behind his back, but that would soon seem like paradise if he tried any kind of a double cross. When a gruff voice barked 'Yo' down the other end of the line, Hunter loosened the gag and held the phone to the gangbanger's mouth.

'I gotta talk to the boss—get him to call me back on this number,' said Cassius, reeling off a string of digits before his eyes darted back to Hunter. 'It's done. Niggah be off to call Dread. You gonna let me outta here or what? I'm gettin' cramps all over…'

'That's it? Talk about the dying art of conversation.'

'Fuck conversation—gimme my fix.'

The gangbanger might have been talking tough but he couldn't hide the desperation in his tone. Hunter reached into his pocket and pulled out the crack pipe he'd confiscated earlier, along with a vial he'd been keeping safe for the occasion. Facilitating another man's drug habit wasn't something that was usually on his to-do list, but the gangbanger had been through enough for now and the trunk of the 'Cuda was no place to go cold turkey. Besides, if Cassius was high then he might behave himself for the next fifteen minutes or so.

'Angel—keep an eye on the bakery,' Hunter directed, before turning his attention to the gangbanger. 'I'm going to untie your hands so you can do what you gotta do. Just don't try anything.'

'All right, man, I be cool, I swear…'

Hunter untied the gangbanger's hands and stepped back, eager to put some distance between himself and the fetid creature before him. As he watched on, Cassius manoeuvred his aching appendages around to the front and started to work some life into them. As soon as his fingers showed signs of being able to function, he was cupping his hands out like a beggar asking for alms. Hunter tossed him the vial and watched as he set about preparing his fix. When the first cocaine hydrochloride fumes rose into his nostrils a look of relief shone out from his face.

'Hunter—we got movement,' called out Angel.

'Lights out,' he said, as he pushed Cassius down and

closed the trunk. When he looked across to the bakery he saw that an almost spherical black man was standing in the entrance, trying to light a smoke.

'Stay here and make sure he stays quiet,' Hunter said. 'That's gotta be our guy.'

'Be careful,' Angel replied, laying her hand against his cheek. 'I can't lose you as well.'

His heart pounded against his ribcage as they held eye contact. Thoughts of a shared future flitted across his mind, then he banished them and got his head back in the game. The next half-hour was all about Gracie—everything else would have to wait. He broke away and crossed the road, his gun held low behind his back. Up ahead, Dreadnought's switchboard operator was now waddling down the street, presumably in search of the nearest payphone. Hunter increased his pace and began to close the distance, regulating his breathing as he strode forward in order to ready himself for confrontation. With any luck, this would go down quick and easy. He had the element of surprise and his target was way out of shape. When the distance between them was down to forty feet, the black guy made a slow turn, like an oil tanker at sea, to detour down an alley.

Hunter broke into a light jog. This was the perfect opportunity to take Dreadnought's man down in a more private location. When he came to the head of the alley he paused and ducked his head quickly around the corner. The fat guy was twenty yards ahead and still oblivious to the fact he was being tailed. Hunter loosed the safety on his gun and set off in pursuit. When he was five yards behind him he made his move.

'Hold it right there and keep your hands where I can see them!'

The fat guy froze on the spot then raised his hands high above his head.

'Now turn around nice and slow—you and me are going to have a little talk.'

The big guy shuffled his blubber-filled carcass around to reveal that he was sporting a wide grin.

'What's so funny, Shamu? You've got one minute to give me Dreadnought's phone number otherwise I go Ahab on your ass…'

'You ain't huntin' nuthin', boy,' he said loudly.

'Oh, yeah? Why's that?'

'Coz you got enough guns trained on you right now to blow you halfway into next week…'

Hunter looked deeper into the alley then risked a quick glance behind him to confirm that the two of them were alone.

'What the hell are you talking about? Just because you're the size of five men doesn't mean you're not alone.'

The big guy looked heavenwards. Hunter followed his gaze to find that four semi-automatics were trained on him from a second-floor window.

'I hear you've been looking for me,' called down a large shaven-headed figure from above. 'The name's Dreadnought. Move one fucking muscle and you're dead.'

Hunter weighed up his options and realised he was fresh out. Shamu had led him into a kill zone. He dropped his Beretta and raised his hands. How in the hell had Dreadnought known he was coming? Stone.

The Indian must have sold him out. But why? He wanted to bring down the gang as much as Angel. At least she was still safe. But what would she do when he failed to return? He hoped she'd have the sense to realise that something had gone wrong and hightail it the hell out of there.

'Keep him covered,' shouted Dreadnought. 'I'll be right down.'

The big guy pulled a Colt from his sweat pants and trained it at Hunter. The two of them stood facing each other in silence until a side door in the building burst open to allow Dreadnought and his men to emerge. The gang boss walked over to Hunter and eyeballed him up close. He was a bull of a man, three hundred pounds of pure muscle, wearing an expensive suit that somehow managed to look good on his oversized frame. His head was shaved to the bone, and he had a diamond stud in his right ear, plus three tattooed tears under his right eye.

'I don't suppose there's any chance those tears reflect your sympathy for my predicament?' asked Hunter.

'Nope. They're for the three punks I killed back when I was in the belly of the beast. But if anyone asks, I never met 'em,' he said with a conspiratorial wink. 'Enough of this small talk—where's your buffalo-hunting, peace-pipe-smoking, totem-pole-dancing, tomahawk-throwing inbreed of a sidekick?'

As Hunter went to answer he saw a slight burst of movement at the head of the alley. He dropped his gaze to the ground as if his spirit was broken, then glanced slowly upwards to stare off into the distance. Angel. There she was peeking around the corner, her chestnut-brown hair hanging down over one side of her face. He willed her to leave, to run and never look back, but instead she took a step forward, then another, then another, until she was walking right towards him. What the fuck was she doing? Couldn't she see that the bakery had been a trap?

'Where the hell's Gracie?' she asked, marching right up to Dreadnought to jab him in the back. 'I kept my side of the bargain, now you gotta hand over my daughter.'

Hunter's jaw fell open. He couldn't believe what he was hearing. It had been Angel who'd sold him out. She must have cut some sort of deal with the gang boss in order to facilitate the safe return of her daughter. After all they'd been through. After all he'd done for her. He'd put his life on the line for her time and again these past few days so that she might be reunited with Gracie, and this was the way she repaid him? Selling him out at the first opportunity she got? He snapped his jaw shut and swallowed hard. Just moments ago he'd been thinking about making a go of it with her. Giving her another chance to get out of the gangs. Giving her a chance to give Gracie a brighter future. Talk about being played for a sucker. His blood began to boil, but he did his best to hide his inner turmoil. This was no time to show weakness, not when Dreadnought held all the aces.

'I ain't gotta hand over shit,' rumbled the gang boss, pushing Angel away with hands that looked like they could crack walnuts. 'You promised me the red man and he ain't here.'

'But I got you Hunter plus your weasel Cassius is back there in the trunk—surely that's enough?' she pleaded.

'Angel, what the hell are you doing?' cried Hunter.

'Shut the fuck up—she got you so pussy-whipped you don't know which way is up,' barked the gang boss, before turning back to Angel. 'What you brought to the table ain't enough. This guy don't mean shit to me, and I'd have taken care of Cassius in my own sweet time anyhow. It's the Indian you was meant to deliver, and you failed.'

'But what if I—?'

'What if you what? You ain't got nothing left to offer me, apart from the obvious,' he said, running a lecherous glare up and down her body. 'A word of advice—don't play all your cards up front otherwise you'll end up sucking hind tit for the rest of your life. I should have known not to deal with a goddamn spic. I'd be running my 'hood from the comfort of my own home if it weren't for you and the Mexican Mafia.'

'But I'm done with all that, I already told you…all I want is my daughter back.'

'Well, what you want and what you're gonna get are two different things,' said Dreadnought, turning to one of his henchmen. 'Cyclops—have her show you where Cassius is then stick them all in the back of the van. One way or another they're going to tell us what they know about the Indian.'

Hunter looked straight at Angel but she refused to

meet his gaze. A solitary tear trickled down her face as the one-eyed brute called Cyclops went to lead her away. On one level his heart went out to her and on another he was as angry as he'd ever been. She'd ripped out his heart and stomped all over it. He'd trusted her—she'd double-crossed him. She'd let him walk straight into a trap. Angel had gambled everything to get her daughter back and she'd come up short, and it looked like her decision to betray him would cost them all dearly.

CHAPTER FORTY-THREE

'YOU guys sure like to travel in style,' said Hunter, as
the van careered around another corner to slam its
human cargo against the metallic walls of the back.
Cyclops, the gangbanger that had been tasked to guard
them en route, just stared back with his one unblinking
eye, seemingly oblivious to his prisoner's rapier-like
wit.

'How about you? You're awful quiet,' Hunter said to
Angel, who was sitting on the floor alongside him.
'Shame you couldn't manage that earlier.'

She stared straight ahead and refused to acknowledge him, having slipped into a near catatonic state
since being taken captive. Despite everything, Hunter
was still worried about her—having risked all and made
a deal with the devil, she'd realised too late that the deck
was stacked against her, and now that the prospect of
being reunited with her daughter was further away than
ever, she was perilously close to breaking point. While
he could understand why she'd felt compelled to take
the steps that she had, her betrayal had still cut him to
the bone, but he couldn't waste time thinking about that

now, because surviving the night was going to require all his ingenuity plus a large dose of luck.

'Jeez—it's like a morgue in here. C'mon, Cassius, you're usually the life and soul. Why don't you do that impression of Dreadnought again—you know, the one where he's got his fat ass jammed in a doorway. Man, that one always kills me…'

Hunter was pleased to see Cyclops's eye narrow. If he and Angel were to have any chance, the first thing he had to do was sow some discord amongst Dreadnought's men. Maybe an opportunity to escape would present itself if they were busy fighting among themselves. For his part, Cassius continued to shiver and shake on the other side of the van. In line with the other captives, his hands were secured with plastic restraints, but that was where the similarities ended. The drug-addicted gangbanger was curled up in a fetal ball and drenched in sweat, his body racked with spasms as he suffered through the cravings once again.

The journey thus far had been short and Hunter had been trying to keep track of where they were headed, but he'd soon lost all sense of direction, not that it really mattered. Both his and Angel's cellphones had been confiscated before they'd got into the van so, with no means of calling in the cavalry, a list of directions was pretty superfluous. When the van lurched to a stop, everyone bar Cyclops shifted a few inches across the sheet-metal floor. Hunter flexed his wrists against his restraints but there was no give in them. The rear doors were yanked open, then the one-eyed mute began to throw them out into the moonlight. Cassius went down

like a sack of shit in the gutter, Hunter landed face first
to his left, then Angel landed on top of him a moment
later. As Dreadnought's crew encircled them, Hunter
took in his surroundings. The residential area that he
found himself in was rundown and shabby. A couple of
the streetlights blinked on and off, while most of the
available wall space was covered in graffiti. The buildings themselves were old-style apartment blocks—
square in design, three storeys high, and fashioned from
cinderblock. All but one had lights shining out from
their windows, and it was to this shadowy structure
that Dreadnought now gestured.

'Get them inside and make it quick,' he barked at his
men, who proceeded to hoist the three prisoners to their
feet and shove them down a path towards a dark
concrete passage.

'Take it easy back there,' Hunter muttered to the guy
who was shoving him from behind, but that just seemed
to encourage him more. He emerged into a courtyard
to find an oval-shaped fountain straight ahead and two
external stairwells on either side. The fountain was
clogged with leaves, while the render on the stairwells
was crumbling away in large chunks.

'Bring 'em up,' said Dreadnought, leading the way to
the stairwell on the left. With their hands tied behind their
backs the ascent wasn't easy, and by the time they'd made
it to the top both Hunter and Angel had stumbled on more
than one occasion, while Cassius ended up having to be
dragged after his legs gave out on the second flight.

'Line 'em up,' said Dreadnought, gesturing to the
side wall that overlooked the courtyard. Cyclops

dumped Cassius on the floor as directed, then placed Hunter and Angel alongside him. 'And someone go fetch me some sheets.'

'Up past your bedtime?' asked Hunter, 'coz, trust me, you could use some more beauty sleep.'

'You've got a smart mouth—let's see how funny you are later when I'm torturing you for information on your scalp-collecting partner,' responded Dreadnought. 'I'll get to you soon enough, but for now I wanna concentrate on this piece of shit right here.'

The gang boss swung one of his Timberlands and kicked Cassius in the ribs to elicit a grunt of pain, which was swiftly followed by a sobbing litany of woes.

'Why you done play me like this, Dread? Ain't I always done what's best for the 'hood? Knights always came first with me, Knights is my family, and you my brother, yet y'all got me tied up like some dog, and now you're putting the stomp on? Why, Dread? What I done to deserve this?'

'Look at the state of you! What did I tell you about using? You're a smoked-out mess. It's no wonder you've been fucking things up. If you'd have been straight, we'd have had the Indian by now, and half my crew wouldn't be on injured reserve. Because of you, our security's been compromised and sales are down.'

'Security? How the fuck's security been compromised when you be hiding up here like some punk?' responded Cassius, suddenly remembering where his balls were. 'And as for sales, is that all you care about these days? I remember when the 'hood was all that mattered, but you ain't even set foot there since you been on the outs. I ain't no traitor to the Knights, you are! You only in it for the money and the power.'

Dreadnought silenced Cassius's tirade with another boot to the torso. Hunter glanced around the rest of the crew to note the hungry looks on their faces. The pack was feasting on one of their own.

'I'm sorry, Dread, I din't mean it,' whined Cassius, doing a complete one-eighty. 'You know I got your back, I always have. An I'm sorry 'bout the whole Geronimo thing…I never knew the kid had a brother…'

'What fucking kid? What the hell are you talking about?'

'I dunno, Dread, my head hurts so much… If I could just get a fix, just to straighten me out…'

Dreadnought nodded to one of his lackeys who reached into his pocket, withdrew a small bag of blow, then cut up a line on the concrete walkway.

'Try that,' said the gang boss.

Cassius slithered over to the cocaine and used his nostrils to suck it up like a vacuum, then a loud sigh escaped his lips and a sated expression fell over his face.

'Now start talking. Who's this kid you were talking about?'

'Li'l Indian kid…run up on me at school…wanted to earn some dough…how was I s'posed to know that shorty had a psycho big brother,' said Cassius, the buzz from the coke seemingly having convinced him that he could talk his way out of trouble. 'It weren't my fault, D, it weren't my fuckin' fault…'

'Okay—you went after the lunchbox market, and

the Indian got pissed 'cause you had his kith and kin selling drugs,' said Dreadnought, somehow keeping a lid on his fury, 'but that doesn't explain why he's come after us so hard.'

'Coz the drugs I gave him to sell were bad, D, suppliers done fucked up the mix. Shorty ended up dead along with a bunch of his classmates…'

Cassius was spouting his story as if he was glad to finally get it off his chest, as if in telling the sorry tale he'd somehow make good on his past mistakes, but Hunter had no idea what he was hoping to achieve. If the banger thought his boss was going to throw open his arms and welcome him back to the fold then he was in for one hell of a rude awakening. Dreadnought didn't look like the forgiving type.

'And let me guess—you got these bad drugs from one of your side deals that Angel told me about?' asked Dreadnought, the veins in his forehead standing proud.

'Niggah just trying to make a li'l extra money, D, you know how it is…'

'A little extra money? So for a few bucks you managed to get some psychotic Indian on our case? You're the whole damn reason that half my crew's been taken out? What the fuck's happened to you? You used to be solid. Your crack pipe's fucked you like the class tramp on prom night.'

'I can get straight, D, I swear I can, then everything'll be cool…you just gotta give me a chance…' Cassius pleaded.

'You've had all the chances I'm gonna give you,' said Dreadnought, his expression hardening. 'You've fucked yourself, your crew and your 'hood, you've left me no other option. Cyclops, tie those sheets together.'

'I swear I can make this right, D…'

Dreadnought took hold of the knotted bed sheets and secured an end to one of the concrete columns that supported the roof of the walkway, then walked over to where Cassius lay snivelling on the ground and tied the other end around his scrawny neck.

'D, you can't be serious, we go way back, you ain't gonna play me out like this…'

'You brought it on yourself, Cass,' said Dreadnought, hauling the prone man to his feet. 'You're a fucking liability. You've been high for so long, it's time you came back down to earth. '

'D, no…you're my brother…'

Cassius began to kick and struggle as Dreadnought lifted him off the ground, but within seconds the gang boss had manoeuvred his former right-hand man into a sitting position on the side wall that overlooked the court-yard.

'See you on the other side,' he said, before pushing Cassius into oblivion.

The gangbanger fell like a stone as gravity took over, or at least he did until the makeshift noose around his neck brought his descent to a sudden halt. He ended up suspended against the side of the building, his legs scrabbling desperately against the brickwork as he slowly asphyxiated, while Dreadnought's crew moved forward to get a better look, each of them eager to observe the death throes. Cass gave out a series of gurgles as the life was choked out of him, then his kicks grew steadily weaker until finally they ceased alto-gether.

'Right—time to get busy,' said Dreadnought. 'All this action's making me hungry. Stash those two in one of the apartments, have someone stand guard out front, and have someone else go out for pizza,' Dreadnought commanded Cyclops.

'What about him?' asked the one-eyed henchman.

'Leave him be for now—flies gotta eat. And as for you two, how about you start making a mental list of everything you know about the Indian because once I'm done eating, I'll want some answers.'

Cyclops grabbed Hunter and Angel by their upper arms and hustled them down the walkway until they were outside apartment 3b. He pushed open the door then shoved them inside. Despite the gloom, it was clear that the room had been uninhabited for some while. The ceiling had collapsed in one corner, half the floorboards were missing to expose the water pipes that ran underfoot, and a musty scent hung heavy in the air.

'Smells like a pussy died in here—let's hope it was your mom's,' muttered Hunter, earning a painful punch to the kidneys for his troubles.

'Sit down, back to back,' commanded Cyclops. Once they were in position, he looped another plastic restraint through their bonds and proceeded to fasten it around one of the pipes, then he rose to his feet and headed for the exit.

'Leaving so soon?' asked Hunter over his shoulder. 'But we were having such fun…'

Cyclops slammed the door on his way out, leaving the two of them in total darkness.

'What's with the wiseass act?' asked Angel, her back bumping into his as she shuffled her ass on the floor. It was the first time she'd spoken to him since he'd learnt of her betrayal.

'I'm trying to knock them off guard. If I joke around long enough they might stop taking me seriously—maybe I can take advantage of that.'

'Sounds like a long shot.'

'Long shots are all we've got. Why'd you do it?'

'If you want an apology, you're not going to get one.'

He waited for her to continue.

'I did what I thought was best for my daughter. If I'd delivered Stone then Gracie and I would have been home by now.'

'No, you wouldn't. Dreadnought was never going to let either of you walk away from this. You know too much. You should have trusted me. My plan would have worked. But there's still one thing I can't work out—why did Dreadnought choose you in the first place? Why take Gracie? Why was he so damn keen to spark a gang war between the Ghosts and the Vipers?'

'Search me.'

Angel entwined her fingers in his, and he made no move to stop her. What had Dreadnought said? That he was pussy-whipped and didn't know which way was up. Maybe the gang boss had been right. Ever since he'd picked up the phone and heard Angel's voice one week ago his emotions had clouded his judgement. Looking back, he realised he'd made mistakes, chief amongst which had been his failure to insist that she go to the cops. His growing feelings for her had been the main problem, but he'd also wanted to turn back the clock and change the past—he'd still wanted to rescue her from the gangs, to give her a future that involved more than just bullets and funerals, and for a while that had seemed like a real possibility.

The past. Why hadn't she quit the gangs back then when he'd first offered her the chance? What had she gotten out of her role as an informant? A bit of cash and some help in controlling her competitors. Was that all she'd really been after? It didn't seem like much. She hadn't even wanted any payment for the best piece of intel she'd provided. Then the truth hit him like a sucker punch to the gut. The reason why she'd first come into his life all those years ago. The reason why he'd been her bitch since the very first day they'd met.

'You used me,' he said coldly, withdrawing his hands from hers.

'What?'

'Back when I was trying to get you out of the gangs.'

'I don't know what you're talking about.'

'All those snippets of info you sold me on your gang rivals were just bait, because your real target all along was your own boss. You used me to get him out of the way. You set him up for a murder rap by planting a head in his freezer, and once he was gone, the field was wide open for Lunatic to take over.' His face hardened as his tone became ever more bitter. 'How long did it take for your partner to become boss? Another six months? A year? And all the while you were pulling the strings, the power behind the throne. You played me for a sucker from day one.'

'You're deluded.'

'I don't think so. You never had the slightest intention of leaving the Ghosts—that was all just bullshit to keep me interested. You worked out what I wanted to hear then spun me a story to reel me in. How about this time around? Has it been nothing but lies all over again? What aren't you telling me? When you fucked me in the shower, was that your new way of getting the hooks in? Did it all mean nothing to you?'

'No,' she said quietly. 'It meant something. It still does. But my daughter's missing and I'd do anything to get her back. Anything. Okay, I've done some stuff I'm not proud of, but I'm from the streets, and the first thing I learnt was that I couldn't rely on handouts—I've had to fight every step of the way.'

Hunter lapsed into silence as he replayed the events of the past week in his head. Sure, Angel had been through hell, and her emotional responses had largely been in keeping with that, but there was still something in her behaviour that jarred with him, some reaction that didn't ring true, but no matter how hard he thought about it, that something remained just out of reach, dancing right on the edge of his subconscious. He was still searching for an answer when he felt her stiffen against his back.

'Someone's coming,' she said softly, a tremor of fear in her voice.

So this was it. One torture session courtesy of

Dreadnought and his thugs coming right up. Their choices were simple. Hold out for as long as possible and then die in agony, or give up Stone and die in agony anyhow. Hunter set his jaw and readied himself for the pain.

CHAPTER FORTY-FOUR

'YOU!' gasped Angel.

Hunter craned his neck around to look at the doorway, and when he saw the towering figure that stood there, a smile crossed his face.

'Where the hell have you been?' he asked.

'Busy,' replied Stone, before stepping outside for a moment to return with one of Dreadnought's henchmen draped over his shoulder. He dumped the unconscious man in the corner of the room, then walked over to the captive pair with his hunting knife at the ready, leaving his two Akitas to stand guard by the entrance.

'So why didn't you meet us at the bakery?' asked Hunter.

'I was there, just not where you expected me to be. I had a hunch that things might turn out this way. When Angel was on the phone to the kidnappers back at my place, she made a point of moving out of earshot, and she stayed on the line a little too long. I was worried that she might pull something like this.'

'You didn't trust *me*? You son of a bitch!' spat Angel.

'It's not a matter of trust—never underestimate a

mother's love for her child,' he said, as he sawed through their bonds. 'I watched Dreadnought capture you, then I followed you back here.'

Once he was free, Hunter rose to his feet, shook Stone's hand, then turned to Angel.

'What now?' she asked. 'You're not just gonna leave, are you? You're still gonna help me, right? Help me find Gracie? You promised, remember…'

'I remember. Although, given your recent behaviour, you can count yourself lucky that I'm a man of my word. Besides, I think Stone's got some unfinished business of his own to attend to.'

The Indian gave a slow nod as Angel surprised Hunter by wrapping her arms around him in a tight embrace.

'Thank you,' she said, pushing her chest against his. 'I won't forget this.'

Hunter eased her away, marvelling at how she was still using her sexuality as a bargaining chip.

'I'm not doing it for you—I'm doing it for your daughter. Gracie's an innocent. She doesn't deserve to be hung out to dry. But we've got to move fast, and we've got to move quietly. Our only chance is to take them out before they realise what's happening. Stone, do you know where Dreadnought is?'

'The gang boss and most of his men are in the apartment at the eastern end of this floor.'

'Most of his men?'

'That one was standing guard outside,' Stone said, gesturing to the unconscious man in the corner. 'While one of the others went into the room at the western end, as far away from the boss as you can get.'

'If Gracie's here, then that's where they've got her stashed—Dreadnought wouldn't want a screaming kid anywhere close by.'

'My Gracie don't scream,' bristled Angel.

'Whatever—we'll go for her first. What did you do with the guard's gun?'

Stone pulled a Micro Uzi from the back of his jeans and hefted it towards Hunter.

'Nice,' he said, catching it cleanly. 'This oughta even things up a little.'

'What about me?' asked Angel.

'You wait here.'

'Like hell I will—she's my daughter!'

'Okay, but keep back and keep quiet. Let us take care of the guard, then you can take care of your daughter. C'mon, let's get going.'

Hunter ducked his head outside to check that all was quiet on the balcony. Other than the swinging corpse of Cassius, there was no one in sight, so he headed west on the balls of his feet with Stone and his dogs next in line and Angel bringing up the rear. When they neared the final apartment they found that the sole window had been boarded up, and an annoying electronic jingle emanated from the room. Hunter stationed himself to the right of the door, grabbed a firm hold of the handle, then gestured for Stone to take the lead. The Indian whispered something to his dogs and they responded by planting their hindquarters on the floor, then he nodded to signal his readiness.

Hunter turned the handle slowly, one tiny increment at a time, then he eased the door open a fraction to allow an ultra-thin shaft of light to spill out across the balcony. Stone stepped forward and put his eye to the crack, then he motioned for Hunter to continue. Little by little the door swung inwards until finally there was just enough space for Stone to squeeze through. Hunter slipped into place behind him with Uzi at the ready and marvelled at the scene that greeted him. One of Dreadnought's men was on the sofa with his back to the door, while a small girl was perched alongside him. Both of them were staring at a portable TV where a bunch of colourful cartoon characters were zipping around a racetrack in their go-carts. The girl had short brown hair that was cut in a bob, and even from behind Hunter knew that the search for Graciela Cortez was finally over.

'You ain't never gonna catch me!' cried the gang-banger, his body swaying to the left in tandem with one of the vehicles on the screen. As they played on, Stone continued to advance, his lightness of foot impressive in such a large man. Hunter tensed as the Indian closed in, four feet away, then three, then two. At the very last moment Gracie's guard realised that something was wrong but by then it was too late, as Stone stepped forward to jam the serrated blade of his knife against the guard's windpipe while simultaneously placing his other hand over Gracie's mouth to choke off her nascent scream.

'Make one move and you die,' he whispered to the gangbanger.

Hunter followed the Indian inside and patted down the prisoner, relieving him of two Ruger handguns in the process, then he knelt down in front of Gracie, whose eyes were as wide as saucers as she squirmed against Stone's hand.

'Hey, kid, remember me? I'm here to rescue you— I'm a friend of your mom's.'

He kept his voice calm as he tried to ease her fears, which wasn't easy as at that moment a wave of emotion was crashing through him. He'd found her. He'd found the six-year-old girl who was being used as a pawn in the gang wars. He'd completed his mission. He'd saved an innocent. Gracie stopped struggling as a look of recognition passed over her face.

'You wait here for just one second, okay? I'll go get your mom—she's right outside.'

He headed back out to the balcony and called Angel over.

'Get in there and go to your kid,' he said softly. Angel's face lit up, then he stood aside to let her through.

'Gracie! Gracie, it's Mommy, don't be scared,' she said, running across the room to kneel in front of her daughter, tears of joy welling in her eyes. 'When the nice man lets go of your mouth, I want you to stay as quiet as you can, okay? Can you do that for Mommy? Can you be a brave little girl?'

Gracie gave an almost imperceptible nod, so Stone slowly removed his paw from across her mouth, and when no scream was forthcoming he raised his arm over her head to give her a free run at her mom.

'Mommy!' she whispered.

The gamepad she'd been holding fell from her hands as Angel scooped her up and showered the top of her head in kisses. Hunter watched the family reunion with a lump in his throat. Angel's love for her child was plain to see, and while that didn't totally excuse her betrayal, it did go a long way to explain it.

'Mommy, that's too tight…'

'I'm never gonna let you go again, princess, you hear me? Mommy's sorry she wasn't there for you, but I promise I'll make it up to you, I promise that everything's gonna be okay.'

'I missed you, Mommy. Where have you been?'

'I've been looking for you, baby girl—it's been like a big game of hide and seek, you know, like we play at home sometimes?'

'With Daddy?'

'Yeah, with Daddy,' replied Angel, her voice cracking a little. 'Are you okay, Gracie? Has anyone hurt you?'

'Hurt me? Of course not, Mommy. I've just been playing with Dexter,' Gracie said, pointing to her guard. 'He's real good at 'Tendo, and we get pizza every night!'

'Talking of which, what are we going to do with him?' asked Stone, the blade of his knife still pressed firmly against the neck of the guard.

'Here's the deal,' said Hunter, squatting in front of the gangbanger to look him straight in the eye. 'You keep quiet, you live. Think you can manage that?'

The gangbanger nodded once.

'Smart move,' said Hunter, as he began to unlace the prisoner's sneakers. Once he was done he stood back and levelled the Micro Uzi at the centre of his chest. 'Now stand up.'

Stone removed the knife and allowed the gangbanger to rise to his feet.

'Tie his wrists,' said Hunter, throwing Stone the laces. 'And make it tight.'

'My pleasure.'

Once Stone had finished Hunter pushed the gangbanger back into the corner of the room and handed Angel one of the confiscated Rugers.

'I'm gonna need you to stay here,' he said, 'to make sure this guy stays quiet.'

'Sure,' she said, her eyes still fixed on her daughter.

'If he moves, you shoot…got that?'

'But if I shoot I'll blow your cover.'

'I can help with that,' said Stone. 'Caleb! Joshua! Heel!' The two large dogs were at their master's side in an instant. 'You see these dogs, boy? These are Akitas, and there's enough power in their jaws to bite clean through your arm. You make the slightest move and they'll be on you in an instant. You'll be chopped liver by the time they're through.'

The gangbanger stared at the two animals as if they were related to Cerberus himself.

'Caleb! Joshua! Guard!' Stone commanded. The two dogs rose to their feet as one and took up flanking positions in front of the gangbanger, their canine faces a study in concentration.

'Nice,' said Hunter. 'Now stay here and look after your daughter. When it's safe to come out we'll come get you. If the door starts to open and you haven't heard my voice, shoot first and ask questions later. You want this?' he asked Stone, offering him the second Ruger.

'No.'

'We'll be going up against some serious firepower.'

'My guardian spirit will watch over me.'

'Okay.' Hunter shrugged. 'You ready?'

'More than you'll ever know.'

'Then let's do it.'

CHAPTER FORTY-FIVE

HUNTER and Stone moved like ghosts along the balcony until they were ten feet shy of the room where Dreadnought and his crew were holed up. The door was wide open and light spilled out into the night. Hunter stilled the Indian with his hand and thought about sneaking a peek through the window, but quickly ruled it out. While it would be nice to know what they were walking into, they couldn't risk being seen, or they'd lose the element of surprise. He pointed first to the window and then to the floor, obtaining a nod of the Indian's head in response. When he sank to his knees, Stone followed suit, then the two of them began to crawl forward, each man taking care to ensure that his head remained below the level of the sill. Having cleared the obstacle successfully, Hunter rose to his feet and sidled up to the doorway with Micro Uzi at the ready. As the adrenalin surge began, he took three deep breaths to steady his heart rate, then swung into the opening.

'Nobody move!' he yelled as he stepped into the room. Dreadnought was sitting dead ahead of him on a leather sofa with a pizza box in his lap, while two of his lackeys were stretched out on the floor to the right, leaving Cyclops by the window on his left. For a fraction of a second they all made like statues, and then one of the prone gangbangers reached for a gun.

Hunter responded instantly, swinging the Micro Uzi around in a smooth arc, his finger pressing down on the trigger just as it reached its target. The sound was near deafening in the small space and the carnage it wrought was near biblical. Bullets ripped out of the barrel to riddle the gangbanger's torso with lead, sending a series of bright crimson splashes across the wall. As the first gangbanger slumped lifelessly to the floor, the man alongside him brought his weapon to bear, so Hunter nudged the Uzi onwards to even the sides yet further, then the next thing he knew he was being shoved aside as Stone entered the fray in a hurry.

The Indian's knife arm was drawn back and his attention was focused on Cyclops, who by now had freed his gun and was set to fire. Stone's arm flew forward in a blur as he let the weapon fly; his aim was true and the knife whistled through the air to embed itself in the one-eyed monster's chest. Cyclops stumbled backwards into the wall then slid down it until he was sitting on the floor with a look of surprise on his face. For his part, Dreadnought remained motionless, a slice of pizza held halfway to his mouth.

'Thanks,' said Hunter, acknowledging the fact that Stone had just saved his life, but the Indian marched straight past him towards his nemesis.

'You killed my nephew!'

Dreadnought took a bite of his pizza and chewed it slowly as he appraised him.

'You got the wrong man, Tonto. The man that did for your kin be twistin' outside in the wind.'

'But you were the supplier! You put that poison on the streets in the first place!'

'Wrong again. I don't be sellin' no poison drugs—it's bad for business. I want my clients high, not dead. Cassius was off on his own trip, he cut some side deals, kept me out of the loop. You wanna know where those drugs came from, go ask him.' The gang boss shrugged.

Hunter found himself marvelling at Dreadnought's demeanour. Here he was, his crew in pieces all around him, facing a man who wanted nothing more than to see his head on a plate, yet he was as cool as a cucumber.

'All this time you been hunting me down for something I never did. How about you say sorry, fuck off back to the reservation, and leave me the hell alone?'

'You're a goddamn liar!' yelled Stone, drawing back his fist.

'No, he's not,' Hunter said quietly. 'He's telling the truth.'

'Then why the hell…?' began Stone as he turned back round, but before he could finish his sentence his eyes were widening in shock.

Acting purely on instinct, Hunter began to swing the Uzi around to where Stone was staring to discover that the knife in Cyclops's chest wasn't quite as terminal as they'd first thought.

Finding himself momentarily unguarded, Dreadnought

sent his pizza box flying skywards to reach for the .44 Bulldog that lay hidden beneath.

As Cyclops made a desperate lunge for his own weapon, Hunter squeezed down on the Uzi's trigger.

Dreadnought raised the Bulldog until it was aimed at a point midway between Hunter's shoulder blades.

A ragged line of bullet holes appeared in the wall as the Uzi continued on its arc.

Dreadnought's finger tightened on the Bulldog's trigger.

When the line of bullet holes made it as far as Cyclops, both his face and his life force were obliterated.

Then a lone shot rang out.

CHAPTER FORTY-SIX

THE bullet took him high in the torso, punching a hole clean through his chest. The gun slipped from his fingers and he started to cough up thick red fluid as his lungs filled with blood. He'd lived his life on the edge for thirty-odd years and this was the first time he'd ever been shot. And probably the last.

Dreadnought reached up with one of his huge hands and poked at the opening in his thoracic cavity. The blood pulsed out in viscous waves between his fingers as he slumped back onto the sofa. Hunter and Stone turned towards the entrance to find Angel in the doorway, her hair streaming out behind her, a Ruger clasped tight in her hands.

'You're welcome,' she said, to the two men whose lives she'd just saved.

Hunter walked over to the gang boss and kicked his weapon away.

'Looks like you're checking out, partner,' he said. 'But before you go, there's one thing that's still bothering me—why take Angel's kid, Graciela? Why go to all that trouble to start a gang war between the Ghosts and the Vipers?'

'Ask her,' coughed Dreadnought, the blood running freely down his chin. 'She knows what this been about…'

'He's lying,' said Angel, striding forward to silence the gang boss once and for all, until she found her path blocked by six feet three of Native American.

'Whoever sells the drugs makes the money,' began Dreadnought, his once booming voice now little more than a whisper. 'But whoever controls the territory controls the drugs. I got talkin' to a Latino when I was back in the pen…he say Mexican Mafia getting greedy… EastLos ain't big enough for 'em no more. It don't matter that LA was founded by brothers—the spics are all over this shit now. Mex bosses sent word down from on high that their soldiers had to make a move on South Central…Ghosts and Vipers tasked to take my crew out…had to buy myself some time…get the spics fightin' amongst themselves…so's I grabbed Lunatic's kid so I could force him to take out Venom…wanted to make some money then disappear…I was gonna go legit… leave all this bloodshed behind…'

Hunter's heart sank. He'd suspected that Angel had been holding something back, but this? The events of the past week flashed through his mind like a film on fast-forward, and he ended up freeze-framing on the way she'd responded to two separate pieces of news.

First, the reaction she'd displayed on hearing that Lunatic had attacked the Vipers had been beyond shock and closer to utter disbelief—little wonder when she thought that the two gangs were brothers in arms who were about to march on South Central.

And, second, on hearing that Cassius, a member of the Imperial Knights, was involved in her daughter's abduction, she'd shown no surprise whatsoever. She must have guessed that the Knights had somehow become aware of the Mexican Mafia's plan, and that they'd forced Lunatic to kill Venom as a way to forestall the danger.

When he turned to look back at her he found that her head was already bowed.

'You knew who had Gracie all along.'

'No, I didn't—I swear. I had no idea what was going on until you started to uncover the truth. Even when you told me that the Knights were involved, there was nothing I could do about it, as Dreadnought had gone to ground.'

'She a lying bitch…' spluttered the gang boss, managing to spit out one final insult before his eyes glazed over and he passed away.

'But you knew about the plan to attack the Knights—that's why you were so keen to keep the police out of it. There was no way that the Mexican Mafia would have allowed you to call in the authorities, so you did the next best thing and called me.'

'What was I supposed to do?' she sobbed. 'My baby girl was missing, my husband wasn't telling me a goddamn thing—I had nowhere else to turn.'

'You could have told me the truth.'

'I wanted to, but I was scared…scared that you'd lose all sympathy for me and walk away.'

'You know, for a while there, I was starting to think that we had something.'

'We did…'

'Mommy?' asked a tiny voice from the doorway.

'Mommy's coming, sweetie, you just wait out there like I told you.'

'I'm glad that Gracie's okay,' said Hunter, as he walked Angel out to the balcony. 'Now it's time for you to take her home.'

'So this is it?'

'I guess it is.'

'Gracie, come here now,' said Angel, squatting down to take her daughter by the hands. 'And say thank you to Uncle Zac.'

'Why, Mommy?'

'Because he's done more for us than you'll ever know. Just thank him, honey.'

Hunter knelt down alongside the two of them and summoned up a reassuring smile.

'Thanks, Uncle Zac.'

'You're welcome, Gracie,' he said, his throat suddenly dry. 'You be a good girl for your mom now, you hear?'

Gracie nodded solemnly and the two adults rose to their feet. Angel wrapped him in a tight embrace, then planted a lingering kiss on his lips.

'Thanks for everything,' she said softly, her big doe eyes just inches from his, the tears running freely down her cheeks. 'And if you ever change your mind, you know where to find me…'

With that, she turned tail and walked out of the room. He stood and watched her leave. In another life, maybe things might have worked out differently between them, but in this one she ran with a street gang, which meant she was up to her neck in all the violence, drugs and duplicity that her world entailed—and that world had just got a little bit bigger. With Dreadnought dead and the Knights leaderless, the Latino march into South LA could now begin in earnest.

'I think it's time we left too,' said Stone, as he withdrew his hunting knife from Cyclops's chest and wiped it clean on the dead man's shirt. 'With all this gunfire, the cops will be here soon.'

The two men exited the room and headed back along the balcony.

'I thought you'd be pissed at me for not telling you that it was Cassius who sold the drugs to your nephew,' said Hunter.

'A journey may have many twists and turns, but once you reach your destination, they are all soon forgotten.'

'Meaning Cassius is dead, so you're happy?'

'Exactly. Caleb! Joshua! Heel!' Stone barked as they neared the stairwell, prompting the two dogs to explode from the apartment down the way and race back to his side. 'But there's one thing that I don't understand. Back there, you said that Dreadnought wasn't the source of the poisoned drugs. If it wasn't him, then who was it?'

'I think I can help you with that, but first you're gonna have to ask yourself what you really want. Do you want vengeance for your nephew, or do you want to make a real difference?'

'Both,' replied Stone. 'For the last couple of months I've witnessed the drug trade at first hand. Gang bosses run their empires while kids die hard on the streets. It's a war zone out there, and the schoolyards are on the front line. That has to stop.'

'Well, we're gonna have to move fast. And bring him along too,' said Hunter, pointing at Cassius's swinging corpse. 'I've got a feeling he might come in useful.'

CHAPTER FORTY-SEVEN

'THIS is fucked up,' said Diaz, working his Desert Eagle free from its leather holster.

'You're telling me,' agreed Mason. 'But what choice we got? You saw the text message that piece of shit sent me—"Bring cash money to the gym at Acorn Elementary or I go the cops." Who the fuck does he think he is? Trying to put the squeeze on us. But you know what beats me? After all the months we've been working with him, why wait till now to threaten to drop a dime?'

Diaz shrugged his shoulders in response then busied himself with plucking a piece of lint from the lapel of his designer jacket. The two men were on the sidewalk outside Acorn Elementary School with a chain-link fence in front of them and Mason's beat-up Oldsmobile at their backs. The moon was waning high overhead, the midnight hour having long since departed.

'You think my wheels will be all right if I leave 'em here?'

Diaz gave the car a withering look then cocked an eyebrow in his partner's direction.

'Fuck you,' Mason responded, before clambering

over the chain-link fence to enter the schoolyard. 'Let's see you get your fancy suit over that in one piece.'

Diaz backed up a few yards, broke into a sprint, planted his hands on the top of the fence and vaulted over gracefully, then favoured his partner with a dazzling smile.

'Fucking Olga Corbett,' grumbled the shorter man as he spun on his heel and headed for the school's entrance.

'Why the hell does Cassius wanna meet us here? And at this time of night? Gangbanger musta lost his mind. I'm tellin' you, Diaz, he's a fucking liability. It's time we cleaned house.'

When the two men made it as far as the entrance they found the door slightly ajar.

'Little fucker's got himself some lock-picking skills,' Mason muttered. 'Say, you think this is where he's been holed up for the last couple of days?'

He drew his gun without waiting for an answer and stepped through the opening. The corridor was masked in shadow, the moonlight glinting off the metallic lockers that were situated dead ahead. He turned to his right and began to edge forward, leaving Diaz to cover his six. His eyes flicked nervously around the space, and every time he came to a classroom he paused for a moment to check that the door was locked. After advancing in this tortuous fashion for the best part of ten minutes, he arrived at his destination. The large double doors ahead of him were made of wood, as was the sign that hung over them. The sign read 'Gymnasium'.

'This is it,' whispered Mason. 'Let's get it over with.

I'm gonna sleep a whole lot easier once that weasel's got a bullet in his coked-up head.'

Mason put his shoulder against one of the doors and waited for Diaz to join him, then the two of them exploded into the gymnasium as one, Mason heading low and to the right with his gun tracking around for a target, with Diaz doing likewise going high and to the left. After a second or so, both men's weapons came to rest on the figure that was slumped in the far corner of the auditorium, just to the right of the retractable bleachers. They set out warily towards it, their footsteps on the maple hardcourt echoing around the cavernous space, but by the time they'd covered two-thirds of the distance their guns hung loose by their sides.

'He's all fucked up!' exclaimed Mason. 'Talk about making things easy for us.'

Cassius was sitting in the corner with his back against the wall. His head was slumped forward on his chest, a piece of black flex was knotted just above his elbow, and a hypodermic needle hung lazily out of his scrawny biceps.

'See that?' said Mason, gesturing at the tangled mass of bed sheets that lay alongside him. 'Motherfucker *has* been laying low here. Probably injected all that dope we gave him 'stead of selling it. You think he's still alive?'

Diaz reached for the gangbanger's wrist with a distasteful look on his face, probed around for a moment, then shrugged.

'I'm gonna put a bullet in him to be sure. That Mexican Tar was primo shit. If he's whacked out on it, it might have slowed his vitals right down. We ain't got no call to be takin' chances.'

Diaz stood clear while Mason took careful aim. The gun barked once, sending a bullet clean through Cassius's temple to explode out the back of his head, showering the wall in blood, grain and gristle.

'Goddamn terrible—who woulda guessed that li'l Cass would wind up just another victim of the inner city gang wars,' muttered Mason, putting on a faux sympathetic tone. 'It's a shame to lose him—he used to be a good little earner—but I guess we got plenty of other applicants for the position. C'mon, let's haul ass and ditch this gun down the nearest storm drain.'

When the two men turned to leave, they suddenly found they had company.

'Hold it right there!' yelled a voice through a megaphone, as a cluster of heavily armed police officers burst through the gymnasium doors. *'Surrender your weapons and get down on your knees!'*

Mason placed his throwdown piece on the hardwood floor, then kicked it away to send it skittering off into the shadows. Diaz watched it disappear then muttered just one word before following suit.

'Fuck…'

CHAPTER FORTY-EIGHT

'TURN it up,' said Stone, pointing at the TV. 'This is it.'

The two men were kicking back on the leather couch in Hunter's home, way up high in the hills that ringed the north side of the city. Outside, the sun had just started to rise, and the golden rays now streamed in through the sliding glass doors to bathe them in a warm glow. Hunter had a half-empty bottle of Coors grasped in his hand, while Stone was working on a bottle of Evian. The two Akitas, Caleb and Joshua, were lying out on the floor, chewing noisily on some rawhide bones. Hunter reached for the remote, turned up the volume, then settled back to enjoy the show.

'And now I hand you over to Veronica Lane, reporting for K-CBS News, direct from the scene…'

The face of an attractive brunette filled the screen, her eyes still sparkling despite the fact she'd been up all night. She had every right to be amped, as she'd just bagged lead reporter status on the biggest news story to hit LA since Rodney King had taken a baton bath back in 1991.

'You join me here outside Acorn Elementary School,

where two Los Angeles police detectives were arrested for the murder of an unnamed black male in the early hours of this morning. Just minutes ago, a police spokesman reported that officers were acting on an anonymous tip-off when they apprehended Detectives Nic Mason and Eduardo Diaz at the scene of the crime. Detective Mason was found standing over the victim with a smoking gun in his hand, in what is sure to be seen as another hammer blow to the LAPD's already tarnished public image. While the coroner has yet to make an official report, sources at the scene have revealed that the victim was not only shot, but was also found with a hypodermic syringe in his right biceps and severe bruising around his neck. Our viewers may recall that Acorn Elementary School was the source of a terrible tragedy just three months ago, when seven of the pupils died from an overdose of crack cocaine that had been contaminated with strychnine, the pesticide most commonly found in rat poison. And in a further stunning development, I have recently learnt that a per-functory search of Detective Mason's car has uncovered a significant amount of crack cocaine, leading commentators to suggest that the two disgraced officers were somehow involved in the local drugs trade.'

'Just wait till they run the lab tests on it and find it's full of strychnine,' muttered Hunter.

'I'm going to have to stop you there for a moment, Veronica,' cut in a talking head from the studio, his face dominating the screen as the roving reporter's visage was relegated to picture-in-picture. 'As I've just heard that there's been another exciting development in the case. Here at K-CBS News we've just received an envelope containing a number of long-range photos of the two detectives currently under investigation, in discussion with a man identified only as Cassius, who, it seems, may be none other than the murder victim found with them tonight.'

When the photos appeared on the screen, Stone sat up in his seat in surprise. 'How the hell…?'

'Oh, yeah, I forgot to mention I borrowed a couple of your surveillance snaps,' said Hunter. 'Hope you don't mind, but I had a street kid drop them off at the news station an hour or so ago. I like the way you've got all three of them in the picture—Cassius, Mason and Diaz. They've been really well framed…'

'I figured those two were just customers—I never even gave them a second thought.'

'These pictures add further credence to the theory that the illegal distribution of narcotics was somehow involved,' continued the news anchor, 'as they clearly show that the two officers had a prior relationship with their victim. The police commissioner has already promised that a full inquiry will be launched immediately, and he reiterated his continued faith in the vast majority of law-enforcement officials that police our city…'

Hunter snapped off the volume and took another pull on his beer.

'You did the right thing,' he said to Stone. 'If you'd put a bullet in their heads, everything would have been brushed under the carpet. Mason and Diaz might still be drawing breath, but by going public we're shining a light on all those other cops who think that the law doesn't apply to them. It'll help make a difference. Lives will be saved.'

'Children's lives,' added Stone. 'How long have you known that those cops were involved?'

'For a coupla days or so—I started to get suspicious when I realised that they'd tipped off Cassius about a Winnebago on a drug run from Mexico. Their intel was way too good for them to be lowly street thugs. Then I remembered that I'd made a note of their licence plate back when I first saw them in Imperial Courts. I got a friend of mine at the DMV to run the plates, and guess what I discovered? Their day job was to protect and to serve—but while Gracie was missing I had more pressing matters to attend to.'

Hunter paused as a vision of Angel swam into his mind's eye. She might be out of his life, but she wasn't yet out of his head. The anger he'd felt over her betrayal had begun to fade, but the hurt would live on for a while.

'It wasn't until you came along that I started to realise how they fit into the picture. They'd been supplying Cassius with drugs that they'd either confiscated or stolen from other dealers, and his role was to sell them on the street to release the profits. At some point they got their hands on a batch that had been cut up with strychnine, which in turn found its way to your nephew, Daniel, via Cassius. When you caught Daniel with the backpack full of drugs it was lucky you kept them, otherwise we might have had trouble making everything stick.'

'Luck had nothing to do with it. I kept the drugs for a reason, remember? I was planning on feeding them to the man responsible for Daniel's death.'

'Either way, those drugs came in handy. Nice job on the plant, by the way—whereabouts in Mason's car did you stash them?'

'I taped them to the underside of the wheel rim while he was inside the school with his partner. Had to be quick as I didn't know when the cavalry was going to arrive.'

'And I bet you had a big grin on your face as you did it?'

'Let's just say I was happy to return what was rightfully theirs…'

'Look, man, I never really thanked you—until you showed up at Dreadnought's lair I thought I was a goner.'

'Think nothing of it—without your help I'd have never found Dreadnought in the first place. Not to mention the fact that it was you that told me about Cassius, Mason and Diaz.'

'So what's next for you?'

'Now that my nephew has been avenged, I'm going to head back to the reservation to pay my respects at his graveside.'

'What sort of reception you figure you'll get from the rest of the tribe?'

'That remains to be seen. I've gone some way to atone for my errors, but I have many miles to go before I can even begin to approach redemption.'

'Are you coming back to LA when you're done at the res?'

'I expect so.'

'I'll see you then,' Hunter said, rising to his feet and offering his hand.

When Stone hauled his large frame off the couch, Caleb and Joshua dropped their rawhide bones to stand alongside him. The Indian grasped Hunter's hand in a tight clench and pumped it once.

'Count on it,' Stone said, as a new day dawned in the background.

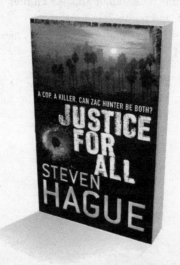